The Calvarymen

Author: Adam Love

Book One

Eyes of Gold

Edited by: Kayla Martin

Illustrations by:

Blanca Love

Whitney Lightsey

thecalvarymenadamlove.com

Contents

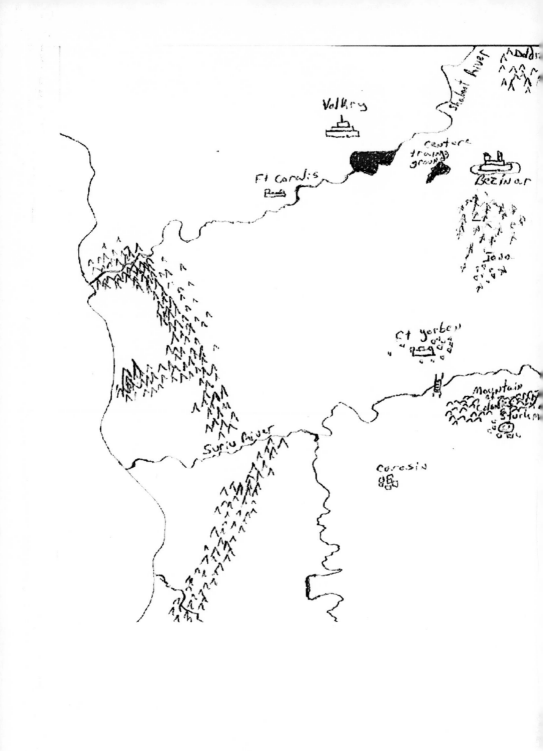

Prologue

We knew this day would come--the day when the people of Qanas would forget who the true ruler was. As a result, wickedness spread throughout the land and throughout every kingdom. The Creator became enraged, sending a supernatural being to destroy all the wicked and to spare the few who still believed in Him. However, after many years, Qanas thrived once more. As the population increased, resources diminished, causing an outbreak of war and chaos. When all seemed lost, a wise group of beings called the Nephilim entered the region. No one knew where they came from, or why. A gifted race, the Nephilim brought order to the realm. They were superior to the people of Qanas, and placed themselves as kings. These Nephilim leaders were called Centurions, and through them, peace endured for centuries. However, in time, their greed for power caused a civil war among the Centurion leaders. Knowing the Centurions could not be trusted, three kingdoms broke away and headed far to the north during the war. After the war, the grand capital Fenris was rebuilt. One Centurion remains, ruling all of Qanas and the neighboring lands, using the people as his footstool to conquer all in his way. To ensure his reign would not be cut short, he killed all siblings and descendants of the Nephilim...except one, who must choose his own fate.

The fall of Sturkma

There have been many wars through the ages, but this time it was different. This war was not due to a lust for gold or power, but the annihilation of all. Stories of past wars were frightening--especially the Centurion War, when the three kingdoms broke away. Peace reigned within the three kingdoms for years, but this war would decide the fate of all. It would not take place in some distant battlefield, but among everyone, where children could learn from it with their own eyes.

There were many towns and cities in the kingdom of Bezinar, but the City of Sturkma was unique. It was in the middle of a valley--a safe haven--surrounded by mountains. Families had lived in this valley for many generations and were proud of their city, despite it being on the outskirts of the kingdom. Since yesterday, people had been gathering gear and supplies. It had been reported that the Geol army was sighted two days ago. The Geols had already destroyed several cities to the south, and Sturkma was next in its path. Felden, the leader of the Shadow Scouts, brought the people warning of the Geols approach. At sunrise, many of the people left when the gates opened. The sun was well above the tree line but had not cleared the wall. The wall was made of gray stone and stood twenty feet high, circling the entire city. The King ordered the wall's construction about twenty years ago, after the city and outside villages had been pillaged. Soldiers occasionally came to check on Sturkma. However, since an army of Geols was in the area, the King had sent a small group of soldiers to stay and protect the city. The question was, why such a small force? He has been on the throne for about forty years and had done well keeping the kingdom intact. The city air was full of quarreling families yelling at each other and the clanging of pots and pans. But one family seemed to have more trouble than the others and was lagging behind.

Naughton grew restless waiting for his family. He stood on the wall, looking into the distance watching villages burn. The smell of smoke filled his nose as ash rained down on his head. The Geols had withdrawn some time ago, but he knew their prize still awaited them. He held his bow firmly and wished he could stay and help, but his father would not allow him. He looked to his left and saw the guards gathering at the gate, hurrying people out so they could be closed. Archers rushed by him; one stopped to look at him, his hands on his hips. "What are you doing up here?"

"Nothing."

"Exactly! If you wish to fight, then come with us. Otherwise, leave!"

Naughton turned around, putting his bow on his back. He went down the ladder and ran to his house, dodging the frantic crowd. His feet pounded against the dirt as he ran by shops and buildings, trying to reach his house in one piece. Their house was made of brick and taller than most buildings, allowing them to enjoy the view of the city. When he reached the city square, local soldiers were taking up arms and marching down the street. Most were volunteers with very little training, and Naughton knew a few of them. He waved at them as he ran by. After several more blocks, he reached his house. He leaned over, panting, as his father stepped out. His father was short and thick, with arms and legs as stout as an ox. He had short, salt–and–pepper hair. "How much longer?" grunted Naughton, as he stretched his back.

"I'm not sure--your mother and sister are *women,* I remind you." A loud boom echoed to the southwest and his father rubbed his face. "Go ask the guard how much longer they will keep the gate open, and see where your cousins are."

Naughton took a breath. "Why? I'm sure they are quite capable of taking care of themselves."

"Just go, Naughton. I will hasten your mother

and sister."

Naughton took a deep breath and began making his way through the streets, fighting the crowd once more to the gate. When he got close, he heard people screaming outside the walls. Suddenly, a soldier yelled, "Arrows…arrows…get behind something!" An arrow hissed by Naughton's head. He turned around and ran as fast he could up the main street to his cousin's house, dodging the panicking crowd. He saw his little cousin Lili wearing a long brown travel dress, with her hair hanging down either side of her face. She was tan and lean, with light brown eyes that sparkled.

"Hey, Naughton is coming!" said Lili, pointing at him.

"Quit standing around! The village is under attack! We must leave!"

Suddenly, a loud thud sounded on the small wagon behind him. Jesper was looking at him, his arms crossed. His hair was black and reached below his neck. He was slightly shorter than Naughton, but more muscular. He was dressed in dark pants and a dark black robe. He raised an eyebrow. "I'm not done yet."

"Did you hear what I said, Jesper? The gate guards are dead; it's time to go!"

"Alright!" yelled Jesper, throwing his hands up

10

in disgust.

Naughton looked around. "Wait, where are the others?"

"They're coming! They went to get food," said Lili.

Naughton looked down the street. "Jesper, you and Lili go to my Father's house. I will get the others."

As Naughton ran towards the store, he heard a faint chant in the distance that echoed off the buildings. As he rounded the corner, he saw arrows in the ground. One of his cousins, Cana, was on the ground, an arrow through her neck. Grief overwhelmed him as he saw the bright red blood. He clenched his fists. "Muir...what happened?"

"I--I--It's all my fault--"

"Come on, Muir, you can't help her. We must go!"

Muir stood in shock as agony seized him. "I can't leave her..." Naughton grabbed his bow off his back and hit Muir in the back of the head, knocking him unconscious. He threw Muir over his shoulder and ran back towards his house. The chant was getting louder and people were running around in a state of mass confusion. Naughton's legs began to burn as he ran back. When he saw his father and family in the distance, he gritted his teeth and urged on.

"Uncle Berton, I see Naughton!" yelled Lili.

"You said that a second ago. You sound like a parrot," said Jesper.

Berton turned around. "What took you so long, Naughton? And where the blast is Cana?"

"I'll explain later, but now we must go. The Geols are in the city!"

Berton's eyes widened as he grabbed his pack. "Everybody stay together and run towards the horse stables."

"What about the wagon?" asked Jesper.

"Leave it. We can't take it where we're going."

The chanting had ceased. There was the sound of metal clashing and villagers screaming. Naughton's hair stood up on the back of his neck. Berton led them toward the North wall. Naughton was last, his legs trembling as he carried his cousin. "Why are we going to the horse stables? It's a dead end."

Berton shook his head. "No, there is a secret passage underneath that a guard showed me in case something like this were to happen. They are getting close. Hurry!"

Jesper reached the stables first. "Where's the door, Uncle?"

"Look under the third stable."

Jesper ran to the stable and paused. "What do

you mean 'under'?"

"Boy, move. It's right here!" yelled Berton, agitated. Berton brushed the wood shavings aside and lifted a hidden door. "Everybody jump in the hole and go through the tunnel!"

Lia, Naughton's sister, went first. "Father, how will you fit? You're bigger than us."
Berton gritted his teeth, "I'm not that fat, stop being a hindrance!"

Once Lia dropped down, her mother followed, taking Lili in her arms. Berton went next as enemy soldiers closed in on them. Naughton put Muir down and got his bow ready. Suddenly, Muir grabbed him and punched him. "Now we're even."

Naughton stood up, swaying, trying to keep his balance. "Oh, my head!"

Muir looked at the soldiers coming. "Go in the tunnel. I will close it behind you so they can't find it."

Naughton slung his bow on his back. "But you will be killed!"

Muir pushed Naughton in the hole. "If I can't leave here with my sister then I won't leave at all!" With that, Muir shut the door and covered it with shavings. Naughton got up and started running until he reached the others.

"Where's Muir?" asked Berton. Naughton

looked back.

Berton drew his sword but Naughton put his hands up. "It's too late."

They ran through the tunnel blindly, guided only by a small light at the end that seemed to go on and on. The ground was moist, and a foul stench made Naughton gag as they ran through the mud. As they finally approached the exit, Berton grabbed Jesper. "Wait...Let me go first to see if it's safe." Berton stuck his head out slowly. He moved some vines to the side and peeked around, looking at the hay fields and the tree line. He held his breath, listening for any signs of danger before letting out a puff of air. "Okay, listen-- run straight to the trees. Let's get some distance from the city, and then we will catch our breath. Naughton, make sure nobody else is left behind, or so help me...Everybody, on the count of three: one...two...three!"

With a jolt, they took off running across the hay fields and into the woods. Naughton was last. He leaned against a tree, looking back to make sure no enemies were following. He saw smoke rising above the wall of Sturkma and heard faint screams. *Why us?* he asked himself as more smoke rose. He looked to the right of the city and saw a group of soldiers making a sweep through a village towards the hay fields.

Naughton pushed himself off the tree and ran deeper into the woods, catching up with the others.

Berton was panting like a dog. "Wait...wait. Stop, Jesper. Let's rest a bit."

Jesper slowed his pace. "But we are not far enough yet!"

Lili grabbed Jesper. "We have to stop--I can't breathe!"

"Fine, but just for a few minutes," he said, kneeling down.

Berton caught his breath and leaned against a pine tree. "Naughton, where is Muir? And what happened to Cana?"

Naughton went to speak but hesitated for a moment. "Cana was shot in the neck, and Muir covered the door for us so we could escape."

"You mean you left him behind to die?" said Lia, as tears formed in her blue eyes.

"Enough!" Berton yelled.

Lili cried out, "What about Cana, Aunt Teras?"

Teras touched her warm cheek. "She will not be forgotten. We will mourn for them when the time is right, but for now we must keep moving."

The group looked around for a moment, gathering their thoughts and their bearings. Berton pointed north. "Naughton, take us to the Mountain of

Colonies."

Naughton's eyes widened as he looked up the slope. "Many of our ancestors died trying to cross those mountains. The terrain is perilous; we won't survive if a snow storm hits up there!"

"Exactly. It's the last place the Geols will come looking for us."

"I agree with Uncle Berton, Naughton," said Jesper.

Naughton gestured his hand toward the mountain. "What do you know, Jesper? You have never been up there before! I have hunted up there for years. You have no idea what it's like, especially at night."

Berton clenched his fist. "Boy, stop arguing with me and do as I say! Just lead us in the lowest paths of the mountain and we can avoid a big portion of it." Naughton shook his head as he began walking at a quick pace. The others followed reluctantly up the mountain.

Mountain of Colonies

The sun was setting giving Oynst Peak to the east an orange glow. Pink clouds surrounded the peak, covering it with snow. Some had made the attempt to climb it, but all had failed. Oynst was unlike any other mountain. It curved at the top slightly arching back toward the earth. It reminded Naughton of death, for no man had ever been its conqueror. As far as he knew, it was the tallest mountain in all Bezinar, and just walking around the base of it was as close enough for Naughton. The group was getting tired as they walked slowly up the mountain. Naughton did not slow his pace, for a fear was in the back of his mind that they were being followed. The dead pine needles crushed under his feet as he weaved around the thick forest of pine trees. Over and over he thought about Muir, wishing he had shot the soldier when he had the chance so Muir could be with them. As he pondered he kicked pine cones, watching them roll down the slope.

He looked back at his father who was bringing up the rear, and Berton waved at him to wait. He slowed down to let Jesper pass. "Jesper, take the lead and stay on this course. I have to talk to my father." Jesper nodded, taking point as Berton approached.

"I believe our group has had enough for today.

Make camp."

Naughton looked behind them, straining his eyes. "Not yet...I feel like we're being followed."

Berton raised an eyebrow. "I have the same feeling. I will watch over us tonight."

"So what is the plan once we clear the mountain?"

"The only plan I have is to head Northwest to Fort Yorben. There we will come across an old friend of mine. He is in charge of the fortress and he will update us on the situation with the war and where we can go."

Naughton smirked. "If you're talking about who I think you are, he is cracked."

Berton gave a slight grin. "Yes, he is a little...different, but he's not stupid. Yorben is a long way from here. It will take at least eight days to get there and it will give me time to think. Find us a place to sleep."

Darkness was upon them and the sounds of night began. Crickets and owls sang their tune as the branches creaked. The whistle of the mountain wind was frightening, yet soothing at times. The tall pines were swaying in the light wind, with pine cones falling every once in a while giving a soft thud. It was a sound that Naughton was accustomed to after many hunts. He enjoyed the tranquility of the forest, as it brought peace to his mind. He found a small opening with grass and they all sat down in a circle. Teras grabbed some bread and water and began passing it around. Everyone ate in silence, fighting the cold as they shivered in their blankets, but no one complained.

Jesper sniffed the air. "What is that awful smell?"

Berton laughed. "Do you remember what we ran through in the tunnel?"

Jesper gave a disgusted look at his feet.

Lia looked at her feet. "Yep. It's horse poop alright."

After dinner Lia and Lili began gathering wood for a fire, but Naughton stopped them.

"We can't build a fire; it will be seen by the Geol soldiers."

Lia threw down the wood in disgust. "Then how will we stay warm?"

Naughton smiled. "Looks like you're going to have to huddle."

Lia gave him an evil glare, but Naughton just shrugged his shoulders. "At least you will be warm."

After the group settled for the night, Naughton saw his mother Teras leaning against a tree looking up at the stars. Her dark curly hair was pulled back, revealing her smooth, tan face. She wore a green tunic made of wool that reached down to her knees. Naughton sat near her. She seemed calm, revealing a slight grin. After a moment, Teras sighed. "They say many of our ancestors were buried up here when they came from the kingdom of Bezinar."

"I remember the story," Naughton said, peeling bark off of a tree. "A snow storm hit, killing many of them when they came over the mountain, and that is why it was named after the colonies. But why would they want to leave the kingdom?"

"Because it was getting too crowded and our people loved the open fields."

Naughton lowered his head, "I'm sorry about Muir and Cana, Mother."

Teras smiled. "It is not up to you who lives or dies. Remember what our elders used to say: our Maker is in control and has a reason for everything."

"I feel like I could have done more," said Naughton, throwing a piece of bark into the darkness.

Teras grabbed his chin and looked him in the eye. "Quit thinking about such things," she said, and then winked. "Get some sleep. You have to lead us tomorrow."

Naughton grunted and found a big tree to lean

up against. He pulled his thick blanket out from his pack and put his quiver under his head, gazing at the stars. Eventually, everyone was asleep except for Berton.

Morning came. There was frost on the ground, and everybody was wrapped tightly in their blankets. The sun shone on the frost, making it glitter like jewels. The air was still with few birds to be heard. Lili opened her eyes and froze; staring at her, ten feet away, was a skunk. The skunk picked up his tail, about to spray, but suddenly a rock skipped past and scared it away. "Thank you, Uncle Berton."

"You're welcome. I've been watching him for a while," replied Berton as he stood up. "Get them up, will you? I'm going to go ahead a little. Tell Naughton to meet me at the rock that has a face on it. He will know what I'm talking about."

Lili slowly got up, knocking the dead pine needles out of her hair. "Okay, Uncle."

Lili roused everyone and Teras had everybody drink some water. After gathering their gear, they followed Naughton to where his father requested. They approached an oddly shaped rock, with unique crevices and lumps. It was dark grey, with lines of dried sap on it from the pines which gave it wrinkles like an old man.

Naughton stood, puzzled. "Where is he? He said to meet here."

Lili yelled, "Uncle!"

Naughton put his hand over her mouth. "Shhh! We don't know who's around." Lia looked around and saw Berton standing beside a tree that had fallen. She pointed, and they walked.

"Why did you leave us early?" asked Jesper.

"Settle down. I went to the cliff to see if we were being followed and--"

"And what?" Teras interrupted.

Berton slowly wiped his face from his forehead to his chin with agitation. "I'm getting to it. I spotted smoke two miles behind us. I guess they camped last night, but they are nowhere near our path. I don't think they're on to us." He looked out to the South. "However, we must push on until we gain some distance from them."

Berton took the lead and Naughton brought up the rear, bow in hand. They continued walking north all day, taking small breaks to eat and drink. Gradually they turned northwest, and the terrain became more rigorous with loose stones hidden underneath pine needles. At night, they would stop and rest until the moon had risen. The pines got thinner the further up the mountain they went, exposing the loose stones allowing for better footing. Fortunately, the snow was farther up and they could avoid it by staying on the lower ridges.

The third night came and Berton went to a cave where he had taken Shadow Scouts for training. The cave was small and cozy, with the opening facing north. They put their packs in corners and circled a small fire pit in the middle. Berton took the water sacks from Teras and threw them at Naughton. "Go along the ridge and you will find an opening and a spring."

Naughton picked up the sacks and grabbed his bow. "I know where it is."

Lili walked around, investigating the cave. "Please tell me we can build a fire?"

Berton bit his lip. "I am hesitant, but I don't think we are in any danger." He rubbed his belly, pondering. "Very well, but keep it small, and put it in the pit so it will conceal the glow."

Naughton walked to the exit of the cave. "While I'm getting the water I will try to get some supper as well."

Berton laughed. "Good luck. None of the men I trained could kill anything near that spring. The deer always seem to know when danger is near."

Lia jumped up. "Can I go?"

Naughton started to say no, but had a change of heart as he looked at her. She wore a dark blue travel dress with brown pants with stains on the knees. She had freckles on her cheeks and long brown hair with bangs that were just above her brown eyes. "Can you keep quiet?" he asked.

Lili began to giggle and Lia looked at her. "What's so funny?"

"You," replied Lili. Everyone started laughing, but Lia did not find it amusing. Naughton grabbed his quiver, snickering. "We will be back in a little while."

Naughton and Lia went west walking along a ridge at a slow pace. The pines swayed with a low hiss above them.

Lia spoke. "So where are we going, Oh Great Hunter?"

"Shhh...not so loud," replied Naughton, grimacing.

Naughton approached the spring. It was surrounded by tall grass and a few bushes. Lia followed him slowly, staying low. Naughton pointed at the ground. "Sit here and keep quiet." He sat on a stump alongside her watching both ways, judging the distances for a shot.

Hours had passed when two deer approached the opening to get a drink of water. The first deer was small and careless; however, the second was very cautious, looking in every direction. As the deer walked behind some bushes, Naughton drew his bow and waited for the shot. He let the first one pass, waiting for the second. Finally, it stuck it's head out from behind the bush and stared in Naughton's direction. He thought to himself, come on come on, step out! He waited what seemed like hours to him as the deer smelled the air and continued to move its ears. Naughton's arm started shaking from holding the string back so long. His muscles ached and he could not hold it much longer. He aimed at a small gap in the bush, guessing where the deer's body would be. He let out a breath of air as the arrow flew and disappeared. The deer ran and fell to the ground about a stone throw away. Naughton started laughing hysterically and mocking in a deep voice what his father said. "None of the men I trained could kill anything up there. Bah!" Naughton pushed Lia. "Get up. We've got work to do."

Lia woke, yawning. "What, you got one?"

Naughton put the bow on his back. "Yep."

Lia slowly got up, stretching. "What do you mean, 'we'?"

"Why do you think I let you come with me?" replied Naughton as he went to the spring and filled the water sacks.

They made their way back to the cave, dragging their prize. Berton got up, drawing his sword. "Well, I can't believe it. I figured they would smell you."

Naughton smiled. "Nope. Lia saw them before they got too close." Lia smiled and winked at Naughton.

Berton and Jesper prepared the deer while Teras and Lili prepared for supper, spreading the leftover bread. Naughton and Lia sat back, leaning against the stone wall and enjoying the view, watching them work. Naughton poked Lia. "I can get used to this." Instantly they both gave a soft laugh at the rest of the group.

Everyone filled their bellies and after an hour of conversation passed they went to sleep--except for Berton and Naughton, who stood outside the cave, talking. Berton was smoking his pipe with his arms crossed and Naughton was leaning against a tree, looking south and rubbing his bow, feeling for any cracks. Berton gripped the hilt of his sword and held his pipe. "Well, son, I have to say I am impressed."

Naughton smiled. "You taught me well."

Berton blew a ring of smoke. "I have a feeling you will use the skills I've taught you soon. I will not be around forever and you will have to face challenges on your own."

Naughton stopped examining his bow and looked at his father with concern. "What are you talking about?"

Berton continued smoking his pipe. "I'm getting old, Naughton, and one day you must make your own destiny. I made mine by tracking and surviving in the wild. Not to brag, but I was the best woodsmen in the region. Your mother would be worried sick for days when the King requested my help at times."

Naughton's face went blank. "What--you helped the King?"

Berton started picking bark off a tree, examining where bugs had eaten through the bark. "There are many stories I wanted to tell you when you were older, but it seems there is no longer time for waiting. I served King Irus as a Shadow Scout. When I started raising a family, I trained a new leader for the Shadow Scouts so I could stay home."

"You mean Felden?"

"Yes. The King understood and gave me his blessing. We stay in touch. He is a good friend, but lately I have not heard from him. I'm afraid this new enemy has put him in great peril. The Geol army is a fierce group with many legions of men. I do not know who commands them or where they come from, but I'm sure King Irus does."

Naughton sat on the ground with his bow in his lap, holding it tightly and listening to every detail his father was saying. His father had never opened up this much. It was hard to get him to tell as much as a bedtime story and Naughton wanted to ask questions, but was afraid his father might not say any more.

Berton looked at Naughton, surprised. "You're not going to ask me anything?" Naughton seized the opportunity.

"I heard a story once when I was at the city trade center. Some of the King's soldiers came in and talked about the King asking for help in some place, but messengers are too afraid to go there because no one returns."

Berton took the pipe out of his mouth, staring at Naughton. Then he raised an eyebrow. "Really now…we are in more serious danger than I thought." Naughton waited for more, but his father put the pipe back in his mouth and puffed before changing the topic completely. "I have decided what actions to take when we get to Fort Yorben. If we are winning the war, we will take the Shaboot River and stay with your grandmother far to the north until this war blows over."

Naughton un-strung his bow. "What if we are losing?"

"Then we will stay in Bezinar and assist the King any way we can."

Naughton stood up. "I don't think we're winning the war. The Geol army took our city in a day without any resistance; perhaps the King does need help." Naughton was trying to get his father to tell him more, but it did not work.

Berton put out his pipe. "We will see, but for now we must rest."

The days wore on, and the company continued traveling in the lower parts of the mountain. They finally began going downhill on the sixth day with the snowy mountain peak Oynst to their backs. The trees were increasing in number again and the loose pine needles did not help their footing. The water sacks were low and the food was gone. Lia and Lili complained more day by day, wanting to know how much further. They staggered on occasion, with Jesper and Naughton having to carry them on their backs. Most of the time Berton was in front, leading the group. Naughton was last, making sure no one fell behind.

The night of the seventh day came and everyone was exhausted. Once again they sat in a circle and Teras gave portions of water to everyone. Berton walked over to Teras. "How is the water supply?"

"It is low; it will be gone by tomorrow. Are you sure it takes eight days to get there?"

Berton picked up a water sack, feeling the weight. "Of course. We will reach Fort Yorben tomorrow night."

Teras looked at the group, wondering if they would make it when she noticed Naughton was missing. She jumped up. "Where is Naughton?"

Berton looked around and yelled his name, but there was no reply. Berton clenched his jaw. "That boy knows better than just go wandering around without telling us. Wait here. I will go look for him."

Berton left the camp, going back the direction they came from. He dashed through the pines and stood still to listen at times. There was no sound except for the music of crickets. The moon was fading, making it hard to see. "I can't believe he would do something this stupid. When I get a hold of that boy I'll--" suddenly he was interrupted by a voice from behind him.

"You taught your son well."

Berton pulled out his sword as he turned around. Staring at him was a man in a dark green hood, with a bow on his back and a sword on his hip. His face was narrow with a peppery beard, and he had green eyes that sparkled with the fading moon. His hair was dark and well combed, going past his shoulders. His body was lean and toned--unlike Berton, who was short and heavy set with trimmed hair. Berton sheathed his sword. "Good grief, Felden, are you trying to give me a heart attack?"

Felden laughed. "You're not that old. Come with me and I'll take you to your son."

Berton followed Felden, continuing south. They walked for some distance when Berton started to hear laughter. As they got closer, he could see a fire with men standing around while Naughton told a story. Berton ran ahead of Felden, grabbing hold of Naughton's shoulders. "Have you lost your mind? You had me worried sick, boy! Why didn't you say something before you left?"

Felden walked up. "Easy on him, Berton. Let your son explain." Berton released Naughton, waiting for an answer.

"Father, I thought I heard something behind us, so I looped around to see what it was and I saw someone following our tracks. I slipped up behind him with my bow and took him by surprise, and then I realized it was a Shadow Scout." Felden and the other men began laughing at Naughton's victim.

"Well, Jayus, how does it feel to be at the mercy of a boy?" Jayus threw a rock at Felden, missing him by inches before stomping off. Felden walked up to Naughton, patting him on the back. "Your son is very skilled. He will make a fine Shadow Scout."

Berton shook Felden's hand, smiling. "It is good to see you, old friend, but what are you doing here?"

"Before I explain, let's go back to your family. We have water and food for them. Then we will talk."

Naughton and Berton walked up to the group an hour later with the scouts behind them. Jesper stood up. "Look! Shadow Scouts!"

Teras jumped up in tears. "Oh, thank El you're safe! How could you just leave us like that?"

Naughton hugged his mother, then Berton hugged her. "Relax, Teras, the boy has a good reason for his actions and I am pleased."

"He better have a good one."

Felden appeared with his men behind him. "My lady, it is good to see you again."

"Likewise, Felden."

Lia ran up next, hugging her brother and father.

She then approached Felden and gave a slight bow. "Mr. Felden, it's good to see you."

"Ah, little Lia, I have something for you and Lili." Felden pulled out a cupcake from his pouch.

"Wow, for us? Thank you, Mr. Felden!"

Felden smiled, looking down at the olive skinned, dark haired girl. "Of course, my little lady. Now who is this? Ah, yes. Jesper, you have grown much since we last met." Felden pulled out some bread and fruit from his pack. "Give this to your brave group. My men have water as well." Jesper began sharing the food while the scouts gave the water.

After building a fire, Berton sat down, pulling out his pipe with Teras and Naughton at his side. "Sit down, gentlemen, and tell me what you know." Felden sat down across from Berton with his men behind him. Of course, the children were curled up in their blankets, ready to listen to the story. Felden was chewing on an apple as he began the story.

"Well, we picked up your trail and have been following you for three days. I guessed it was you since the tracks had children's footprints and were heading in the direction of Fort Yorben."

Berton nodded as he blew smoke. "I had a feeling someone was following us but I was not sure. I saw smoke behind us one day."

Felden took a bite from his apple. "That was not us. It was a Geol patrol--a small one, I might add--but we took care of them."

"I see. What about Sturkma?"

"The city fell with little resistance. The Geols went through the small defense in minutes. They are nothing we have encountered before and they have strange markings on their dark armor."

Jesper interrupted. "What kind of markings?"

"A red flame with a snake curled around it. Many people escaped before the siege began but were cut off and taken prisoner. The others within the city and outer villages were shown no mercy either. Those that resisted were killed."

Teras gasped and brought a hand to her chest. "This is madness! Why did the King send us such a small force to help us?"

Felden took another bite from his apple. "I'm not sure, my lady. That is why we are going to Fort Yorben as well to find out. I and the six men you see came from Bezinar with orders to see how big the Geol army was. That was two weeks ago."

Naughton spoke. "Does the King not care about us?"

Suddenly, without warning, Berton slapped Naughton in the back of the head. "Silence, boy! Do not question such actions without knowing the King's intentions. It will get you in trouble."

Felden raised his hand. "We have asked ourselves the same question. It is vital to get to Fort Yorben and get our answers. Tell me, Berton, are you still friends with Mohai, the Commander of Fort Yorben?"

Berton puffed his pipe. "As far as I know, yes."

"Good. We can go straight to him when we get there, but I'm sure the guards will give us trouble. As you know, they do not care for Shadow Scouts. Mohai and I are on good terms, but those blasted guards give me trouble constantly."

Berton raised his right hand. "They won't bother us." On his hand was a ring that was solid white gold, except for the blue plate with two half shaped moons on it and a leaf in the center.

Felden gazed at the ring. "You have the Crescent ring? I forgot King Irus gave you that. We can go anywhere we want!"

Felden stood up with enthusiasm and his men did the same. "I suggest we get some rest, for tomorrow will be a long day for all of us."

Berton stood up as well. "Agreed, but I would like to talk to you alone if you don't mind." Berton and Felden left. Naughton wanted to follow and listen to their secrets, but he knew better, and feared the back hand of his father.

Mohai

Before the sun rose they were on their way down the mountain bearing north. Teras, Lia, and Lili were full of energy from the delicious food Felden and the scouts gave them. The scouts led the group while Berton and Felden conversed. Naughton was bringing up the rear as usual, but he had noticed that Jesper had been acting strange the past few days and was worried about him.

He caught up with him and slapped his back. "What's wrong with you? You have been very quiet lately."

Jesper glared at him, snapping a twig in his hands. "I'm fine."

"No, you're not. I know you too well. What's troubling you?"

Jesper grabbed another stick and started breaking it in many pieces as they walked. "I am anxious to get to Fort Yorben. As you know, my father was killed there. Lili was very young when it happened. Your father was the one who told us about it, but he did not know exactly what happened. I hope I finally get an answer."

"I remember him telling me about Uncle Tulios, but as you say, my father knew very little or withheld the information. You know how he keeps his secrets. Either way, I will help you get an answer, Jesper. I promise," said Naughton, giving a warm smile.

"Thank you. I am feeling a little better knowing I have help." Naughton dropped back to give Jesper his space.

The day waged on, and by midday they made it to the plains with few trees in sight. The tall grass was swaying from the wind hitting their waists. Birds scattered, chirping as the group intruded upon their territory. As they pressed onward, the grass got thicker, making it difficult to keep a steady pace, especially for Lia and Lili. People took turns carrying the little ones when they got tired, and few breaks were taken; being in the open made the scouts cautious.

Finally the afternoon came and the southern Suriu River was in sight. Going through the plains meant they were getting close to Fort Yorben. The Suriu River traveled a great distance, covering half the country of Bezinar. It traveled from northeast to southwest and gave great opportunity for transporting supplies from one region to another. They went to the only bridge that crossed the river in the region, which was guarded on both sides. It was made of stone and pillars and a wooden draw bridge that could be raised and lowered with ease. The bridge was also equipped with lookout towers so enemies could be spotted in the distance. To wade or swim the river was unwise due to the strong current.

As the group approached the bridge, a horn sounded, and two horsemen dressed in bright silver armor rode toward them. "Halt! State your name and destination," demanded the horseman on the right.

"I am Felden, lead Shadow Scout. These are my men."

Berton lifted his right hand, showing the horsemen the ring. "I am Berton. We are on our way to Fort Yorben to seek council with Commander Mohai."

The man jumped down from his horse and approached Berton. The man gazed at the ring. "Berton, you say? I have not heard your name in a long time, but I recognize Felden and his company." The man looked at Berton's family. "You may pass, but take heed: the Commander is not in the mood for company since learning of the fall of Sturkma."

The man jumped back on his horse and rode back to the gate, giving orders to lower the bridge. Felden led the way and the group crossed the bridge. The water rushed underneath them, forming foam around the pillars and spraying them as they traveled across. Eagles flew gracefully along the river hunting fish. The tower guards kept a sharp eye on them. As soon as they crossed, the bridge was raised, making a loud creaking as it lifted. Berton walked up beside Felden. "Well, it seems we have come at a good time."

"What are you talking about? If Mohai is mad he will be difficult to talk with."

Berton laughed. "You don't know him as I do. When he's mad he vents like smoke, and we will learn everything we want to know."

"If you say so," replied Felden, shaking his head with concern.

As sunset, Fort Yorben came into view, and Naughton was astonished at its majestic size. It was three times bigger than the city of Sturkma. The grey stone wall was at least a hundred feet high, with archers along every side. Some buildings could be seen peering over the massive walls. The towers stood twenty feet higher than the fort walls, with catapults mounted on them and archers all around each one.

The main gate was well guarded, with soldiers and horsemen that were decorated with thick armor and spears. Above the gate were slots where hot oil could be poured and stones could be dropped on approaching enemies. Behind the fortress were many villages and fields wealthy in livestock. Many roads were scattered around the fort, with some directed towards the river for wagons transporting supplies. Once again a horn sounded and horsemen rode up and escorted them into the city. Within the fort were many buildings made of stone and wood. The ground was covered in small brown pebbles that crunched beneath their feet.

Barracks were scattered within the fort, along with houses and various shops such as blacksmiths, bakers, and butchers. The people looked rugged yet humble, and were very polite, as if no war was in their midst. Children were running around playing with wooden swords. It reminded Naughton of his youth, when he and his cousins would play back home.

After passing the first barracks within the fort, a thin, tall, red-haired man dressed in a blue robe approached Felden. "Felden, it is good to see you escaped from Sturkma. I have been ordered to bring you to the Commander immediately for questioning. He is very upset because--" He paused, and looked at Berton. "You...I know you. El be praised, is it really you, Berton?"

"Of course," Berton said, laughing. "You look ridiculous in that blue bird outfit, Bane."

Bane grabbed his robe, shaking it. "It's not

funny. I feel at any moment people will start throwing birdseed at me, but this is what the King desires his scholars to wear. Is this your family?"

"Yes, but I'm afraid I cannot properly introduce you. We need to speak to Mohai. Will you tend to my family while we meet with him?"

Bane bowed. "They will be well taken care of."

Bane led them away, but Berton stopped them. "Naughton, Jesper, come with us. I want you to meet Mohai." Naughton and Jesper followed them without question.

They walked toward the center of the fort where the tallest building stood. Soldiers eyed them as they walked through. Naughton whispered to his father, "What is their problem?"

"Many soldiers do not care for Shadows," Berton replied in a soft voice.

"But why?" asked Naughton.

"I will explain later, but for now keep silent unless spoken to."

Felden approached the headquarters where Commander Mohai was located. The building was made of stone, much higher than the walls that provided its protection. The guard blocked the door. "Mohai has not summoned you, Shadow Scout. You will have to wait."

Felden crossed his arms. "I have heard otherwise."

"Regardless of what you have heard, you cannot pass."

Berton put the ring in the guard's face. "Stand aside before I make you!" The guard gripped his spear, clenching his jaw as he moved aside.

Felden led the group up a nearly endless flight of stairs to the top floor where the main chamber was located. Naughton heard yelling, but could not make out what was being said. As they reached the top of the stairs there were guards standing at attention. Mohai's personal guard stopped them at the door. "Wait here a moment, Felden. Commander Mohai is having a discussion with a Captain." They could hear every word that was being said. Mohai was yelling at the Captain in a deep voice that shook the halls.

"Captain, do not make assumptions! I told you that you and your men were on alert in case I had to send you to another fort or city for reinforcements. Remember what happened to the city of Sturkma. You and your men left due to a mere rumor, and when an order came to send you to Sturkma, you were not here, were you? Those people died because of your stupidity. Your assignment is to be prepared as reinforcements only! The King is furious over the loss of Sturkma, and guess who he was angry with? Me, you moron! Do not leave this fort unless I give you orders to do so, is that understood, Captain Hubin?"

"Yes, Commander."

"Get out of my sight! Morons! I'm surrounded by morons!"

Mohai kept yelling as the Captain stepped out, glaring at the scouts as he walked away.

The guard stepped in. "Commander, the Shadow Scouts are here with guests."

Mohai yelled, "Well, it's about time. Let them in!"

Felden and his men walked in, followed by Berton, Naughton, and Jesper. Mohai sat down in his large chair made of oak and gold, with two guards by his side. His personal guards wore red and gold armor and were armed with long spears. Their heads were covered with silver plated armor with slits for their eyes.

Mohai was a large man, with long, black, unkept hair that passed his shoulders. He had a well trimmed beard, and his face was plump and aged, with wrinkles on his leathery skin. His eyes were blue, with bushy eyebrows resting above them. He wore silver, lightweight armor with the crest of an eagle imprinted on the gold breastplate. His leggings were brown and

44

lined with gold down each side, and he carried a large sword on his hip. "Ah, Shadow Scouts, what news have you brought me?"

Felden and the scouts knelt. "Commander, I guess you heard that the city of Sturkma has fallen?"

Mohai slammed his fist on the arm of his chair. "Of course I've heard. That damn Captain left the fortress without my consent and the city fell without resistance. This mess is on my hands. The King was fond of that city, and now I have let him down."

Felden stood while the other scouts knelt on the ground. "Commander, do you know why the King was fond of that city?"

Mohai stood up and started pacing, holding the hilt of his sword. "Because of an old scout named Berton. He used to aid the King. Berton was a good friend of mine, and apparently had a precious item on him that the King needed, and now he is dead!"

Berton started laughing. "Well, it seems I am still somewhat important, then."

Mohai gasped, his mouth open like a fish. "I know that voice! Is that you, Berton? I did not recognize you with that short, peppery hair of yours!" Mohai walked up and bear hugged Berton, squeezing the breath from his body. "How did you escape Sturkma?"

"It's a long story, but if you don't mind I would like to check on my family. I just wanted to let you know that I was here."

"Of course. I will send for you when dinner is prepared. You can tell me what happened to Sturkma later."

Felden and Berton bowed. "Thank you, Mohai."

When darkness approached, Bane came and led the family to Mohai's dinner hall, which was one level below his main chamber. There was food of all kinds, from beef to fruit, and a variety of drinks. They sat at a long oak table that even had two special chairs that were taller than the others so Lia and Lili could reach. Mohai sat at the head of the table, with Felden and Berton on either side. Teras blessed the food and the feast began. Naughton tasted everything; he had never seen so much food in his young life. They laughed and enjoyed the fellowship and forgot about the worries of the world. Mohai waved a servant over, whispering, and moments later the servants brought in dessert for the girls. Lia and Lili's faces glowed while they tasted the dessert and started giggling.

An hour later, everyone was full to their heart's content. Mohai stood up. "It is an honor to be in the presence of such fine folk. Ladies, if you would excuse us, we have many things to discuss. However, Teras, you are welcome to stay."

Teras bowed. "No thank you, Commander. My husband will inform me of all I need to know." With that, Teras and the girls left the hall.

Mohai sat down and ordered the guard to show in the officers of high rank, and then he ordered the servant to bring in the ale. "Well, gentlemen, it's time we discuss recent circumstances. Felden, if you will, please tell us what happened to Sturkma."

Felden took a swill of water to clear his throat. "Sturkma was destroyed without struggle. The Geol army assembled southeast of the city and began their attack at midday. People were trying to escape and were taken prisoner. Those in and near the city were taken as well; those that resisted were killed. The small group of soldiers that defended Sturkma was overwhelmed within minutes.

An officer blurted out. "Why did you and your fellow scouts not help them, Felden?"

Felden turned and glared at the officer. "My orders were to not engage the enemy, only to study their tactics."

"Well, that figures. What else would you expect from a Shadow?" said another officer.

Mohai stood up and bellowed in his deep,

powerful voice, "Silence! We will need everyone the King sends our way. You will all honor these Shadows, or you might as well stick your head in a bucket full of water, breath in, and rid us of your stupidity!"

The officers sat in silence and Felden continued. "Many of the Geol soldiers were average sized men. They wore dark armor that had a flame with a serpent around it on the breast. There were a few commanding them that were not normal--at least, not man-like. They stood at least nine feet, but were slightly arched over, with spikes on their necks. They were covered in wide, thick armor that seemed like it was part of their body. They carried giant hammers and long, two-pronged spears on their backs. Their armor was black with a marking I did not recognize. The oddest thing about them was their eyes--they were blood red. Their language and dialect is something I have never heard before, almost a deep gurgling sound.

Berton pulled out his pipe and started packing it with tobacco. "Were their faces like ours?"

"No, their heads were shaped like an armadillo, but slightly broader, and their eyes followed the contour of their heads, sloping downward."

Mohai leaned back in his chair, rubbing his

beard. "You mean…they weren't human? I have never heard of such."

"As far as we know they are no breed of man, Commander. We were at least sixty yards away when some passed us in the woods."

The officers started arguing among themselves about what actions should be taken. Berton sat in silence, thinking to himself, while Mohai and the officers talked. An officer spoke out. "Commander, what about the other forts? Have we heard anything from them?"

"I'm afraid not. There have been no messengers from the other two for some time, and I'm afraid even if they requested reinforcements that we would not be able to respond fast enough."

Berton puffed his pipe for a long time, deep in thought, forgetting his surroundings. Naughton stared at his father, wondering what he was thinking. Jesper nudged Naughton. "What is wrong with your father?"

"I don't know, but I would like to ask the Commander a question."

"Well, what are you waiting for?" Naughton raised his hand. Mohai gestured his hand, making everyone silent.

"Speak, Naughton."

Naughton took a deep breath and had a sudden

chill. "Why don't we ask for help the King truly needs, since the messengers are too afraid to do so?" The entire room fell silent, except for Berton, choking on his pipe. Everyone stared at him in shock.

Mohai crossed his arms. "And where did you hear such things?"

"I heard it in the Sturkma trade center when some soldiers came through."

Berton cleared his throat. "Son, now is not the time for such questions."

Mohai interrupted. "On the contrary. I think now is the best time since you're here, Berton."

Berton shook his head. "Only the King can give such a request, and I swore secrecy on the matter."

"The enemy is knocking on our doorstep and your concern is secrecy!" yelled Felden.

Mohai raised his hand. "Calm down, Felden."

"No, I will not. I want to know the whole story."

Mohai stood up. "Indeed, but this topic does not need to be heard outside this room."

The officers started arguing. "That's just a myth. He doesn't exist, and no one has ever returned from the Seraph Lands."

Mohai laughed. "One did return, and he's sitting in this room." The entire room fell silent again.

Mohai tapped his fingers on the table, "Well Berton? We're waiting."

Berton waited a long time, drinking his fresh brew and puffing his pipe. Finally, he answered. "It is true." The officers sat speechless, but Mohai and Felden were not surprised. Naughton could not believe his ears, that his father had been to the Seraph Lands.

In the midst of his own agitation, Naughton exclaimed, "What is in the Seraph Lands? I have been left in the dark for years, and I want an answer!"

Berton narrowed his eyes at Naughton. "Quiet! I suppose now is as any good time as any, however, I ask everyone to leave the room except for Naughton, Jesper, Felden, and you, of course, Mohai. I swore secrecy to the King on this matter and there are few who know this story."

Mohai cleared the room of the officers and guards. The officers started grumbling, but gave no trouble.

When the room was cleared, Berton drank more ale and gnawed on his pipe for a moment. Mohai slammed his mug on the table. "Now, out with it!"

Berton put out his pipe and put it in his pocket. "Years ago--before I met your mother,

Naughton--I was in the King's service after the Centurion War. He asked me to lead a group of soldiers and scholars to the Seraph Lands in search of his messengers that had never returned. He sent them to ask for help from this so-called supernatural being, which dwelled in the Seraph Lands. I thought he was crazy to think such a being could possibly exist. We do not have a name for him, and no one knows where he came from. Many say he does not exist, but the King was told otherwise and was desperate for help to prevent the collapse of his kingdom. Some scholars believed that thousands of years ago, this being was responsible for the destruction of great corrupt civilizations. One was called Qanas. Rumors were that he dwelled in the Seraph Lands, among a perilous landscape of deserts, mountains, and caves. Ours was a long journey that lasted for weeks. When we reached the Seraph Lands, we learned from the Samhas that there was only one path that you could take to avoid a swift and painful death. We lost two men along the way. The scholars found clues that were written in a language I had never seen before. It was called Hebrew. Luckily, the scholars could read it, and they guided us during our journey.

I will not get into the discussion of the clues because of strange circumstances I can't remember.

The heart of the Seraph Lands was surrounded by mountains. We found a massive temple deep within. We spent three days searching for the entrance. We felt as if something or someone was watching us, so we took turns at night keeping watch.

On the fourth day the door revealed itself to us and opened by itself. We were immediately surrounded by a swift, cold wind. As soon as we entered the temple, the door quickly shut behind us and blew out our torches. We could see nothing; it was so quiet you could hear our hearts beating. After a moment, when our eyes adjusted, we could see a glowing hallway. I touched the walls and they felt smooth, solid, and cold. It soon dawned on me, they were made of gold.

We followed the hall for what seemed like forever. There were many rooms and halls, all dark. We kept following the glowing hallway until it came to some stairs that spiraled downward. The steps were also glowing, and it seemed like hours before we reached the bottom. Once we reached the last step, there was no more light except for the steps that lay behind us. We stood there for a few minutes and then I saw two small golden lights staring at us from the distance. I was not sure, but it looked like a pair of eyes. I told everyone to be still and listen, but there was no sound. I eventually heard movement around us, but could not see anything. The two golden lights disappeared and then I realized that they were, in fact, eyes.

All was quiet and then a voice spoke in our tongue. The voice was smooth and calm, and I heard these words: 'Ye are not welcome here.' Suddenly, there was a flash of bright light. I looked around, and everyone was dead. Some with holes through their heads, and some had no heads at all. I was the only one alive. Something hit my chest and fell to the ground. I picked it up, and it was a necklace that had a jewel attached to it. The jewel is this."

Berton pulled from around his neck a necklace. It was a solid gold chain, and the jewel was shaped like the sun, with five golden rays extending out from the diamond–filled center shaped like a drop of blood. He passed it around, and everyone looked at it in awe. Naughton was the last, and he held it for the longest. It was very light, and the red diamonds were smooth and showed no evidence of cutting.

"What happened next?" asked Naughton.

Berton took the necklace from Naughton and continued. "The last thing said to me was, 'Tell your king that my King will only help those who believe, only the sun may return.' And then I awoke in Samha.

My gear was beside me and there was bread and water. I returned and told the King what happened to me and my men. He swore me to secrecy, and after that day the King dispatched his scholars throughout the kingdom, and they taught from the Bindings of El that we know of today."

Berton pulled his pipe back out, stuffing it with tobacco, and began smoking again. The group sat for a while, taking in everything Berton said.

"What Bindings of El?" asked Naughton

"It's a book that is heavily guarded at the castle. Apparently, there is only one left in the world," answered Felden.

"But why send scholars out to teach the Bindings of El?"

Berton replied. "The King assumes that the supernatural being and the Bindings of El are related because of the Hebrew writing. It has stories in it that tell of our history and who created us. The King had scholars study it and teach the people throughout the kingdom. However, many do not believe."

Felden drank a sip of water. "How can the sun jewel return if nobody takes it?"

"I don't know. I have thought about that statement every day since."

"It's a riddle, then?" asked Jesper.

"I suppose," replied Berton, gnawing on his pipe.

Naughton stretched out his hand. "Father, can I see the jewel again?" Berton pulled out the necklace and gave it to him. He examined it again and flipped it over, looking at the smooth gold plating with words engraved on the back. "What do these words mean?"

"Quit joking around," said Berton.

"I'm not."

Berton yanked the jewel back and looked, but there was nothing there. "Boy…I told you to stay away from that ale, there is nothing here. I know it like the back of my hand!"

Naughton stretched his hand out. "Apparently, there have been recent changes. Give it here and look on the back." Berton placed the jewel in Naughton's hand and suddenly words appeared. Naughton did not realize it the first time he held it. Suddenly, a cold chill went up his spine and he began to sweat.

"What!" yelled Berton, jumping out of his chair. "That is impossible!"

Felden looked at the words. "I can't read this."

Mohai leaned over Naughton."Nor can I."

Jesper took Naughton's hand and examined it close. "Maybe it's Hebrew, since everything else you encountered was Hebrew."

Mohai slapped Jesper on the back. "Well done, Jesper. We must find someone who can read this. Guard!"

The door guard ran in. "Yes, Commander?"

"Where is Bane?"

"He left a while ago on an errand. He is expected to return in the morning."

Mohai banged his fists on the table. "Blast it! Very well, have him report to me in the morning."

"Yes, Commander," replied the guard, giving a bow.

Mohai rubbed his beard. "I suggest we get some sleep. Tomorrow we will get our answer." Naughton gave the necklace back to his father, who was still stunned, and the words disappeared.

Berton stared at the jewel and Felden spoke in a soft voice. "To think that it is your boy who must go back."

Berton clenched his jaw. "Do not jump to conclusions. We do not even know what these words mean."

Mohai stood up. "I agree. Let us wait for Bane before we worry the boy." The others stood up and left the hall. Berton, Jesper, and Naughton went to a small brick building inside the fortress where the rest of the family was staying.

Teras put her hands on her hips. "What took you so long? It's been three hours!"

"Tonight has been...different, and I don't know if it's good or bad."

"I'm tired of surprises," said Teras, closing the door once they entered.

"Naughton, give me your hand," said Berton with a calm voice. Naughton outstretched his hand and Berton placed the jewel on it. Once again, the words appeared on the back.

Teras grabbed Berton's arm. "How can this be?"

"I don't know, but tomorrow I'm hoping we will get an answer."

Teras could sense her son's fear and hugged him. "It will be fine, Naughton. Get some sleep."

Jesper whispered to Naughton. "Maybe I should not have encouraged you to ask the question."

Naughton ignored him and thought about what was going to happen to him tomorrow. He replayed his father's story in his mind, thinking of every detail, and eventually fell asleep wishing he had never asked a single question.

Knocking at the gate

Naughton woke to a loud horn blast and soldiers yelling. Berton leapt out of bed and ran to the window and saw soldiers grabbing their weapons. "Oh, this can't be good. Naughton! Jesper! Get up! I think the fort is under attack." The pair dressed themselves as Teras immediately began to prepare Lili and Lia. Naughton strung his bow and took a deep, readying himself for whatever might come. Berton opened the door. "Jesper, Naughton, you two follow me. Teras, stay here with the girls. We'll be back."

The three took off toward Mohai's headquarters. Archers were manning the walls and preparing the catapults while soldiers slid deftly into formation, swords and shields in hand. Minutes later, armored horsemen exited the fort and headed west. They disappeared into the dust, the gate closing behind them.

When Berton approached the door to Mohai's quarters, he heard someone shout his name. He stopped to look, and there stood Mohai on top of the southern wall next to the gate waving them over. They ran upstairs to the top of the wall. Mohai was in full armor, his golden eagle shining in the sun. His guards were all around him, spears and shields in hand, providing his protection.

Mohai gave a big smile. "Well good morning you lazy oafs," he said. "I see the horn woke you."

Berton looked to the south and saw dust rising in the distance. "How did they get here so quickly?"

"This is another force. Our guards spotted them coming from the west along the river. I ordered them to draw the bridge and fall back to the fort. Felden has already observed them and returned; he says it's the same size that attacked Sturkma. If that is the case, we will have no problem holding them."

Naughton looked at the surrounding villages and saw people leaving with wagons full of supplies and heading north. As he gazed at their faces, he was flooded with the memories of leaving his own family behind and felt sorrow.

Felden came running up the steps. "My Shadows have returned from their flank. They say all they have is infantry, archers, and a few of those creatures behind them. I think this is merely a test of our defense."

Mohai turned to the archer nearest to him. "Do not fire the catapults until they are double within range!"

The archer looked at him, confused. "But Commander, that will put their archers within range."

"I know. Stop questioning me!"

"Yes, Commander."

"But why wait?" asked Naughton.

Mohai grabbed the boy's shoulder. "I don't want the enemy to know how far the catapults can reach," he explained.

Bane finally reached the stairs. Out of breath, he took a moment to compose himself and then stated, "Commander, all families within the fort have been relocated in the shelters--including yours, Berton--and the villagers are fleeing to Iona."

"Thank you, Bane," replied Berton, shaking his hand.

Felden grabbed hold of Bane's arm to get his attention. "Do you know how to read Hebrew?" he asked.

Bane cocked his head to the side like a bird. "Hebrew...I haven't read or spoken that language in ten years. Why?"

"Now is not the time for such questions!" Mohai snapped. "We have another problem right now--fighting off the Geols!"

"Oh, you grumpy old goat, I just wanted a yes or no."

Mohai waved Bane closer. "Where did you go last night?"

"I had business in one of the villages and I--"

"Irrelevant," Mohai interrupted. "From now on let me know where you're going."

"As you wish, Commander."

Mohai turned to glare at Naughton and Jesper, who had begun murmuring to themselves while watching the exchange. "I think it's time you boys became men," he announced. "Captain Ruros!"

"Yes, Commander."

"Take these boys to the armory and prepare them for battle. We have at least an hour before the enemy arrives--make sure they're looked after."

Naughton and Jesper's eyes grew wide as the captain grabbed them. "Yes sir!"

Jesper's mouth opened wide in shock. "But I am no warrior..."

Mohai glanced at Jesper. "Very soon you will be. Now go! Also, tell the Centores to stay out of this battle. I don't want the enemy to know they're here."

The captain began dragging Naughton and Jesper down the wall to the barracks near the gate. He opened the door and led them passed various beds and closets to the back, where another door stood open. Inside lay a vast array of weaponry. Naughton went to the bows hanging on a wall and immediately began rifling through them like a child. Jesper headed for the swords, which were sitting in racks in the middle of the room. Ruros was digging through a chest searching for armor to fit the young men. Lo and behold, he found four sets of armor that would prove suitable for the task at hand. "Well, gentlemen," he said, motioning toward his findings. "This is all we have that will fit you. What is your choice?"

Jesper walked over to examine the armor. Two sets were made thin for agility, with one coated in silver and the other gold. The other two sets were thick for heavy combat. They both were coated in silver, though one set also had gold emblazoned on the shoulders. Jesper touched it lightly and asked, "What about this one?"

Ruros looked Jesper up and down contemplating. "This is Centore armor. I don't think they will mind you wearing it; however, it will be a little heavy on you."

Jesper grabbed the armor. "Nah…I can handle it."

Naughton grabbed a bow hanging towards the top. Ruros looked at him, concerned. "Are you sure about that? That is an osage bow; it's one of the hardest to pull back." Naughton struggled stringing the bow, but he pulled it back with ease. Ruros smiled. "Very well, then. Come pick your armor."

Naughton ignored the heavy armor and eyed

the two thin sets. The silver was plain with some battle markings, but the gold had an eagle claw coated in silver. Naughton ran his fingers over the eagle claw on the chest plate. Ruros nodded in agreement. "I think this is fitting for you, Naughton. You are an archer, and the claw represents picking victims from the sky."

Jesper finished dressing. The armor felt bulky but comfortable. Ruros laughed. "Well, turtle, you haven't picked your weapon yet."

Jesper walked over to the swords again. "I'm having trouble deciding. Which one should I pick?"

The captain examined the swords; there were all different shapes and sizes. He veered to the left of the rack and opened a dusty closet full of long swords. He pushed a box aside. "Aha! This will do nicely." The captain brushed the cobwebs off the hilt of a sword and brought it down from a high shelf. Unsheathed, it appeared to be about three feet long. He wielded it with ease, swinging at a piece of firewood cutting it like butter. "No one uses this sword for some reason, and I think it's time for a young man like you to revive it."

This sword had a different shape than the others. The blade curved towards the end with sharp teeth on top curling back towards the hilt. He passed the sword to Jesper, and it felt heavy in his hands. The blade was three inches wide including the teeth. The tang was large enough for two hands, and the grip was made of black leather. The pommel had a polished gold emerald. Captain Ruros looked them over, pleased. "Well, gentlemen, I think it's time to test your skills. Come with me."

Jesper followed, clinking and clanging out the door. Naughton put his old bow on his back--he refused to leave it behind because of its sentimental value. Ruros waved an archer over. "Take this young man to the range and work with him."

"Captain Ruros," Naughton interrupted. "I have handled a bow my whole life."

"These are not targets that stand still like deer, Naughton. You're shooting at men that shoot back."

"As you wish," Naughton replied with disgust.

The archers ran off to practice and Jesper tugged on the Captain's arm. "What about me? I don't have a clue what I'm doing."

"I figured as much the way you're clanging about in that armor, Turtle," Ruros laughed. "I'll take you to some men over here who will train you."

Ruros walked toward the north gates where a small squad of soldiers stood Jesper noticed they were unlike the others. Their armor was similar to his, but had strange colored markings on them. Each had a different color such as green, blue, and orange on their shoulders. The leader, however, had red shoulder armor and a skull was imprinted on it.

Ruros approached the red shoulder. "Nemian, I need you to train this young man to fight."

Nemian glanced at Jesper. "A gold shoulder Centore? I did not realize Thorg trained more. It's been a while since we've had green horns with us."

Ruros raised his hand. "This is not what it seems," he explained. "I brought him to you because you are the best, and he has never seen battle."

The Centores stopped laughing and Nemian gave a grave look. "Then why is he wearing Centore armor?"

"He chose it and it fits him well."

"This deception is punishable by death. Only Centores can wear our armor!" Jesper swallowed wetting his dry throat as he looked at Nemian.

"He is a child, Nemian!"

"I know. This... is ill advised. It takes months of training to become a Centore. Most of the soldiers do not pass our training, and you think we can teach him in one hour?"

Ruros became aggravated. "Nemian, I cannot order you to keep an eye on this boy, but I know he will be safe with you and your men. Besides, Mohai has ordered you and your men to stand down this fight; he does not want to reveal how strong we are."

Nemian gripped the pommel of his sword and went to speak, but cut himself off in frustration. "Fine! But after this battle is over, I demand to speak with Mohai. We will be inside the headquarters if you need us." Ruros bowed and left. Nemian took off his helmet and looked at the young man with stern, hazel eyes; he was not pleased with his new assignment. Jesper stood in awe as he looked at Nemian from head to toe. He was slightly thicker than the others, with a bald head and a rugged tan face. Jesper noticed he was missing his left ear, but did not stare. "How old are you?" Nemian asked.

"I'm...seventeen sir," Jesper replied stuttering.

"Seventeen...I might as well put a diaper on you! Well, son, what is your name?"

"Turtle," Jesper answered without thinking. "--I mean Jesper, son of Tulios."

The Centores began whispering and Nemian spun around. "Shut up!" He turned back to Jesper. "You say your father's name is Tulios?"

"Yes, sir."

Nemian observed Jesper closely and looked at the sword. "Give me your weapon." Jesper unsheathed the sword and gave it to him. Nemian studied the blade closely. "How did you come by this?"

"Captain Ruros gave it to me in the armory."

"Did he now?" Nemian twirled the sword with ease as it glittered in the sun. He placed the blade in its sheath on Jesper's belt with a flash. "Come, we will drink all Mohai's wine and see what you're made of, Turtle."

While Jesper was getting acquainted with the Centores, Naughton was practicing with his new bow. After several shots, he managed to finally hit the target. His trainer worked with him to take cover when necessary, as well as how to hold the bow correctly. The new bow could be pulled back much farther than his old one. When he pulled back the bow creaked, but when he released the arrow all was quiet. The trainer looked at his target with satisfaction. "That bow is very powerful. The more you shoot it the less sound it will make. Osage bows are strange; it seems they get more powerful the more you use them." His trainer gave him a quiver full of arrows as a sign that he was ready.

The horn sounded again and all soldiers and archers became quiet. Captain Ruros retrieved Naughton and they ran back to Mohai to the top of the wall. "I put Jesper with the Centores

Commander, but where should I put Naughton?"

Mohai looked at Berton. "Where do you want him?"

Berton dressed himself with armor and took up a bow. "He will stay by me."

"Very well." Mohai ordered two guards over. "Guard these two with your lives."

The guards saluted. "Yes, Commander."

Felden pulled out his bow and grabbed an arrow from his quiver. "They will be in range within minutes. I'm going to the north gate with my men to help the archers. El be with you!" With that, Felden sprinted off, his cloak flapping in the wind.

"Where do you want us, Mohai?" asked Berton.

"Go to the other side of the gate on the wall and wait for my signal to open fire."

The Geols numbered five thousand strong and Fort Yorben had over seven thousand. The Geol army was a mix of archers and infantry in dark armor with red flames on their chests. The infantry took their shields off their backs and lined up, marching in unison. The Geol archers lined up behind them for cover.

One of the officers started yelling. "Commander, they're in range! Can we fire?"

"I said wait until they are double within range!" yelled Mohai, in his deep voice. The Geol archers unleashed their arrows and they rained upon the fortress. "Take cover, shields up!" The archers took cover behind the walls and the soldiers hid behind shields. Screams echoed throughout the fortress as some of the Geol arrows made it past the defenses.

The officers began to panic. "Permission to fire back, sir?"

"Not yet, you idiots!" yelled Mohai with rage. Another rain of arrows came down. "Shields up!" Mohai raised his hand. "Hold…hold…fire!"

Instantly, Fort Yorben unleashed fury on the Geol army. Arrows hissed through the air and many Geol soldiers fell to the ground screaming in agony. The catapults released fireballs that exploded on impact, devastating their lines. The Geols could not keep ranks. Arrows found gaps in the Geols' shields and pierced their armor. The entire fortress unleashed hell on the Geols and it was obvious that the fort had the upper hand.

Naughton, shaking, had difficulty placing the arrow on the string in the midst of action. Berton was calm, placing his arrow without delay and firing within seconds. He glanced at Naughton. "Breathe, son. Use your palm to guide the arrow to the string;

control is difficult in the heat battle." Naughton understood, and after a few tries his firing rate increased. "Very good," said Berton, as he let loose an arrow. "Now shoot at their necks or under their arms if you can."

The second wave of Geols came, but they held their ranks and eventually reached the wall. The Geols shot grappling hooks, hitting the top of the wall on the first try. The soldiers were cutting the ropes in an effort to keep the Geols from climbing. Under the cover their archers provided, the Geol foot soldiers began to climb the wall. Berton looked into the distance behind the Geol army and saw the dark armored creatures. They were not advancing, but rather observing the battle. Berton ran over to Mohai. "Do you see those creatures?"

"Yes...I've been watching them for some time now. This is surely a test!"

After several attempts, a few Geol soldiers made it to the top of the wall, but were greeted with swords and spears. The clanging of metal began ringing through the air as they fought on the wall. Naughton was shooting as fast as he could, hitting mostly shields. Every once in a while he hit his target knocking soldiers to the ground in pain. He became agitated, not hitting his intended targets often. Berton watched him closely, and then moved close to his son. "You must point at their necks and underarms, not aim. Aim small miss small, do you understand?" Naughton nodded and took a deep breath as he continued to fire, his aim steadily improving with every shot. Suddenly, a wave of arrows came raining down on them. Naughton looked up, and dread filled his heart as he realized there was no escape. Berton, however, remained calm as he grabbed a shield on the ground and raised it above them. The guards instructed to protect them did the same, forming an overhead barrier. Multiple arrows thudded against the shields and a few screams filled the air. When the barrage stopped, Berton laid the shield down and resumed firing, unfazed by the attack. Naughton speechlessly stared at his father, knowing that they could have just died. His father glanced at him. "Shoot, son."

Though the soldiers of the fort seemed to have the upper hand, Mohai spotted a mass of shields approaching. After a moment, he realized they were carrying a battering ram to the gate. Mohai whistled loudly to get the attention of his soldiers and shouted, "Man the gate!" The men immediately began placing support posts; others lined up to apply steadying force. By the time the battering ram reached the gate, men from above were hurling rocks and hot oil over the wall. The Geol shields gave little resistance as the oil seeped its way through the cracks, scalding their skin. As some ran, flaming arrows hit their backs, igniting the oil. Rocks continuously bombarded the few stragglers left carrying the battering ram.

Eventually the Geols abandoned the idea of breaking down the gate, but others kept trying to scale the walls. Mohai signaled his armored horsemen in the west to attack. The horsemen charged in from the fields, flanking the Geols catching them by surprise. The horsemen plowed over them, decapitating and gorging them in droves. After almost three hours the Geols retreated out of range of the archers and catapults. The men guarding the fortress cheered, laughing at their enemies. "Hey, come back! We have plenty more for you!"

Mohai slapped Berton on the back. "The battle is ours and we didn't even show them half of what we can do. They have no idea what awaits them next time. Captain Ruros!"

"Yes, Commander?"

"Order the men to stand down and care for the wounded, and then give me a count of casualties."

"Yes sir!" replied the captain, as he took off down the steps.

Naughton put his new bow on his back

alongside his old one. He was still breathing heavily and his hands were shaking. He had never been in a battle. He took a deep breath. "I take it we won?"

Berton winked. "Yes, today we did. However, this was a mere test and next time will not be so easy. Come with me to help our injured."

By sundown the fortress had regrouped and injured men were being cared for in barracks throughout Yorben. The air filled with smoke as bandages soaked in blood were burned, while fresh bandages came from hot water buckets. The less fortunate were lined up along the wall and covered with blankets. Families who lost loved ones could be heard wailing in the night. Berton and Naughton went to see Teras and the others to let them know they were okay. Teras was caring for the injured soldiers while Lia and Lili were running errands for her. Eventually, Berton and Naughton met up with Mohai and Felden at the south gate. Berton shook Felden's hand. "How did the north gate fare?"

"They didn't even scratch it. No battering ram came at us, but the Geols were consistent in trying to scale our walls."

Mohai looked to the south deep in thought, then stretched his back. "Let's go to my headquarters; I have scheduled a meeting to get an update of our situation." Mohai led the group and as they went upstairs they heard laughter coming from the dining hall. Mohai opened the door. There was Jesper, getting knocked down like a rag doll as the Centores took turns training him, between chewing on turkey legs and drinking wine. Mohai's veins bulged from his forehead with anger. He gripped the hilt of his sword. "What is this? You Centores are all the same, taking anything you want without asking and showing your asses!"

Jesper quickly got to his feet. "But Mohai, I have enjoyed their training, and learned much."

Mohai puffed out his chest and glared at Jesper. "Boy, do you have any idea what you're getting into? These men are nothing like other soldiers; they have no fear of anything and constantly disobey my orders!"

Nemian stood up. "That's enough, Mohai, and you know that is not true. We are trained to obey orders from the King and fort commanders. I can understand why you are angry with us eating and drinking your wine, but we will do what we like when we are unable to engage the enemy!"

Mohai walked up to a Centore and yanked the food from his hand. "I could care less about the food and wine, but you could at least help the injured soldiers!" Nemian raised an eyebrow at Mohai and silence filled the room. Mohai poked Nemian's chest, "I will speak to you alone on this matter later, but for now I want you in my meeting. You other Centores will go and inspect the fort and help my soldiers any way you can."

The Centores looked at Nemian. He nodded and they left the dining hall. Jesper ran to Naughton. "What happened, and how many did you kill?"

Naughton shrugged his shoulders. "I don't know. I lost count, but you will hear everything in the meeting."

They all met in Mohai's upper room headquarters along with captains and officers. They all sat down at a long table as Mohai threw his armor on the floor and sat back in a chair. "Let's start off with the captains. I want to know how many we lost."

Captain Ruros stood up. "I lost twenty-four."

Captain Hubin stood up. "I lost fourteen."

Captain Yezun stood up. "I lost thirty-seven."

Mohai tapped his fingers on the table. "So we lost seventy five. How many injured?"

One of the lower officers stood. "We have two hundred and seventy-eight injured."

"That leaves us approximately seven thousand men strong. We are very fortunate," said Mohai, crossing his arms. "This was a test, gentlemen. As of now we must assume they are regrouping with a different strategy and will call for reinforcements."

Captain Ruros raised his hand. "Did anyone see those creatures in the distance?" Everyone mumbled and nodded yes in unison.

Felden spoke, "I believe it will be sometime before they attack again. They had many casualties and my Shadows say they crossed the Siriu River and are traveling northwest in a hurry."

Mohai pointed at Nemian. "What say you, Centore? Why are the Geols so quick in leaving the area?"

"Perhaps their companions had better luck attacking one of our other forts and they are going to give reinforcements."

Berton nodded. "This is quite feasible; why else would they leave in such a rush?"

Captain Hubin slammed his fist on the table. "Why are we sitting here? We should be giving chase and keeping them from helping their comrades if this is the case!"

The outburst caused several other members of the meeting to begin shouting at once. Mohai watched them for a moment before shouting, "Silence!"

Once again they were quiet, until Felden began

to speak. "Perhaps the captain has the right idea. My men and I could follow them undetected to see what has caused their hasty retreat."

Discussion immediately took place among the men to see if such actions were advisable. Nemian let out a quiet laugh, causing them to fall silent. "What's so funny, Centore?" asked Mohai.

"I think you are missing a great opportunity."

Mohai leaned forward with interest. "Speak your mind."

Nemian clasped his hands with a wry smile. "If the Shadows follow the Geols and not allow themselves to be seen, it is likely that at least a few will take off to send word to their leader. That would give us a chance to see where the Geols hail from and who commands them."

Everyone--even Mohai--agreed in unison, but Berton sat in silence thinking on the matter. Felden noticed Berton and quieted the men. "Berton, I'm sure you have an opinion of this idea?"

Eventually, Berton shook his head. "I must advise against it. We know they come from Qanas. If you and your Shadows are discovered and captured, they will torture you without mercy. Their leader will learn all our strengths and weaknesses, and most of all, our secrets."

Felden stared at Berton for a moment. "So, you're saying we should just stay in the dark and hope for the best? We cannot stay on the defensive Berton."

Berton gave Felden a sharp glance. "No, I'm saying you must ask yourself if it is worth the risk."

The room fell silent once more with the weight of the decision. Minutes went by before Jesper broke the silence. "I have an idea, Uncle Berton, but it may sound crazy."

"What is it?"

"What if you led a young company of Shadows? That way, if you are captured, they won't learn anything because you've been out of the loop so long. You don't know that much information and neither do the young scouts."

Naughton became enraged. "What? Surely you are not suggesting my father take such a quest! How could you think such a thing?"

Nemian, however, was impressed. "You have spoken like a Centore, Jesper."

Naughton pointed at Nemian. "With all due respect, sir, my father knows more than you think. He has more secrets than you can imagine!"

Nemian narrowed his eyes. "Boy, I knew your father long before you were even an itch."

Berton placed his hand on Naughton's. "You're missing the point, son. Centores are trained to only think about victory, no matter what the cost. They care for others, but victory always comes first-- otherwise it would jeopardize their mission. They would rather die than return home having lost a battle."

Nemian beat his chest. "You honor me, old Shadow, and you know us well."

"You are crazy!" Captain Hubin blurted out.

Nemian clenched his jaw to keep from hitting the captain over the head. "No, we make sacrifices so others may enjoy freedom."

Naughton crossed his arms, avoiding eye contact with Jesper. Mohai leaned back in his chair and the room was quiet. Felden spoke with a low tone, "Jesper's theory is somewhat sound; however, it is a dangerous and many would advise against. What Naughton says is true. You know many secrets, Berton." Berton nodded in agreement. Felden paused tapping his fingers on the table. "I will go with you if you choose to go, Berton, but it is a gamble. We could learn much from our enemy if we succeed, but if we are captured they in turn can learn a great deal from us."

Captain Ruros slammed his hand on the table.

"This is outrageous talk! There must be another way."

Mohai raised his hand. "No...there is no other way. Berton must choose his own fate; no one can ask or order him to do it."

Berton rubbed his chin in deep thought and finally spoke. "I must pray on this and talk with my wife."

Mohai stood up. "Very well then, but make haste. For now, I want everyone to keep a sharp eye and be ready in case the Geols return. You are all dismissed."

All the officers and captains left the hall except for Nemian, who wanted to speak to Mohai alone. Naughton stood up and left angrily, refusing to look at Jesper. "It seems my cousin is angry with me, and he has the right to be," said Jesper.

Berton looked at Jesper. "Do not worry about Naughton. He'll be fine. Your words gave great counsel to our situation. Felden and I must speak alone. Will you excuse us, Jesper?"

"Yes, Uncle." He left to look for Naughton. He went outside, searching, but could not find him. Instead, he went back to the brick house to await Naughton's return.

Naughton walked around the fort and came across families taking their dead loved ones out the north gate to bury them. He avoided looking at the devastated faces of the families; no words could ever ease such suffering, only time. He eventually made his way to the south gate, only to discover it was closed. He asked the guard if he could go for a walk outside. The guard hesitated as he looked at his spear. "Very well, but return in an hour and we will open the gate for you." Naughton exited the gate and walked toward the river. The smell of death overwhelmed him as he stepped over the dead bodies of enemy soldiers, sending chills up his spine. Most of the Geols were pierced with arrows, but some were scorched from the catapults and oil. Still others were gored by swords and spears. He did not know if he could go on. The smell was becoming almost more than he could bear, but he wanted to reach the river to hear the rushing water. Naughton gazed at the dead men, wondering where they came from and who lead them to their fate. He squatted down next to a dead Geol and looked at his armor. There was a red flame imprinted on his chest with a snake curled around it. As he looked around he heard a faint whisper.

"Help."

Naughton froze.

"Help me."

Naughton walked toward the sound when

something grabbed his foot. He jolted straight up in the air, grabbing his bow. Looking down, he saw a Geol soldier, grasping at him weakly. Naughton kneeled and looked at the soldier. He had an arrow through his right chest plate, and there was dried blood around the arrow as well as his mouth.

"You must...you must...help my people," the dying man gasped out." We had to swear allegiance or...he...he would kill our families."

Naughton grabbed his hand. "Why did you not resist?"

The soldier coughed, blood dribbling from his mouth. "You...don't understand. He has creatures and men that fight...fight for him and he is ver...very..."

Naughton waited for more, but the man let out one last breath before his eyes went dim. Naughton placed the soldier's hands over his chest and closed his eyes. After a moment, he began searching the body and found a map. Half of it was burned, and some parts were stained with blood. He glanced over the map, but the damage made it difficult to interpret. He put it in his pouch and began walking towards the river.

He made his way to the rushing water and sat down on the bank. He gazed at the sky in hopes of seeing the stars, but found that the clouds were blocking them. The sound of the river helped him find peace as he pushed the battle out of his mind. He pulled out his father's sun jewel and felt it with his fingers as he relaxed in the night air. The night was cold with no wind, and the dead bodies behind him made Naughton feel as if he were in a tomb.

Suddenly, he heard footsteps approaching from behind. He put the sun jewel back around his neck and tucked it under his shirt. He readied his bow, turned around, and did not move. He could see someone, but could not make out who it was. Finally, he recognized Nemian. "You should not be out here alone, son of Berton. There could be Geols still around you know." Naughton lowered his bow, refusing to respond and wondering if the Centore would go away. Nemian looked around. "You should not be mad at your cousin, Naughton. Jesper was trying to help in the matter and he gave good counsel," said Nemian in a soft voice.

Naugthon turned and stared at the Centore with tears in his eyes. "How would you feel if your father went away, unlikely to return?"

Nemian sat next to him. "I would probably feel as you do, but I have learned much since my youth." He looked up at the dark sky. "You must understand that you should not be selfish but rather supportive in this matter. You may show concern and express love, but support him in whatever decision he makes. Your father has a difficult choice to make; he could be leaving and risking his life for you, your family, and friends. He is the only one who could pull this off because of his experience and it would be selfish not to help us. On the other hand, it would be selfish to leave you and your family behind wondering if he would ever return. Like I said, I knew your father long before you were born. Believe me when I say that if your father accepts this quest, it would be for the greater good--not for his selfish ambition." Naughton sat silently looking down at the ground, annoyed with Nemian's presence. Nemian gripped the hilt of his sword. "Naughton, I came out here because I have a matter to discuss with you. What do you know of Jesper's father, Tulios?"

Naughton curled his legs up to his chest and wiped away his tears. "We are not sure what happened to him. All we know is that he died at Fort Yorben and no one knows how."

"Did he know what his father was?"

"No," replied Naughton in a stern voice. "All he knows is that he would leave for months at a time and would not say much when he returned."

Nemian unsheathed his sword and stuck it in

the ground. "Look at the hilt of the blade and tell me what you see." Naughton pulled the Centore sword out of the ground and angled it so he could see, but no light was available. Feeling along the hilt with his fingertips, he made out an engraved C 2.

Naughton handed the sword back to Nemian. "C 2. What does it mean?"

Nemian sheathed his sword. "It means Centore unit number two, leader of the second unit. Each unit is commanded by one leader who wears red shoulder armor, and each unit has at least a hundred men. The leader of unit three died a tragic death saving the King's niece, who was kidnapped a decade ago and held for ransom." Nemian paused before explaining. "The leader's name was Tulios."

"The Centore three unit was sent to rescue her. They snuck in the fortress and found she was being held in a high tower. When the Centores entered the room, she was thrown from a window by an assassin. Tulios jumped out of the window after her, caught her, and used his body to save her from the impact of the water below. Whether or not he knew the moat was there, his actions were brave. It worked, but the shock of hitting the water knocked him unconscious and he sank to the bottom drowning. She survived with a few bruises. He is highly honored, and the story was only shared by Centores. His sword is held by the King's niece to this day, and no one has taken his place as commander of the Centore three unit."

Naughton was stunned. "You mean Jesper's father was a Centore? But how do you know it is the same Tulios? Surely it could be someone else."

"That is highly unlikely. The story you gave me fits perfectly. Tulios said he was from Sturkma and he died ten years ago."

Naughton was speechless--his uncle was a Centore Commander! "I have to tell Jesper."

"Say nothing to him!" Nemian said, sharply.

Naughton leapt to his feet in frustration. "I promised him I would help find out what happened to his father!"

"No matter what oath you gave, you cannot tell him."

"But why?" Naughton asked, clenching his fists.

"Boy, sit down and be quiet before you draw too much attention and get an arrow shot through my head!" Nemian hissed. Naughton sat down and crossed his arms, waiting for more commands from the stubborn Centore. "The reason you cannot tell is because you will dishonor Tulios. Commanders are not allowed to have romantic relationships or families while we serve; it is our law. If word gets out that Tulios married and had children during his command, his honor will be tarnished. I used to wonder why he would disappear at times, but now I understand. I knew Tulios like a brother, and I will not allow this to be revealed to anyone. My men grow curious, but I will assure them that Jesper's father is not the Tulios we know. I do not believe your father even knows of this matter. You must remain silent."

"But Jesper has a right to know!"

"No. The time will come when he will learn of his father, but for now he must remain in the dark."

Naughton threw a rock in the river. "What else must I deal with tonight?"

Nemian stood up. "I am returning to my men, but remember to keep quiet. I have something in store for Jesper if he so chooses, and he can learn about his father in time." Nemian began walking and then paused, turning to the boy. "I would not linger here, Naughton." With that, he disappeared into the dark. Naughton sat in frustration, skipping rocks in the river wondering how he would keep this secret.

Naughton woke suddenly to his father standing over him, hands on his hips. "Have you lost your mind spending the night out here? You had your mother and I worried all night. Nemian had to tell me where you were. Get up! We have matters to attend to with Mohai and the others."

They walked toward the gate. "Father," Naughton began, "I am sorry about my anger last night. I was just upset at Jesper's suggestion."

"I know, but next time try to calm yourself in safer places--this is no place for folly. All it takes is one mistake and death will be upon you. There could have been one or more soldiers out here playing possum who could have killed or captured you. Come on, quicken your pace. We will be late for the meeting."

They entered the dinner hall and were greeted by their family, as well as Felden, Mohai, Jesper, and Bane. Dinner was eaten in relative silence until it was broken by Mohai. He locked his eyes on Naughton. "Did you enjoy your stay out in the battle field? My gate guards say you didn't return all night. You had us worried, lad."

"I'm sorry. I just had a lot on my mind."

"Apparently!" blurted Teras. "Your disappearing acts always cause unwanted stress. What were you thinking? I have enough grey hair as it is!"

Felden held out his hand towards Naughton. "If you would, let Bane examine that sun jewel."

Naughton pulled it out and gave it to Felden, who handed it off to Bane. Bane examined it thoroughly. "Where are the words?"

"Oops," said Felden jumping to his feet. "Come here, Naughton, and let him see."

Naughton walked over and Bane put the sun jewel in his hand. "Incredible!" said Bane, his eyes wide. When he picked up the jewel again, the words disappeared.

"Is it magic?" asked Lili.

"Nonsense! There is no such thing as magic," said Bane as he studied the words closely. "This is amazing!"

Felden paced in the room. "We know that already, you goof. What do the words mean?"

"I have no idea. I haven't seen this language in years."

Felden gritted his teeth. "I thought you were a scholar?"

"I am, but I must admit I got lazy and just taught from memory," said Bane, remorsefully.

"Well, that's just great!" yelled Felden.

Mohai laughed. "You Shadow Scouts always blow things out of proportion."

Bane raised his finger. "I have to go see the King; I am sure that the scholars there will be able to read this."

"No, my son is not traveling in the midst of

war," objected Teras.

Berton shook his head. "Teras, the boy must go so that this matter may be resolved. The kingdom is in peril and we must do whatever we can to aid King Irus."

"Fine, I will go with him."

"No, you will not!"

"But Berton, you are leading the Shadow Scouts."

"You're going?" Naughton interrupted.

Berton wiped his face from his brow to his chin with agitation. "Blast it, Teras, I wanted to tell the boy myself." He looked at Naughton. "This must be done. Felden is going with me, along with several capable Shadow Scouts. You must understand the situation at hand. This will be our only chance to find out where the Geol stronghold is and who is leading them."

Naughton pulled out the map he found. "I might have an answer to that question."

Mohai stood up, reaching out his hand. "Where did you get that, lad?"

"I found it on a dying soldier."

Mohai grabbed the map, Felden and Berton examining it alongside him. "This map is useless--it is burnt where the enemy stronghold is located," said

Mohai, disgusted.

Felden pointed at the map. "But it does reveal what direction they came from. It looks like they came from the south, way past Sturkma. Look at this; they have the locations of Fort Coralis and Fort Estmere. They even have the paths to the City of Valkry. They have been planning this a long time. It would appear that there are spies among us. Look here, where the blood stains are--here, give me that candle."

Berton handed the candle to Felden, who put it behind the map. The ink shown through the blood stains. "Look to the southwest. There are many villages and towns outside the kingdom of Bezinar. We can only assume that these people have either aligned themselves together in order to destroy us, or that they have been captured."

"Yes and no," Naughton interjected.

"What do you mean? There are not two answers here," said Mohai.

"The soldier spoke to me."

"Out with it, lad!"

"He said we must help his people, as he would have killed their families if they did not ally with the Geols."

"Who is this 'he'?"

"I don't know. The soldier died before telling

me."

Teras ordered a servant over and had Lia and Lili removed from the dinner hall and escorted back to the lodge. Lia put up a fuss. "I believe we are old enough now to listen to your secrets!"

Mohai smiled. "Not quite yet, my brave ladies. Not quite."

Once they left, Teras spoke. "How can we repel this evil? Not only does this mean the Geols are very powerful, but that they have amassed an army from many enslaved regions. We will be greatly outnumbered. There is no way the King can build an army big enough for a defense."

Berton took the map and sat down. "The soldier said that they were forced to serve the Geols. This means we could help them and they in turn can help us."

"It's possible," interrupted Mohai. "But first things first, we must see where the Geol stronghold is located so we can assemble an assault. Berton, Felden, and his Shadows will trail the Geols. Naughton will go with Bane to see King Irus."

"I am going with Naughton," said Teras.

"No," countered Berton in a calm voice. "You must take Lia and Lili far north to the mountains, where you will be safe until the war is over. You know Ruby is worried about us and wants word of our health."

Teras stared into her tea cup. "Why can't we just send a messenger to let her know that we're okay?"

"Because I want a clear mind while I am tracking the Geols," Berton responded, scrubbing a hand across his face.

Teras closed her eyes, gripping the cup. "Fine."

Berton looked at Mohai. "Can you spare some men to send with my wife and family to ensure safe passage?"

"Consider it done."

Jesper raised his hand. "What about me?"

Mohai raised an eyebrow and gave a slight smirk. "Nemian has a proposition for you, Jesper. He wants to know if you want to become a Centore." Naughton then realized what Nemian meant about keeping the secret and it being revealed to Jesper.

Jesper leaned back in his chair. "But how will I be accepted? I have never seen battle and they only accept soldiers who have seen combat."

Naughton patted his cousin on the back. "I think you would be a great Centore."

Jesper was surprised. "I thought you would never speak to me again?"

"Oh, I'm alright. I just needed time to calm down and accept what has to be done."

Jesper was unsure. "I wish to speak with Nemian first."

Mohai jumped to his feet in excitement. "Excellent! Tomorrow, at the sound of the battle horns, we shall each adjourn to our fates. But tonight, we shall feast." Everyone left to prepare for the journeys that would change their lives forever.

Naughton was gathering gear and packing food for his four day journey when Teras caught him in a fierce hug. "I have a gift for you." Naughton looked at her, noting her drawn mouth and watery eyes. Teras handed him a necklace. It was made of leather, and hanging from it was a deer horn carved in the shape of an arrow head. "Your grandfather made this and wore it when he was a scout many years ago. He wanted you to have it for your twenty-first birthday, but eighteen will do."

Naughton put it on and looked in the mirror. The necklace hung just below his shoulders beside the sun jewel. He noticed his blonde hair was thicker than it once was. His eyes were dark green, unlike his family who were all brown eyed and dark haired. His face was tan with a prickly beard trying to grow. His body, however, had changed since they left Sturkma. His torso was slender and his legs were thicker from all the walking, but his upper body had lost muscle mass from the lack of timber work he and Jesper used to do, swinging axes, and hauling wood. Jesper, on the other hand, was now thicker and slightly shorter than Naughton. Jesper always had the advantage of cutting a tree down faster than Naughton because of his brute strength, but Naughton was more agile and could climb trees quickly. Naughton remembered those days fondly as he turned and hugged his mother. "Thank you. It will remind me of you and where we come from."

Teras smiled. "It is to remind you to be brave." She went back to Lia and Lili, helping them pack for their trip to Doldram where her mother Ruby was waiting for them. Berton began packing. He gathered rope, a knife--anything he could possibly think of that would be useful on his journey. He also packed extra tobacco for his pipe and hid it from Teras, knowing she hated his habit. He strapped on his sword and kept the bow he had gotten from the armory during the attack. To camouflage himself in the woods he also packed a green robe, which could be inverted to reveal a brown rabbit fur underside to blend in fields. The Shadow Scouts wore similar robes.

After packing, Naughton and Jesper went to investigate the fort. They walked along the west wall and saw blacksmiths pounding away on anvils shaping medal to their desired shapes. As they reached the north gate, they noticed caretakers grooming the horses in the most immaculate stables the boys had ever seen. The horses had shiny coats and they were each provided with fresh hay and water. "These horses are truly cosseted. I wish I had someone to rub me like that all day--preferably a woman," said Naughton with a chuckle.

Jesper smiled. "I'm sure you wouldn't mind at all."

"You men are all the same," they heard someone say from behind one of the pampered beasts. Looking at them was a woman with long golden hair and soft blue eyes, wearing brown attire. She was working on its hoof. "Do you think we are your slaves?"

"Why, no! I was just making a joke," said Naughton.

The woman shook her hair out of her face. "I see. So we are here for your entertainment?"

"No, no...I was just saying that--"

"Shh..." the woman said, standing suddenly and placing a finger over Naughton's lips, silencing him. "You're just digging yourself a hole of which I will be delighted to bury you in." The woman patted the horse and walked off to tend to another that needed attention.

Naughton watched her walk away. "I would say she is a little sensitive."

"I suppose you don't want her to groom you then?" Jesper said, smirking. They continued walking down the stables and saw Bane packing his saddle bags and watering his horse. "What horses are we riding, Bane?"

"Greetings, gentlemen. A bit anxious, are we?" replied Bane, not looking at them.

"A little," replied Naughton as he started rubbing the horse's neck.

"Your horses are at the front where you came from. Asha, I believe, is preparing your horses for the journey. Did you meet her?"

"If you call that a greeting, then yes."

"Don't worry," Bane laughed. "She won't bite. She just has a lot on her mind. Most of these horses have seen battle; some are wounded and others did not return. It agitates her when the horses she tends to get hurt or killed after spending so much time in her care."

"That explains things," said Jesper.

"Well, gentlemen, I have errands to run before we leave in the morning. I will have one of the caretakers bring you your horses at sunrise. Farewell," he said, nodding to the both of them before heading toward the food storage.

Jesper and Naughton continued on around the fort. When they reached the courtyard, they heard soldiers laughing. Heading toward the sound, they saw many men drinking their fill from the barrels of beer situated around the fire. The soldiers looked towards Jesper and Naughton and raised their drinks. "Well, well, look at the young Centore." Naughton and Jesper looked around but did not see any Centores. "Hey, come here and show us what you've got, kid." Jesper realized that they were talking to him.

Naughton answered instead. "Sorry, but we're on an errand."

"What's the matter with your friend? Does he need his armor to keep him safe?" asked a soldier. "Wait, didn't the Captain refer you as Turtle?" The rest of the soldiers laughed.

Jesper curled his fists. "I think I can take him."

Naughton stared at him. "Have you lost your mind? He is a soldier, and I hate to remind you but you have never actually been in a fight."

"That's not true! The Centores gave me some

lessons during the battle."

Naughton shook his head. "Fine, let them make a fool of you!"

Jesper approached the soldier. He was the same height as Jesper, but with a thicker build and broad shoulders. Jesper squared up with him, ready to fight. The soldier finished his beer and met him head on, fists clenched so hard the knuckles were white. The others moved back to give them plenty of room. Naughton perched himself on a nearby barrel, hoping his cousin wouldn't get his head pounded like a drum. The soldier ran at Jesper to tackle him. Jesper stepped to the side and pushed his head down, making him flip onto the hard ground. The soldiers laughed, which agitated Jesper's opponent; he stood up and reset himself. The soldier swung a fist at Jesper, who blocked the punch. Jesper swung at the soldier's face, but he ducked and punched Jesper in the stomach. Jesper curled in on himself, grabbing his gut. The soldier kneed Jesper in the face, knocking him to the ground with blood pouring from his nose. The soldier grabbed a barrel and stood over Jesper, ready to hurl it at him. Instead, Jesper kicked his feet out from under him and the barrel collapsed over his head, spilling beer over the ground beneath them. Jesper stood up and kicked the soldier in the face knocking him out.

"That was a cheap shot!" yelled the soldier's comrades. They swarmed Jesper, knocking him to the ground and kicking him.

Naughton stood up, ready to charge in to help his cousin. Before he could take a step, a hand grabbed his shoulder and pushed him back down on the barrel. Naughton turned and saw Nemian, watching with a grin. Behind him stood almost a hundred Centores. The Centores rushed in together as a single unit, mercilessly throwing the soldiers like rag dolls and beating them to a pulp. The soldiers scattered like quail and were chased off by the Centores hurling barrels at them, laughing in their wake. Nemian made his way to Jesper, who was covered in dust and had blood dripping down his chin. Nemian pulled him off the ground, and all the Centores returned to examine Jesper. "It seems Turtle paid attention to his training," said a Centore.

Nemian gave a small, proud smile. "Indeed."

Jesper grimaced, spitting blood onto the ground. "Apparently not well enough. I just got belted like a dog."

Nemian dusted him off. "No, boy. The point is that there is no such thing as a fair fight, and you beat that soldier on your own. We watched the whole thing. You did well. We only came to your aid when you were unfairly outnumbered. Now come on, before one of the captains discovers what happened. I don't feel like explaining our actions." Nemian led them to his quarters near Mohai's command post while the Centores took Jesper's fallen opponent and tied him naked to a pole in the middle of the courtyard.

Nemian cleaned Jesper's face and examined his nose, which had mostly stopped bleeding. He turned Jesper's head to the side. "Well, your nose isn't broken, just a little battered. You'll be fine," said Nemian as he put the bandages away.

Naughton looked around Nemian's room; it was small, but cozy. It was furnished with a bed, a desk, and a single cabinet. On the wall was a picture of a forest, and in the corner of the room was his armor. "Do all leaders have a skull marking on their shoulders?"

"No, it was engraved because of an action in Samha. By order of King Irus, we killed a corrupt King who had enslaved his people for years."

"Where is Samha?" asked Naughton.

"It is northeast of here, just beyond Hightop forest. The new King's name is Mel, and he is very respectable and wise. The people there have recovered and live in peace now. They honor us and King Irus to this day for helping them. As a matter of fact, King Mel gave me that painting on the wall."

"Is that Hightop forest?" asked Naughton.

"Yes," Nemian answered as he sat in his chair. "I am fond of that place. It is like no other I have seen."

"How so?" asked Naughton.

"The forest has a very tall canopy and the animals are massive. Why, I have seen a rabbit as large as a dog."

"How's that possible?" asked Jesper.

"No one knows. But know this: if you ever visit, be cautious, as some of the predators will consider you for their dinner." Nemian looked at his armor, lost in thought. Then he snapped his fingers. "Before I forget, did Mohai tell you of my offer, Jesper?"

Jesper took a deep breath. "He did...and I accept."

Nemian leaned over, looking solemnly into Jesper eyes. "Good. But I must warn you this, training will be the hardest challenge you will ever face. Your trainers will inflict immense pain upon you--not because they want to hurt you, but because they want you to stay alive. Very few men make it through the training. Some men don't even make it out alive."

Naughton watched Jesper as the two of them spoke, noticing his newfound confidence. He appeared to have overcome much of the fear he had suffered in Sturkma. He knew his cousin was not the violent type, but recent events had changed him greatly. Jesper approached Nemian's armor and touched it lightly, looking at the red shoulder. "I want to do this. I feel as if it were in my blood." Nemian and Naughton glanced at each other, but remained silent.

Nemian reached in his desk and pulled out a sealed document. "Here. You will need this. Give this to the Centore instructor named Thorg when you reach Bezinar, and hopefully he will accept you into the training."

"Nemian," Captain Hubin asked, barging in abruptly. "What is this all about?"

Nemian stood up. "What do you want, Captain?"

"Explain to me why your men tied up one of my soldiers in the middle of the courtyard bare ass."

"I guess one of your men got out of line, Captain."

Hubin crossed his arms. "My men are well disciplined. I will not just sit around while you Centores get away with such actions!" He then left, slamming the door behind him.

Nemian smirked. "It looks like I have some explaining to do before things get out of hand." Nemian began to escort the young men out. Suddenly, the battle horn sounded.

Nemian turned back to grab his armor, but Jesper stopped him. "Wait! Mohai said he would have the horn sounded when it was time to eat."

"That is ridiculous!" yelled Nemian. "That horn is not a dinner bell! I have to go tell my men." Nemian ran off, and Naughton and Jesper headed to the dinner hall.

The table was set with an astounding array of food. Everyone was there, including Mohai and his officers, Felden and his company, Bane, and all of Naughton's family. Bane arose to bless the food, and then the feast began. Musicians played songs of old that none of the young ones knew but that the elders knew by heart. They sang, ate, and drank, enjoying the fellowship and telling stories. Felden began to dance with Lia around the room. Mohai's softer side shown through as he, in turn, danced with Lili. Eventually everyone was dancing--though not all were good at it. Naughton danced with one of the servant girls.

Jesper sat to the side watching his friends and

family twirl around the floor. Suddenly he felt a tap on his shoulder and turned, only to find Asha. She was wearing a red and green dress, her long golden hair in a braid. Jesper felt his stomach tighten as he stared at her, speechless. "Is something wrong?" she asked.

"No, of course not," Jesper answered, voice wavering. He cleared his throat. "I just--I didn't recognize you, is all."

"I see. I suppose I look a little different when I clean up."

He looked at his companions dancing and finally mustered some courage. "Would you care to dance?"

"Not tonight. I am tired from caring for the horses. Perhaps another time." With that, she disappeared into the crowd, leaving Jesper feeling very foolish.

After a long night of entertainment, Mohai whistled for everyone's attention. "My friends, it has been an honor to be in your presence. We all come from different places, but we are all Bezinarian. We are people free from tyranny and slavery. We come and go as we please, not worried about the dangers of the world because we are protected within our borders. Until now. Now, the Geols threaten our peaceful existence and bring with them the cloud of death. We have forgotten that freedom does not come without sacrifice. Other kingdoms have not been as fortunate as we. Many lands have fallen at the hand of this new enemy, their peoples enslaved and killed. They have been working toward this attack on us for years, and we must rise up together once again. Now it is our turn to make sacrifices, like those of our forefathers so many years ago during the Centurian wars. We must trust in one another, no matter our differences. May our mighty El be with us as we crush the Geols into dust!"

A mighty cheer rang throughout the hall. Toasts were made, and afterward everyone left to rest for the journey ahead. Naughton walked out into the night air and saw his father waving him over to the gate. Once he reached him he caught him in a fierce embrace, knowing that this could be the last time he would ever see him. Berton grabbed his shoulders. "My son, I know I haven't spent much time with you since we got here. As you can see, we are about to make history. It is up to you to make your own destiny. Tell me, Naughton, what do know of the Bindings of El?"

"I only know of what mother has taught me."

Berton gave a small smile. "Do you remember me telling you of the day my life was spared?"

"Yes."

"I believe I was allowed to live because of my belief in the Bindings of El and its teachings. You cannot just learn El's teachings, my son. You must believe in every word. I know you don't know much, but know this: El has always taken care of me, and you must come to trust Him as I and your mother have. He will not leave you in the dark. At the kingdom of Bezinar you can study His teachings for yourself and gain wisdom. Here, take this." Berton pulled off his Crescent ring and gave it to Naughton. "I was told this ring is the key to all of Bezinar. It came from the heart of Valkry and has been passed down for generations. It will gain you access throughout the kingdom without confrontation. Remember your teachings from me about tracking and survival. Do not trust anyone by just their words, but by their actions as well. Trust your instincts like you always have. Another thing," he said, looking sternly, "what you did on the wall when the Geols attacked can never happen again. You must never hesitate during battle or let your emotions cloud your mind. Focus on the task at hand and you will survive. I will be gone before you wake in the morning, so I will tell you now. Farewell, my son. I love you, and I am very proud of you."

With a slow pace they went to the brick house.

Naughton went to bed early, but did not sleep as he tried to listen to his parents whisper through the night.

Paths to follow

Naughton woke to a banging at the door. He rubbed his eyes and answered it. Before him was Asha dressed in travel attire, wearing a long brown cloak and dark green pants. She was equipped with a bow and quiver on her back. Her hair was up and pinned back. "It's sunrise, you lazy ox! Hurry up and get going. Bane is waiting for us at the gate!"

Naughton shut the door in her face. "Oh, why her?" he muttered. Naughton woke Jesper and they readied.

Teras was already up preparing breakfast. "You better hurry. Bane will leave you without regrets." Teras placed the food on the table while they got dressed.

"Mother, when are you leaving?"

"We will leave at noon. Mohai and his guards are escorting us to Valkry, and we will go on boat from there."

"What does Valkry look like?"

"I thought I had told you."

"You did, but it has been a long time."

She poured some hot tea. "Very well. Sit and eat." Naughton and Jesper took bites of eggs. "Words cannot express its beauty. Every time I go there, I come across structures I've never seen before. It would take weeks just to explore the whole city, for it seems each level has its own culture. The tower is teal and taller than any other structure known to man. Endless streets surround it, with walls higher than the trees, except for Hightop forest. It has the biggest trade market in all the land, with items unseen by most. Traders throughout the countryside bring their very best items to sale." She got up and retrieved some baked bread from the stove. "One day I am sure you will see it."

Jesper took the bread. "Why does the King stay at Bezinar Castle when Valkry is more majestic?"

Teras shrugged her shoulders and sat back down. "He says if ever an army were to invade, he would rather have the castle destroyed instead of Valkry. It is home to thousands of people and the city has been there longer than anyone can remember. But the King, I'm sure, has his secrets. Some sections are closed off to the public." Naughton and Jesper swallowed their food and drank it down with water. They strapped on their gear and headed for the door. Teras stepped in front of them. "Forgetting something?" Naughton and Jesper kissed her on the cheek and started to walk out, but Teras grabbed Naughton. "Be sure to use your heart, soul, and mind in every decision you make." She hugged him, and they smiled at each other. Naughton gave a wink and walked out.

The horses were being held by Asha. "Come on already. Bane will be agitated with us for being late!" Naughton and Jesper got on their horses but they looked at Asha oddly. She noticed. "What?"

Naughton spoke. "You are coming with us?"

"Of course. I go with Bane often to Bezinar Castle to visit. You don't think I just stay here all the time, taking care of horses and shoveling excrement, do you?" Naughton and Jesper looked at each other, smirking, and they rode to the gate.

Finally they reached Bane and he was wearing his blue robe with a brown cloak. "Well, it's about time!"

"Sorry, Bane," replied Asha.

"No apologies. We have to reach the town before sundown." They exited the north gate in a light trot, going northeast toward Iona. The road passed through open fields and forests, and several villages. The weather was nice for traveling when the sun was out, but when the clouds came they brought with them an unwanted chill. Bane led the group, not looking back once, as if he and Asha traveled all the time. As Naughton and Jesper followed Bane, they had a hard time not laughing. Bane's stirrups were too short, making his knees stick out like an ostrich.

At noon, they stopped under a tree to eat. Bane passed around some dried meat and bread as Asha pulled out the water sacks. They ate in silence for a moment until Bane spoke. "Well, Naughton, that necklace you have is very odd, and I am quite curious what it has to say."

Naughton nodded, chewing his food. "Me and you both."

Bane continued, "I'd advise you to keep silent about it until we reach the castle. We don't want to draw attention to our quest." Naughton looked at Asha, though she seemed to care nothing about the topic.

She noticed him staring at her. "I already know about your secret, sir."

Naughton was surprised. "Who told you?"

"Bane, of course."

Bane swallowed some water. "Don't worry, Naughton, I trust her completely." Asha winked at Naughton. Jesper sat in silence, deep in thought about what awaited him in Bezinar, but would often glance at Asha.

They continued on until nightfall, reaching Iona. It was a small town, with short wooden walls that stood about fifteen feet high. Bane led them inside the gates, and the guards gave them no trouble since they recognized him. Iona was quiet, with little movement on the streets except for a few who gave strange looks to the group, considering how late it was. Bane led them to an inn that looked cozy and well kept, called Hermits. Jesper shook his head, laughing at the sign.

Bane looked around. "Mind what you say here. There are strange folk about, hence its name." Asha took the horses to the stables while the others found rooms. After getting settled, they sat in Bane's room to eat and keep out of sight. Bane went to the kitchen and got some food from a cook he knew. The cook gave him meats and fruits without question.

They began eating while Jesper made a fire. "I can't wait for it to start warming up. I'm tired of this cold."

Asha warmed her hands. "I love the cold. The air is cleaner without all that pollen."

Bane looked at Naughton. "Let me see that jewel so I can examine it," he said. Naughton pulled the jewel from around his neck and gave it to him. Bane studied each side of the jewel. "This is solid gold except for the red diamonds in the center. These five rays...you think they would break easily--and should have, by now--which makes me think they are made of some other type of metal that is very strong. Here, Naughton, let's see what the letters look like again." Naughton held out his hand and the words appeared on the back. "Let's see here now…there are three words here. I know the last word is "holy" but I can't make out the rest. What did that being say to your father when he received the sun jewel?"

"That only the sun may return."

Bane scratched his head. "I've been studying my Hebrew ever since I found out about this thing, and I will continue to do so. Remember what I told you: say nothing about this jewel until we reach Master Nellium."

"Who's that?"

"He is the head scholar at Bezinar and is very wise. I suggest we sleep. We will leave at the first sign of light."

Asha got up. "Do I have to wake you in the morning?"

"That isn't necessary. Goodnight, Asha." She left, and Bane handed the sun jewel back to Naughton as they made their beds.

Naughton laid his head down, suddenly missing home. He rarely left the boundaries of Sturkma. He watched the fire dance in the fireplace until the flames died. As the embers began to dim, he fell asleep.

Morning came quickly, and they were on the road leaving Iona well before sunrise to avoid suspicion. They kept a steady pace, and at noon they stopped and unsaddled the horses to rest off the road. Asha leaned back against her saddle, eating dried meat and bread. Naughton sat next to her, sharing the water. "You surprised me by showing up to Mohai's dinner. I thought you hated us from the very start."

Asha glared at him. "Did you sit here to start an argument?"

"No, I was just starting a conversation."

Asha drank some water. "Well, you're failing. Try another topic."

Jesper began chuckling as he listened to them, yet he felt slightly jealous. Naughton threw a pebble at him. "I'm glad you're finding this amusing."

"You never were good with the ladies." Naughton glared at Jesper, then suddenly, he charged. He tackled Jesper and they rolled on the ground, wrestling. Asha's mouth opened in shock. They wrestled for several minutes trying to hold each other down, but after a while they got tired and quit moving. Bane sat back and enjoyed the show, laughing. "It seems we have a tie. Now knock it off, it's time to go!"

They got up and dusted themselves off. "We

will finish this later, Jesper!" said Naughton as he walked to his horse.

The road had changed from open fields to woods. Old oaks, hickory trees, and other timber were covered in moss which gave the forest a gloomy look. However, it was quiet but for a light wind blowing every once in a while.

Nightfall was upon them, with a storm approaching from the west. Bane pulled out a large cover when they stopped, and everyone helped strap it down. Once they had tied the horses, they built a small fire under the shelter with their blankets prepared for the night. Naughton was curled up in a ball with his blanket wrapped around him, deep in thought. He wondered how his father and Felden were doing. Jesper quickly went sound asleep when it began raining. Bane kept to himself, studying a book trying to catch up on his Hebrew.

As the night passed, lightning flashed periodically. Asha was looking at Jesper with curiosity. She did not speak until the rain stopped and all was quiet. "Tell me about yourself, Naughton." Naughton had dozed off, and she kicked him in the foot. Naughton awoke to find Asha looking at him. "Tell me about you."

He blinked and rubbed his eyes. "What do you

want to know?"

"Where do you come from?"

"We came from Sturkma. My family and I escaped before the city fell. I lost many friends, including two of my kin there, Muir and Cana."

"I'm sorry." She leaned back, shutting her eyes. "How did your father know of Mohai?"

Naughton tightened the blankets around him. "I guess they are old friends from when they served King Irus together. My father is very secretive and never told me of his expeditions."

Asha put her hair in a ponytail and put a hood over her head. "Tell me about Jesper."

Naughton gave her an odd look. "Do you always ask this many questions?"

"I just wanted to know more about the company I'm with since I am stuck with you for a while."

"Very well then," replied Naughton, taking a deep breath He felt uneasy about sharing information with someone he barely knew. "Jesper is shy at first, but he opens up once he gets to know you. We grew up together as brothers, and he has a sister named Lili."

"What about his parents?"

"His mother died of an illness and his father

was…" Naughton thought for a moment. "Killed in Yorben, I think."

Her face became saddened. "That's horrible. Are you sure he was killed in Yorben?"

Naughton hesitated. "I'm pretty sure he died there, but we are not certain."

She looked at Jesper, making sure he was still asleep. "He looks so familiar. He reminds me of someone." She looked away for some time in deep thought as mist formed around them. She glanced back and noticed the ring on Naughton's hand. "Is that the Crescent Ring on your finger?"

Naughton raised his hand. "It's my father's, given to him by King Irus."

Asha's eyes widened. "Interesting. Your father is of great importance if King Irus gave him that."

She lay down and curled up in her blanket, closing her eyes. "I'm sure your father had good reason for not telling you everything. I have learned that too much information can be a burden."

Naughton gazed at the fire. "Then again, not knowing is just as dreadful." Asha went silent, falling asleep with a calm expression on her face. Naughton leaned back and curled up under his blanket, while Bane stayed up studying his book.

Bane woke everyone at sunrise, and they

continued riding through the misty forest at a steady pace. All was quiet, with the exception of the horses' hooves pounding in the mud. There were no birds or wind to be heard, as if a dreadful hush had fallen on the forest. Naughton kept getting the feeling that they were being followed, and he soon became uneasy. He kept turning around and looking behind them, but nothing was in view. He couldn't take it any longer as he pulled on the reins. "Wait. I think we're being followed."

Everyone stopped and looked behind them. "Why do you think that?" asked Bane.

"I just have a feeling."

Bane squinted, his eyes looking in the fog and shook his head. "We cannot go off your feelings, Naughton. We can reach Bezinar tonight if we continue our pace."

Jesper got off his horse. "The last time you felt this way, you were right."

Asha jumped off her horse, but Bane was reluctant as he tapped the horn of his saddle. "I say we continue. Don't forget, I am in charge of this expedition." Asha glared at him, and Bane got off his horse, mud splattering on his boots.

"What do you suggest we do, Naughton?" asked Asha.

"Leave us. Jesper and I will catch up."

Asha strung her bow. "Absolutely not. We will stay together."

Bane patted his horse on the neck. "Give me the horses then." Naughton and Jesper pulled their armor from their packs and geared up. Bane took the horses over a hill and hid, waiting to see if anyone was following. They sat for an hour, hiding behind some trees and bushes. As the sun rose, the mist began to dissipate and Bane started getting impatient. "This is flat out foolish; we could be well on our way by now."

Jesper put his hand over Bane's mouth. "Shh...Someone is coming." Jesper gripped his sword. Naughton and Asha got ready to pull their bows back, readying for targets. Suddenly, six men appeared on horses. They were dressed in black and had a red flame mark on their cloaks. They were looking at the ground and started slowing down. They came to a halt as the horses flared their nostrils, catching their breath. One of the riders got off his horse and stared at the ground. He then kneeled, touching the mud and suddenly looked up in their direction. The man on the ground pointed at the tracks without saying a word. Instantly, his companions got off their horses and continued walking towards them. Asha poked at

Naughton and whispered. "Kill the leader if you can. I'll shoot the others." Naughton pulled his bow back and Asha did the same. They waited to release once the men were in range. Naughton took aim at the Geol tracker and released the arrow, hitting him in the chest. Asha released her arrow, hitting the one next to him. Both men fell to the ground, crying in pain, while the others jumped behind some trees. Asha and Naughton ducked, ready for them to return fire, but no arrows came. Naughton stuck his head up to see if he could see anything, but all was clear.

They sat for a few moments, though it seemed like hours to them. The entire group was breathing heavy, ready for the unexpected. Naughton heard a limb crack and turned around. A Geol was right on him, about to stab him, but Jesper blocked the blade with his sword and swung at the Geol, cutting his head off. Jesper froze in shock at his first kill. The other three Geols saw Jesper standing there. "A Centore!" one yelled. Asha stood up and tried to pull Jesper down, but he was in a deep trance. The Geols shot arrows at Jesper and Asha. Naughton jumped up and pushed them down. When he did, an arrow went through his armor, piercing his left shoulder. Naughton hit the ground in pain. The remaining Geols jumped on their horses and rode off in fear that more Centores were around.

Bane ran to Naughton, placing his hand over the wound. "We must stop the bleeding! Asha, go get my horse and give me the right saddle bag!"

Jesper was in shock. "What have I done?"

Bane grabbed Jesper's hand and put it over Naughton's wound. "Not now! Here, keep pressure on it while I break the arrow." Bane snapped the front of the arrow, and Naughton screamed as pain jolted through his body. Bane examined the exit wound and bandaged him. "He is losing blood. We must get to the castle!" Asha jumped on the horse, putting Naughton in front of her. Bane yelled at her. "What are you doing?"

"I am lighter than all of you and we will be faster. Keep up if you can, but no one else will die because of me!" Asha rode off while Jesper and Bane mounted their horses to follow.

Within hours, Naughton became weaker and he passed out from the loss of blood. Asha's arms were getting tired from holding Naughton's broken body, her arms and legs burning from exhaustion. Tears began to run down her face from the pain, but she did not stop and kept kicking the horse, demanding more speed. The sun began to set as the castle came into view. Asha rode through the villages without slowing as Naughton's blood covered her clothes. The villagers screamed as they jumped out of the way to avoid getting trampled. Guards rode in on horses, thinking the two of them were thieves or pillagers, but soon realized that was not the case. The guards moved out of the way, allowing the company to pass and the gate guards opened the gate.

Asha was greeted by soldiers. "Lady Airah, we did not know it was you."

She jumped off her horse and her legs nearly gave out. "Get Winsto this instant and take this man inside. He has an arrow through his left shoulder!"

"Yes, my Lady!" Bane and Jesper gave their horses to a servant and followed Naughton, who was being carried in the castle as his blood dripped to the ground

Shadows

Berton woke before daylight and put on his gear. He looked at his wife as she slept, lost in dreams. He leaned over, kissing her lightly on the forehead. He looked upon the children, admiring them, hoping it would not be the last time he would see them. After a long stare, he went to the door, opening and closing it lightly, and made his way to the gate. There he met with his seven companions: Felden, Taxon, Rubus, Jayus, Cimson, and Hundar.

Felden gave Berton the reigns to his horse. Without a word, they exited the south gate, disappearing into the darkness.

As they crossed the Siriu River, the sun's golden rays appeared over the horizon, and they began looking for tracks. In a short time they discovered footprints following the river northwest. "A child could follow this," said Rubus, in a low voice. The Shadows followed, going southwest along the Siriu River during the day and tracking well into the evening. Come nightfall there was no moon, and it was too dark to track so they made camp.

They made the horses lay down in the tall grass and covered them with blankets. They put on their cloaks to keep warm and to stay out of sight, spreading out and taking turns keeping watch through the night.

When daylight broke they began to track again. The tracks continued to follow the river until the eighth day, when one small group of tracks broke off to the south. The Shadows stopped and Berton pulled out the map Naughton found. Berton and Felden looked at it, trying to decide which set to follow. Berton pointed. "I suggest we follow the tracks going south. They may be reporting to their superiors and could lead us to their stronghold. Although, there's still a chance that they are just a scout party."

Felden scratched his face. "There's nothing to scout to the south--they have conquered everything." The group agreed and followed the tracks headed south. The tracks led them around the Mountain of Colonies, through the valley, and back to Sturkma. The Shadows only stopped occasionally to water their horses. Berton was a gifted tracker, but Felden was stealthier. He often used the Centores in his training at times to see if they could find him. Through trial and error Felden had learned to keep silent in various types of terrain. For instance, he was talented at walking in mud without being detected, which was difficult for most. He found that the trick was twisting his feet as he walked so the suction from the mud would release without producing sound. Now that Felden was in command of the Shadow Scouts, he had trained many to use the same techniques.

They followed for five days through fields of tall grass and eventually came upon what was left of Sturkma. The Shadows waited until dark before moving. Four Shadows followed Berton and Felden into Sturkma, while the other two waited with the horses. Berton led the way and the others followed quietly. They went through the tall grass slowly, staying low. They came up to the first outer village of Sturkma and detected no movement. The villages were pillaged and burned to the ground, bodies lying in the open. Berton burned with anger, for he recognized several victims. They passed through the second village, and again there was only silence. The smell of the rotting corpses was unbearable as they drew closer to the city. As they passed through the last village they came to the city wall. When they approached the gate, they could see a fire burning within the city. Berton and Felden ordered the others to stay and have their bows ready in case they were discovered. Felden went first, leaving the tall grass and ran to the stone wall. Berton followed him.

They slowly entered the city, keeping to the shadows and sneaking from one building to the next, swords in hand. The buildings were burned and debris was everywhere. In the remnants of the courtyard they saw a fire. They scaled a building and crawled on the top of the roof to see a dozen men sitting around, trying to keep warm as they spoke to one another. Berton could not make out their words, nor could Felden. Felden poked Berton. "Wait here. I'm going to get closer so I can hear them." Felden climbed down and made his way up the street, sneaking from one pile of rubble to another until he could hear them. He found a hole in the floor of a building. He crawled in and peeked out at the Geol soldiers.

"Why did we have to come back here?"

"Because we were ordered to. They wanted to make sure that any surviving villagers did not come back."

"They are not that foolish. They are probably hiding in Bezinar castle right now."

"Don't worry, the day is coming when we strike. For now, he wants to keep looking for him."

"Shh…you're being too loud."

"You worry too much, Xata. No one is here."

"You don't know that. Keep silent about our mission. I don't want to be fed to the Spikers. We must report soon. Tomorrow we leave for Crubitz and then to-" he cut himself off abruptly. "Did you hear something?"

"No, you are just being paranoid."

The soldiers sat for a while and started talking again, telling old war stories and comparing battle scars. Felden heard enough and returned to Berton unnoticed. Berton and Felden retreated back to the fields where the rest of the Shadows were waiting with their horses. They all sat in the tall grass and discussed the situation while Jayus kept watch. Berton pulled out his pipe then decided against it. "What did you learn?"

Felden swallowed some water from his sack. "They are stopping by a city called Crubitz and then reporting in to their superiors at another location, perhaps Qanas if they continue south."

"Qanas...surely not. That city was destroyed many years ago," said Cimson.

"That name sounds familiar," said Rubus.

Berton sarcastically chuckled. "Of course it should. That's where the greatest kingdom thrived. I guess it has been rebuilt."

"How do you know this?" asked Hundar.

"An old scholar taught me while I was in the King's service. You see, the legend says that every civilization was destroyed within that kingdom because of their disobedience to El. The problem is, no one knows the details of its destruction. Some say it was a natural disaster of some sort, but some say that it was destroyed by a supernatural servant of El."

Felden held up his hand. "With your permission, Berton, can I speak of your encounter in the Seraph Lands?"

"I see no reason why not," replied Berton.

"Good. Do you think it was the same being you found in the Seraph Lands?"

"Given the recent events, it's possible."

Hundar stood up abruptly, putting his hands on his hips. "I hate to interrupt, but we must deal with the present. What shall we do now that we know where they come from?"

Berton looked at him and raised his eyebrow. "We will continue to follow these Geols and see the size of their stronghold. If we can discover how many men they have, and how many of those creatures, we will have a better understanding of what we are dealing with."

Felden snapped his finger. "I forgot, they also mentioned that they were looking for someone."

Berton's eyes narrowed with great curiosity. "Did they give details?"

"No, the leader ordered them to keep quiet about the matter."

Berton reflected on his thoughts for a moment

rubbing his short hair. "I would hardly think they destroyed this city just to find one person."

Felden raised a finger. "Perhaps that's why they set traps for those people fleeing the city."

"The circumstances give a good indication of the matter." Berton stood up, adjusting his cloak. "Either way, we must follow and see exactly what we're up against. I want everyone to sleep, but take turns keeping watch. I will go first." The group dispersed as usual and slept, taking turns watching the city.

Jayus was the last on watch before sunrise and saw the soldiers leaving the city. He alerted everyone and they prepared to follow. As soon as the soldiers were out of sight they continued following the Geols, keeping their distance. The soldiers were predictable. For six days they headed southeast, always stopping and taking breaks about mid-afternoon and resting at night. They continued following the Geols, though they eventually lost track of where they were. The burnt map was useless and Berton had never gone this far south. The terrain changed from rolling hills to flat plains and dense forests. On the seventh day, the Geols approached a city in a valley north of some mountains in the distance. The city had no walls or any sign of defense. The buildings within the city were made of timber and looked rugged and old. Some were grouped and some were scattered, standing much taller than others. The city was vast and stretched along the valley. There were some villages on the outskirts of the city where people were caring for livestock. The Shadows stopped on the edge of the forest and observed the reaction of the villagers when the Geols passed through. The villagers were not frightened by them and most did not acknowledge their presence. The Geols rode into the city and the Shadows lost sight of them.

Felden leaned forward in his saddle, stretching his legs. "I'd say we've reached Crubitz."

"Well, any ideas?" asked Jayus.

"Do you think the villagers will know what we are?" asked Hundar.

Berton shrugged his shoulders. "Who knows? We could go around and wait for them to come out, but they may stay in there for days."

They sat in silence until Jayus came up with an idea. "What if I go in acting like a traveler and see what I can find out? We are running out of food."

"That is risky," said Felden. "If you are discovered, the Geols may change course and ruin our mission."

"I agree with Felden," said Berton. "It is not

worth the risk. That hill is a good look out point. I suggest we camp there and see what happens. As for food, we will go into the villagers' store houses at night and take what we need." The group agreed. They stayed in the forest going around the villages, making their way to the hill.

The Shadows reached the hill at sunset leaving their horses tied to trees in the forest. The hill was covered in bushes and tall grass allowing them to hide with ease.

At nightfall the city lit up, and a loud horn blast seemed to call people into the city. Taxon noticed a glow in the middle of the city and saw smoke rising up. "Look, Felden, they're building a huge fire." Felden looked at the fire and saw an oddly shaped statue illuminated by the flames, but could not make out what it was.

"It seems a celebration is in progress," said Taxon.

Berton stared at it as well. "What are they doing?"

"It's too far to make out," said Cimson.

"They're throwing something in the fire but it's not wood...it's something else."

Jayus grabbed a bag. "I'm going down to the store houses while they're distracted."

Felden grabbed him and then released him. "Alright, but be quick. We don't know how long this will last." Jayus ran down the hill and snuck into one of the villages, but he did not go into store houses. Berton and Felden watched him intensely, wondering what he was doing. Jayus cut the bag and put it over him like an old brown cloak, and then rubbed some dirt on his face as he began walking into the city. Rubus jumped up to go after him. Berton tried to stop him but was unable.

Felden cursed. "Those fools! They are going to get us all killed!"

"Let's just pray they don't get caught," said Berton. Jayus entered the city and walked in as if he was one of the villagers. Soon after, Rubus did the same thing, and eventually the Shadows lost sight of them. The people in the city were chanting and more objects were being thrown in the fire. The chanting carried on for hours until they heard screams echoing off the buildings. While the people gathered around the statue, the Shadows spotted a giant creature dragging a person by the arm toward the fire. The villager was kicking and screaming, trying to get away. The creature pinned him to the ground and took out a long spear stabbing the man in the chest. The creature raised his victim and started drinking his blood. People

135

were chanting and worshipping the statue. Once the creature finished, he cut off the man's head and threw it in the fire that surrounded the statue. The body was thrown to the crowd and was torn apart. The creature disappeared into the shadows and the chanting continued.

Berton, Felden, and the rest of the Shadows looked at each other, horror in their eyes. "Did you see that?" asked Cimson.

Berton blurted, "Of course we saw it! May the powers of El help us all, that creature just...and the people ate that man!"

Felden ducked down and drew his bow. "Someone is coming," he whispered.

The Shadows hid and waited. Moments later, Rubus approached. "It's me," he announced, panting.

Felden stood up and punched him. "You jeopardized our lives and our mission! Where is Jayus?"

Rubus stared at Felden with tears in his eyes. "Jayus was caught...he got too close."

Berton stood up and grabbed him. "What do you mean, caught? Speak!"

"The villagers discovered him. All villagers had a mark on their foreheads, and he was noticed by a child. A creature came and dragged him to the fire and the creature--he--"

Berton pushed him away. "Enough! Say no more, we saw it from here!" Felden sat down in shock as the rest stood speechless.

Felden finally asked, "What were they throwing in the fire?"

"Heads…human heads," replied Rubus in a shaky voice.

Some of the other Shadows lowered their heads and mumbled, "We are doomed."

Berton unsheathed his sword. "We will not have that kind of talk! I did not come all the way out here to run back like a coward. Our families and friends are depending on us to accomplish this quest." Berton pointed the sword at all the Shadows except for Felden. "If any one of you does anything stupid like Jayus did I'll kill you myself! You will obey my command. I will not die because of your stupidity! I have more experience than all of you put together, you got me?" They all nodded in unison.

"Very well," said Berton, sheathing his sword. "Rubus, you will not be punished because you tried to save a companion, but I will be watching you. Now, did you see the soldiers we have been following?"

"Yes, I saw them sitting in a corner resting and watching the fire."

"What was the statue?"

"It was a creature with spikes coming from its neck carved in marble. The base of the statue had letters but I was too far away to read."

Felden stood up and took a deep breath as he began to walk away. "We will remain here until the soldiers leave so we can follow. I will take first watch."

The Shadows tried to sleep, but the recent events haunted their dreams. Felden went to some store houses and collected what food he could find. He sat on a rock and took first watch of the city as he mourned the loss of Jayus. The city was quiet, with only a few people walking around the perimeter. Felden put a piece of straw in his mouth and tried to enjoy the night air. He sat looking up at the constellations, when suddenly he heard movement coming from ahead. The sound kept getting louder, rustling the tall grass. Felden was too far to rouse his company, so he hid and readied his bow. He knelt down, hiding beneath his cloak, and waited to see what was coming. He strained his eyes but saw nothing, until finally he saw a dark image emerge. The image walked slowly and stopped several times being very still. The wind blew in Felden's face and he smelled a foul stench. It was the same smell from when he saw those creatures at Sturkma. Felden's heart began pounding and sweat started rolling down his face. The creature got closer and Felden could see its red eyes glowing. Its body was massive, like a giant bull, but had armored plating all over its body as if it was part of its skin. Its head was broad at the top and narrowed toward its nose. It had three giant fingers with claws on the tips that looked razor sharp. The creature stood arched over with its neck spikes flaring up, smelling the air as it continued walking up the same path Rubus walked. The creature's feet were wide, but had four toes with talons curving forward. The giant creature pushed the bushes aside with its left arm. It was holding a massive shield and staring at the ground.

Felden knew he had to do something or his companions would not stand a chance. Felden stayed low waiting to be sure that it was alone. Once it passed by, he looked for a weak spot in its armored plating. He made his choice and aimed the arrow just below its head. He let out a breath and released. The arrow slapped against its armor and fell to the ground. The creature turned around and stared at Felden with its glowing red eyes.

Felden drew his sword and held it up, ready to strike. The creature pulled out its two pronged spear and charged. It thrust the spear at Felden and he dodged it, swinging his sword. The sword slammed against its armored skin, vibrating the blade, and the creature hit Felden with its shield, knocking him into the air, he landed on the ground hitting his back. The creature ran up with its spear held high, about to strike, when suddenly arrows hit it in the back and bounced off. The creature turned around, and there were Felden's companions shooting at the creature. They continued shooting as the creature made a low grunting sound, as if it was laughing at their pointless effort. The creature charged at the Shadows, pulling its hammer off its back and swinging violently. The men dodged the hammer by inches, trying to keep from getting pounded into the ground. Felden ran behind the creature and jumped on its back, narrowly avoiding the spikes as he stabbed at its neck, but the blade would not penetrate the skin. As he was stabbing away, the others continued slashing at the creature, but their blades glanced off and left no marks. Berton ran to his horse and readied a rope. He threw the rope with a giant noose at the creature's feet, hoping it would step in just right. As soon as it did, he took off with the rope tightening around its feet. The creature's feet were pulled out from under it and it toppled to the ground, throwing Felden backwards. Berton spurred his horse, dragging the creature into the forest.

It began kicking and swinging its arms trying to grab hold of something. The others followed on horses as they led the creature away from the city. "Berton, how are we going to kill this thing?" yelled Rubus.

"I don't know, but it must have a weakness!"

They rode a great distance and came to a halt when the creature quit thrusting. It was bleeding from its nostrils and was breathing rapidly, moving side to side as it tried to get up, but was too tired. The Shadows surrounded it and threw ropes around its appendages. Berton walked up to it, pointing his sword in its face and asking, "Can you understand me?" The giant creature flexed its spikes and locked its narrow red eyes on Berton. It snorted blood at him. "I'll take that as a yes. I will make your death swift if you tell me where your stronghold is located." The creature stared for a long moment before laughing with a deep gurgle. It flexed its spikes and muscles, trying to break free from the ropes, but it was hopeless. Berton kneeled next to it. "What the hell are you?"

The creature opened its mouth, revealing a forked tongue and large fangs that came forward. It spoke in a deep, hollow grunting voice. "You will all die, for I serve the last of his kind." Berton stood up and suddenly started stabbing in different places, looking for a weak spot, but the sword would not penetrate anywhere. The creature continued laughing while Berton kept jabbing away with rage. Felden grabbed the creature's two-pronged spear and pinned it behind the head. He pushed down, trying to choke the creature. Instead, its neck stretched, exposing flesh between its neck plates. Berton saw the gaps and stabbed its neck. The creature howled in pain and orange blood gushed out. It kicked in an attempt to break free, but five other Shadows jumped on top to keep it still. Berton continued to stab at the creature, until finally it died, letting out a long horrific roar. The Shadows backed away and stared at each other. They were covered in orange blood and the smell was almost unbearable.

Felden wiped his face. "It took six of us to bring this thing down!"

Berton withdrew his sword from the creature's flesh. "You mean the only way to kill these things is to expose its neck?"

"I guess so. I stabbed everywhere on that thing earlier."

"So what did it say it was?" asked Taxon.

"It serves the last of his kind," replied Berton as he began cleaning his sword.

"Who is that?" asked Cimson.

Berton shrugged his shoulders, "I fear we will know in time." The Shadows sat and rested as they cleaned themselves. Berton looked up and saw that sunrise was approaching. "We must make our way back to the city and watch for the soldiers. We cannot lose them now."

"What if they heard the sounds from this thing?" asked Taxon.

Berton jumped on his horse. "We will take one matter at a time. For now, let's get back to our lookout point."

They got on their horses and left the creature to rot, getting back to their position before the sun came up. The city was still quiet and seemed normal. As the sun rose, the city and villages came to life with people walking around and working as if nothing happened. The Shadows ate the potatoes, corn, and nuts that Felden gathered. The day grew warm as the sun reached high noon, making it difficult not to fall asleep. Felden looked in the water sack. "We're running out of water. Food we can go without for some time, but not water." Berton nodded as he stared into Crubitz.

Once again night fell upon them, and the city was quiet. There was no activity and no worshipping. Berton took first watch that night and others in turn.

Taxon was on the last watch when he saw the soldiers leaving the city. He roused the others and they followed, keeping their distance as usual. The soldiers' pace was swift and they took no breaks, as if they were running late. The terrain started to change from forests and fields to mountains and pines. The soldiers made their way upward and continued going south. For three days the Geols kept a steady pace, only resting at night. Two more days passed and they finally came across a stream. They filled their water sacks and continued on, encountering snow the further up the mountain they went. The snow seemed relentless as it became deeper and the temperature dropped. The pines stood tall, swaying in the wind and becoming fewer as the elevation increased. They could see each other's breath, including the horses that were exhausted from fighting the snow. At night they curled up in their blankets and cloaks, fighting the cold and unable to build a fire in fear of being detected.

On the third day, after filling their water sacks, the Geols approached a mountain face and they disappeared into a small crevice. The Shadows left Hundar behind to guard the horses and approached slowly, using caution in fear of an ambush. Felden saw some snow fall from a tree and stopped. The others did the same. Berton crept up next to Felden. "What do you see?"

"I think something is in that tree over there, but I'm not sure."

Berton looked to the snow and saw no other tracks except the ones they had been following. "What do you suggest?"

Felden sat silent for a moment, thinking and staring at the tree. "We wait for the cover of darkness to approach. I would hate to come all this way and ruin our chance." Berton agreed, and the Shadows pulled back and settled behind what few trees they could find. They lay still, covering themselves with their cloaks and letting the falling snow cover them.

By nightfall the Shadows were completely covered in snow, but their patience paid off. Before dark, a man came out of the cave and walked up to the tree. A lookout came down and went into the cave while the other took his place. Felden and Taxon went around, creeping up to the tree slowly while trying to suppress the sound of the crunching snow under their feet. They looked up the tree but could not see the man hiding. Felden hid behind a boulder about a stone's throw away while Taxon started scratching the bark on the tree. There was no reaction at first, but soon after, the tree started moving and snow fell from it. The lookout made his way down slowly, and when Felden saw him he shot him out like a squirrel. The man fell out of the tree and Taxon jumped on top of him, covered his mouth, and stabbed him. The other Shadows ran up and got ready for other Geols, but no one came. Taxon dragged the body away and buried him in the snow as Hundar brought up the horses. The Shadows approached the crevice, slowly entering the cave. It was a tight squeeze for the horses. The cave was dark and humid, a silent vortex. The only sound was the air moving across the entrance behind them. Heat was rising from deep within the cave, hitting their faces and making the horses nervous. Hundar smelled the air. "It smells like goat butt in here!"

Rubus wrinkled his nose. "How would you know?"

Berton lit a torch that he had prepared earlier, then slapped Rubus in the back of the head. "Shut it!" The Shadows led their horses into the tunnel, their hooves making loud, deafening clacks on the hard stone. They ripped pieces from their blankets and covered the horses' hooves to muffle the sound. They walked for over an hour as the tunnel widened and narrowed many times. The ceiling was full of sharp, jagged formations and the smooth stone walls became slick as water trickled down their grooves. After some time, the tunnel split in two directions, and Felden had no idea which one to take. Berton held the torch up to the tunnel on the right, and the torch was not affected. He took it to the tunnel on the left, and it flickered. "This way. Follow the air."

They took their time and paused on many occasions to listen, but the cave was silent. They continued until the tunnel opened up into a cavern. Several torches were burning along the walls and the Geols' horses were tied to a post. The Shadows approached with bows and swords in hand, ready for an ambush. They walked, no one in sight, as their shadows filled the cavern. Berton looked around for another path, but found nothing. "Where did they go?"

Taxon whispered, "We have a problem." The Shadows gathered around him. He was looking down a hole at a ladder descending into the darkness. Berton shone the torch into the hole and the ladder disappeared into the abyss.

Felden rubbed his rough, bearded face. "You have got to be kidding."

"Who wants to go first?" asked Rubus sarcastically.

Berton grinned. "I believe a young fellow like yourself would be willing, since you like to dive into the realms of chaos."

Rubus snatched the torch from Berton. "Fine, but if I lose my head I'll be sure to haunt you for the rest of your lives." Rubus went down into the hole as his companions watched, the torch get smaller until it disappeared into the darkness.

The longer they waited the more tense they became, especially Felden. "I am going down there after him."

Berton glared at him. "And just how do you plan to see where you're going?"

"My eyes will adjust."

Berton snickered. "You're not a owl, you goof. I suggest we wait a little longer."

"No, I'm going. If I don't return soon, leave and go to Yorben," said Felden as he descended down the ladder.

Berton sighed. "We stay together. Just hurry up."

Felden went down, feeling his way to each step. The air was rushing upward, drying the rungs. He kept descending, and his last step down came as a surprise. There was a faint glow behind him. He slowly approached it when suddenly he was grabbed, a hand covering his mouth. "Shh…you're going to get us caught." Felden turned his head and Rubus moved his hand. "Follow me, but stay low."

They crawled up to a ledge and looked down. Below them was a vast cavern. There were thousands of men coming and going in and out of tunnels. The cavern was full of fire pits and several buildings where blacksmiths pounded away on new weapons as various ores were brought to them by the crate. The horses squealed as they pulled the heavy metal filled carts. Felden looked at Rubus. "How in the world are we going to stand against this?"

Rubus shook his head. "We can't, unless we know the layout of these tunnels."

Felden started crawling back. "We mustn't linger. We need to get back to the others." As they approached the ladder they heard faint voices coming from behind them. They stayed low and leaned against the wall, covering themselves with their cloaks. A torch appeared and Geol soldiers were coming toward them. Felden and Rubus did not move, hoping that the Geols would pass by without noticing them. The soldiers walked by them and entered a tunnel. Felden and Rubus followed the soldiers to a fire-lit room, with a table in the center covered with food. The soldiers sat down and started looking at a map.

"What did you find, sir?"

"Nothing. Sturkma remains empty. We stopped

by Crubitz to observe the sacrifices and rested."

"What about Fort Yorben?"

Xata took a bite of bread. "The fort is going to be tough. We will lose many men trying to take it, and our slaves had no chance at all! I sent the rest of them to fight at Fort Coralis."

"I see. I will get word out. Have you heard from Brytak?"

"No. He is still deep in Bezinar territory acting as a scholar."

The soldier examined the map closer and eyed Xata. "Did you find any trace of him?"

"No! Keep silent on the matter. Our master grows impatient and I do not want any rumors going around."

"Sorry, sir."

"Now go, and be sure to keep a good watch on the south crevice. I don't want any surprises."

The soldier bowed, and he and the others disappeared down a tunnel, leaving the map on the table.

Rubus winked at Felden. "I'm getting that map." Felden nodded and readied his bow in case the soldiers returned. Rubus approached the room, staying along the wall. He waited to make sure it was clear and ran to the table. He grabbed the map, rolled it up, put it in his pouch, and ran back to Felden. "Come on, let's get out of here before they realize their map is missing!"

Felden and Rubus ran to the ladder and began their ascent. The climb up seemed longer than their trip down. As they approached, their companions heard movement and readied their weapons in case it was Geols. Instead, it was Felden's head that popped out. "Whoa, point that bow somewhere else."

They crawled out and Rubus ran to his horse. "We must leave immediately! There is no way we can scout these caves without being detected."

Berton crossed his arms. "What did you see?"

Felden grabbed a torch off the wall. "First of all, we stole a map, which will raise suspicion. Secondly, the hole leads to a cavern that contains thousands of Geols, as well as endless tunnels. An army is living down here and preparing for war. I believe we fulfilled our quest."

"You stole a map?" asked Berton, rubbing his face agitated. "That was very foolish!"

Felden grabbed his horse's reins. "Relax, old friend. We can escape if we leave now."

Cimson sheathed his sword. "Let's get out of here!"

The Shadows left the small cavern and made

haste to the entrance. As they approached the entrance, Cimson thought he saw an object standing in the way, but guessed it was a shadow from the torch. Just as they put out the torches and exited the cave, there were several red eyes staring at them. The Shadows froze. Geols and Spikers were waiting for them.

A Geol soldier approached them wearing a black hood over his head. "Give us your weapons and you will be treated fairly."

Rubus laughed sarcastically. "I doubt that. You will have our heads on platters and be drinking our insides within seconds."

The soldier chuckled. "Oh, no. Only our Spikers do that, but if you don't throw down your weapons, we can arrange it." The six Shadows were surrounded and stood in a circle, backs to one another.

Berton took a deep breath, smelling the pines and letting the cold air fill his lungs. He thought about Teras and his children playing in the fields of Sturkma and smiled. He stepped up to the soldier. "I would rather die than be anyone's slave or dinner!" Berton swung his sword high and brought it down on the soldier's head, splitting his skull. The Geols sprang into action, and the battle was on. The sounds of clashing metal rang in the air as sparks flashed. The Shadows stayed together, keeping their backs against one another. Some soldiers were thrusting the torches at them, trying to burn them, as others were swinging their swords. Each Shadow was fighting two or more Geols at once. Felden screamed as he was burned on his left arm, but kept parrying with his right. The Shadows killed several Geols before losing Taxon. He was knocked to the ground and a sword went into his abdomen, but he kicked the feet out from under his foe and stabbed him in the chest before the others finished him. The Shadows were down to five, and then four, until only Berton, Felden, and Rubus were left.

There were two Geols left, and the three Spikers stayed back, waiting their turn. Berton looked at Felden and moved his eyes toward the Spikers. Felden and Berton instantly ran towards the one in the middle, while Rubus fought the last two Geols. Felden and Berton caught the Spiker off guard and knocked it to the ground. The other two swung their hammers at them, missing and hitting their companion on the ground, crushing its body. Felden jumped on one of the Spiker's back and grabbed its head, pushing upward. The Spiker flexed its spikes, scratching Felden while it swung around violently, trying to throw him off.

Berton was dealing with the other one, parrying its spear. Rubus killed the other two Geols and ran over to the dead Spiker, grabbing its spear. He ran up to the Spiker Felden was holding, staying low, and pinned the spear between its legs, making it fall to the ground. Felden landed on the snow, which cushioned his fall, and quickly got to his feet. The Spiker started to get up but Rubus pinned it down, holding the spear to its neck and pushing up, revealing its flesh. Felden raised his sword and slashed its neck. Blood flew into the air and the Spiker howled in agony. As Felden and Rubus were finishing the Spiker, Berton screamed as he was knocked into the air, hitting a tree. It ran up to Berton and pinned him to the tree, using its long two prong spear. The Spiker raised his hammer to finish him, but Felden jumped on its back, distracting it from Berton. The Spiker swung around, throwing Felden to the ground. He hit a rock, which knocked him unconscious. Rubus ran up in front of the last Spiker and pointed the long spear at it. The Spiker snorted and swung its hammer at Rubus. He dodged and parried, trying to tire the Spiker, but it showed no sign of fatigue. Meanwhile, Felden woke up and saw Berton pinned against the tree. He ran to him and tried to pull the spear loose, but it would not budge. Felden heard voices. He looked up and saw other

Geols approaching.

Berton pushed Felden away. "Get out of here. My time has come."

"No, I will not leave you to die!" yelled Felden as he shook the spear, violently grinding his teeth.

"You must survive so you can tell what you have seen. Too much has been lost to go back with nothing." The Geols started closing in, and Felden had to make a decision. He looked at Rubus and noticed he was getting tired from fighting the Spiker. Felden knew they would not be able to fight off the other Geols.

He grabbed Berton's hand. "I will return for you!" With that, Felden ran toward the Spiker and threw snow in its face, blinding it long enough to grab Rubus and start running. They raced down the mountain on foot, tripping and stumbling through the snow as they tried to gain distance from the Geols. The Spiker gave chase, but was too big to run through the deep snow. As they ran, Felden looked back and saw Berton being tied up and carried away by the Geols.

Resurrection

Naughton woke, opening his eyes slowly and adjusting to the light, which was just a faint glow from a fire. He tried to lean forward, but pain shot through his body from his left shoulder all the way up to his head. He cringed as his eyes began to water. He remained still until the sharp pain subsided, but his shoulder constantly throbbed. His eyes wandered trying to figure out where he was. The room was dark with wooden walls. He turned his head toward the glow and saw the fire dancing in the fireplace. To the side of the fire he thought he saw a statue shaped like an angel, but realized it was a woman sitting in a chair.

He gazed at her in wonder as the fire illuminated her face. She had dark hair that went just below her shoulders. The glow revealed her smooth skin, with a few freckles under her eyes and across her nose. She wore a green dress with gold lining along the edges. Her eyes were fixed on her book and she breathed slowly, grinning contently every few moments. The light from the fire made her brown eyes sparkle and her lips resemble curled red rose petals tucked in missing the sun. She looked up and saw that Naughton was staring at her. He felt himself blush as she closed her book. "Ah, you're awake. You have been asleep for over a week." Her voice was soft and soothing as she looked at him with concern. "Are you okay Naughton?"

When he spoke his voice was raspy, his throat sore. "Yes, did you say a week?"

"Yes, I'm afraid so. How do you feel?"

Naughton shivered. "I feel cold all over."

She rose from the chair to examine him. Naughton stared into her eyes in awe as she touched his forehead with her soft hands and warm skin. He breathed in, and she smelled like a sweet incense of mint and honey. It made him relax as he closed his eyes. She threw another blanket over him. "You still have fever, but you will overcome it in time. Now that you're awake I must tell the others." She began walking out of the room.

"Wait, what is your name?" asked Naughton.

She looked at him, giving a warm smile. "I'll be right back." She walked out, and Naughton started feeling warm thanks to the second blanket. He laid still in fear that pain would shoot through him again. In spite of the fear he took his right hand up to his chest to check the sun jewel. It was gone. He started to panic, his hands moving up and down in search of the necklace. It seemed like forever before company returned. The door opened, and in walked Jesper, grinning ear to ear. Naughton grabbed him and pain shot through his shoulder as tears rolled down his face. "Where is the sun jewel?"

"It's okay, Naughton, it's safe. We are the only ones that know about it, we hid it until you recover." Naughton relaxed and laid motionless, waiting for the pain to stop. "Naughton…I am so sorry about what happened in the woods. It's my fault that this happened to you."

Naughton shook his head slowly. "No, do not apologize. You saved me first, remember?"

Jesper smiled. "You still have a sense of humor I see."

Naughton laughed and pain shot through him. "Ouch…don't make me laugh." When the pain stopped, he stretched his legs. "Where am I?"

"Bezinar castle. You gave us quite a scare, cousin."

Suddenly a voice yelled, "My lady, he's awake!"

Naughton looked at Jesper. "Who's coming to see me?"

"You will see," replied Jesper, snickering.

A second later, Asha entered with a physician. The physician, a large man with dark skin and a bald head, carried a small leather bag. He gave a humble smile as he walked up and touched Naughton's shoulder. "Agh! What are you doing, you dope?"

yelled Naughton.

Asha spoke softly. "Be nice, Naughton. This man saved your life."

Naughton gritted his teeth. "Who are you?"

"It's okay. I'm a doctor, and my name is Winsto," replied the physician.

"Why is it every time I am around you people I feel pain?"

"Oh, quit being a baby," said Asha.

"Tell me exactly how you feel," said Winsto.

"I have hot and cold flashes, my shoulder throbs, and my throat is dry."

Winsto touched his head. "You have an infection in your shoulder which is why you have a fever. Your throat is my doing because of the medicine I've been giving you." Winsto removed some bandages and looked at the wound. "The infection is going down and--I don't believe it-- you're healing much quicker than I anticipated. Why, the way it's healing you won't even have a scar! But if you do, the ladies will love it, especially when..."

Asha interrupted, "Winsto, that's enough."

"Sorry, my Lady. I was just trying to get the boy in good spirits."

Naughton looked at Asha. "Is that true?"

"Absolutely not. Well, some do, but enough of

that nonsense!"

Naughton's eyes wandered again. "I must be losing my mind, Asha. I thought the King was going to walk in, but it was just you." Asha smiled big and everyone began to laugh. Naughton was puzzled. "What's so funny?" Jesper continued laughing, and Naughton glared at him.

Jesper gestured his hand at Asha. "Cousin, you are looking at a princess. Her actual name is Airah, and she is the King's niece. She had us fooled the whole time!" All the color left Naughton's face replaced by a blank stare.

Winsto checked his pulse. "Are you okay, Naughton?" He gave no response. His only thought was that Jesper was standing next to the girl his father saved. Winsto put new bandages on his shoulder. "I think Naughton has had enough excitement for one day. He needs rest. I want everyone to leave him alone; only Airah's servant can stay with him."

"But I have slept a week," said Naughton.

Winsto pointed a finger at his patient. "Your body will only heal if you rest. When you've healed enough, Airah's servant will work with your shoulder, and I will check in on you periodically. Do the exercises exactly how she shows you, or you will tear muscles."

Everyone left the room and the servant returned, sitting down in front of the fire and continuing to read her book. Naughton looked at the girl. "So can I know your name?"

She glanced at him. "I will give you my name when you recover."

"Women and their games," he muttered.

She raised an eyebrow. "You will get no name with that attitude, mister."

Naughton closed his eyes and sighed. "At least the doctor is gone."

Naughton slept for many days before beginning his exercises. The first day was pure agony, and his shoulder was stiff as a board. Many times he thought his shoulder would rip off when Airah's servant moved it in certain directions. He exercised his shoulder twice a day. Eventually it started getting flexible and the pain decreased. His new friend was strong-minded and would never tell her name, no matter what bribes Naughton attempted. He enjoyed her personality; she was laid back and kind, but had no problem keeping Naughton in check when he started getting agitated. She understood, considering he was cooped up all the time. Naughton talked to her about many topics, but eventually they would run out of things to discuss. At first Naughton had a hard time with Airah's servant, for she was secretive and did not like discussing her private affairs. After some time, however, she gradually warmed up to him, giving some information like her favorite color, which was blue, and her hobbies.

Some mornings the servant did not come and Jesper would take her place, keeping Naughton updated on all events. "How are we feeling today, cousin?"

Naughton moved his shoulder around. "I feel stronger each day, but my shoulder still hurts."

Jesper went to the door and took him down the hall to a window. He opened the curtains. "I want you to see this."

Naughton's eyes adjusted to the bright light and he could finally see. He walked up to the window and he was baffled. Before him was a beautiful landscape, full of trees, fields, and rolling hills. There were villages everywhere in the distance. He looked down; he had not realized how high his floor was. The people down below were like ants scurrying around, busy with their day-to-day tasks. He looked side to side and saw other towers next to him. The castle was vast, with tall towers and massive walls. It was made of grey and white stone. Flags were flying on the towers. Some had balconies and many windows on them with people waving at him. It was surrounded by a city that had buildings made of bright stone and wood in all shapes and sizes. There were markets, streets, houses, and other buildings that looked ancient. The city and castle were surrounded by a giant wall that stood two hundred feet high, with multiple towers. Each tower had two catapults, and the walls had spears sticking out preventing anyone climbing over. The gate was twenty feet wide and forty feet tall.

"This place is enormous!" said Naughton, as he was leaning over. "Never in my dreams could I fathom such a place."

"I figured you would like to see this," said Jesper. "They should have allowed you to see this already, but they have been only worried about your health." Naughton looked around a bit more and returned to his room, sitting down on his bed. "Have you learned the servant girl's name yet?"

"No, she refuses to tell me. I assume you know it?"

"I'm not allowed to tell you. She gave me a nasty threat if I did," replied Jesper, giving a wink.

"Fine." Naughton lay down. "So have you and Lady Airah hit it off yet?"

Jesper gave a perplexed stare. "What are you blabbering about?"

Naughton rolled his eyes. "I'm not blind, and I've seen how you look at her." Jesper's face turned red. Naughton started laughing. "Nevermind, your face reveals everything."

Jesper threw a blanket over his face. "It's none of your business!"

"No need to get fussy, I was just curious."

Jesper put on his coat. "She seems to avoid me."

"Perhaps she needs to get to you know you better."

Jesper nodded. "Maybe, but I have other matters to be concerned with right now. I am suppose to meet the Centore instructor today. I'll see you tomorrow, cousin." Jesper walked out the door and down the hall, passing the servant girl.

"Did you tell him my name?" asked the servant.

"Of course not. Though I think Naughton is fond of you. I've never seen him so curious. Farewell." The servant girl blushed as Jesper bowed and left.

Jesper continued down the hall, passing several rooms. He came to a stairway and started his long descent, which was several flights to the main hall. The stairway had various colorful mosaic designs and stained glass windows. When he reached the bottom floor in the main hall he made his way to the front door, passing large pillars of marble and statues of warriors and past kings. The hall was enormous, with tall ceilings painted gold and red and covered with paintings of heroes in the past. People were standing in the upper levels discussing various topics with their voices echoing through the halls. A guard was standing at each pillar, armed with a long spear and dressed in gold armor, as if protecting each king. They wore silver helmets that completely covered their heads, with gold outlining and a slit for each eye. Jesper went out the front door made of dark oak and walked down the steps, making his way to the front gate of the castle where many guards were posted. The castle itself had a wall constructed all the way around, including the garden, and was guarded by archers and soldiers that patrolled constantly. As he approached the gate, the guards opened it for him, giving him a nod and they shut it behind him with a loud clang.

He went down the main street into the city, eventually making his way to the west wall, which took him about twenty minutes to reach. There was a building marked with a sign that had a long red sword with four colored shields around it: gold, orange, green, and blue, just like the royal guards described it when they directed him. There was a long line of soldiers signing a book and leaving. He got in line and waited for his turn, getting strange stares from the men around him. When his turn came up he grabbed the quill, but the recruiter sitting on the other side of the table grabbed his hand. "You're wasting your time, son. Only soldiers can sign up."

"But I was ordered by Nemian to come to see your leader," blurted Jesper.

"Sure, kid. People say many things. Why I am I supposed to believe you?" demanded the recruiter. Jesper reached in his pocket and showed him the letter that was sealed with a certain emblem on it. The recruiter glared at Jesper. "How did you come by this?"

"I told you! Nemian, Commander of the second unit gave me this."

The man looked at the seal. "Come with me." The man stood up, leading Jesper in the building. They went down a long hall and the recruiter knocked on a door.

"Who is it?"

"Sir, there is a boy here with a valid letter to see you."

"Not now, I have matters I am attending to!"

"But sir, this letter is from Nemian," said the recruiter, looking at the letter again.

"Nemian, you say?" He paused for a moment. "Come in." The man opened the door and there was a bald, well-built, yet lean man sitting behind a desk. He had a short peppery beard and was wearing a black robe. On the right of his chest was a patch containing four colored shields. There were parchments stacked high on his desk, and his room was full of books and scrolls. "What do you want?"

Jesper replied with a shaky voice. "Sir, my name is--"

The man interrupted, holding his hand up. "Don't call me sir, boy. You are not under my command...yet. My name is Thorg. Let me see that letter." Jesper handed him the letter, and Thorg broke the seal and began reading. Thorg's face was stern, his eyebrows moving and nose wrinkling. "His nickname is Turtle...ha ha! Well, this is the most outrageous thing I've heard yet. Nemian never ceases to humor me. However, he never asks for favors. I don't know why he is fond of you, but I'll see what I can do. But I must ask, do you have any idea what you're getting into?"

Jesper nodded. "Yes, Nemian gave me an idea of what to expect, but gave me no details."

"Good, he's not supposed to. Come back here in three days and I'll let you know if you're in," said

Thorg, folding the letter.

"I will sir--I mean Thorg." replied Jesper with excitement. Jesper left the building and made his way back to the castle, excited but nervous about his fate.

Winsto allowed Naughton to walk around the castle as long as he was escorted, and he had to promise to keep his arm in a sling. Airah's servant led him around, taking her time, allowing him to see all the sights. She led him to different rooms, one of which was a meeting room with large maps on a long table where they strategized attacks. One room was a library two stories high full of books and scrolls. There were scholars studying and talking about different topics of which Naughton had never heard. She led him downstairs toward the sanctum room where two royal guards, like the ones he saw in the great hall, were guarding a steel door. "What's in there?" he asked.

"Lady Airah wanted me to show you this. It is where the Bindings of El are held, and where only the King and master scholar Nellium are allowed passage. I am sure your father told you about this place?"

"Yes, but I know very little of it."

The last stop was the garden. They walked around and looked at all the plants and flowers, but few had blooms in the winter. One, however, caught his attention. It had dark green leaves with blue flower petals and red swirls on it. The center had a gold bulb about to bloom. "What is this?"

She walked over and pulled the flower closer. "This is called a Rerasa; it comes from the Seraph Lands. It is a very rare rose." As she looked at the flower, Naughton looked at her. She had a warm smile, and her soft brown eyes looked peaceful as she smelled the rose.

"Well, since you won't give me your name, I will name you," said Naughton.

She giggled and looked at him curiously. "And what is that?"

His heart started pounding and his stomach felt odd. "Rerasa."

She blushed and smiled, smelling the rose again. "That is sweet of you. I've never been named after a plant."

"A plant--I did not mean it to sound like that. I was referring to the rose," said Naughton, biting his lip.

She laughed. "I'm just giving you a hard time. Thank you." She led him back to his quarters and a meal was prepared for him. There was fruit, meat, and bread. "If you need anything, a guard is right down the hall," she said, exiting his room.

Naughton sat down. "Wait, will you keep me company while I eat? Eating alone is unhealthy where I come from."

She smirked. "I suppose." She sat down across the table from him and he handed her a plate.

"So how long have you served Airah?"

"For many years. My family lives in the castle as well; we are good friends of the family." She took a bite of bread. "So what kind of name is Naughton?"

"It's a long story that is a family secret, but maybe sometime I will share it...when you tell me your name."

She smiled. "You and your bribes."

"No, I just want to know the name of the person I'm telling the secret to. So, why did you leave Samha?"

"When our King started enslaving the people," she replied, eating small bites of fruit. "My parents offered their services to King Irus, and now he is fond of us."

Naughton was pleased she was opening up to him. "What do your parents do?"

"They are cooks!" she replied with joy.

"Do have any brothers or sisters?"

"I have one sister who is older, but she moved

away to the west with a boat captain."

Naughton knew the next question he wanted to ask, but was hesitant. "And what about you, is there someone special?" She glanced at him. "Maybe, but I'd rather not talk about it now."

"Oh....too private, huh?"

"Not necessarily, but I would rather not say anything right now," she replied, wiping her mouth. Naughton clenched his jaw, frustrated and uneasy with how she had dodged his question. She stood up. "I think I'm going to bed. I have many duties to attend to tomorrow. Goodnight, Master Naughton."

"Please, don't call me that. Just call me Naughton."

"As you wish. Goodnight." She exited the room, not giving him the chance to respond. He took a few more bites and lost his appetite. He blew out the candle and looked out his small window. The kingdom was glowing down below with the dim light of street lanterns. He could just barely see some of the townspeople still moving about, some alone and others in roving groups. He lay down and stared up at the ceiling, wondering where the sun jewel and the necklace his mother gave him were. He missed his parents and Sturkma, but his last thought was of Rerasa.

Naughton awoke to a knock at the door. There stood Bane, dressed in a blue robe and gold tassels. "Time to get up! At last we can find out what those words mean on your jewel."

Naughton yawned. "Wait...I don't have it. Jesper said they hid it until the time was right."

Bane looked at him oddly. "Are you mad or delirious, Naughton? It's right behind you." He turned around and there on his bed was the sun jewel, hanging from the bed post. Naughton stood there, baffled.

"It wasn't there last night! Who could have-- and how?" Naughton muttered to himself.

Bane stood there looking at him, arching one eyebrow. "Perhaps...we should wait until you feel better."

Naughton whipped around. "Absolutely not! I'm tired of being cooped up in this room."

"If you say so," said Bane, shrugging his shoulders. Naughton grabbed the jewel and put it around his neck, tucking it under his shirt. They went downstairs to the main hall, making their way to the library. There they descended another set of stairs that spiraled down, lit by few candles hanging on the wall. They reached the bottom, and Bane led Naughton down a dark hallway that had several rooms. They went to the last door and Bane knocked as he opened it.

When they entered, there was a pot boiling in a fireplace on the opposite side of the room, and scrolls were stretched out on a round table before him. The room was cozy and well lit with candles. It had a couple of cushioned chairs around the table in the center of the room. In the corner sat an old man with a narrow, wrinkly face and a pointy chin. He had bushy white eyebrows matching his long mustache with little hair on his head. He wore a white tunic with blue tassels hanging downward. He gestured with his cane at the pot in the fireplace and Bane took it, pouring soup into three bowls. He put the pot back in the fireplace. Bane pulled out a chair and motioned Naughton to sit on the other side of the table.

The old man looked at Naughton from under his bushy eyebrows and pulled on his mustache. When his spoke his voice was soft, but full of wisdom. "Well, sonny, are you going to try my soup or sit there like a codfish?" Naughton grabbed the bowl and put it up to his mouth, but Bane nudged him, holding a spoon. Naughton grinned, feeling stupid, and took it. He dipped it and put some in his mouth. The soup burned his mouth and he dropped the spoon. The old man laughed. "This dingbat is not too bright! Let it cool, sonny. It just got off the fire, didn't you see that?"

"Yes sir, I did," replied Naughton wiping his mouth.

"Use your brain the mighty El gave you! Common sense for instance." The old man got up, pouring some water and giving it to Naughton so he could cool his mouth. The old man examined Naughton up and down for a moment before speaking again. "You look nothing like your father. You are somewhat skinnier than he was when he was your age."

Bane leaned forward. "Naughton, I would like to introduce you to master scholar Nellium. He knows all about the Bindings of El and the history of the kingdom."

"It's nice to meet you, sir."

"Likewise, sonny. So I hear we have a puzzle to solve, eh?"

"Yes, sir."

"Well, let's see what we can do," said Nellium, as he sat at the table and took a sip from his soup. Naughton pulled out the necklace and gave the jewel to Nellium, who pulled out a magnifying glass from his pocket and began studying the artifact. He sat for several minutes before saying anything. "From what I can see, your father took good care of it, but I see nothing different than last time."

Bane laughed hysterically. "I know master Nellium, but look what happens when he holds it."

Nellium reached over, putting the jewel in Naughton's hand. "I see nothing of importance."

Bane lifted a finger. "Look on the back master."

Nellium flipped it over, and instantly the words appeared.

Nellium yanked Naughton's hand under the glass, knocking the bowls off the table. "Well, I be flabbergasted!" Nellium picked up the sun jewel and the words disappeared. He put it back, and once again the words reappeared. The old man examined it for a minute and released Naughton's hand. Naughton got back in his chair, holding his shoulder. Bane picked up the bowls. Nellium grabbed his cane. "Sorry about that sonny, I got a wee bit excited." Nellium poured some more soup while Bane cleaned the floor. Once they were settled, the old man looked at Naughton with uneasy eyes. "You have a long road ahead of you, I'm afraid."

Naughton's face turned sour. "What do you mean?"

"The words are only revealed when you hold it, which means the words are meant for you."

"Yes yes, but what does it mean?" blurted Bane. Nellium looked at him with a sharp eye under his bushy eyebrows, and Bane relaxed. "Sorry."

Nellium continued. "That supernatural being wants something from you." Naughton's face went pale and his mouth opened. His heart started pounding and sweat started to form on his brow. Nellium touched Naughton's hurt shoulder very gently. "Calm down, sonny. It's not the end of the world for you, but a great honor. However, it may be the end of the world for the rest of us." Naughton was taking deep breaths to calm down and leaned back in his chair.

"How--how do you know he wants something from me?" asked Naughton.

The old man took a sip from his soup and swallowed. "Because it says 'Honor the Holy'."

Naughton curled his lip. " 'Honor the Holy.' But what does he want?"

The old man laughed. "Now how am I supposed to know that, dingbat?"

Bane crossed his arms. "I thought Holy was the first word?"

Nellium shook his head. "I see you have not kept up your lessons."

"What do you mean?" asked Naughton.

Nellium wiggled his mustache. "The Hebrew

language is written backwards, right to left."
Naughton was puzzled. Nellium held up his hand.
"Don't ask, I don't know why it's different than ours."

"Wait, did you say for others it could be the end of the world?" asked Bane.

"Yes, I did. The last time he was seen, he destroyed a powerful kingdom. Only few people were spared, one being King Irus's forefathers." Nellium grabbed Naughton's spoon and gave it to him. "Eat, sonny. This soup will help your shoulder, unlike that nasty medicine Winsto gives you." Naughton started eating, even though he had lost his appetite.

Bane was stirring his soup. "What do we do now Nellium?"

"I haven't the foggiest idea. The last time I sent scholars with Berton that supernatural being killed them all. Except for Berton, of course. I don't know anyone who'd be willing to go help solve the riddles that Berton mentioned along the way."

"I will go with him!" exclaimed Bane.

The old man laughed sarcastically. "You? You don't even know how to read Hebrew anymore, much less memorize every word in the Bindings of El. No no, you will just get yourselves killed."

"But I can relearn the language! It should come back to me since I knew it before, and I have been studying ever since I left Yorben."

"Perhaps, but you will need help. I just have to think of someone who might be crazy enough to go with you."

Naughton was almost done with his soup and his shoulder started feeling better. "The soup has helped my shoulder."

"Well, naturally," replied Nellium, giving a slight grin.

"What's in this?"

Nellium shook his bony finger. "Ah, it's a secret recipe handed down for generations. Maybe I'll teach you before you leave, if you pass your studies."

Naughton looked at him confused. "Studies?"

"Why yes, boy. You can't expect to confront that being without some wisdom. We must also try to figure out what he wants from you. He will kill you for sure if you know nothing." Naughton remembered what his father told him at the gate of Fort Yorben about why he was spared.

"I guess I will study then," said Naughton, with very little enthusiasm.

"There is no guess; you will. Be here in the morning. As for you, Bane, I want you to continue your studies. I will tell the King of what we have discovered, and I'm sure he will want to meet you,

Naughton. Now I have other duties to attend to, so be off with you." They started to walk out the door and Nellium spoke. "Don't be late."

Naughton bowed. "I won't."

They went back to the main hall and Bane had to leave. "Naughton, I have to go the main library. I'm sure you can find your way around." With that, Bane walked away, and Naughton started exploring the castle.

Naughton had all afternoon to look around, so he decided to look for Airah since he had not seen her in several days. He asked guards if they had seen her, but no one knew where she was. He walked all around the castle and could not find her, so he decided to explore the city. He walked through the streets and saw many people coming and going. He saw shops that had fine clothes for sale, and other items such as jewels, gold, and silk. He made his way to the stables, looking at all the horses as the servants cared for them. He was about to leave when in came Airah, riding her horse. "Hello, Naughton. It's good to see you're up and about." She jumped off the horse and a servant took it away.

Two guards rode up behind her. "Lady Airah, you cannot leave us like that! Your uncle would have my head if something were to happen to you."

"My apologies," she said, walking up to Naughton. She hugged him and looked at his shoulder. "How's the arm, hero?"

He moved it around. "It's coming around, and I am no hero."

"Ah, but you are. You saved Jesper and I. My uncle wants to meet you soon. He has been very busy lately with the war issue."

Naughton whispered. "Why did you disguise yourself in Yorben?"

"Isn't it obvious? My uncle is very protective. I sneak off to Yorben occasionally with Bane, acting like a servant when I want to leave this place. Something happened to me when I was a child, and my uncle worries constantly for my safety."

Naughton grinned. "I see."

Airah narrowed her eyes. "You grin as though you carry a secret."

"No, no secrets, Lady Airah."

"I will visit tonight with Jesper, and we will all have dinner."

Naughton bowed. "I would be honored." She gave a wink and went to tend to her horse.

Darkness was approaching and Naughton made his way back to the castle. He went to his room, did his shoulder exercises, and took a hot bath to relax. He leaned back and breathed in the steam as his shoulder started tingling. He began to forget the world, when suddenly there was a knock on the door. "Who is it?"

"It's me, Jesper."

"Come in."

Jesper entered and immediately turned away from Naughton in shock. "Why did you tell me to come in? I'll come back later!"

"Relax, if I have something different than you, then shoot at it."

Jesper laughed. "I came to tell you that we're eating in Airah's room tonight. It will be you, me, Airah, and Rerasa."

"You call her that too?" asked Naughton, giving a blank stare.

"Yep, she is enjoying teasing you, it seems."

"Hmph...it doesn't matter anymore what I think now," said Naughton, sinking lower in the tub.

"Why do you say that?"

"Because she is taken,"

Jesper sat on the bed. "Oh, I see."

Naughton changed the subject. "Well, are you going to be a Centore?"

"I find out tomorrow. I'm supposed to report back in the morning. What about you? Did you find out what the sun jewel means?"

Naughton's lip twitched. "It says 'Honor the Holy'."

"Huh?" asked Jesper, tilting his head to the side.

"I have no idea what it means, but Nellium says I have to see him."

Jesper looked glumly at his cousin. "You--you mean you have to go see that thing that killed all those people?"

"I guess. That is, of course, when we find a group of people to go with me."

Jesper headed for the door, already worrying about Naughton. "Well, let's not go into details. I'm sure Lady Airah will want to hear." Jesper threw a towel at Naughton. "Hurry up, we're running late." With that, Jesper walked out.

Naughton got dressed and walked out where Jesper was waiting on him. They went down the hall and up the stairs two levels. There were only two rooms on that level; one was Airah's, and the other the King's quarters. The hall was heavily guarded with several guards parked in front of the King's door. They walked by the King's door and the guards paid no attention to them. Jesper walked up to Airah's door and a guard let them pass. They entered the room and there were Airah and Rerasa, sitting at a small table with all kinds of food. Airah's room was vast and had colorful arrangements. The bed was sitting on a dark wood frame, with a cream silk canopy and a purple quilt cover. Her room had chairs and couches in front of the fireplace, along with a bookcase full of books and journals. There were paintings of landscapes and animals hanging all around her room. "The food is getting cold," said Airah, gesturing her hand to the seats at a square table.

They sat down, and Naughton went to grab a huge turkey leg, but Airah popped his hand. "Not until we bless it." Airah blessed the food, and they started to eat. Naughton stuffed himself, happy to get away from the food he had to eat when he was sick.

Rerasa handed him a bowl of meatball soup. "My mother made this." Naughton dipped his spoon and took a sip. A few seconds later his mouth was on fire.

"Agh....this stuff is spicy!" Naughton grabbed his mug and downed his drink. "What's in that?"

"It is a special recipe my mother made long ago," she replied. "Do you not like it?"

"It tastes good, I just have to eat it in small quantities or the results will disastrous." They all laughed at Naughton as his face turned red, trying to escape the fires of the soup. He took a break and ate

other delicious foods, such as pork covered in a red
sauce that Rerasa's mother made as well. Naughton
ate the entire plate and leaned back, rubbing his belly.
He looked at Rerasa.

"Tell your mother that I enjoyed that
tremendously."

She gave a slight grin. The others finished eating
and servants came to take the plates away. They
walked over to the fireplace and sat down. Naughton
stretched out on one of the large couches and relaxed.
Jesper and Airah sat on a couch together, and Rerasa
sat in a chair.

"Naughton, I heard you found out what the sun
jewel says," said Airah.

Naughton leaned forward and pulled out the
sun jewel. "Yes."

"Well, are you going to tell us?" asked Rerasa.

Naughton gave a smirk and raised an eyebrow.
"Not with that attitude." She crossed her arms and
gave a stare. Naughton continued, "It says 'Honor the
Holy'. I have no idea what it means, but Nellium told
me that I have to see him." Airah's jaw dropped.

They all sat in silence until Rerasa spoke. "You
mean you have to go through the Seraph Lands?"

"It seems I have no choice. But believe me, I'm
in no hurry to go to a place that is cursed," replied

Naughton, rubbing his shoulder.

"I wouldn't say cursed, but a place where only the chosen may go," said Airah.

Rerasa stared at Naughton's chest, looking at the jewel. "Where are the words?" Naughton flipped it over so she could see them. She examined it closely, and Naughton quit looking at the sun jewel and instead stared at Rerasa. His heart started pounding and his stomach tightened like it had the first time he saw her. She touched the sun jewel. "It never had words when I was holding it for you."

Naughton sat up and looked at her sternly. "You had it the whole time when I was sick?"

"Well yes, but I was--"

Airah interrupted. "Naughton, I swore her to secrecy on the matter. I told her to hold onto it until you recovered. I did not want anyone to know about the sun jewel."

Naughton shifted back from Rerasa, puzzled. "What about the other necklace I wore? It was an arrowhead made from deer horn."

Rerasa's face saddened. "I don't know about that." Naughton looked at the others and saw they did not know where it was either.

Airah spoke. "I guess it was lost when Winsto started working on you. My only concerns were you and the sun jewel at the time."

Naughton leaned back and took a deep breath, looking at Rerasa, "I'm sorry." She looked down and nodded, accepting his apology. Airah spoke to Jesper to take attention from Naughton.

"Jesper, do you see the Centore trainer tomorrow?"

Jesper gave her a strange look. "I already told you that I was seeing him tomorrow." Airah raised an eyebrow and glanced at Naughton. "Oh...but I don't know any details of what is yet to come." Jesper looked at his cousin. "I heard you start your lessons tomorrow with an old scholar."

Naughton grunted. "I start my studies in the morning, but I must say, Nellium is a strange man."

Airah laughed. "He means well, he is just old and somewhat senile. But he is no fool. Be sure to listen to him. It is rare that he gives lessons these days, so feel honored. Well, if you would excuse me I must sleep. I have to see my uncle tomorrow." Airah stood up and escorted her company out, begging their pardon as she shut the door. They went downstairs and Naughton headed to his room.

"Wait, Naughton," said Rerasa. "I want to speak to you."

Jesper looked at Naughton and gave a wink.

"Goodnight, cousin," and continued down the stairs.

Naughton and Rerasa went to his room and Naughton sat on his bed, letting his arm stretch out. Rerasa sat down in front of the fireplace and warmed her hands. "I am sorry I did not tell you I had the sun jewel. I made a promise to Lady Airah."

"No need to apologize," he replied in a soft voice. "I understand your situation completely."

Rerasa clasped her hands together. "What do you mean?"

"I have a secret myself that I'm not allowed to tell."

Her eyes became curious. "Really? What is it?"

"I'm not trying to bribe you, but how can I trust someone when I don't even know their name?" She stared into the fire with no reply. He lay down. "I'm sorry about getting upset in Airah's room."

Naughton closed his eyes, thinking she was going to leave, but instead she walked over to Naughton. "May I ask you a question, if you'll keep your eyes closed?"

"Of course," Naughton kept his eyes closed, having no idea what to expect. He cleared his mind and relaxed, waiting for a complicated question. He hoped she was not playing a game with him. She touched his hand, and it seemed like forever until finally she moved again, and he felt a touch of warm, soft lips on his. Instantly, his body went numb. She leaned back, and he opened his eyes just in time to watch her walk out the door. He was completely stunned. He felt something in his hand and looked down. It was the necklace his mother gave him, along with a piece of paper that simply said Eirmosa. He smiled and lay motionless, feeling his body tingle from head to toe.

Warriors broken

At sunrise, Jesper strolled through the city streets as the lanterns flickered. All was quiet. He made his way to the recruiting station and knocked on the door. "Greetings, Jesper! Come in," said the man in the front of the station. He escorted Jesper back to Thorg's room and knocked.

Thorg yelled, "Enter!" The man stepped aside and opened the door for Jesper. "Come in and have a seat," said Thorg, pointing at a chair. Thorg stood up, grabbed a bag, and threw it at Jesper's feet. "Open it, Turtle." Jesper opened it, and there lay his armor. Thorg sat down and looked at Jesper, waiting for a response.

"How did you get this? It was locked in my room."

Thorg crossed his arms, his muscles bulging. "First of all, it's not yours--not yet. You must earn that armor, and in order to do that you must undergo the toughest training known to man. For twelve weeks you will be trained to become a Centore. There are strict rules you must follow, and there will be no exceptions. Know this: there are few men who pass this training and they were soldiers in the field already. Are you sure you want to do this?"

Jesper looked at the armor and then looked into

Thorg's eyes. "Yes."

"Very well. Report here before sunrise with your clothes only. I will see you in the morning." Jesper stood up and was making his way to the door when Thorg told him, "Good luck."

Jesper left and walked back to the castle, deep in thought. He began to wonder if he was up to the challenge. "Is this something I really want to do?" he asked himself. He went to his room and was gathering clothes when there was a knock on the door.

He opened it, and there stood Airah. "What did he say?"

"I'm in."

"Oh...that's good."

Jesper looked at her curiously. "You don't sound happy for me."

"I am. It just happened so quickly and I didn't get the chance to know you."

Jesper continued packing his bag. "I'll be back in twelve weeks, don't worry."

"No, you will be sent to a unit when you're done, and I will never see you again." With that, she walked out and did not look back.

Jesper paused, deep in thought, and then continued packing.

That same morning, Naughton went to see Nellium down in his secluded room where there was peace and quiet. He knocked and the old man replied, "Come." Naughton entered and Nellium was sitting there, smoking a pipe and looking through rolls of parchments. "You managed to be here on time, sonny. Have a seat." Naughton sat down and stared at the papers. There were strange writing and markings all over them.

Naughton let out a skeptical laugh. "You expect me to learn all of this?"

"Of course not. I've managed to round up many scrolls that we have recorded from the Bindings of El."

"We are not studying from the original copy?"

Nellium coughed up some smoke. "I will not risk anything happening to it. There is only one left, let me remind you. Perhaps I will allow you to see the book one day, but for now these copies will do. You will learn the story of our history and where we come from, and I expect you to take this seriously. Your life will depend on it when you reach the Seraph Lands. I have not yet found another scholar to go with you-- except Bane, of course. By the way, you're meeting the King tonight."

Naughton's eyes widened. "What?"

"Easy now, sonny, just relax. It's time to learn ya something. Keep in mind this will take many days, and it will be a slow process, so be patient. We will have breaks through the day so you can do your shoulder exercises." Naughton nodded. The old man leaned back and took a puff from his pipe, squinting his bushy eyebrows. He grabbed a piece of parchment and began his lecture to Naughton.

"According to the Bindings of El, mankind has been around thousands of years. Nations and kingdoms have thrived and fallen because of power, greed, knowledge, lust, betrayal, and sacrifice. Man is always rising and falling because of such things; it is an endless cycle. History always repeats itself, it seems."

Naughton interrupted. "If history repeats itself, why can't we learn from it?"

The old man grinned. "Because it is our sinful nature to put oneself above others, instead of loving one another like the Bindings of El command. Not all people have the same goals, Naughton. Each human being seeks individuality. They forget at times, if not forever, how they are supposed to live. Therefore, history repeats itself due to the stupidity of those that think they can do it better the next time. It is the way of things in this world."

Naughton sat back. "So is that where evil comes

from?"

Nellium blew a puff of smoke. "Somewhat." The old man went to a shelf and pulled out an old painting, laying it in front of him. Nellium sat next to him observing the painting. There were two people standing in front of a tree in a garden. One was a man and the other was a woman, and they were naked. Naughton pointed at the painting. "You mean evil came from naked people?" Nellium laughed so hard he almost fell out of his chair.

"Of course not, you nimwit! Look at the tree, do you see that serpent?"

"Yes," replied Naughton, not appreciating the old man's criticism.

"Well take a good look, because that is where it all began for us and our turmoil." Naughton was totally confused, but waited patiently for an explanation. "According to the Bindings of El, the serpent was the craftiest creature of all. Do not be fooled by its appearance, for it is an evil angel who was cast out of heaven for his treachery. The evil angel transformed himself into a serpent, and persuaded them to eat a piece of fruit from the tree. But this tree was no ordinary tree; it was the tree of knowledge, which gives the power to distinguish between good and evil. El instructed them not to eat from the tree so that they would not have to worry about such things--for our mighty El would take care of them--but the serpent convinced them it was okay to have such knowledge. The man and woman ate from the tree of knowledge, and thus began the battle between good and evil. El was displeased, and threw the woman and man out of the garden, cursing them and the serpent forever."

"What did the angel do to become evil?"

Nellium's eyes hardened. "The angel tried to overthrow El, and he was cast down from heaven. Do you understand that clearly?"

Naughton leaned forward. "Clear as mud, but let's keep going."

By the end of the night Naughton's head was full. Before meeting the King, he decided to walk in the garden to get some fresh air and relax. Under the dim glow of a torch he could see Airah and Eirmosa sitting on a bench talking. As he approached, they looked at him and suddenly got quiet. "Everything okay?" Naughton asked.

Lady Airah spoke. "No, but I will manage. Thank you."

Naughton crossed his arms. "What's the matter?"

Eirmosa looked at him and then at Airah.

"Perhaps he can help." Eirmosa suggested, and then stood up. "I think you should talk to Naughton about this, my Lady. I will see you two in the dinner hall." She walked by Naughton, giving him a kiss on the cheek and walked off. Naughton sat next to Airah. A slight breeze blew; there was a chill in the air.

Airah rubbed her arms and smirked. "I see you learned her name."

Naughton winked. "I thought she'd never tell me. So what's troubling you?"

"We were discussing a secret." She reached below the bench and withdrew a sword in a sheath, sitting it on her lap. The sheath was gold with white pearls down the sides. The pommel was pearl white with swirls. The grip was black and the cross-guard was gold. She pulled the sword, exposing part of the blade. Engraved on it was C3. Naughton locked his eyes on it and gasped. Airah noticed his reaction. "You do know my past!" He looked down, clasping his hands. "I apologize for the deception, but I swore an oath. What I'm about to say must stay between us no matter what, do you promise?"

She nodded her head and then put a finger up. "As long as you never lie to me again." He looked around and lowered his voice.

"Do you know a Centore by the name of

Tulios?"

"Of course I do."

Naughton continued. "He was the one who jumped from the window to save your life, was he not?"

Airah's eyes grew large. "How do you know this? It is a sworn secret!"

"Jesper and Tulios were very close, and if I'm not mistaken, that is Tulios's sword."

Airah gripped the sword. "I demand you tell me everything this instant!"

"I'm trying, if you will allow me."

Airah's eyes hardened, and then she relaxed. "I apologize. So Jesper knew Tulios?"

"Yes, but he did not know that he was a Centore."

Airah rubbed the pommel, following the white swirls. "How close were they?"

Naughton looked at her steadily. "He was Jesper's father."

She released her grip on the hilt and smiled. "I knew his face looked familiar."

"I wanted to tell you sooner, but Nemian swore me to secrecy."

She stood up and began pacing back and forth. "He has the right to know. He must know that his father saved me."

Naughton grabbed her and sat her down. "Keep it down! Centore commanders are not allowed to have relationships, much less children. If word gets out that Tulios had children, he will lose his honor. Jesper has no idea, and must not until the time comes."

"But that is ridiculous. Jesper must have his father's sword!"

Naughton shook his head. "I understand, but Nemian told me that he will know when the time is right. For now we must remain silent."

"You do realize Jesper's wrath will come upon me in the future."

"On both of us. But I promise, he will understand."

Airah stood up and cradled the sword in its sheath. "It's funny....ever since Tulios rescued me, I have kept this sword secret and waited for a sibling to claim it. I never would have thought a son. Now I must wait even longer knowing who it belongs to. I told you knowing things can be a burden."

"That you did," replied Naughton, standing up.

"I must return the sword to its hiding place. Wait for me here and I will escort you to the dining hall."

Shortly after, Airah led Naughton to the royal

dining room, which was being guarded. The table was shaped like a horseshoe with an empty seat for the King, who sat in the middle so he could see everyone. Most of the company Naughton recognized, but there were others he did not know. Naughton sat beside Eirmosa and Jesper, while Airah sat beside the King's empty seat. Jesper whispered to Naughton. "Airah is acting odd."

"How so?"

"I don't know, just....distant."

"Have you said anything offensive?"

"Of course not! At least, I don't think."

Eirmosa leaned over. "Perhaps you should apologize."

"How can I apologize if I don't know what I did?"

"Are you blind or stupid? It is obvious she is fond of you and you're leaving."

Jesper's forehead wrinkled. "But what should I say?"

"Something is better than nothing."

"But that makes no sense."

Naughton chuckled softly. "Of course not. They're women."

Eirmosa pinched him. "That's enough!"

Suddenly, a squire entered and announced the King's

entrance. Everyone stood up except Naughton and Jesper, who did not know of local traditions. Eirmosa grabbed them both by the ear and lifted them up. "You're supposed to stand when he enters the room," she whispered.

Naughton rubbed his ear. "How about you just tell us next time."

"Shh, here he comes." The King entered the room, and everyone bowed in unison--except Jesper and Naughton, but no one noticed. The King was short, Naughton noticed, and he had a white mustache. His hair was short and grey and he wore a gold and silver crown on his head, which was covered in emeralds. On the front of the crown were two crescent moons facing away from each other with a leaf in the center. The King wore a red and gold robe that dragged on the floor behind him. Strapped to his belt was a sword that had a blue jewel on the end. The King sat in his chair and everyone else followed. No one spoke until he spoke.

"I would like to apologize to our guests, Naughton and Jesper, for not saying hello to them when they arrived. I have been very busy dealing with matters to the south." Naughton and Jesper sat in silence, staring at King Irus. Airah looked at Eirmosa and motioned for her to make the boys speak.

Eirmosa leaned over and whispered to Naughton. "Say something, you goof."

"Oh! It's okay, your Highness, I understand completely. We came from the south, and know the matters there need your utmost attention," said Naughton. Airah slapped her forehead with embarrassment.

King Irus laughed. "What's wrong, Airah?" King Irus grabbed her hand. "You choose your friends well, and they speak exactly what's on their mind. Well, Naughton, I hope you and Jesper can give me more details. Bane has told me of your adventures traveling from the south, and of your injuries, but we will discuss that later. Bring in the food!"

Servants entered with plates, trays, and drinks. They sat the food on the table and the drinks were poured. King Irus stood up and raised his mug to make a toast; others did the same. "May El watch over us and keep us safe from evil that dwells around us, and may he give us strength to overcome the wickedness that is coming," he said, and with that, the feast began. There were endless choices of food and Naughton tried everything that looked appealing.

Naughton pointed at a piece of meat and asked Eirmosa, "what is that?"

"That is roast duck," she replied.

"Roast duck!" said Naughton with dismay.

"You mean you have never tried roast duck?"

"Why...no, I have never heard of it."

Eirmosa stood. "I'll be right back." She went through a door and moments later came back dragging a cook behind her. He had short, coarse peppery hair. He was well-built with impressive arms, for he was a hard worker and took every project seriously. However, cooking was his specialty. He was a charming man with a pronounced chin and a sincere smile that stretched from ear to ear.

"Naughton, I would like you to meet my father, Paston."

"Hello, Mr. Paston," said Naughton.

Mr. Paston was holding a knife. "You don't like my duck?"

Naughton's eyes became focused on the knife. "I haven't had a chance to try any."

"You scared to try my duck? That is my favorite dish; here, don't be scared. Eat!" said Paston, pushing the plate closer to him. He cut some of the duck and put it on Naughton's plate. Naughton took a tentative bite and was surprised at the rich taste. It was the highlight of his meal. "You see, there is nothing here that tastes bad. Don't give me no more trouble or I'll make you wash dishes!" Paston laughed, and then returned to the kitchen.

The meal lasted for over an hour and was full of chatter and laughter. As the meal came to a close, King Irus raised his hand and everyone got quiet. "Thank you for coming and fellowshipping with me. These events bring us joy in times of chaos; keep these memories so you can smile." Everyone clapped, praising King Irus for his council, and remained standing as he exited the dining hall. Naughton, Jesper, and Airah followed, and were escorted by King Irus's guards to his library and they sat. King Irus rubbed his belly. "I must admit, I have never seen Airah smile so much. You bring her joy."

"Uncle!"Airah shouted.

"Relax, my dear, I'm just having a bit of fun. So, Naughton, I understand you are the son of Berton?"

"Yes, sir," replied Naughton.

"He is a good man. I hope my ring gave you passage without quarrel."

"It did indeed."

The King clasped his hands. "Good. How is your shoulder?"

"I'm almost back to full strength, but Winsto insists I wait longer before trying anything that would stress the muscles."

King Irus nodded. "I must agree with him. He is very wise in the practice of medicine. Now word has reached my ear that the sun jewel has returned to my castle, but with different applications?"

Naughton pulled out the sun jewel. "Yes, sir. Here it is."

The King rubbed his mustache. "Nellium has explained to me what the sun jewel says when you hold it, and what actions are necessary. But the question has not been asked." King Irus leaned back, interlocking his fingers on his belly. "Do you want to go to the Seraph Lands?"

Naughton hesitated before answering. "I don't have a choice it seems, sir."

The King raised an eyebrow. "Oh, but you do have a choice. No one is forcing you to go. This choice is yours alone." King Irus looked at Jesper. "I understand you start your Centore training tomorrow?"

"Yes, sir," replied Jesper.

"Ah, I owe much to them," said the King, winking at Airah. "They are the finest warriors to ever walk this earth. Why do you wish to become a Centore?"

"Well, it's been on my mind since Fort Yorben when I met the Centores, especially when I met

Nemian."

"I see. Nemian is an excellent leader and gives good counsel when I call. It is not an easy task to become a Centore. But if you succeed, you will be honored wherever you go within the kingdom, and feared by all enemies. They have served the kingdom for generations." The King slowly rose and stretched. "Naughton, walk with me. Airah, will you be so kind to escort Jesper back to his quarters?"

"Yes, Uncle."

The King gestured to the door. "Come, Naughton. I would like to speak with you." Jesper and Airah were left to sit by themselves. They sat in silence, until finally Jesper spoke.

"I'm sorry."

She looked at him, her eyebrow arched. "What are you sorry for?"

"I've noticed you have been distant. If I have offended you, I apologize."

"You've done nothing of the sort. Much is on my mind with this war, and many things have transpired since we've met. Pay no attention to my actions; it is nothing personal. Come, I will escort you to your room."

Airah led him upstairs to his room. She opened the door and gestured her hand. "Sleep well, Jesper. I hope you prevail in your training." Jesper stepped in, and Airah slowly closed the door in his face. Jesper stood speechless, staring at the door as he heard her walk away.

He clenched his fists. "Apologize, ha! Silence is golden."

Rain or shine

Jesper made his way to the recruiting building, walking anxiously down the silent streets. The air was still and his stomach was tight; he was unsure of what awaited him. It was well before sunrise, and when he turned the last corner he came up on a large group of men gathered in the street. They stood around talking and appeared to be waiting for further instruction. There were at least seventy men, all of them expecting the same thing: to become a Centore. As Jesper approached, they glared at him briefly before continuing their conversations. Jesper was standing off to the side when a tall, dark-skinned soldier approached him.

"I don't recognize you. What regiment were you with?"

Jesper hesitated, but told the truth. "I wasn't in one."

The soldier raised an eyebrow. "Who did you know?"

"What? I don't understand."

"It takes politics to get into this ordeal and you must know someone of great importance, considering you're no soldier."

"I see your point. Nemian helped me."

The soldier shrugged his shoulder. "No matter.

Everyone you see here has some political connections, even me. My name is Gideon."

"Jesper."

"Where do you hail from?"

"Sturkma, or what's left of it."

Gideon shook his head. "I am sorry to hear that. Perhaps when this training is over your sword can taste the flesh of Geols. Speaking of training, I will give you some advice: never look them in the eye, and keep a low profile."

Suddenly, a group of horses came around the corner pulling wagons. The horses' hooves pounded against the earth, echoing off the buildings. A cold chill went down Jesper's spine; it was time. The first driver pulled on the reins and did not look at them. "Good morning, gentlemen. Get on the wagons and we will take you to the training grounds." The soldiers loaded themselves onto the wagons and the horses pulled them out of the city towards the western countryside. They rode for hours until they came to a group of wooden buildings in the middle of a field. "Get off!" the driver yelled. The men jumped off with their belongings and the wagons left them standing there. Everyone looked around wondering what to do. The cold wind howled around them as the stars began to fade with the rising sun.

One of the men spoke, "I guess we put our things in this building." Everyone went inside to find beds and cabinets for their clothes. The men put their stuff up and got settled in, waiting for more instructions. They waited all day for someone to come, but by nightfall they had seen no one. Jesper was uneasy and had a hard time going to sleep. He kept thinking about home and the last things he and Airah said to each other. His mind jumped from one thing to the next, but eventually he fell into a fitful sleep.

In the middle of the night, Jesper woke to a fully armored Centore staring him in the face. The Centore grabbed him and threw him off the bed. Other Centores were in the room, giving the other men the same treatment. "You were told not to bring things! Who said you could sleep in here? Get your asses outside! Move move move!" The men ran out of the building in a panic. Jesper ran toward the back of the group in an effort to stay out of sight. They stood outside, torches surrounding them. Ten Centores, whose shoulders bore the red symbol of leadership, came out of the building. They lined up, battle-ready, and deployed shields. A man behind the panicking group spoke, and Jesper recognized his voice, it was Thorg. He was dressed in black clothes and he wore a sword.

"I'm sorry, did we disturb your sleep?"

A man spoke out. "No, sir!"

Thorg walked over to him. "That was a rhetorical question, you idiot!" Thorg's voice was deep, powerful, and authoritative. "From now on, you don't speak at all unless spoken to. You will not look us in the eye. You will stand battle-ready just like the Centores you see in front of you. These Centores will aid me in training you and make your lives a living hell for the next twelve weeks." Thorg stood in silence for several seconds. "What are you waiting for? Form lines! Battle-ready!"

Those that were not in correct formation were thrown to the ground. "It's not hard, people! Bend your knees--lower, lower! Now put your right foot behind your left, quartering yourself towards the direction you're facing. Spread your feet just outside your shoulders. Lift up your left arm as if you're holding a shield. Most of you are soldiers and should know how to do this already. No wonder soldiers die so quickly. You have become lazy!"

The Centores walked around, continuously inspecting the men. Over and over they would push men to the ground. "Wrong...do it again!" Jesper got pushed over repeatedly. "Use your peripheral vision!

Your arms must be the same height as everyone else's; you must match each other!" Some of the men would look around to see what the others were doing, but the Centores would hit them in the head. "Look toward your enemy. Use your peripheral vision!"

The abuse went on and on into the morning when the sun was clearing the horizon. Everyone's legs burned from standing battle ready for so long. Their arms shook as their muscles cramped. Many men fell to the ground from exhaustion, but would immediately get up again to resume the training. Jesper's entire body was shaking from the cold and his muscles ached as he tried to keep his stance. His body was screaming to stop, but his mind told him no. I can't go home. I will lose the respect of everyone I know. I would rather die first! The Centores, including Thorg, mocked their efforts.

By noon, Thorg raised his hand for them to stop. "I've seen enough of this madness; sit on the ground." All the men collapsed to the ground, some even lying down in the grass.

The Centores would kick the ones lying down. "He said sit. Can you not follow simple instructions?"

Thorg walked around and observed the men. "I have trained thousands of men and I must say, you people are the worst I've seen yet. You could not hold yourselves up, and you weren't even wearing armor or holding a shield! I don't know why you are here and at this point I don't care, but I can tell that some of you better rethink your reasons for being here. We can look into your eyes and see doubt and fear, such things make you weak. You will jeopardize yourself and the men standing next to you. Those of you who are ready to go home can just walk over to those poles, engrave your names, and be done with this insanity. Many have done it before and many will do it again and again." Thorg walked slowly around the group, eyeballing them closely and with no remorse. It was as if his heart was formed in the pit of hell; he showed no sympathy. "I will tell you this: no one will sleep until someone leaves. You will go inside and find clothes and gear that we have given you. You have one hour to put up your clothes and gear in an orderly fashion. They must be identical to each other. Now move!"

They ran inside and began organizing their clothes and gear. After an hour had passed, the men ran back out to see the Centores pouring water all over the ground. The men stood around looking at each other, wondering if they had to sit in the mud. Jesper ran out of the building and sat in the mud without a second thought, waiting for further instructions. A few others did the same as Jesper and suddenly Thorg yelled, "those of you who are standing, get in a battle stance!" Thorg clapped his hands and servants appeared, giving food and water to the men sitting on the ground. They started stuffing their faces without chewing.

Some men standing in battle stance began grumbling, and the Centores knocked them to the ground. "Did you say something? We couldn't hear you."

When Jesper and the others finished eating, Thorg walked over to Jesper and looked him in the eye. "Was it good, Turtle?"

"Yes, sir," replied Jesper in a low voice.

"Stand up and speak to me, bonehead!" Thorg yelled, suddenly angry.

Jesper leapt to his feet. "Yes, sir!"

Thorg asked the others and they all jumped up and yelled, "Yes, sir!"

Thorg smiled. "You see what happens when you follow simple instructions? You are rewarded. Alright, all of you get in lines and in battle stances."

The day waged on and on without mercy. Thorg and the Centores were relentless and made them stand in battle stance for hours until nightfall came. As the sun set, the cold took its toll on the trainees. Jesper's bones ached and his skin was numb.

He never thought he could tolerate so much pain. Over and over he told himself, I can do this.

"Go to that water bucket and drink; you have five minutes. Then, line up in two lines facing the forest and wait for further instructions." The men ran to the water and drank as much as they could, then lined up in the dark, barely able to see one another. Jesper was exhausted, his eyes closing, wishing he could just sleep for an hour.

The Centores rode up on horses and walked around with torches in their hands, keeping an eye on everyone. Thorg appeared on horseback as well. "You are to follow me and do exactly what I say. If anyone falls behind, the Centores riding behind you will punish you severely." Thorg kicked his horse, walking toward the forest. The men stayed in two lines with Centores riding around them.

After a short time, Thorg increased his pace and the men started jogging. Jesper tried to block out the pain in his lungs from breathing the cold air. His feet stung with every jolt and his knees felt like they were going to snap. His eyes were watering from the cold wind. Trees passed by him like a hazy dream, tripping him with their roots. He thought of past times with his family and spending time with Airah. Once they were deep in the forest, Thorg took a slow path for the men to follow behind. They were all panting like dogs and trying to catch their breath, but it seemed impossible.

A Centore took the lead so that Thorg could inspect the men. "Someone will leave tonight, I promise you. To help encourage you, let me tell you our laws. You are not allowed to talk about any of our missions. Commanders are not allowed to marry and have children. Once you serve your time with us, I could care less what you do. If you survive our training, you will obey these laws or you will be exiled." Jesper's mind continued to wander, and he began to forget his pain. He was glad Thorg was giving a lecture, for his legs felt hollow and his stomach was cramping.

Thorg continued his lecture. "If you become a Centore, you will be assigned to a unit and be under the command of a red shoulder Centore. If your leader sends me a complaint about you, there will be consequences. If it happens twice, you will be exiled. If you die in battle or choose to retire, which is only allowed after seven years of service, you will be known as Guardians and will be honored for the rest of your lives. Do I make myself clear?"

Together they yelled, "Yes, sir!"

Thorg kicked his horse. "Very well. Push on, boneheads."

Thorg increased his pace again and the men ran behind him, trying to keep pace. Eventually some of the men fell behind, and the Centores had their way with them. They threw a powder on the stragglers that made their skin burn, and they screamed as they tried to catch up. Thorg eventually led the group to a lake and ordered the men to jump in. The water was cold and dark. A dozen men covered in powder dove in without a second thought, and were relieved when the water washed away the powder. Thorg and the Centores stood on the shoreline, watching them closely. Thorg shouted, "get out and line up!" Everyone was moving slow and were in no hurry to line up. "You have thirty seconds, maggots!" Thorg yelled, impatiently. The men rushed out of the water and lined up, waiting. Jesper was one of the last to get out of the water. Thorg kept a close eye on him, making sure he was okay. "Push on!" he yelled.

Thorg rode at a quick pace and the men followed in agony, hoping that the run would end soon. They continued through the forest, and once again some men fell behind and had powder thrown on them. A man began screaming, "I can't do this! I submit!" The Centores threw water on him to end the burning on his skin and returned him to the poles. Thorg continued without looking back and increased his pace. More men fell behind and the Centores continued throwing powder on the stragglers. Four more men submitted and were carried off by the Centores. A Centore took Thorg's place leading while Thorg himself rode around the group.

"Who's next? Only the strong can be a Centore! I will take no weaklings!" The men remained silent and continued running. Jesper ran and dared not fall behind in fear of the burning powder. The screams alone drove him to run faster, ignoring the pain.

Finally, at sunrise, they made it back to the buildings. Everyone was arched over, gasping for air. The Centores poured water over the ones who still had powder on them. Thorg got off his horse. "Let's see…that's five less children to worry about. Clean yourselves and I'll let you sleep for five hours. How's that sound?"

"Yes, sir!" they replied in relief.

Thorg looked at them and crossed his arms. "Get out of my sight." All the men took off running to their beds.

Jesper collapsed onto his bed, and right before he passed out from exhaustion, said to himself, "what have I done?"

Knowledge is wisdom

Naughton continued his studies with Nellium, learning all about El, angels, and the realms of evil. Sometimes Nellium took Naughton outside to teach him, because he could tell Naughton was having a hard time staying focused when he was stuck in a room all day. Weeks had gone by with Nellium teaching key points to Naughton. Sometimes he had trouble understanding certain topics, such as the plagues of Egypt with Moses leading the Israelites to freedom, the story of David and Goliath, and the book of Job.

Nellium wiggled his mustache. "I know I'm throwing a lot at you, but you must relax your mind and quit thinking so much. Sometimes it's better to just listen and let it sink in before analyzing it in your mind. Remember what I told you about the man and woman. They ate from the tree and gained certain aspects of knowledge, but not all. If that were not the case we would be just as wise as El. For instance, there are some things you must accept even though you can't offer up explanation. Gravity, for example. Can you see gravity?"

Naughton crossed his arms. "Yes."

Nellium stuffed his pipe. "Really? How so?"

"Because when I drop a rock, it falls to the

ground."

Nellium lit his pipe. "No, there you see the effect of gravity. Another example: can you see wind?"

Naughton rolled his eyes. "No, but I can feel it."

"Exactly, just like how you feel gravity. Believing is not seeing; it is feeling what's in your heart." Nellium noticed that Naughton was getting tired. "I think we will continue tomorrow. I want you to do something creative and go relax your mind."

Naughton jumped up. "I will." Nellium slowly got up from the bench, leaving Naughton with his thoughts. Naughton stretched his legs and decided to go see Eirmosa. As he was making his way there, he heard a whistle. He looked to his left, and there stood Eirmosa, waving at him from a well. He walked over and hugged her.

"You were gone a long time," said Eirmosa. "Nellium must have really worn you out."

"You have no idea. The stuff he is teaching me is hard to believe sometimes."

She put her hand on his arm. "It's because you're being overwhelmed with so much information. He would not push you so hard if it were not necessary. In time, it will all come together for you.

Just have patience."

"How can you be so sure?"

She smiled. "Because it came together for me."

They held each other in the night on a wooden bench beside the well, watching for falling stars as people came and went. The castle was illuminated by torches and lit windows, and birds were darting back and forth in the light, catching bugs. From within the castle, a long-haired woman came to the well.

She approached them with her arms wide and Eirmosa jumped up to hug her. "Naughton, this is my mother, Lena."

He stood up to shake her hand, but she hugged him instead. "Pleased to meet you, Naughton. So this is the young man my daughter has become smitten with."

"Mother!" yelled Eirmosa, stomping her feet.

"I hear you must make a dangerous quest soon, young man."

Naughton noticed that Eirmosa looked much like her mother. "I fear I must leave soon."

Lena hugged him again. "Fear nothing. I have heard great stories of your courage, such as saving Lady Airah and your cousin. I'm sure your bravery will be rewarded. It has been a long day; I will leave the two of you to discuss my future grandchildren." With a wink, she left.

Eirmosa blushed with embarrassment. "I'm so sorry. She can be very forthcoming."

"It's okay," replied Naughton. But deep down, Naughton was terrified. He moved his shoulder around, and it suddenly occurred to him he had not shot his bow since Fort Yorben. He stood up. "Have you ever shot a bow?"

Eirmosa gave him a sarcastic smile. "Of course I have."

Naughton grabbed her hand and pulled her up. "Good. Now is the time."

Eirmosa pulled her hand away. "No, Naughton! Winsto said not to strain your shoulder for another four weeks."

"My shoulder feels fine, and I am tired of sitting around. I want to do something fun."

Eirmosa thought for a moment. "Very well, but this never happened. Where can we shoot at this time of night?"

"I have an idea. Come on."

They went to his room to retrieve the osage bow and then to the outer walls of the city and put up a hay bale. He hesitated before drawing the bow, remembering the pain he felt when he first met Winsto. He took a deep breath and pulled back slowly. There was no pain. He aimed at his thirty yard target and hit it dead center.

Eirmosa took the bow from Naughton and tried to pull back, but couldn't do it. "I can't pull this thing back! How in the world did you do that? And how did your shoulder heal so quickly?"

"I don't know, but it feels great!" he replied, moving his arm around. "Here, let me help you." He stood behind her and helped pull back the string. She took aim. "On three. One…two…three!" They released the string and the arrow flew, hitting the target. "Nice shot. What do you say we go hunting?"

"Hunting! Are you brainless?"

Naughton started walking into a small patch of woods along the wall. "No offense to your father's cooking, but I'm craving deer meat."

"Where in the world are you planning on finding deer, and how will you see them?"

"I've seen them eating beside the wall under the torches." They crept through the woods until they spotted their prey eating a patch of grass beside the east wall. They stalked as close as they could without being seen or smelled. Once in range, Naughton took aim and fired. They followed the blood trail into the woods. "Here it is! This thing is--oh, no."

Eirmosa ran up next to him. "What do you

mean, 'oh, no'?"

"It's got a collar on it," replied Naughton, kneeling down.

"What?!" Eirmosa looked at the deer. "I ought to beat your head with that bow! This is one of the villagers' pet deer!"

Naughton threw his bow down. "You mean they have pet deer around here?"

"Of course, you nimwit!"

"Why didn't you tell me?"

"I thought you knew," replied Eirmosa, throwing her hands in the air.

He touched the deer's shoulder where the arrow had entered. "What should I do?"

Eirmosa put her hands on her hips. "Are you serious? How would I know? Like I go killing pet deer in the middle of the night!" Suddenly they heard someone yelling a name and eventually they saw an old lady and a child walking along the wall.

"Clover! Here, Clover!" Naughton looked at Eirmosa, disgusted with himself, knowing he ruined their night. Suddenly the old lady yelled, "Guards! Guards! Someone has shot my deer!" Moments later the guards ran up.

"What's wrong?"

"Someone shot my pet deer! Look, here is the

arrow with blood on it."

The guard looked at the arrow. "How do you know it's your pet deer?"

"Because we can't find her!"

The guards looked at the ground and began following the blood trail.

Naughton looked at Eirmosa. "I want you to run deep into the woods and go around back to the gate. I don't want you involved in this."

She glanced at the guards. "Absolutely not."

"Please go, Eirmosa. This is my doing."

She lowered her head, putting her hands over her face. "Fine."

She ran off deep into the trees, staying in the shadows as Naughton waited for the guards. He cut off the collar on the deer and sat next to it. The guards came walking up with torches. "Here is the deer, but it doesn't have a collar," said one of the guards.

"Yes, it does," said Naughton, standing up from behind the bush holding the collar.

The guards whipped out their swords. "Who are you?"

"I am Naughton, son of Berton, sir."

"Naughton...the one who saved Lady Airah?"

"Yes, sir," replied Naughton with a grim face.

The guard slapped his forehead. "Why on my

shift…why?" The guard turned around and yelled. "We have a problem, Captain!"

"Just bring it out here, Tirus."

He sheathed his sword. "I'd rather not," mumbled Tirus. "Come on, Naughton. You two grab the deer." Naughton was escorted by the guards back to the wall. "Captain, we found the deer and violator." The old lady looked Naughton up and down in disgust, and then the little boy yelled at Naughton,

"You killed my pet deer!"

The captain turned around. "Settle down, boy."

Naughton handed the collar to the old lady. "I'm sorry. I did not know there were pets around here."

Her face seemed to wrinkle even more around her eyes as she snatched the collar from Naughton's hand. "Obviously!"

The captain looked at the violator. "What is your name?"

"Naughton, son of Berton."

The captain's eyes widened. "Oh no…why on my shift?"

"That's exactly what I said, Captain."

"Shut up, Tirus!" The captain rubbed his head.

"My lady, do you want the deer?"

"Oh, no. That would not seem right, eating one of my pets."

"Very well. Tirus, take this deer away."

"Where to, Captain?"

"I don't care, just get rid of it. And as for you, Naughton...come with me."

The guards escorted Naughton back to the gate, not once looking at him. Naughton's heart pounded and sweat rolled off his face. He had never been in trouble of this magnitude and he knew his father would whip him till sunrise if he were there. They continued to the guard headquarters. They saluted as they let them in. The captain and Naughton sat down at a table with two other guards standing beside him. As soon as the door shut the captain and guards burst into laughter. "I have been guarding this place for years and I have never seen such craziness!" said the captain, gasping for air. "Do you know how hard it was for me to keep a straight face?" Naughton felt the weight lift from his shoulders. The captain took off his helmet. He had short red hair and a narrow patch of red hair on his chin. He was very tall and broad, like a bear. "By the way, I am Captain Anor, and I must say it's a small world, Naughton."

Naughton looked up. "Why is that?"

"Because I will be going with you to the Seraph Lands."

Naughton's face was puzzled. "I thought only a couple of scholars were going with me?"

"You will need some protection, and the King picked me and Tirus to handle that task. I am a Guardian and Tirus used to be one of the King's royal guards. He knows us well and saw fit that we go with you. Come to think of it, have you decided when to leave?"

Naughton rubbed his head. "You mean you use to be a Centore?"

"Long ago; I had enough of sleeping on the ground being cold and hungry. Now, when are you leaving?"

"Whenever I complete my studies," said Naughton.

"I see," said Anor, gesturing his hand towards the door. "Well, I have to take care of the mess you've made, but I will see you again soon."

"Yes, sir," said Naughton, feeling embarrassed. He stood up and the guards escorted him back to the castle. Naughton went straight to his room sat down and took a deep breath, grateful he wasn't taken to the dungeon.

"Naughton! Naughton, wake up!"

"Ugh...who's there?"

"It's me, Nellium, you dingbat! You have had me waiting for over an hour. Get up!"

Naughton opened the door. There stood the old man, gripping his cane. "I am sorry, Nellium. Last night was a long one for me."

Nellium pointed the cane in Naughton's face. "I know. I told you to relax, not go around killing people's pets!"

Naughton walked away from the door and sat down. "It was an accident. You see, I--"

Nellium interrupted with a loud pop from his cane stabbing the floor. "I know what you did. Anor told me all about it. Let's go. We have much to cover today." Naughton washed his face and followed Nellium to the library. When they entered, Nellium ordered everyone out and went toward a table. The library was two stories high with multiple rows of books and parchments. Nellium sat and raised a bony finger. "King Irus has just learned that Fort Coralis fell three days ago, and he is growing very weary. I fear, Naughton, that you will have to leave sooner than we planned. Today we will talk about our history. Grab that map." Nellium laid some parchments beside the map. "Naughton, what I'm about to share with you is vital. This lesson explains how our kingdom came into existence. In fact, some have forgotten, but it is important that we understand where we come from."

Nellium stood up and leaned on his cane, tapping his fingers on the handle. "Years ago, a kingdom to the South called Qanas was very powerful, probably the most powerful kingdom in existence. However, in time, El became displeased with his people because of their disregard for Him. Qanas fell within months, leaving few survivors. In time, Qanas was rebuilt and became even larger before."

Naughton was skeptical. "How do you know all this?"

"Stories passed down from one generation to the next. But Bezinar is becoming powerful itself, and people are forgetting how we got here to begin with."

"What do you mean?"

Nellium's eyes narrowed. "You mean, you don't know how Bezinar was formed at all?"

"No."

Nellium bit his pipe. "I thought Berton knew better! Why on earth did he not tell you about the Centurion wars?"

"He told me very little of it. My father kept many secrets."

"It is no secret. Let's see here now, how can I explain it--ah, yes. After Qanas was rebuilt, and the people were thriving again, evil filled the land. There was no king, therefore no order; people were fighting over territory, food, gold, and so on.

A unique clan moved into the lands. They were different than we were. They were taller, stronger, wiser, and did things that were considered unnatural. In battle they were unstoppable, and no one could kill them. The people grew to fear them, and they seized the opportunity to claim territories. Their leaders were called Centurions and declared themselves kings. Peace reigned for many generations as the Centurions ruled different territories, for they were very wise and able to resolve disputes with little conflict. However, all good things come to an end. In time, greed filled their hearts and the Centurions turned on each other. War broke out over the land as they tried to claim territories and the city Fenris. However, our ancestors knew better than to follow the Centurion that ruled them. They broke away and found land to the north. From that point on three kingdoms were established: Bezinar, Samha, and Getaria. All three were allies, but we have not heard from the Getarians for some time."

"Why Fenris?"

Nellium rubbed his beard. "Fenris is not just

any city--it's a safe haven with an impenetrable wall and defenses much greater than Valkry. A sea is next to it, allowing ships to carry resources constantly." He raised an eyebrow. "As far as I know it still exists."

"No one goes there?"

"Why should we? We have lived in peace here for generations. Now, though, it seems we have made a mistake in not keeping an eye to the south."

"So what happened next?"

"Rumors were the Centurions went extinct, killing each other off. After the war, the people united under one banner and became the Geols."

"So who rules them? Surely they have a king or leader."

"We don't know. That is why your father decided to go with Felden and the Shadow Scouts."

Naughton leaned back for a moment, thinking about the last time he saw his father. "Is it possible that a Centurion still lives?"

Nellium's eyes widened and then relaxed. "I have thought of the matter, but many years have passed and we would have heard of such by now."

Naughton began turning the ring on his finger that his father gave him, remembering their last conversation. "How did Qanas fall to begin with?"

"You mean before the Centurions ruled?"

Naughton nodded his head. Nellium sat down, putting his hands on the parchments. "I told you already, El destroyed it."

Naughton held out his hands. "But how exactly?"

Nellium rubbed his long white mustache. "Many scholars have debated over the issue, because nowhere does it say exactly what happened. Keep in mind, it happened thousands of years ago, but there were clues. These parchments have the clues recorded and have been passed from one generation to the next, as I said. Look here," said Nellium, pointing his bony finger at a drawing. Buildings were on fire, smoke rising high above the horizon. Bodies lay in the streets, crows eating them.

Naughton looked closer at the bottom of the drawings and noticed letters. "What does this say?"

Nellium took a puff from his pipe. "I don't know. It's a language that no one can translate." He rubbed his hand over the words. "There are many more writings, but it's useless to us. We can only go by the drawings and guess what happened." Nellium unrolled another parchment and pointed at a drawing. "Look here."

In the drawing stood a man unsheathing his sword. Rays of light came from the sword, and the people around the man were covering their eyes. Nellium unrolled another parchment. "This one is very interesting. Tell me what you think it is describing." Naughton leaned over, studying the drawing closely. People were building multiple structures while many others were on guard, staring toward the desert at the sunset.

Naughton sat back. "Why are they looking at the desert?"

Nellium pulled the pipe from his mouth. "Use your brain. Why are they standing guard?"

"To look for danger, but…" Naughton paused and pulled out the sun jewel. "After my father went through the Seraph Lands, he mentioned a flash of bright light when everyone around him died in a temple."

"Exactly! Your father's experience in the Seraph Lands leads me to believe that he found the same being that did this to Qanas."

"But how did anyone know where he was to begin with?"

Nellium grabbed his cane and started pacing. "Have you not been paying attention? These drawings represent that he lived in the desert, and there is only one in the region. It was I who told the King of that being's possible whereabouts."

Naughton ran his hand through his hair. "You mean the Seraph Lands?"

"Yes, the Seraph Lands. No other desert exists in the area. However, it is very vast."

"But why is it called the Seraph Lands?"

"Open your ears, boy. I just said it's a desolate wasteland."

Naughton became agitated. "I know, master, but why the word seraph?"

"I suppose that deserves an answer. The word seraph is the name of a celestial being--a high ranking angel. People say that desert is not passable. The heat is unbearable. No water, no plants, just sand and sinking pits as far as the eye can see. Not once has a human being crossed it and lived. Therefore, it was named Seraph Lands for they are the only ones who could ever live through such a journey. Your father proved this theory wrong when he returned."

Naughton looked at the sun jewel. "So this being could be a Seraph?"

"I'm not sure, sonny. He could be an angel or a supernatural being of some sort..or a Centurion who escaped and turned from evil. Whoever he is, he has remained unseen for a reason. This is merely a myth now."

"Why didn't he help the people during the

Centurion wars?"

"Who knows? Either way King Irus is desperate. He feels this being is the only one who can save us from the Geols. The King has been trying to unite all three kingdoms to fight, but so far he has been unsuccessful. The messenger that came from Fort Coralis said that the Geols have legions of men, and creatures with great powers. Fort Coralis was the same size as Fort Yorben, but it had more men. There are two forts left in the outer perimeter and then the city of Valkry, which is well guarded. The city has better defenses, but by the way the messenger described the fall of Fort Coralis, it is safe to say those defenses will be tested."

Naughton put his elbows on the table and covered his face with his hands. He wiped his face and leaned back in the chair. "When must I leave?"

"As of now, the King is getting a group together to escort you. You have already met Anor and Tirus."

Naughton's face went pale and he felt his stomach tighten. "I did not expect to leave so soon. I have learned so little."

Nellium's voice was encouraging. "I know, sonny, but remember this: you were summoned to the Seraph Lands. It is a great honor to be called upon by this being."

Naughton stood up. "Can we go see the King?"

Nellium narrowed his bushy eyebrows. "Why?"

"I wish to say farewell to my cousin."

Nellium leaned on his cane giving a nod and then led Naughton to the Crescent hall where four royal guards stood guarding the door. When they approached, the guards moved to the side and opened the doors. As they entered, Naughton could see the King sitting on his throne with many gathered before him. A general with broad shoulders stood before the King. "My King, I request permission to lead an army to Fort Coralis and take it back."

"Absolutely not!"

"But why, my King?"

"The Geols took Coralis without much struggle. I will not send our army in the open to fight them. Instead, break up the army into two units and reinforce Fort Yorben and Fort Estmere."

"What about the city? The fall of Coralis has left Valkry vulnerable."

The King scratched his head and readjusted his crown. "If Valkry is attacked, it can hold its own for some time, and we can send more Centores there. Fort Yorben and Fort Estmere must be protected."

The general bowed. "Yes, my King."

The King looked up and saw Naughton and Nellium standing by the door. He motioned to them as everyone stared at them. "What brings you to my hall?"

Nellium bowed. "Naughton wishes to speak to you."

"Of course."

The hall was quiet and King Irus leaned forward.

"I am sorry to trouble you, but I was wondering if you had word from my father. Has he returned to Fort Yorben?"

The King's face saddened. "I'm afraid not, son. I will send a messenger to Fort Yorben immediately to see if there is any news."

"Thank you, sir. With your permission, I have a request." The King cocked his head to the side.

"Would it be possible to see Jesper before I leave?"

King Irus stood up. "We will go this instant. Everyone is dismissed!" The crowd bowed and left the hall. King Irus walked up to Naughton as he waved the guards over and ordered them to get a chariot ready. They walked out the front doors of the castle and the chariot awaited them. It was fifteen feet long, made of heavy oak with gold trim, and pulled by six horses. Guards surrounded the chariot on foot and horseback to protect the King. The chariot made its way out of the city as people shouted his name and bowed. Naughton watched the crowd throw roses and other flowers in front of the chariot. King Irus touched Naughton's shoulder. "Do you fear the journey that lies before you?"

"I would be lying if I said no, Sire."

"Ah, yes you would. Any normal human being should be afraid of that place. I would like to give you counsel if you will accept it."

Naughton's eyes opened wide. "By all means."

The King smiled. "Then listen well. I will pray for you, son of Berton, because you carry a heavy burden on your shoulders. Go to the Seraph Lands with confidence. Do not doubt your beliefs or your abilities. Your father and mother raised you well. You are humble and brave, a natural leader. The men I'm sending with you are loyal and will obey your commands without question, despite your youth. But I would consider their counsel at all times." The King shook his hand firmly and continued waving to the crowd.

Naughton looked out the chariot window. "Sire, is it possible that a Centurion still lives and is leading the Geols? Nellium finds it unlikely."

"We have discussed the matter before many times. If one were still alive, he would have attacked us many years ago, I believe. What all did Nellium tell you?"

"Only that their race were very powerful, bigger than us, and supposedly killed each other off."

King Irus stopped waving for a moment. "They were the most feared beings to exist, especially a Centurion. Centurions were well trained and could kill thousands of soldiers. The Centurions and those under their command never tired, rarely slept, and had powers that were...unnatural to this world."

Naughton's stomach began to tighten. "What do you mean, unnatural?"

"They could wield weapons that normal men could not lift. Their speed, agility, the ability to take multiple wounds and not die...was not normal." The King leaned back, gazing out the window. "To my knowledge, no normal man has ever killed one." The King laughed sarcastically. "In fact, that is where our Centores got their name. It's a derivative name that inspired our soldiers to become better warriors so they could kill a Centurion if the time came." The King winked and continued waving to the crowd.

Finally they arrived at Centore valley. King Irus and Naughton stepped out, and the leader of the royal guards spoke. "My King, no one is here. They must be out training."

"We will wait for them."

The guards bowed and formed a perimeter. Naughton and the King sat in the middle of the field and talked. When night came, the guards became weary. "My King, request that we return tomorrow? We cannot protect you in the dark."

The King laughed. "Relax, Captain. The Centore training grounds is one of the most protected regions in the kingdom." About that time, they heard singing coming from the forest and saw torches in the distance.

"Call out the army, call out the cavalry, but we'll be standing long after they're dead! Death before dishonor, glory to the Creator, Centores never die!"

King Irus and Naughton stood up, watching the men running toward them in formation. Thorg was leading the men on his horse and saw a chariot. "Who put this piece of junk on my grounds? Speak!"

The King and Naughton walked up behind Thorg. "It was I," said the King. Thorg snatched a torch from a Centore and pointed it towards the voice.

"My King! Everyone kneel, the King is among us!" Everyone knelt, including the Centores. Thorg jumped off his horse and knelt.

"So you don't like my chariot?" asked the King.

"Sire, forgive me. The dark played tricks on me."

King Irus began to laugh. "It is somewhat ugly, isn't it?"

"My King, what brings you out this time of night?"

"We wish to speak with Jesper."

"Of course. Turtle, get up here!" Jesper ran up with a big smile on his face and hugged Naughton.

"Cousin, it is good to see you."

The King raised his hand. "Rise." Everyone rose and stood silent. "Thorg, would you excuse us for a minute?"

Thorg bowed. Naughton and Jesper walked away from the group while the guards stayed close to the King, keeping a sharp eye.

"What brings you out here, Naughton?"

"I am leaving soon for the Seraph Lands and I wanted to say goodbye."

"Goodbye? You talk as if you won't return."

"I may not, but if I do you may be gone to your unit when I get back."

Jesper looked at his comrades. "That's true. Have you heard from Berton or Felden?"

"No word, but the King is going to send a messenger to Fort Yorben." Naughton looked at Jesper from head to toe and wrinkled his nose. "You smell like a yak! How is your training going?"

Jesper laughed. "Thanks. They're trying to get rid of all the weaklings first before they start training us. It has only been four weeks."

Naughton glanced at the King. "I need to go. I'm sure the King has duties he must attend."

"It was good to see you, cousin, but I must ask you a question." Jesper got close to Naughton and whispered. "Has Airah mentioned me?"

"Once or twice."

"What did she say?"

"Wondering how your training was going," replied Naughton, keeping his voice at a whisper.

"That's it?"

"Yep."

Jesper threw his hands in the air in anger. "Figures!" Thorg glanced at Jesper from the distance and continued talking to the King. "I can't get her out of my head."

Naughton looked at him with concern. "You've got it bad. Don't do anything stupid."

"I won't," replied Jesper with a grunt.

"I know you well." He poked Jesper in the

chest. "Don't go sneaking off to see her, or you will risk bringing dishonor to yourself just like--" He cut himself off, realizing his error.

Jesper put his hands on his hips. "Like who?"

"Nothing, don't worry about it. Just don't do anything stupid."

"I'll do what I must."

Naughton shook his head and smiled. "Would you like me to give her a message?"

Jesper thought for a moment. "Tell her I am well and maybe soon I can visit her."

Naughton smirked. "That's all?"

"No… I mean yes, for now." Naughton began to chuckle. Jesper clenched his fists. "Are you going to tell her or not?"

"Calm down, I will tell her." Naughton grabbed Jesper's arm and shook his hand. "Let's go."

Jesper ran to King Irus and bowed. "Thank you, my King, for allowing me to wish my cousin a safe journey."

"The honor is mine, young Jesper. Farewell." Jesper ran back to the group and got in formation.

Thorg bowed. "Would you like us to escort you?"

"That would be fine, Thorg."

Thorg turned around and yelled, "Form a

perimeter around the chariot!" The chariot made its way through the plains. When they reached the end of the training grounds the Centores broke off running into the darkness, only one face looked back.

Do or die

Felden and Rubus continued running down the mountain, fighting the snow and rough terrain as they tried to gain distance between them and the Geols. It took five days before they were off the mountain and deep in the forest. They were tired and soaking wet, but were glad to get away from the cold mountain. Rubus unwrapped Felden's arm to look at the burn. "It's not bleeding anymore, and it looks like it's trying to heal." He put another field dressing on and sat down. They sat in silence, fighting the cold and their hunger. Rubus searched through his sack. "Our strength will continue to diminish without food."

"I know," said Felden, feeling hopeless. "It's entirely my fault. If only--"

Rubus interrupted, "Don't start. A lot of things went wrong up there. It's a miracle that we even escaped. Try to think ahead, Felden. The past is the past and we need to survive so we can tell Mohai what we're up against. I have looked at the map many times and it shows all their strongholds, including where they're from."

"I'm glad you're here, Rubus, it's just I have lost an old friend. He taught me everything I know."

"He is not lost! Now come to your senses. Do you think we lost the Geols?"

Felden grabbed his cloak and pulled it around him tighter. "I doubt it. They are probably tracking us as we speak. We cannot remain here. The village we came across, Crubitz, has store houses. We will get food there. Be sure to fill up the water sacks; we can't survive long without water."

Rubus got up cautiously, moving slowly through the crunching leaves under his feet to the water. He looked at his face in the small pool. His face was scruffy with a dark mustache. His skin was dark and his cheeks sunken from the lack of food. His short, dark hair was frizzy from the damp air. He filled the water sacks and put them in his bag. He crept back to Felden. "I feel like a rabbit being hunted by hounds. The closer we get to Fort Yorben, the better I'll feel."

Felden stood up, cradling his arm. "For once, I will be glad to see his guards."

The next morning they left the creek and continued walking through the forest, trying to stay out of sight. Every so often, wildlife would scatter at their intrusion. They traveled during the day and rested at night, knowing the enemy would not be able to trail them in the dark. They avoided fields and kept to the woods. Each day seemed longer than the last. Their bellies ached and their muscles felt like jelly.

Each night they fought the cold air with no fire to keep them warm, afraid to give away their location. The wind numbed their faces and hands as they tried to sleep. Felden's arm ached continuously but was healing well, considering the conditions. They took turns keeping watch as the feeling they were being hunted began to consume them. Every sound was a Geol.

The terrain looked familiar when they neared the city of Crubitz. Rubus took point while Felden followed. On the eleventh night, they could see the glow of the city, and they approached with caution. They went to the hill to look down upon the city. When Rubus reached the lookout point, his mouth dropped and he knelt to the ground. He waved Felden to come up and he stood speechless when he saw what Rubus was staring at. Before them was a massive army camped around the city, roughly fourteen thousand strong. Felden sat down, feeling his weakness. "Where did they all come from?" Rubus pulled out the map they stole and tried to guess.

"There are other strongholds apparently. One to the southeast and another to the southwest, but they are further to the south than the one we found." Felden took the map and looked at strange symbols above the locations. He continued looking at the map to find a way around to avoid the army and city.

"We can't go back the way we came when we discovered the city; I'm sure the path is crawling with soldiers. We need to go northeast to the other side of Sturkma, and then go over the Mountain of Colonies."

"Are you crazy? You know they will be watching Sturkma. By now they probably have an outpost there with many soldiers. I suggest we go around completely."

Felden gave the map back to Rubus. "No, that will take too long. Besides, the Mountain of Colonies is only a ridge. The further east you go, the bigger the mountains get, which takes you to Oynst Peak. We are certainly in no condition to make that attempt."

"Then what do you suggest? Just sit here and hope the army leaves soon?"

Suddenly, Felden came up with an idea. It was crazy, but if they could pull it off they would reach Fort Yorben in no time.

"I have an idea, but you won't like it."

Rubus put his hand on his forehead, looking away from Felden. "Please spare me…"

Felden pulled his hood over his head. "I'm sure the Geols have scouts. After we learn their pattern, we will sneak in, kill two, and take their places. Their armor will be our pass to Fort Yorben."

Rubus put his hand on Felden's forehead as if checking for fever. "Yeah, sure, let's just sneak in and kill them and hope their comrades don't recognize us. And while we're at it, let's talk to them like we have known them for years! Oh yeah, best pals, we'll be fine...Are you mad? That's insane! We will be caught and tortured without mercy, and then they will eat us! That is the worst idea I've ever heard. It's worse than what Jayus tried to do!"

Felden narrowed his eyes and readjusted his burnt arm. "Are you in or not?"

"We're going to die, but fine. Let's just commit suicide and get it over with!"

"You have no hope whatsoever, Rubus?"

"Hope? I'll show you hope." Rubus grabbed his legs and pulled his head down, putting it between his knees.

Felden stared at him. "What are you trying to do?"

"Kiss my ass goodbye."

Felden shook his head and grinned. "You're an odd fellow, my friend."

"Me? Odd? No, say it ain't so! You do remember that we're being tracked right now, and we probably have two days before they find us?"

Felden stood up. "Then you better hurry and start learning their patterns while I sneak down to the store houses. Meet me here in the morning."

Rubus marched off toward the other end of the hill, mumbling, "Hope we don't taste good. Agh…they will probably castrate us before they eat us anyway."

All night they studied the Geol patrols, who were easily traced thanks to the light of the moon. Sometimes they lost them when they went deep in the forest, but they would return after time getting back in formation. When the sun started to rise they met and discussed what they saw and took turns sleeping. They studied the patrols one more night and readied themselves during the day with food and rest. Under the cover of darkness, they snuck down before the moon rose. They crept through the villages and up to a tent where the patrol soldiers stayed. They crawled as close as they could in the tall grass, using their cloaks as camouflage. They found one sleeping and another eating at a table. They looked around to see if it was safe and snuck around the tent. The candle glow gave a shadow of where a soldier was sitting. Rubus pulled out his knife and started meowing like a cat. The guard stood up and when he lifted the tent flap, Rubus cut the soldier's throat so he could not scream.

Instantly, they ran in the tent and killed the other soldier while he was sleeping. They took their clothes, weapons, armor, and put on the helmets to hide their identities. They wrapped the bodies in their cloaks and hid them in the tall grass.

They walked toward the horses and started to mount when a soldier yelled at them, "Hurry up, you're late!" They rode to the squad, taking a place in the rear of the formation, and kept their heads down as much as possible.

The leader looked toward the rear. "If you two are late again, you will be whipped like dogs!" They passed glowing tents and thousands of soldiers, as well as a few Spikers as they rode around the outskirts of Crubitz. Their pounding hearts matched the pounding hooves of their horses and sweat poured from their faces. Finally, the time came to break formation, and two by two the soldiers broke off to make their rounds.

Once they got some distance, Felden whispered, "Rubus, be sure to take a right up here and we can make a run for it."

"I know, just keep up. It won't be long before somebody discovers the bodies." The turn came, and instead of turning left like the routine required, they turned right, gaining distance from the Geol army and

Crubitz. They ran the horses all night, and when the sun rose they slowed pace, giving the horses a chance to catch their breath.

Felden looked behind them to make sure no one was following. "Put your helmet back on and quicken pace. I'm sure they know by now."

They continued riding until the following morning. They stopped next to a stream to let the horses drink and made them lay down in the bushes to rest. At noon they began riding again. They veered off the trail to hide their tracks as much as possible. The forest was thick and unforgiving, forcing them to slow their pace. Finally, they reached the plains and were able to let the horses stretch their legs once again. They were making good time; however, being in the open gave no comfort. On the fourth day, they spotted a squad of Geol soldiers headed west. After that, they decided to travel only at night.

Each day they grew more nervous as they approached Sturkma, knowing they would come across Geol patrols. "I have a bad feeling about this," said Rubus, as he observed his surroundings.

Felden rubbed his arm, "we have no choice."

"So be it, but my skin is raw," said Rubus, kicking his horse. He adjusted his armor, trying to keep it from rubbing his skin.

Golden rays pierced the horizon and they
stopped to rest. They finished what food they had and
drank the last drop of water. They sat in silence,
listening as Rubus began sniffing the air. "...I smell
smoke."

"Coming from Sturkma?"

"Possibly. Don't you smell it?"

Felden rubbed his nose. "I can't smell anything,
but I'll take your word for it." Eventually he heard
pounding hooves. He jumped up and woke Rubus.
"Get up, they're coming!"

They jumped on their horses and rode east to
lower ground. When darkness fell, Rubus could barely
see a group of soldiers riding from Sturkma to the
south. In the cover of darkness they rode to Sturkma,
staying off the hills as much as they could and using the
tall grass for cover. When they reached Sturkma, they
found it to be much worse than they had feared.
Sturkma had become a fortress for the Geols. They
stood in shock at what had become of the city.
Felden's heart mourned. "Berton would be disgusted
if he saw this. He would rather it be in ruin than be
used for the Geol forces."

"How many men do you think there are?"
asked Rubus, rubbing his neck.

They mounted their horses and continued to

the Mountain of Colonies, staying east of Sturkma and looping around. They ascended the same path they had used when following Berton and his family.

On the third night after leaving Sturkma, they stayed in the small cave where Berton's family had stayed. They sat in silence, thinking about Berton's family and how this mess began. Morning came with no breakfast, but thanks to the horses they had two days left before reaching Fort Yorben. The forest became dense again with loose hidden stones, and snow gave their horses trouble. The swaying pines rustled loudly, making it difficult to listen for approaching hooves.

As usual, they took turns sleeping. Rubus was on watch, peeling pinecones and trying to stay awake when he heard the faint squeal of a horse the distance. He froze, a cold chill running down his spine. He jumped up and kicked Felden while running to his horse. Without hesitation, Felden rushed to his horse, which was tethered to a tree. Felden caught up with Rubus. "What did you hear?"

"A horse squealed not far from us."

"How far?"

"Half a mile at the most."

They rode until morning, reaching the other side of Mountain of Colonies and stopping on the outskirts of the forest. Felden looked behind him to see Geols on horses racing toward them. "How did they track us in the night? No scout can track in the dark!" They kicked their horses toward the Siriu River, but the tall grass made it difficult for the horses to run. The horses were constantly jumping and lifting their legs high, trying to overcome the tall grass. When they reached the Siriu River the horses were exhausted, and it dawned on Felden that they were still wearing Geol armor. "Stop, stop! Take off this stupid armor before our own men shoot us!"

The bridge guards were on approach with spears and swords drawn.

Felden and Rubus raised their hands high, yelling, "Wait, we're allies!" The guards ran up and surrounded them, blades out and ready to be jabbed into their flesh.

"I am Felden, leader of the Shadows, and this is Rubus." The captain looked at Felden and recognized him.

"You're an idiot, Felden. You almost got yourselves killed."

Rubus interrupted, "I hate to break up our family reunion, but look behind us!"

"To the bridge! Quickly!" The archers drew their bows, waiting for the Geols, but they stopped out of range. Suddenly, a voice rang out.

"We have your friend, Shadows, and for this treachery he will suffer greatly!" The Geols turned around and returned to the plains.

The chosen

The next morning, Nellium was in the library surrounded by scholars. At times they yelled at one another, and the guards had to warn them several times to lower their voices. Maps were scattered all over the table, and some lay on the floor. "No one will go, Nellium! The quest is suicide! We remember what happened last time you sent scholars out there and you expect one of us to go?"

Bane banged his fist on the table. "You're all cowards!"

"Bane, you should not even be in this council," said a scholar.

Nellium raised his hand, and everyone fell silent.

"Calm yourself, Bane."

"Master Nellium, you know as well as I do that most people in this room don't even believe in the Bindings of El. They only study them to gain political power." Grumbling and whispers filled the room, leaving Nellium perplexed.

He rubbed his long white mustache.

"Those are some serious accusations, Bane, but this meeting is to decide who goes with Naughton. He does not have enough knowledge to embark on this journey alone. I honor you for going with him, but we need someone else to go in case something happens to you. If you remember Berton's story, each riddle was complex and required much thought. Keep in mind that the four scholars I sent were very wise." The room was silent and everyone looked at each other, wondering who was going to step forward. A loud bang filled the air when Eirmosa burst through the library doors. Nellium acknowledged her. "Greetings, Eirmosa. What can we do for you?"

Eirmosa crossed her arms, glaring at the scholars. "You can grant me permission to go since they are all afraid." The library filled with laughter.

Bane became furious. "How dare you laugh at someone who will go into such peril when full grown men will not!" The men continued laughing at Eirmosa, until suddenly a giant sword was jabbed into the table, forcing everyone to fall silent.

There stood Captain Anor and Tirus. "Are you finished?" asked Anor. The room remained silent and Anor looked at Eirmosa. "I would be honored for you to come with us." Anor pulled his sword out of the table. "Where is Naughton, and why is it none of you will go? You're going to die someday. Make your death honorable."

Nellium stood up with his hand raised. "Captain Anor, we are greatly honored to be in the presence of a Guardian, but I must object to Eirmosa going. As for Naughton, he is on an errand with Lady Airah. I did not want him in this council, for reasons I will explain later."

"Why can't I go?" demanded Eirmosa.

"Because the road is treacherous and I don't think the King will allow it."

"But I have as much to lose as all of you. I have studied the Bindings of El more than half the people in this room, I read Hebrew, and I also believe in it!" Nellium admired her, for she was passionate about her beliefs.

"Very well, Eirmosa, but we must consult the King. He will decide your fate."

Anor sheathed his sword. "The kingdom is at stake, with the Geols tightening their noose. Everything you know of will perish. Our women, our children--everyone you hold dear will die." A young scholar stepped forward and everyone looked at him. He was lean and lanky with bright green eyes and short black hair. He was dressed in a long sleeve tan shirt with dark pants.

"I will go."

Nellium gave the young scholar a perplexed look. "You, Zealot? Why?"

"Because I know Anor very well. He saved me

and my family once when he was a Centore. I will repay him now when he and his companions need me most."

Nellium gave a warm smile, "I am humbled by your bravery, Zealot. It is decided, then. Anor, Tirus, Bane, and Zealot will escort Naughton. Eirmosa's fate will be decided by the King. I would love to go with you, but I don't think my bones will stay together. This mission is to be kept secret." Nellium went to the door, gesturing with his cane for the others to leave. Once they were alone, he sat down, and behind closed doors he swore them to secrecy about a topic that was not to be shared, even to Naughton.

Lady Airah and Naughton returned that evening from their errands. They reported to Nellium in a small room upstairs above the great hall with the selected group. Nellium greeted them. "Have a seat, you two." They sat down and Anor chuckled.

"My men enjoyed that deer Naughton. Next time, though, try not to kill a pet." The entire room started laughing and Naughton grinned.

Nellium banged his cane on the table. "Enough of this silliness. We have serious business to discuss."

"Okay, old man. You're the boss."

Nellium stood up and went to the map on the wall, officially beginning the meeting. "First of all, the

King has decided that Eirmosa will only go as far as the city of Samha, in the east. She will then be escorted to Fort Estmere where she can return to Bezinar."

Eirmosa became enraged, and Airah touched her arm in an effort to calm her. Nellium continued. "I am sorry Eirmosa, but the King has spoken. The journey will take many days, perhaps months. The King will enter in a moment to give us details about the Geols, thanks to the Shadow Scouts."

Nellium pointed at the map with his cane. "Your first goal is to reach the kingdom of Samha. The King there is an ally, and he will aid you in any way he can. Once you reach Samha, you will continue southeast and cross Mara valley. It is a dry bitter land, with no vegetation and deep crevices. A guide from Samha will escort you through safely to the edge of the Seraph Lands. There you will find your first riddle that will guide you. According to Berton, each riddle will lead you to the heart of the Seraph Lands where you will find this supernatural being.

"You make it sound so simple," said Tirus, picking his teeth from a previous meal.

"What is beyond the Seraph Lands?" asked Zealot.

Nellium looked down, gripping his cane tightly. "I am not sure." Suddenly, King Irus appeared. Everyone stood at attention while Nellium apologized. "Forgive me, Sire. I did not know you were there."

"It's alright, Nellium. You amuse me when you get mad." Everyone greeted the King, and he had them sit down. "I bring news of the Geols, and it is disturbing." He walked up to the map and hung his head for a moment. "After the fall of Fort Coralis, the Geols have regrouped to attack Fort Yorben. Their strategy is to take out the fort so they won't be cut off from reinforcements. I have sent an army to Fort Yorben and to Fort Estmere. What is odd is that Fort Estmere has seen no Geols. I am going to wait before I send more Centores to the city of Valkry. If things go ill for us, I hope you make it back with help before they attack Valkry. Now, if you cannot get help and the kingdom is falling, I want you to continue to carry out your assigned duties."

Anor shot to his feet. "My King, I am a Guardian. I cannot just leave!"

The King smiled. "Anor, I understand your oath, but I need you to do this for me." Nellium gave Anor a hard stare.

Anor sat down with a heavy sigh. "Very well, if that is your wish." Naughton noticed Nellium's stare and began to wonder what was going on.

Naughton raised his hand, and King Irus gestured for him to speak. "King Irus, what duties are you referring to?"

The King looked at Naughton for a long moment. "I promised your father long ago to keep you out of harm's way, and I must keep that promise, even if I have to send a unit of Centores with you." The King clasped the hilt of his sword. "I thank each of you for the journey you are about to take. The people of all three kingdoms are relying on you, whether they know it or not. But remember this: in the end, it's all up to El." The King bowed and then left them to their thoughts.

Nellium opened the door. "Be in the gardens before sunrise. Dismissed." Everyone but Naughton got up and went their separate ways. Eirmosa noticed and sat next to him.

"What's wrong?"

"There are secrets being kept from me."

"There are some things in this world that you should not know until the time comes. Remember Jesper's situation."

Naughton gave her a puzzled stare. "What are you hiding from me?"

"I can say no more. Just know we are here for you." With that, she walked away.

Naughton propped his head on the table, thinking about all that had happened since Sturkma. Each day he felt more distant from all he knew. His home was burned to the ground, into a pile of dust and ash, and his friends grew farther away all the time.

That night, all was silent until a messenger ran into the great hall, yelling for Naughton. The guards seized him and put him in a room to calm him down. "What is it?"

"I bring news from Fort Yorben, and I must speak to Naughton."

"Why?" asked the guard.

"Because Berton has been captured by the Geols!"

The guard's eyes widened. "Wait here." A few minutes later, King Irus entered the room with his royal guards.

"My King, I bring grave news. Berton has been captured and only two Shadows survived!"

"Who?" demanded the King.

"Felden and Rubus, Sire. They said they saw mass armies in the mountains to the south, and that the city of Sturkma has been rebuilt as an enemy fortress."

"My King, should we summon Naughton?" asked a guard.

The King turned around with rage in his eyes. "Absolutely not! Say nothing to the boy. I order you to all be silent on this matter. Naughton must have a clear conscience on his quest. There is nothing we can do for Berton right now. Captain!"

"Yes, Sire."

"I want Thorg here at once."

"It will be done."

As the guard left, King Irus continued talking to the messenger.

Several hours later, Thorg arrived to greet the King in his meeting hall. Thorg entered the hall wearing his black cloak and his sword strapped to his hip. He bowed low. "You summoned me?"

"Yes, Thorg. Sit down." The wooden chair creaked as he sat. "How is your new class going?"

"My King, I have not had enough time to estimate the strength of this class. Why?"

"We are in more peril than I thought. Berton has been captured and the Geols are larger in number than what we estimated. I need you to create a Centore unit that can retrieve Berton."

Thorg sat speechless for a moment before rubbing his chin. "What you ask for is not possible. It would take many months to train these new men for such a quest. The only unit that is trained for doing such is unit three, but we need them here more than ever." King Irus sat in deep thought. Thorg walked over to the King and sat next to him. "Sire, I have known you for a long time. Why is it that we must retrieve Berton? He knew the risk when he accepted the mission." The King sat, staring off into space as if he'd lost all track of time. "Sire?"

The King returned to reality with a start. "There is more at stake than you realize, but I understand what you are saying. When can your new class be ready for combat?"

"It will take eight more weeks at least before they can be assigned to units."

"I see...and how is Jesper doing?"

"He is doing well. He is strong in many ways. He solves our riddles quickly, is good at strategizing, and is proving to be a great leader. He reminds me of Tulios, come to think of it. He looks like him, and is as clever as he was, if not more."

The King rubbed his forehead. "Well, perhaps El has blessed us with another Tulios. He was a great man."

"Indeed." Thorg shifted in his seat. "May I speak freely?"

"Of course."

"Irus, you do not need to rush my training.

One mistake can kill everyone in a unit and if I may be so bold, why in the hell are you not sending Centores head-to-head with this army? We are the best warriors the world has ever known. We will kill every Geol without mercy and win this war."

The King smiled and patted Thorg on the back. "Soon, I will dispatch Centores to various locations, but there is information of which you are not aware. The messenger said that Felden and Rubus discovered one of the strongholds and a city that had at least fourteen thousand strong. They also recovered a map that contained two more strongholds that could be larger. We simply do not know what we're up against. I cannot mount an assault and leave us defenseless." Thorg sat back in his chair in shock. The King looked at Thorg narrowing his eyes. "That's not all. The Shadows also discovered the creatures that lead them."

Thorg leaned forward. "Creatures? What creatures?"

"Felden said that they are called Spikers. I am sending a letter to the King of Samha to join us, or I'm afraid we will all perish before Naughton returns with help--if we get help. Felden and Rubus are on their way here, and I will summon you when we have our meeting to decide what actions to take."

"Very well, Sire."

Thorg got up and left the room. As soon as the door closed, Airah stepped out from hiding behind a statue. "So you do know!"

King Irus turned around in shock. "What are you doing back there?"

"What does it look like? I wondered why you treated Jesper so dearly."

King Irus shook his head. "I have no idea what you're talking about."

"Yes, you do! I know about Jesper!"

The King's face turned red. "Very well, Airah. Speak your mind."

"I'm already speaking it! You knew Tulios had children and you kept it secret for all these years. How was I to know who to give the sword to?"

King Irus rubbed his face. "You were too young to understand, but I suppose I have delayed the truth from you."

"I'll say! When were you planning on telling me?"

"I don't know, Airah! As you can see, I have many things on my mind." Airah glared fiercely at him before she stormed out, slamming the door behind her.

Before sunrise, there was a knock at Naughton's door. There stood Eirmosa and Airah, dressed for the road in brown cloaks. Naughton rubbed his eyes. "Why are we leaving so early?"

"Because Nellium does not want us to draw attention," said Airah.

Naughton walked back to the chair and continued putting on his other boot. On his bed was his pack full of clothes and other materials. He put on his armor he'd acquired at Fort Yorben. The armor had been cleaned and repaired, and shone almost brand new. He put on his pack and osage bow as he headed out the door with a yawn, fighting off the sleepiness. The castle was quiet as they walked through the dark hall. The numerous statues were illuminated by torches, giving Naughton an eerie feeling, as if they were watching him. They reached the back doors and made their way into the gardens where the group was waiting for them. Anor was dressed in Centore armor, but covered it with a black cloak. Tirus wore his royal armor but wore a cloak as well. The rest of were dressed in travel attire and brown cloaks.

Nellium stood up from a nearby bench holding his lit pipe, "well it's about time sonny, and you better put a cloak over that armor." Anor threw him a black cloak, it covered him well.

"What are you doing out here, Nellium?"

"I wanted to wish you a pleasant journey. Your

horses are waiting for you at the back gate.

Wait...what is this? Lady Airah, you are not permitted to go--"

Bane interrupted, "you mean Asha."

Nellium banged his cane against the wall. "Oh, no no no. Your uncle will have me sleeping with the pigs!"

"Relax, Nellium," said Airah. "I will return with Eirmosa when they reach Samha. Just pretend you didn't see me."

Nellium took a puff from his pipe and blew out his frustration. "Very well, but I want you back here as soon as possible."

"I promise, Nellium."

"So be it. Get going, before the sun rises and your uncle sees you." With that, the group walked to the south gate. They mounted, and Anor made a quick speech, keeping his voice low.

"Now listen to me. The King put me in charge and Tirus is next in command. I will lead and Tirus will be last. We must act like common travelers, and no one needs to know our business. If somebody is curious, tell them that we are going to visit family. Remember that there are spies in our lands, and mind what you say."

Asha raised her hand. "I believe I'm in charge,

Anor."

"I'm afraid not, my Lady. The King knows you too well. He knew you would sneak off with us and told me directly not to listen to a word you say." The entire group snickered as they rode east into the glow of the swiftly rising sun.

Rise or fall as one

Jesper wiped the mud from his face and picked himself up off the ground. He kept his shield and wooden practice sword in hand while two Centores constantly circled him. One had a long wooden spear and the other had a long wooden sword. The spearman jabbed at Jesper and he blocked it. The swordsman charged at the same time and swung his sword, hitting Jesper in the leg and making him fall. Once again Jesper was on the ground, his leg throbbing.

Thorg sat on a barrel, watching Jesper and others who were training with the Centore instructors.

"Turtle, how in the world do you expect to survive?" shouted Thorg. "We've been at this for over a week. Move your feet; don't act like a tree waiting to be chopped down! An average Centore is able to take on four to six opponents, and you can't even hold off two. Try again!" The Centores circled him again and Jesper stayed in motion, watching for the first strike. The swordsman charged first, swinging high at Jesper's head. Instead of blocking it with his shield, he dodged it and spun around to the spearman. The spearman jabbed at Jesper. This time, he blocked it with his shield and stepped forward, pushing the spear down and breaking it with his foot. The swordsman came swinging again. Jesper stepped to the side letting the sword come down past him. He then returned with a sword strike, hitting the Centore in the shoulder. "Stop!" Yelled Thorg. "Turtle, come here."

"Yes, sir."

"What was that?"

"Sir?"

"Don't sir me, boy! Your counters are getting better, but you must learn to counter strike to make a kill, not to injure. You must strike to kill and move on. Stab at his vitals, you moron, and keep your feet moving and shield high. Next!" Jesper stood to the side to catch his breath, waiting for his turn again. His arms were throbbing and his muscles burned. His legs felt strange, as if they weren't there. There were forty-seven men left and Thorg was not letting up at all. For some reason, Thorg had become more aggressive and stubborn since returning from his unknown errand.

They practiced for hours day and night. In time, Jesper learned counter killing properly. Instead of two, he took on five Centore instructors and evaded their advances with ease, making proper kills with his wooden sword. He became more aware of his surroundings and learned to trust his instincts, such as when to block or dodge and maneuver his sword with precision. Thorg became pleased with the class and gave them a day of rest, concluding the counter training.

The next day they ate in the field again, waiting for further instructions. Thorg and the Centores came back with ropes in their hands and threw them on the ground. Thorg crossed his arms, walking around the group. "Today you will begin to learn how to work together. A Centore is deadly alone, but he is invincible with his brothers. When facing armies we work as a single unit; one mistake, and you will all die. Get in a circle around us and keep your mouths shut. Move!"

The men got in a giant circle and stood silent. Thorg and the Centores entangled the ropes and tied them to the ankle of each man. "I want you to find your partner who is tied on the other end and separate from the rest of the ropes. If you fail, there will be consequences. You have one minute. Begin." The men were frantic trying to figure out who was on the other end of their rope. They were pushing each other to the ground and yelling at each other while they followed their ropes to the other person. The result was a catastrophic, with ropes entangled far worse than before.

Thorg clenched his fist. "Stop!" The men froze.

Thorg walked among the ropes, shaking his head. "I've been an instructor for a long time, but I believe this is the worst attempt I've ever witnessed. None of you found your partner. I saw one person who was actually doing something right." The men looked at each other to see who he was talking about. "Jesper, you were the only one using your brain. Jesper was trying to gain your attention to tell you what to do. In other words, he was trying to be a leader. The point of this exercise is to see who will lead and who will follow. There are several ways to get out of these ropes. Now, let's see how you do. Begin!" Everyone looked at Jesper for orders.

Jesper took charge and told everyone to grab their rope and hold it chest high, keeping it tight. The men followed the instructions without question. Next, he gave orders to four men to pull the ropes. As they pulled, their partner came directly to them, moving slowly under and over the other ropes. Four by four they went, and the whole group worked together to get out of the ropes. Thorg let them finish even though their time was up.

Thorg clapped his hands. "Well done, but there is one problem: it took you three minutes to get out of these ropes! It should only take thirty seconds. Try again, but know that for every minute you're over is a mile you must run tonight. Begin!" Over and over the group went through the ropes, until finally they succeeded finishing in one minute. Thorg rubbed his bald head. "Not bad. You only accumulated eight minutes. Looks like eight miles tonight. You have one hour to eat and get back out here in formation." Thorg walked to the ropes and examined them. He looked at them, the slowly setting sun warming his face. "Move!" They ran to the food and swallowed it whole, resting as much as they could before reporting back out to formation. By now, Jesper had learned to swallow food without chewing and gulped water without breathing.

Thorg was the only one to be seen when the men got back in formation. Jesper was in the back as usual, trying to stay out of sight and out of mind. Thorg walked around the group, giving a lecture. "Men, I am proud to say that we're making progress. You have made it to phase three of our training. You have learned how to fight alone, but now you must learn how to fight together. Fighting as one unit is not as easy as it looks. It takes trust, practice, and determination. The rope exercise has given you your leaders. Keep in mind this means nothing. Leaders can be picked at any time so do your best. From now on, I will not tell you what to do. I will tell Jesper and

Marxus what to do, and you will take your orders from them, understood?"

"Yes, sir!"

"Now while your stomachs are digesting, I will tell you why our shoulder colors are different." The men remained silent, grateful that they were able to rest. Jesper, however, was a nervous wreck now that he had been named a leader. "As you know, there are four colors that we wear: red, orange, blue, and green. Each color represents a different responsibility to your unit. A red Centore is the commander or leader. The blue Centores are archers, and are also in charge of repairing weapons. The green are scouts. They deliver messages, gather food, and water. The orange are physicians and perimeter security. Centore units usually work alone and at times, no one will come to help us. However, all Centores units can work together to form a single unit using their shields as a giant wall. Each color is assigned to a certain area. The red is in front, of course. The blue is in the back, orange is on the left, and the green is on the right. When the King calls upon us we dominate in every field--swordsmanship, archery, medicine, scouting, and tactics. Next week, you will be assigned a color, and for the next seven weeks we will train you on your duties. There is one color I have not mentioned yet, and to me, it is the most important color. Can anyone tell me that color?" A man raised his hand. "What is it, Marxus?"

"Is it gold, sir?"

"Correct. The reason gold is so important is because it represents a future leader. He is next in command in case the red shoulder is killed. He will be the red Centores apprentice, learning how to lead, and one day he will become a red Centore. Keep in mind, we cannot teach everything here. When you are assigned to your units, listen to your brothers, and they will teach you the many things they have learned." Thorg observed the men closely and crossed his arms. "Good, now get in line and let's get your eight miles over with."

Running for Jesper was like flying with the breeze, now that he'd gotten used to it. His muscles had become toned, and each day he became more confident in his abilities and knew his limits. While running he would put his mind in other places, thinking of home and most of all, Airah. Over and over he wished he could have said something to her. He kept reasoning with himself, trying to find justification for his emotional thoughts about Airah. Day by day the thoughts increased, and they drove him mad. During training, his mind would wander and the Centores developed their ways of bringing him back to reality.

By the end of the week, Jesper was assigned to be an orange Centore. He began learning about the human body, patching battle wounds, and stopping bleeding. Thorg made the men take turns being leaders. By the end of the week, Thorg chose three men--including Jesper--to be leaders on different days. Thorg and the Centores constantly challenged the men, making them work together, and testing their skills under pressure.

Day and night their abilities were pushed to the limit, and they focused on staying together, no matter how painful or hopeless it seemed. One night, they were told to move a heavy object to another location within a time limit, using only two poles, four wagon wheels, and rope. The group had to build a device while the scouts had to find the easiest and quickest path. Each day the materials and transport objects changed, giving each leader a chance to coordinate the men. When they rushed their plan, it fell to pieces and they were punished. Sometimes they took too long on designing a device and did not reach the destination in time. Other times they would fight among themselves. It seemed impossible for the men to work together as a single unit.

One day, the hardest task came on Jesper's turn to lead. They were given two broken weapons, a catapult, and a battering ram. They had only four hours to reach a designated destination and destroy a brick wall built by the Centores. Jesper had to think of a way to combine the weapons to create something that was light enough to transport, but strong enough to destroy the brick wall. All the men waited for Jesper to give orders. He felt their eyes burning his skin. His heart raced, and he could feel the pressure growing, but finally an idea struck him. He drew on the ground with a stick, showing them the device in his head.

"No no no," yelled Marxus. "That will not work. It's too heavy."

Thorg intervened. "Silence, Marxus. It's Turtle's turn!"

Jesper's idea looked sound, but would it work? They built the device with haste, knowing they had a time limit. When it was complete, the men were having second thoughts, but Jesper felt confident. Before them was a device they had never seen before. It was a wagon with a pole in the center that rotated while the wheels moved. The gears and ropes from the catapult were arranged along the wheels that connected to the center pole to make it rotate. On the center pole were long slings that came from the battering ram that held giant rocks. When the men pushed the wagon the gears rotated the pole, twirling the four slings. When they put rocks in the slings, the device became too heavy and it would not move. The men started to grumble. "It's too heavy, Jesper. We need more men!"

Jesper looked to the scouts. "Is there a hill near the wall?"

"Yes, but it is some distance."

"Good, take out the rocks and let's get to that hill." They pushed the device to the hill, but had difficulty getting it to the top.

"It's too heavy!" the men yelled. Jesper ordered them to take out the center pole. Once in place, they positioned the pole back in the center around the gears. They filled the slings full of rocks and got ready to push. Jesper started to get nervous, fearing that their hard work was in vain.

"Alright men, on three! One…two…three!" The group pushed as hard as they could. As the device started to move, gravity took control and rolled it down the hill, twirling the rocks. As it increased speed, the momentum twirled the slings faster and faster. When it reached the wall it was like a whirling tornado, and it bashed through the wall like a heap of dry leaves. The men yelled and celebrated, picking up

Jesper and marching him around.

Thorg and the Centores approached and the men got in formation, silently smiling at their accomplishment. Thorg stared at them for some time before saying anything. "Well, Turtle, it seems you have just created a device that we can use in the future. I am impressed. However, I'm not pleased with you men. It took a victory to make you trust Turtle and each other. You should have trusted your leader and each other in the beginning, without question." Thorg paced in front of the men and then approached Jesper. "I have a question, Turtle. Did you know there was a hill nearby to push the contraption downward?"

Jesper's eyes widened. "No, sir."

Thorg nodded. "I see. So if there had been no hill, your device would have failed, yes?"

Jesper sighed. "Yes, sir. I did not realize the device was so heavy."

Thorg examined the broken wall. "You were lucky. Maybe you should think ahead next time?"

"Yes, sir."

"Since this is your first victory as a unit, I will grant you one day of freedom. Go where you want and do what you want, but be back here tomorrow before noon. Say nothing about your training, or I will personally exile you from these training grounds."

The men looked at each other, thinking it was a trick, and the Centores began to laugh. "That is, unless you want to stay," said one of the instructors. The men took off like a flock of quail, running down the hill to their quarters. They grabbed their gear and found wagons waiting on them outside. They jumped in the wagons and left for the kingdom of Bezinar.

When the men reached the kingdom, they piled out of the wagons and went their separate ways. Jesper ran straight to the castle to go see Lady Airah. He ran through the gates like a wild animal and into hall, startling the guards. He shot past them up the stairs to Lady Airah's room and banged on the door. "Airah, it's me, Jesper!" There was no answer, and his mind flew to all of the places she could be. A guard down the hall approached him.

"She is not here, Jesper. She left with Naughton and his company."

Jesper's heart sank. "She left? When will she return?"

"It will be some time, I'm afraid. Perhaps you should speak to King Irus." Jesper followed the royal guard to the meeting chamber. When they entered the room, there stood Felden and Rubus, well-dressed and trimmed. Jesper ran to Felden and hugged him.

"Felden, Rubus! You're alive!"

"Well, of course we are," said Rubus. "You didn't think we were that easy to kill?" Felden looked at Jesper with watery eyes.

"What is it, Felden?" asked Jesper.

"Sit down, son."

Jesper sat down on the edge of the seat. "It's Uncle Berton, isn't it?"

"Yes. He was captured and I lost all my men. Rubus and I are all that's left." Jesper felt his body ache instantly, like he was going to throw up. He arched over in agony, shaking. Felden grasped his arm. "Jesper, he is not dead. He is only captured. There is still hope."

Jesper looked up with tears rolling down his face. "Do not fill my heart with false hope. You know they will kill him once they are done interrogating him."

"Not necessarily. He is of great importance. They will probably hold him for ransom." Jesper wiped tears from his eyes and saw Felden's arm wrapped in white bandages.

"What happened to your arm?"

"We were ambushed. I was burned, and Berton was pinned by a spear. I could not free him. We had no choice but to leave so we could report our encounter."

Jesper took his sleeve and wiped his face. "What did you encounter?"

Right then, the King entered the room, followed by master Nellium and Thorg.

Felden bowed, cradling his arm, "Sire, it is good to see you again."

"Likewise, Felden. It is a blessing that you have returned. I only wish that--" King Irus glanced at Jesper. "Have you told the boy about Berton?"

"Yes, he is aware of the situation."

"Very well. Let us proceed." The King sat and rubbed his bald head. "Gentlemen, it seems we have underestimated our enemy greatly. Fort Coralis has fallen, leaving the city of Valkry vulnerable. The city of Sturkma has been turned into an enemy fort, and the Shadows encountered giant creatures known as Spikers."

Thorg interrupted. "So what are these Spikers, Nellium?" The old man stood up to speak.

"I have researched the Bindings of El and the scrolls, but nowhere does it mention these creatures."

"What do they look like?"

"They average eight to nine feet tall and have dark skin that is heavily armored," said Rubus. "They have spikes that come out of their necks and their eyes are filled with red hate. They are very powerful, carrying giant hammers and two-pronged spears. They are the reason we lost Berton."

King Irus rubbed his mustache." Who is leading them?"

"Before we killed one of the Spikers, it said 'we serve the last of his kind.'"

King Irus sat in silence for a moment. "The last of his kind...Nellium, do you have any idea what it was referring to?"

"No, your Highness." Everyone fell silent and a sense of hopelessness filled the room. Finally, Thorg let out of a frustrated breath.

"To hell with those giant creatures! El is with us and we will kill every one of those damn things, no matter who is leading them. We Centores will fight to the death before we submit to such evil! It is time for us to be on the offensive! The Shadows have recovered a map that reveals the strongholds of our enemy. I say we attack the place where Berton is being kept!" Jesper felt a massive flow of energy running through him. His heart began to pound as he felt the adrenaline rushing through his veins. One day he would appease his revenge with a bloody sword.

Felden rubbed his burnt arm. "Thorg, I share your enthusiasm. But if you go barging up there they will surely kill Berton, and there are endless tunnels in that mountain. You will be flanked and outnumbered in seconds." Before long the group was yelling at one another, trying to decide what actions to take. The King sat in his chair, deep in thought, ignoring the arguing and keeping his kingly reserve.

Finally, King Irus raised his hand and the royal guard yelled. "Silence!" Everyone stared at King Irus waiting for his council.

"Thorg, I thought you said it was impossible to save Berton?"

"Sire, I have had time to think on this. Berton knows too many secrets! They will wring it from him eventually."

"I see…what if you create a team that can save Berton using stealth instead of brute force?"

"Like I said, Sire, only unit three is trained for such actions. They are leaderless, but somehow they accomplish every mission. My only concern is that they have fifty–one Centores. Unit three has a mind of its own and a tendency to disobey my orders. With your permission I would like to call them in."

The King raised his hand. "No, let them be."

"But Sire!"

King Irus raised his eyebrow. "I said let them be, Thorg."

Felden spoke. "Sire, perhaps there is a better way."

"Go on," demanded the King.

"Rubus and I have been there and know what routes to take. Perhaps we can lead unit three to a remote location and wait for the enemy to unleash from the stronghold. Then we can go in undetected and save Berton. It's only a matter of time before they call for reinforcements from that garrison."

Rubus shook his head. "Berton is a dear friend, but I still think it was a trap to begin with. We were never detected, yet, they knew we were there. They are expecting us to return and will have a plan for us."

Felden glared at Rubus. "I gave Berton my word that I would return for him."

"I know, Felden, I was there. But we must be patient. I believe in my heart an opportunity will arise to get him back." Nellium began pacing around the table, jabbing his cane on the floor.

"Before we go deciding on what actions to take, I should remind you that we have only just now encountered these Spikers. We have no idea what they are capable of or how many there are. After all, Fort Coralis fell in the blink of an eye."

"Enough!" said the King, as he stood up. "Thorg, I want you to dispatch unit six to Fort

Yorben to help units two and four, as well as the army
I'm sending there. Send unit seven to Fort Estmere for
reinforcements--send some to Valkry, too. Felden and
Rubus, I want you to join up with the Shadows here
and send word for all villagers near the remaining forts
to come here. We will protect them. As for unit three,
leave them to me. When the opportunity arises I will
send unit three to go get Berton. Felden and Rubus
will lead unit three when the time is right. All we can
do is prepare for the worst and pray that Naughton
returns with help. Meet me in the great hall tonight
for a feast."

Felden blurted out, "Sire, I have another matter
to discuss." King Irus rubbed his bald head in
agitation.

"Speak."

"While we were on our mission we overheard
some Geols talking in the stronghold. They mentioned
a spy in our borders acting as a scholar and they
mentioned looking for someone."

The King gritted his teeth. "You are sure of this
spy?"

"Yes, Sire. They said his name was Brytak,"
replied Rubus.

"Nellium, do we have any scholars with such a
name?"

Nellium thought for a moment. "None, Sire, that I can think of. But he would not dare use his real name here. I will investigate the situation."

King Irus gripped his sword. "Perhaps this spy sent word ahead of you Rubus, and was ready for you Shadows at the Geol stronghold. Be cautious Nellium. We don't want to spook him."

"I will take great care on the matter."

The King tapped the pommel of his sword. "This person they are seeking, did they give a name as well?"

Felden shook his head. "Their leader was directed to keep silent. Apparently it is a person of great importance."

King Irus looked down gathering his thoughts. "I want everyone to be cautious. Mind what you say, we don't know who to trust." The King left the meeting hall, his long blue robe dragging the ground as his guards closed the door behind him. Everyone left the room except for Jesper and Felden.

"You have come a long way, Jesper. Your uncle would be proud of you. I am sorry I could not save him."

"You have nothing to be sorry about."

With that, Jesper ran out the door to catch up with the King. The guards stopped him. "King Irus does not want to be disturbed, Jesper."

"I have one question to ask him." The King heard him and summoned him.

"What is it, young Jesper?"

"Sire, when will Airah return?"

The King smiled and whispered in his ear. "She will return in two weeks at the most. Be careful of your actions, young Jesper, for you know the code of Centores." The King winked and continued walking to his upstairs chamber.

Jesper's heart was full of grief throughout the day, knowing his uncle was captured and that he would not be able to see Airah. He walked around the city, taking in the cool air and crowds on the streets. Certain smells and buildings reminded him of Sturkma, when he and his siblings used to roam the streets. People were kind, with smiles and friendly greetings. He entered several stores to look at armor, weapons, jewels, and other treasures, but could not find the one thing he was looking for: flowers. As he continued down the street, he saw a little red-haired girl carrying a bundle of flowers. He quickened his pace and tapped her shoulder. "Excuse me, little lady, but where did you get those flowers?"

She looked up at Jesper with a big grin, and her hair seemed to be set ablaze by the sun. "Why, from

Petals."

"What is Petals?"

"You're not from here are you?"

Jesper laughed humbly. "Actually, no."

"It's a floral shop, silly. It's the best place to get flowers--especially roses--around here. This way." The little girl turned around and skipped along the street, carrying her flowers. They went three blocks down and took a right near the north gate. The little girl knew exactly where she was going, and led him along without delay. They approached a two story building with long drapes. There were fresh flowers of all types and roses of different colors in the window. He gazed at the display and the girl tugged his shirt. "Sir, what does she like?"

"What does who like?"

The girl laughed and shook her long, red hair. "You are a strange man, sir. You want to give her flowers and you don't even know her name?"

"Of course I know her name!"

"Good, what does she like?"

Jesper thought for a moment, and realized he had no idea. "To be honest, I don't know."

"What? She's your lady and you don't know what she likes! Are you sure she's yours?"

Jesper laughed. "As of matter of fact she is not

mine…yet." The girl set her flowers down on a table.

"It is good to be persistent. It sounds like you need help from the notorious Nihyah," she said, gesturing to herself. "Come, let's see what we can find." Nihyah entered the store, followed by Jesper, and together they looked through rows of flowers, roses, and other plants. The sweet aroma made him feel at peace and the array of colors filled him with joy. "So, what is her name?" Jesper smiled and was hesitant to share the name with his helper. He kneeled down so he could whisper in her ear.

"Can you keep a secret, Nihyah?"

The girl winked and gave a cute smirk. "Of course, I love secrets."

"Her name is Airah."

The girls face went stern. "Airah. You mean the Lady Airah, the princess?"

Jesper put a finger over his lips. "Keep it down!"

Nihyah grabbed a strand of her hair and started twirling it. "You are aiming for the stars, sir, for she is the fairest lady in all Bezinar…but I suppose anything is possible." Jesper agreed with young Nihyah, thinking that Airah was beyond his reach, but he had to try. Nihyah paused, her eyes looking downward, contemplatively. "I know exactly what to get her."

The girl took off, heading for the stairs, and Jesper ran after her. They went to the back of the store where the sun was shining brightly. She stopped and pointed at a plant.

Jesper's face puzzled. "A plant?"

"All flowers are plants, silly. However, this is no ordinary plant. This is rare, and it is very special. It's called Curado. In the summer its bloom is a giant gold rose. Unlike other plants, it keeps its petals during the winter, and the petals have the power to heal. You can boil the leaves and drink the juice, or rub the leaves on any injury." Jesper looked at the price of the plant and it was fifty shekels.

"I only have thirty shekels on me."

The little girl ripped off the tag, shrugging. "Give me the thirty shekels, then."

Jesper stood stunned. "What? But that is stealing, Nihyah!"

Nihyah gave a quiet laugh. "I knew you were a good person. My parents own this store and you can pay the rest later. Here, take it! And be sure to pick up some red roses on the way out. You can never go wrong getting red roses."

Jesper was humbled by his young friend. "Where are your parents?"

"Downstairs, I'll show you." Jesper followed

Nihyah down the stairs.

"Mother, I have a friend that wants to meet you."

"Be right there," replied a soft voice. A woman with long red hair as fiery as Nihyah's stepped out from behind a wall carrying a pot. "Who is your friend, sweetie?"

"This fellow needs the Curado plant and only has thirty shekels. I told him he can give us the rest later."

The woman set the pot down and narrowed her eyes, "Nihyah, we have been through this. I told you not to do that anymore to customers. You are generous, but how do you expect us to eat?"

Jesper raised his hand. "It's quite alright, I will make another selection. I have plenty of time. I don't have to leave until tomorrow evening."

"Where are you going, if you don't mind me asking?"

"I have to report back to training."

"Oh, you're a soldier?"

At first Jesper was reluctant to tell her but why not. "Well, kind of. I hope to be much more than that."

The woman gave Jesper a strange look. "You're in Centore training, aren't you?" Jesper gave a weary smile. "Don't worry young man, if you become a Commander your secret will be safe with me. I used to help a Centore Commander long ago who did the exact same thing you're doing. I do not agree with their codes, anyway. Love is the greatest gift El gave us. Take the plant and be sure to pick up some red roses on the way out. You can never go wrong with red roses."

Jesper gave the woman his thirty shekels, smiling as she echoed her daughter's advice. "Thank you very much. I will return and give you the rest."

The woman took the money and grabbed his hand. "Forget the rest. Thank you for what you do." She smiled and returned to her work.

Jesper winked at his helper. "Thank you, Nihyah, for your help. I will let you know what she says."

Nihyah giggled. "I already know what she's going to say."

That night after supper, Jesper went to Airah's chambers and the guard allowed him in. He put the Curado plant on her balcony so it would get plenty of sun, and left the roses next to her bed. As he walked out the guard stopped him lifting his hand. The guard smirked. "Just so you know, there are rumors of your actions towards Lady Airah." Jesper's stomach tightened. The guard looked down the hall. "I suggest you take the King's advice. Be cautious in how you proceed, or Thorg will receive word of this. You do not have to worry about me and the other royal guards, but you never know who's watching."

Jesper bowed. "I am grateful, but why are you helping me?"

"I once was in love."

Jesper cocked his head to the side, looking the guard in the eye. "You are a Guardian, aren't you?"

"Yes."

"Were you a Commander?"

The guard laughed. "No, but my Commander was clever." The guard gestured his hand toward the stairs. "You should go, but remember what I said."

Jesper shook his hand. "I am honored to meet you, and I will take your advice." The guard winked and returned to his post.

Jesper returned to his quarters, going straight to bed. He slept throughout the night and the next day, gathering his strength for the next phase of his training.

Samha

The morning was warm as winter was drawing
to an end, and the group was grateful. Bezinar was at
their backs and the sun was in their faces. They rode
through many villages before losing sight of the castle
and reaching the plains. It stretched for many leagues,
with random rolling hills and trees. On occasion they
would pass through small towns, but people paid them
no mind. It was a three day ride before reaching
Hightop Forest, which took two days to go through.

Next was the Nutria swamp that led to the
northern Siriu River, and then Samha. They had an
eight day journey before reaching Samha, which gave
the group a chance to get to know each other well.
Bane and Zealot shared their knowledge of the
Bindings of El, and stories of when they had become
scholars. Anor and Tirus kept to themselves, mostly--
not out of rudeness, but because they took their jobs
seriously. They remained constantly aware of their
surroundings and possible threats. Anor was a good
leader and kept a keen eye on everyone in the
company, while Tirus watched their backs and helped
Anor monitor the group. Naughton was radiating
happiness because Eirmosa was with him. They talked
constantly and about everything, and several times
Anor had to quiet them when passing through villages.

Airah did not say much, which the group found odd, as she was usually chattering away to the point of becoming an annoyance.

The second night came and everyone was huddled around the fire. Lady Airah objected, noting the nearby villages and towns with inns, but Anor was very cautious. Naughton and Eirmosa were cuddling under a blanket, whispering. Eirmosa looked at Airah and noticed she was focused on the fire, paying little attention to conversations. She got up and sat next to her, nudging her shoulder. "You have been quiet lately."

Airah glanced at Eirmosa. "Much is on my mind."

"That is obvious."

"My uncle kept the knowledge of Jesper's secret from me. He always includes me in everything. How am I to assist him if he keeps such secrets?"

Eirmosa thought for a moment. "A king is responsible for many things, including his people. He was protecting Tulios's honor, and after what he did for you, your uncle wanted to make sure he upheld Tulios's name."

Airah rewrapped her blanket around her, frowning. "I hate it when you're right." She gazed at the fire and then gave Eirmosa a small, but genuine smile. "I will be fine."

Eirmosa returned to Naughton. "What's wrong with her?"

"She disapproves of her uncle's actions about keeping Jesper's secret."

"Can't say I blame her. Speaking of Jesper, he gave me a message to tell her, but it will have to wait until we're on the road again."

"Why?"

"She seemed stressed today, and perhaps in the morning she will be more pleasant."

The group ate their share of food and stared up at the stars, enjoying the warmth from the fire. Tirus was curled up in his blanket. "What do you think will happen to us?" he asked, quietly.

Bane glanced over from his position on his own blanket. "What do you mean?"

"Will he kill us like he did the last group?"

"Let's try to be optimistic, shall we? Honestly, I'm trying not to think about it."

Zealot got up and threw another log on the fire. "The question is, why did he spare Berton?" The group sat in thought until Anor broke the silence.

"Perhaps so he could deliver the sun jewel back to Naughton."

Bane sat up. "The sun jewel was a message for

Naughton and more."

"So why does he want Naughton?" asked Zealot.

Bane raised a finger. "Exactly. Where were you born, Naughton?"

"In Sturkma. I grew up there my whole life."

"You are certain of this?"

"Of course! My parents would have told me otherwise." Naughton replied, frowning. Anor glared at Bane.

"Enough! Let the boy be. You're irritating me with all this riffraff."

"I'm just trying to figure out why he chose Naughton."

"We will never know that answer until we reach our destination. Now hush, I'm trying to sleep!"

The group went to sleep, with Tirus taking first watch while the others slept next to the fire.

Morning came with a swift sunrise and the last gasp of the fire. The group mounted their horses and were on their way again toward Hightop Forest. The plains seemed to blend together, all the terrain looking alike. The tall grass swayed in the wind like waves, as far as the eye could see. Zealot's eyes began to get heavy and he yawned hugely. "Why is it called Hightop?"

Anor glanced back. "You'll see soon enough."
The group rode through the rolling plains until finally,
the forest appeared in the distance. Though it had
seemed close, the forest was a two hour ride away. As
they approached, the group noticed the trees, which
were unlike any most of them had ever seen. The high
canopy had made them mistake the distance. The
group stopped to admire the view while Zealot had
quickly realized why it was called Hightop, he still did
not understand why the forest had its leaves in the
absence of spring.

"How is this possible?"

"What is possible?" asked Airah.

"Why do the trees still have their leaves during
the winter?"

Anor stood up in his saddle stretching his legs.
"You're asking a question that no one can answer.
This is the only forest in the region that keeps its leaves
during the winter." The group stared upward in
amazement. Most of the trees stood two hundred feet
and varied in species.

"How do these trees get so big?" asked Eirmosa.

"No one knows," replied Anor, adjusting his
sword.

Naughton noticed Tirus doing the same, and
raised an eyebrow. "Expecting trouble?"

Anor glanced at him. "You can never be too cautious."

"Out with it!" said Airah, crossing her arms.

Anor lowered his head in before staring warily up at the canopy. "I didn't want to tell you unless it was necessary, and chances are we won't have trouble." He moved his head around, stretching his neck. "The trees are not the only large things in here."

"Meaning?"

"The animals. They are...larger than normal."

The group gasped and Naughton suddenly had a thought. "Nemian mention this to me before!" He said, before barking out a laugh.

"You mean squirrels are larger than dogs?" asked Airah.

"Nope, the rabbits are," said Tirus.

The group's eyes widened with shock. Naughton's laughter subsided as he readied his bow. The others got their weapons ready as well. Airah looked at her dagger and then looked at the others larger weapons. "I suppose I will handle the chipmunks."

Anor unsheathed a spare short sword. "Only the mean ones." Airah narrowed her eyes at him, and he gave a wink. He kicked his horse, leading the group into the forest.

As they rode, Naughton noticed just how strange the trees were. Some had slick and glossy bark, while others seemed dark with flakes of bark curving upward toward the sun. Many leaves were as big as a man's chest, with different shapes and patterns on the same tree, as if they were cross-bred. The forest echoed every noise they made, for the leaves were broad and bounced back every sound.

While everyone was distracted, Naughton rode up next to Airah. She smiled at him.   "Yes?"

"I have a message for you."

"What message?"

"From Jesper. I have not had the time to tell you." Her face stayed frozen in a polite smile.

"What did he say?"

Naughton leaned in, keeping his voice low. "He said he is well, and that he hopes to see you soon."

Airah nodded. "Thank you. But I am afraid our journey will delay our visit. I apologize for being distant lately."

"No apologies are necessary. I know that secret is eating you up inside, but it will pass."

"The journey is still young and I'm sure you're right. Thank you." She lightly kicked her horse and quickened pace. Naughton dropped back and looked at Eirmosa, puzzled.

"I don't think she has any feelings for my cousin."

Eirmosa winked. "Don't let her fool you. Remember, she is the King's niece and has many responsibilities."

The first night came in Hightop Forest with no encounters of large animals. They built a fire and huddled close to it. The group was on edge, except Anor, who was sharpening his sword. The wood burned in an array of different colors, almost hypnotizing. Naughton looked around at the trees. "Is this placed cursed or something?"

Anor laughed. "Of course not. I have never seen a ghost or spook while I stayed in these woods. Relax, Naughton. No bear is going to eat you while I'm around."

"No, but a giant rabid raccoon might!" said Airah, holding her short sword tightly. Anor gave up trying to lighten the mood, and eventually everyone went to sleep except for Naughton. He kept feeling they were being watched and constantly bounced his eyes back and forth, looking into the woods. When it was his turn to keep watch, he stayed up the whole night and let the others sleep.

Tirus woke well before sunrise and started

gathering the gear. "Did you keep watch all night, Naughton?"

"Yes, there was no way I could sleep here. I felt eyes on us all night."

Tirus nodded. "Me too. I couldn't sleep at all the first time I came through this forest. At least we only have one more night in here." Tirus and Naughton woke the group and were on their way by sunrise. The giant leaves blocked the sun all day with only a rare beam cutting through here and there, which explained why no shrubs grew. They were more relaxed after their first night in the forest and took in their surroundings with more interest. The birds were beautiful with all shades and hues radiating from their feathers, as if they were born from the colored flames of fire. The various bird songs they sang were nothing they had heard before. Eirmosa whistled and tried to mimic their songs, but most of the birds fluffed up their feathers and changed their tones, insulted.

The group followed Anor like dogs on a leash. The forest looked the same in every direction. There were few leaves on the ground, revealing the dark colored soil, nuts, and acorns. With no shrubs or bushes in the way, the group could see through the enchanting forest for a great distance. "Why are there so few small plants?" asked Zealot.

Eirmosa looked at him like he was an idiot. "Do you not know anything about plants? The giant leaves block the sun, preventing small plants from receiving adequate sunlight."

Suddenly a loud shriek echoed through the woods and the horses came to a sudden halt. The group moved their hands towards their weapons.

"What--what was that?" asked Eirmosa.

Anor strained his eyes. "I have no idea. Lets--" The shriek came again, this time much closer. Birds flew past them, and a rabbit as large as a dog sprang out from behind the trees and dashed by them. Suddenly, noise from above drew their eyes away from the rabbit.

At first, Naughton thought his eyes were deceiving him. Flying toward them was a massive bird. Its wingspan had to have been at least eight feet, and its face was dark brown with black stripes and a curved yellow beak. Finally, the group realized it was a hawk chasing its prize. The horses watched with eyes wide and ears locked as the giant flew over them. At the same time Airah's horse got spooked and ran. She pulled the reigns but with no avail. The horse ran wildly barely missing trees and suddenly the horse tripped throwing Airah in the air. She landed with dirt all over her and sat, relieved she was not hurt. The group finally caught up with her. Anor ran to her and inspected her, "are you injured?"

"No!" replied Airah as she spat dirt from her mouth. Anor noticed the group was staying back and when he looked at them they seemed distracted. He stood up and noticed several large holes around him. Naughton felt a cold snap go through his body and could see his breath for a second.

Anor helped Airah up, "what is this?"

Eirmosa approached a hole and had Naughton help her down. She looked up at the group, "do you want to know now or later?"

"Now!" the group yelled in unison.

"These are graves."

"But there too big," said Bane.

Eirmosa gestured her hand around her and picked up some cloth intertwined with vines, "look at the shape and these old rags."

Naughton helped her up, "but where are the bodies?"

"They have been taken you nimwit," said Airah as she dusted herself off.

"Who would steal bodies and why?" asked Anor.

Zealot was very quiet as he observed the graves,

"you have never encountered this, Anor?"

"Of course not!"

Zealot took steps around each grave, "they were not normal, whoever they were. Each grave is over seven foot long." He looked at the vines that had taken over the graves. "This was done long ago."

Tirus came up with the renegade horse and saw the holes, "what did I miss?"

Airah took the horse, "let's leave this cursed place first."

Before the daylight was gone, Anor picked a camping spot. The group set up camp and started a fire, using the strange, fuzzy bark. It ignited easily, putting off strong heat, and it burned slow with many different colors. Tirus and Bane gathered a big pile of bark for later and got their blankets ready. Anor stared up at the trees. "This forest never ceases to amaze me."

"Why is that?" asked Bane.

"Because trees such as these require lots of water, and I have never come across a single creek or stream."

"That's odd," said Airah.

Naughton rubbed his hand in the soil. "Then why is the soil dark and moist?"

Eirmosa shook her head. "It should be the other

way around, if there was no water, it should be light colored and dry."

Naughton rubbed the moist soil through his fingers and smelled it. "There is water coming from somewhere. It has not rained in several days, but perhaps there is a spring under us."

"That never occurred to me," said Anor. "Maybe this entire forest is on top of a giant spring."

"You think this spring water is affecting the odd growth in here?" asked Zealot.

Bane felt the soil as well. "The Bindings of El have many accounts of strange phenomena. But I have never read anything about water affecting trees and or animals."

Naughton walked around the camp, looking for more wood, when suddenly he tripped in a hole. He picked himself up and went back to the fire, grabbing a stick to use as a torch. The others looked at him oddly and followed him. Naughton waved the torch around, examining the hole. "What are you looking at, Naughton?" asked Tirus.

"This hole I tripped in."

"Please tell me it's not another grave," said Airah.

Anor examined the hole as well before yanking the torch from Naughton. "This is no hole, it's a footprint!" The group circled around, astonished. It was as round as a pumpkin with smaller indentations touching it. Anor knelt down, touching the soil, and stood straight up. "This is a predator."

"So...what is it?" asked Zealot.

Anor walked back to the fire. "Let's return and I will tell you." When the group settled, Anor set his sword beside him and leaned back against a tree. "If Naughton agrees with me, I'd say it's a wolf."

The group sat stunned, looking at one another. "Impossible," said Eirmosa.

"Anything is possible in this forest. Remember the hawk and rabbit?"

Naughton strung his bow. "But wolves do not travel alone."

Anor shrugged his shoulders. "I told you this forest and the animals are odd."

"Odd is not the word I would choose," said Bane.

"I doubt we'll survive the night!" said Airah.

Anor laughed. "Nonsense. I have traveled this forest many times and nothing has happened."

"Yet," glared Eirmosa.

The group talked quietly while they ate. Just before it was time to sleep, Zealot asked to see the sun jewel. Naughton pulled it from around his neck and gave it to him. He examined the jewel closely and the others watched in silence. "The words say Honor the Holy?" Naughton nodded.

Bane examined the jewel next. "What do you think it means?"

"Actually, it's quite simple if we break it down," replied Zealot. "The word honor means to have integrity and to be highly respected. The word holy means to be separated from evil. Since the words only appear when Naughton holds it must mean he must keep his respect and integrity by serving the one who is separated from evil."

"So you're saying that Naughton has to help this being?" asked Airah.

"It seems that way. However, according to the Bindings of El, no human is perfect. We all come up short."

The group fell asleep with Anor on first watch. Naughton, however, remained wide awake and ready for anything the forest presented.

Daylight was breaking when Naughton awoke to Tirus standing over him. "Anor needs you to look at something." He got up and followed Tirus about fifty feet from the camp, where Anor stood with his sword drawn.

As Naughton approached, Anor pointed to the

ground at a set of tracks heading away from the camp. Naughton squatted down and looked at the tracks closely. He touched the foot print. "Whoever this is seems bowlegged or something. These tracks are wider than usual." He looked to where the tracks began and saw markings going up a tree. "And a good climber; there are no limbs to grab this low." Anor kept watching the direction the tracks went, looking for movement. Naughton patted Anor on the shoulder. "Relax, Guardian, whoever it was is long gone by now. And besides, we're going the opposite direction."

"That's what is troubling me," Anor said, grimly. "We have been followed and I want to know by whom."

"Should we tell the group?" asked Tirus.

"Absolutely not! They're having enough trouble getting sleep as it is. Let's just push forward. You will continue following, but keep your eyes open for anything strange. If we change anything, our spy may take notice." They made their way back to the rest of the group, mounted their horses, and continued through the forest.

"Are we reaching the swamp today, Anor?" asked Airah.

"Yes, we will be there before noon."

"Good, the horses will need water soon." The group rode on, with Tirus lingering behind, looking back every so often to see if he could catch their spy.

By high noon the group had reached Nutria Swamp, which stretched as far as the eye could see. The vegetation was tall and the water was covered in a slimy green substance. There was a small path that went through the swamp, avoiding the water. "Let me guess, it's called Nutria Swamp because of all the giant rats?" asked Zealot.

"How did you guess?" said Anor with a grin.

Zealots eyes widened. "What? I was just joking!"

"I'm not. But the rats are not what bother me, it's the other wildlife in here."

"You mean this swamp has giant creatures too?" asked Eirmosa.

"I'm afraid so. There are enormous reptiles."

"What! This is where I draw the line. I'm not going in there!" said Airah, pulling back on the reins.

"We have no choice, my Lady. This is the quickest way to the bridge that crosses the Siriu River."

"Why didn't we take a boat?" asked Eirmosa.

"Because the river flows south, and it would have taken longer to row against the current. On top of that, the Geols are watching the river closely. Now, loosen those reins."

Airah's knuckles turned white, gripping them tighter. "No, I'm not going in there!"

Anor turned his horse around. "With all due respect, Lady Airah, I will bind your hands and drag you every step of the way if I have to. The choice is yours, my Lady, so choose quickly!" The group sat in silence, waiting to see how she would react.

She got off her horse and sighed. "Fine."

Anor gave her an odd look. "How did you know I was going to say we have to go on foot?"

"That's common sense, you meathead!" The group laughed as they got off their horses and followed Anor through the swamp.

The path was narrow, with plants on either side swarmed with massive insects. Some of the plants were covered in thorns, and some had leaves that were sharp as knives. The foul stench of stagnant mud was in the air. Every once in a while the water hissed and splashed, spooking the horses. After a few hours, Anor turned around to make an announcement. "Listen carefully! Do not step off into the water up here. I have seen horses and men fall into this water and vanish into a blood pool." Their hearts sank. The path narrowed even more, with tall weeds brushing their sides and the number of insects increased. The group constantly brushed off the hitchhikers, though some were more difficult than others as they latched onto their clothes. Airah pulled out her dagger, knocking them off in fear of using her hands, and she squealed on several occasions. Anor led them to a small wooden bridge that looked ancient. Below the bridge was a slough full of water with green moss and tall weeds.

Naughton stopped on the bridge and looked closely, seeing a pair of large eyes looking at him from the water. "What is that?"

"Now is not the time to sightsee," said Tirus.

"Fine, but what is it?"

"It's an alligator, I believe."

Naughton leaned over. "I have never seen one before."

Tirus grabbed him, pulling him back. "What the hell is the matter with you?"

"I just want a closer look."

"Well, your horse is going to get acquainted with its teeth if he sees it and panics. Keep moving." Naughton and Tirus caught up with the group, most of whom were standing stock-still, staring at the lake. It had cypress trees all around it with odd stumps coming out of the water.

Anor pointed toward the right side of the bank.

"Do you see them?" The group looked and saw giant rodents on the bank looking right back at them.

Airah squinted her eyes. "Are those...rats?" she asked, disgusted.

"Indeed, but they're called Nutria."

Bane rubbed his eyes. "Those things are huge!"

"They're good eating too," said Anor.

"You must be joking," said Eirmosa.

"I do not joke about good meals. They are delicious."

"Okay, I knew you Centores were crazy, but that is absurd!"

Anor smirked. "You never know until you try. Come on, it's going to be dark soon." Anor led the way around the lake and found a nice, dry spot on a hill. "Set up camp and stay close to the fire."

"Why don't we just go ahead and cook ourselves dinner?" said Airah. Tirus and Naughton gathered what wood they could find and started the fire.

"Use the wood sparingly. There's not much around," said Naughton.

Anor pulled a bag of bark off of his horse. "Use this. I have enough to start fires for the next few nights." The group sat close together that night with weapons at the ready, in case a rodent or beast came for a visit. Throughout the night they heard frogs croaking and occasional screams, with splashes coming from the lake. Eirmosa sat close to Naughton during the night, and he didn't mind one bit.

"So does that lake have a name?" asked Naughton.

Tirus was sharpening his sword, the grinding sound echoing into the darkness. "It's called Nocturnal."

"That's a strange name," said Bane.

Zealot threw more bark on the fire, "I think it fits perfectly. Who could sleep near this lake?"

Anor was sharpening his sword as well. "It's called Nocturnal because that lake never sleeps at night."

"We know what Nocturnal means!" said Airah, holding her dagger tight in one hand and the short sword in the other.

Anor chuckled. "Relax, my Lady, those creatures won't come near the fire."

"You think I was born yesterday?" she asked. Anor began to reply, but Naughton interrupted.

"I wouldn't answer that question if I were you, Anor." The group laughed and it echoed across the lake, making every creature pause in curiosity.

Later, Naughton took the last watch before

sunrise. His eyelids grew heavy, but he dared not close them. He stood up, covering Eirmosa with an extra blanket, and walked around a bit, keeping the fire in sight. He had his bow in hand as he made rounds around the group. He stopped to take a deep breath of the cold night air as his mind wandered back to the night he and his father were on the Mountain of Colonies. He pulled out the necklace his mother gave him and rubbed the horn blade in his hand, trying to stay awake. Suddenly, he heard a hiss in the darkness. He put an arrow on the string and prepared to draw back, looking for a target. He heard the hiss again and he backed away slowly, heading closer to the fire. He grabbed a stick from the fire and used it as a torch. He put his bow away and pulled his sword, waving the torch around, but saw nothing.

He started walking back to the fire when he caught movement with his right eye. He waved the torch and saw a pair of eyes staring at him from the ground. He swallowed, wetting his throat in case he had to yell for help. He walked closer with his sword held high, ready to strike, but then the eyes disappeared. He began to move in the direction he'd seen the eyes, his torch steadily losing flame, and saw a long serpent body lying on the ground. Naughton froze, abruptly aware that he was looking at a giant snake. He felt a tickle on his right arm and when he turned to look, he saw the snake staring back at him. Naughton did not move holding his breath. He was helpless; if he moved, he was sure the snake would strike. The giant snake stared at him as if it was studying him for several minutes before backing away, slithering off into the darkness.

Naughton gasped for air and leaned against a tree. His whole body was trembling from head to toe and lacked the strength to walk back to the fire. The torch went out and he could see the morning glow on the horizon. He stood there, gathering his thoughts, and eventually made it back to the group. He woke Anor first. "Naughton, are you alright? Your face is pale."

"I'm fine, just had a close encounter with a local." Anor got up and woke the others. Eirmosa noticed Naughton's face as well.

She walked over, hugging him tight. "You okay?"

"I think so. Just give me a while and I'll explain."

The group continued on at sunrise, leading their horses around the lake and into the marsh. The path changed its width constantly. At times they saw movement under the water, which Naughton payed extra close attention to since his encounter. At noon, they took a break to eat and drink. Anor threw Naughton some dried meat. "Chew on this. It will settle your nerves."

Eirmosa, and eventually everyone else, began to watch him, waiting. Naughton chewed for a moment before he spoke. "I came face to face with a giant snake last night."

"It didn't strike you?" asked Airah.

"No, it was strange. It just stared at me as if it were studying me or something."

"What color was it?" asked Bane.

"It's irrelevant what color it was, you dope!" yelled Airah.

Naughton reflected for a moment. "It was too dark to make out."

"How long was it?" asked Anor.

"Long enough to swallow me whole!"

Zealot laughed. "Exaggerating a bit, aren't we?"

"I believe him," said Anor.

"Wait a minute. You said it studied you?" asked Eirmosa.

"Yes, and believe me it could have had me for breakfast if it wanted to. It just licked my arm and stared at me."

"That doesn't make sense. Why would a snake

study you? I think you were delirious," said Eirmosa, her hands on her hips.

"I was not delirious! My only guess is that I didn't taste good."

Eirmosa hit his arm. "That's not funny!"

"It's time we push on, but I suggest we stay closer together." said Anor.

The group continued through the swamp, and the further they went the less water there was. A variety of thick bushes with long leaves covered the area. As the day waged on, Airah was getting impatient and was ready to leave the swamp for good. "How much longer until we leave this wretched place?"

Anor shrugged his shoulders. "We have been moving slowly. I'd say by tomorrow." The group was hoping for tonight and everyone started grumbling.

By late afternoon, the group reached solid land. There were a few ponds around, and creeks with cypress trees surrounding them. The tall grass had vanished, putting them more at ease. By nightfall they settled down and built a fire. Anor disappeared briefly, pulling out meat and bread from his pack once he'd returned. He cooked dinner for them, and they ate to their heart's content. "That was delicious, Anor. What kind of meat was that?" asked Zealot wiping his mouth.

Anor chuckled. "I told you it was good."
Zealot looked down at the remains of his food,
realization dawning on his face.

"Did you really sit there and watch me eat rat?"

Anor laughed even harder. "What's the matter?
I thought you liked it?" The group laughed as well,
knowing they had just eaten a giant rodent and there
was nothing they could do about it. Eirmosa felt her
teeth with her tongue.

"I wondered why it tasted so greasy."

Bane pulled out his pipe and leaned back on a
log. "Just think, tomorrow we will be at Samha
castle."

"Speaking of which," began Zealot. "What do
we tell the King of Samha?"

"What do you mean?" asked Tirus.

"Do we tell him of our true errand?"

"Of course. He is an ally and he will help us,"
said Anor. "Nellium said they will escort us to the
Seraph Lands."

"I hate to bring this up, but how will Eirmosa
and I get back?" asked Airah.

Tirus winked at Anor. "You must come back
the way we did." Airah gave an evil look, and he
smiled. "We're just teasing you, my Lady."

Anor shook his head. "The Siriu River flows back to Bezinar, and I'm sure the King of Samha will have you escorted back home."

Eirmosa looked at Naughton. "Please let me go with you?"

Naughton smiled. "That is one thing I admire about you. You are persistent." She glared at him. "I'm sorry but you must go back with Airah. It's not safe where we are going. Like my father says, I must have a clear conscience when I go to the Seraph Lands." She bit her lip and said no more, staring at the fire. Naughton wanted her to come, but he knew he would not be able to live with himself if something happened to her.

Airah changed the subject to help ease Eirmosa's mind. "Anor, I have never asked. Which Centore unit you were with?"

"I was with unit two, commanded by Nemian."

"Now it makes sense," said Naughton. "You helped stop the uprising in Samha."

Anor nodded. "We traveled this route many times to check on Samha, and to make sure everything was in order. The King will recognize me and we will be treated well." The group sat in silence and stared at the fire, thinking about what was yet to come.

Eirmosa contemplated ways to convince Naughton to let her go, but nothing she thought of seemed persuasive. Naughton pulled out the sun jewel, angling it toward the fire so it would sparkle. The group watched as he examined it, and again it was passed around for the group to study, though no one knew quite what to do with it. The group talked into the night, until eventually they fell asleep with Zealot on first watch, practicing his swordsmanship.

In the middle of the night a rainstorm, hit soaking the group and putting out the fire. They huddled together and tried to stay warm, using their wet blankets to block the wind, though their efforts were useless. It was a long night, and they were all soaked to the bone when the storm finally passed after sunrise. Anor tried starting a fire, but it was hopeless with all the wet wood. "It appears that we're going to have to tough it out in our wet clothes."

Airah's teeth were chattering, "I'm--already toughing--it out!"

"If we start moving, perhaps we will warm up," suggested Naughton.

The group mounted their horses and rode toward the Siriu River. When they reached the edge of the swamp, they could see the river. In the night, the rain had made the river rise, flooding the valley.

Anor led the group through the rapid water, then stopped, looking in both directions.

Naughton rode up next to Anor. "What's wrong?"

"I've never encountered this before."

"You can't remember where the bridge is?" asked Eirmosa.

"I'm afraid not, since all the landmarks are submerged. I recognize the trees on the other side but I can't remember where the bridge begins." Out of nowhere, they heard a voice.

"We show you." The group turned around, drawing their weapons. Before them was an odd man with long, shaggy black hair sitting on a mule. His face was rugged and his beard was braided. Anor rode toward the man, and a large snake came up out of the water between him and Anor. The horses reared, squealing, and Anor raised his sword higher, ready to strike. The old man gave a grin. "He not hurt you if you nice."

Naughton yelled. "Stop! I recognize that snake!"

The man laughed. "You do, of course. He like you."

"How long have you been following us?" demanded Anor.

"Me watch you for long time. Me not scared this time, you look like nice folk."

"This time...what do you mean?" asked Tirus.

"Big shiny soldiers come through often, but no see for long time."

Naughton got off his horse to get closer and the snake rose up, looking Naughton in the eye. "What is his name?"

"He named Snipe," replied the man, shifting his weight in his saddle.

"Who gives a damn what that thing is named!" yelled Anor. "That is a huge ass snake and he looks agitated!"

"Calm down, Anor," said Bane. "He could have killed Naughton the other night, he seems friendly." Naughton extended his hand toward the snake, and it slowly moved closer before tasting his hand with its long tongue. It tickled Naughton's arm and made him laugh. The snake backed away and went beside his master. Naughton walked toward the man to shake his hand. While he was trying to be friendly, the group prepared their weapons in case the visit went sour.

"What's your name, sir?"

"Me named Jumbar."

"Jumbar, do you know where the bridge is?"

"Nope, but Snipe do." Jumbar looked at the snake and gave him a hand signal. The snake lowered himself in the water with grace, going around the group toward the river. Jumbar rode through the group and followed his friend, with everyone following in turn. The water got higher and reached the bottom of their saddles as it rushed around them. The group followed cautiously in fear of being washed away by the river, when suddenly the horses' hooves hit the wooden bridge. They crossed the invisible bridge, fighting the cold water, hoping the horses wouldn't slip. Snipe glided on top of the water, with Jumbar riding close behind on his mule. After a few minutes they reached the bank.

"I'm beginning to like that snake," said Anor.

"I think he deserves a treat for his work," said Naughton.

"Are you crazy?" yelled Zealot and Eirmosa in unison. Naughton ignored their warning and sat motionless, waiting for Snipe to take some meat. As Snipe got closer Naughton's horse began to panic, folding its ears back and stepping backwards, so Naughton got off and tried again. The giant snake moved close to Naughton and raised his head up, motionless for several seconds. Within a blink of an eye the meat was gone, and Naughton didn't feel a thing. Snipe licked Naughton's hand and slithered off into the water.

"We go now, bye bye." Jumbar kicked his mule, turning him around. He looked back briefly to say, "Tell me brother to behave."

"Who's your brother?" asked Naughton, but Jumbar did not reply. They watched him and his companion cross the river again, going back to the swamp.

"That was the weirdest thing I've seen yet, and he has a brother," said Airah.

Anor shook his head. "Naughton, you need help, son. No normal human being would have done that."

Naughton smiled. "Define normal."

He looked at Eirmosa and winked, but she just glared at him and muttered, "Idiot."

No one leaves

The morning was cool before sunrise and Jesper had plenty of time to spare, but he did not linger in case the wagons left early. When he returned, half the men were there waiting for departure. No one spoke, fearing the return of pain and misery. Finally, Marxus spoke. "Greetings, Turtle. So, you decided to stick around after all."

"Why not? We're almost done now."

"Perhaps. We heard rumors they're going to be selecting gold shoulders soon."

Jesper laughed sarcastically. "You do realize those rumors are a setup right?"

"I doubt it. My father has good connections with Thorg."

The men laughed. "Your father is probably in on it!" Jesper wanted to be a gold shoulder, but he knew he would have trouble; his competitors were good, including Marxus. Each leader had a weakness and strength. Marxus was gifted in leading the men and was a talented speaker. He was good at boosting their morale. However, he was also slow in coordinating and strategizing. Gideon had the skills that Marxus lacked, but fell short in impressing his own authority. Even so, the men seemed to respect him the most.

Finally, the wagons were ready to depart, interrupting Jesper's thoughts. The men piled in, but three were missing. The group yelled for their absent companions and finally saw three men running up the street. Suddenly the whips cracked, and the horses began to pull. The three men ran with all their strength and one made it, jumping into the wagon as the men pulled him in. The remaining two could not catch up, and were left behind in the light glow of the street lanterns. The clomping of the horses' hooves echoed off the buildings as they pulled the wagons, making their way out of Bezinar and heading toward the training fields. In the far distance, the two men were seen trying to reach the wagon, but their forms faded away as the wagons increased speed leaving the glow of the castle.

They sat in silence, waiting to be thrown back into a world of misery. Before they reached the training grounds, the men made a pact that no one else would leave. From now on, they would work together, no matter the cost. The wagons once again pulled up to the training buildings and they jumped out, ready for the yelling to begin. Once again, no one was there, and the men stood in formation, waiting for instruction. The sun started to rise and the three leaders agreed to have everyone go in and dress for training. As they dressed, they noticed food but dared not touch it, and instead went back outside getting in formation. The sun cleared the horizon and it was getting warm. The men enjoyed the warmth from the sun and stood patiently waiting, glad they weren't being tortured. When the sun was high, the leaders finally decided to have the men go in and eat. As they were eating, Jesper found a note on the back of the door. "Eat the food and be in the center forest at noon."

"Don't eat!" Jesper hollered, panicking. "We have to go! Follow me! Move!" The men leapt to their feet, throwing food everywhere and wondering what had gotten into Jesper as they ran after him. Jesper ran like the wind and the others had trouble keeping up.

"What--is--wrong?" Gideon panted as he finally reached Jesper.

"There was a note saying to be in the forest by noon!"

"Oh no...we're dead!"

Jesper and Gideon were first to arrive. "Get in formation!" Jesper yelled. The men complied without question and waited.

Marxus ran up next to Jesper. "What the hell is the matter with you?"

"There was a note to be here at noon."

"No one is here, Jesper!"

A calm voice came from behind a tree. "Oh, we're here, alright. And you're an hour late." Thorg and the Centores stepped out from behind the trees and surrounded the men. "Who noticed the note?" Jesper raised his hand. Thorg walked over to him. "You noticed it, huh?"

"Yes sir!" replied Jesper, sweat beading down his face.

"I see...and did we enjoy our meal?"

Marxus answered, "Well...no, sir."

Thorg looked at Marxus with a small smile, giving no sign that anything was wrong. "And why not?"

"We did not know it was okay to eat, sir."

Thorg scratched his chin. "So let me get this straight. None of you noticed the note early enough, so you did not eat?"

Gideon answered, "Yes, sir." Thorg walked away from the group, shielding his face from the sun. Suddenly, he clenched his fists, his face turning red as anger swelled within him.

"You are the dumbest men to walk the earth! Always pay attention to your surroundings! Not only that--wait a minute. There are men missing! What the hell is going on around here?" The men began to tremble. Jesper raised his hand.

"What is it, Turtle?!"

"Two men were running late and could not catch up with the wagons, sir."

Thorg walked over to Jesper and glared at him. "You left men behind?"

"Well, sir--I--"

"Answer the question, boy!"

"Yes, sir!"

Thorg's face changed shape before Jesper's very eyes. The veins in his neck began to bulge and his eyes darkened with rage. "What the--you left--" he cut himself off with a gurgle noise. "No one is left behind! Not one!" Thorg bellowed again and grabbed a handful of sticks from the dirt, breaking them and cursing as if possessed. "By the powers of El, I should send you all back home! I thought you were coming together, but clearly I was a fool to think it!" He rubbed his bald head and pointed at the group. "Throw powder on them!" The men howled in pain as the Centores tossed the burning powder at them, tears beginning to roll down their faces. Thorg noticed some men looking toward the lake. "Don't you dare go in that lake, or you're banished!" One man made a run for it, but Jesper tackled him.

"We made a pact! No one leaves!" Thorg and the Centores watched without remorse. Another ran for the lake but Gideon tackled him as well.

"Remember your oaths!" Marxus yelled.

Thorg heard the leaders, and after several minutes of watching the men moan and squirm in agony, he asked, "What is this pack business I hear?"

"Sir, we promised each other that no one else would leave!"

Thorg raised an eyebrow. "Get in the lake, boneheads!" The men ran to the lake and dove in, washing off the powder. Their skin was red and agitated. Thorg walked up to the lake and let the water lap at his feet. "Who came up with this oath?"

Marxus yelled, "We all did, sir!"

Thorg rubbed his beard and walked to the other Centore instructors. After talking with them for several minutes Thorg yelled, "Get out of the lake!" The men ran out and got into formation, silently waiting for punishment. Thorg picked up a big stick and began poking the ground with it. "Well, I see you have come together somewhat, though I am still not pleased that you left two men behind. Get your asses back to the barracks, put on dry clothes, and be in formation when we get there." Thorg gripped the hilt of his sword. "Get out of my sight!" The men dispersed, running toward the barracks.

A Centore instructor walked up to Thorg. "Did you see how fast Jesper and Gideon were running?"

Thorg chuckled and scratched his beard. "I saw them, and Jesper commanded the men very well. Be that as it may, I am not yet convinced that he is to be a gold shoulder."

The men changed and regrouped, getting in formation waiting for orders. Thorg and the Centores rode up on horses and examined the men. "Listen up. While you were on vacation we assigned you colors, and for the next five weeks you will receive training in your specific duties. You will--." Thorg stopped speaking and looked past the men. "Well now, look who has decided to join us."

The men looked to their right, and the two men who had missed the wagon came running up, immediately getting into formation. Thorg laughed long and hard, grabbing his stomach. Then he abruptly stopped and glared at them. "You must be joking! Do you really think you're welcome here? You are banished!" The Centores grabbed them, dragging them to the posts before throwing them on the wagon. The men felt pity for them, but were glad they were gone. They did not want to be punished for someone else's mistakes.

As Thorg continued his lecture, the men felt a load leave their shoulders. Finally, they were going to learn how to fight as an official Centore unit. Thorg approached Gideon, Marxus, and Jesper. "As for you three, we have not yet decided which one of you will become a gold shoulder. You three will go in that building over there where you will be tested thoroughly. You are not allowed to talk to each other for the next week about your tests. Do you understand?"

"Yes, sir!" they yelled in unison.

"Very well." Thorg looked at the other men and pointed to another building, which had previously been off limits. "You children will go in that building and my Centores will equip you. Move!" They ran into the building, leaving the leaders behind. Thorg got off his horse and walked toward the other building, not looking back. "You three coming?" They caught up with him and followed him into the building. The building was bigger than it appeared on the outside, standing at roughly three stories tall. Marxus was sent upstairs, Gideon down the hall, and Jesper downstairs. Jesper was greeted by an instructor, and he followed the Centore downstairs to what seemed like a secret underground floor. The walls were made of red wood and had small candles lit along the way. There were several rooms, one of which had a locked iron door and a sign that read Red Shoulders only.

The Centore led Jesper to a room. "This is your new quarters." The Centore stepped aside, allowing Jesper into the room. He had a bunk and a closet that already housed his clothes. A mirror hung on the opposite side of the room. The last thing he noticed was leather armor hanging in the corner, and a helmet made of bronze that had a gold number three printed on it. Suddenly, the Centore slammed the door. Jesper ran to the door and tried to open it, but it was locked. He sat on his bed, enjoying the sound of silence that he had come to appreciate, as he rarely found a moment of it during training. Minutes seemed like hours as he waited, wondering why he was being held prisoner. To kill time, he grabbed a sheet of paper from the closet and tried to begin a letter to Airah, but changed his mind. He took it to the candle and burned it in fear of getting caught. With no windows he had no idea what time it was. Eventually he returned to his bed and stared up at the ceiling. He wanted to close his eyes, but a small inkling of fear kept him from sleep as he remembered his first night of training.

Jesper jumped to the sound of banging on the door and a Centore entering his room. He wore a black cloak with a shield patch on the left side of his chest, and was carrying a tray of food. "Eat this, then put on that armor and come outside." He left, slamming the door behind him. Jesper swallowed his food quickly and got dressed. To his delight, the armor fit him perfectly. The helmet covered his whole head, and had a small slit for each eye. He ran down the hall and up the stairs, making his way outside. When he opened the door he could see more men in formation. They were dressed in leather armor as well, each with different color shoulders. All were armed with shields, wooden swords, and other various weapons. Thorg waved Jesper over. "Turtle, as of now, you are in charge of these men." He gave Jesper a wooden sword. "They are ordered to obey your commands without question. You and your men are going to undergo a training exercise." Thorg cocked his head to the side with a stern look. "But know this: you have until this time tomorrow to accomplish your mission and return. You and your men are on your own." Thorg handed Jesper a piece of paper with a map. "Let's see what you're made of." Thorg walked away and no Centore trainers were in sight.

The men under Jesper's command gathered around him. "What does it say, Jesper?"

"Attention Centore unit:

We have received word that some of the King's soldiers have been captured and are being held at a fort. Your mission is to rescue the soldiers and bring them back to the training grounds. It is imperative that you are not detected before rescuing the men, or they will be killed.

Jesper looked around. "Where are the other men?" A blue shoulder named Litzer spoke.

"They have been assigned to the other leaders. There are only fifteen of us assigned to you."

"That's it? Well, perhaps it can give us the edge we need."

"It seems that way. You have four green shoulders, five blue shoulders, and six orange shoulders under your command."

"Where are the soldiers being held?" asked one of the men.

Jesper gazed at the map, running his hand along the paper. "From the looks of this map they're southeast, about three leagues from here." A green shoulder named Plonus looked at the map as well.

"That's near the castle of Bezinar, isn't it?"

Jesper pointed. "The map shows a dense forest with a small lake on the far end."

"Shall we get started, sir?" asked Lutzer.

Jesper laughed. "Don't call me 'sir.' I haven't earned that title. Let's go!" The men got in formation and ran toward the forest to the southeast. By nightfall, they could see the castle in the far distance lit up by the torches. It was majestic, like a bright beacon radiating in the abyss of darkness. The large wall was lit all the way around, allowing the surrounding villagers to be seen walking nearby. They stared, enjoying the view for a moment before bringing their attention back to the training exercise.

Jesper gazed toward their destination and saw a small lake glistening from the torches. As he observed the water, he spotted a small building on the north side. A patch of woods and a small group of houses were bordering the south end of the lake. Jesper gathered himself and was about to issue the command, but noticed his men were still daydreaming. They stared at the castle, obviously wishing they could go home just for an hour. "Snap out of it! Time is against us!" His men regained their focus and were ready for orders. "Plonus, do you have any suggestions to avoid being seen by the villagers?

"Why? They are not in this exercise."

"That's what they want us to think. We can't afford to trust anyone during this mission."

"If you say so." Plonus led the team to the villages, staying low and trying to blend in with grass. Birds squeaked and flew into the darkness as the group made their way closer.

Jesper crawled up next to Plonus. "Any ideas?"

"Not unless we can make ourselves invisible. There is no cover from here to those woods. I don't see how we can make it without being seen by villagers." Jesper saw three men herding goats to a wagon. He poked Plonus and motioned at the villagers.

Plonus smiled. "This is going to be interesting." They called the rest of the unit up and Jesper whispered his plan.

"We only have one chance at this, so listen carefully. I want all green shoulders to kidnap the goat herders and bring them here."

"This is a bit much, don't you think, Jesper?"

"Loosen up, Litzer. We're not going to hurt them." The green shoulders took off their armor and began sneaking up on the herders just outside the village. When the herders were distracted loading the wagon, the green shoulders grabbed them, covering their mouths so they couldn't scream. They bound their hands and brought them to Jesper. Jesper observed them and saw fear in each of their eyes. He held up his hands. "We will not hurt you, gentlemen. This is a training exercise for Centores. We will release you when we finish." One of the young herders tried to speak around the hand of his captor. Jesper looked down at him. "Do you swear to keep your voice down?" The young herder nodded, and the green shoulder moved his hand.

"Sir, the ones you're after are in that building over there. I saw men roaming around earlier, but I have not seen them since it got dark."

Jesper smiled. "I appreciate your help young man. Keep silent and we will return for you." They had the herders remove their clothes so that they could take them, except for the child, whose clothes were no fit for any of them. Once they were dressed, they hid the herders in the bushes. "I want two green shoulders to wear their clothes. The rest of us will hide in the wagon with the goats."

"With the goats?"

"Yes, Plonus, with the goats! Now move!" They piled into the wagon, pulling the brown tarp down covering the sides. Their two companions drove the wagon through the villages, and several villagers waved as they passed by. When they reached the forest, Jesper ordered the blue shoulders to get out. "Litzer, what kind of arrows do you have?"

"Our arrows have soft tips on the end with red paint. They told us if we shoot one of their men, their orders are to play dead."

"Excellent. I want you to swim across the lake and take out the archers on the walls while we take out the gate guards."

"Are you sure this is a good idea? If one of us misses, it's all over."

"I have faith in you all. Get going." The blue shoulders went through the forest and started a slow swim through the cold lake, trying to keep from disturbing the water. Jesper waited, allowing his blue shoulders to get in position before ordering Plonus to drive the wagon to the building. As they approached, they saw that the building had a small wooden wall constructed around it and a wooden gate, with three guards holding wooden spears.

The guards approached the wagon. "We told you herders to stay away from here. We're doing a training exercise!" Plonus played along and lured the guards closer.

"We know, sir, that's why we're here. One of their men killed my goats! Have a look." When the guards lowered the wagon gate, Jesper and his men seized the guards and the blue shoulders shot the guards on the wall.

"Hurry, take off their clothes and take their places," said Jesper. Three orange shoulders took the places of the guards while Plonus drove the wagon away to avoid suspicion. "Open the gate when you hear a whistle." Jesper and his remaining men ran along the outside wall and his blue shoulders met them.

Litzer hit Jesper on the shoulder. "I can't believe that worked!"

"Shh…keep it down. This is far from over. We need to get up this wall."

"Why can't we go through the gate?" asked a blue shoulder.

"Are you serious? They'll discover us in no time."

"But we don't have rope. How do you plan on scaling this wall?" asked Litzer. Jesper pulled rope from a bag.

"Where did you get that?"

"From the tarps on the wagon. I tied a herder's staff on the end while we were riding." Jesper started twirling the rope and threw the staff up the wall several times, but could not get it to hook. Litzer grabbed the rope and hooked the wall in one try. Jesper smirked. "Show off."

Jesper went first climbing the wall, which was a

good twenty feet before reaching the top. When he reached the top he climbed over and tied the rope to a post, making sure to stay low. As his men were climbing up after him, he saw the "dead" archers lying down with their eyes closed, just like they'd been ordered to. He looked across and saw two more archers standing on the opposite wall looking in the other direction. He then looked down and saw five guards standing around one of the lower buildings with only a few torches lit. He helped his companions over the wall, ordering them to stay low.

"I need blue shoulders to take out the guards down below with your arrows. Green shoulders, I want you to go take out the remaining archers over there. Orange shoulders with me." As Jesper looked for a way down, his men carried out their duties, taking out the guards and remaining archers. Jesper and his three orange shoulders found a ladder to go down. They grabbed the "dead" guards and took their clothes and armor before hiding them under a pile of hay. One of the guards started grumbling as they buried him in the hay. Jesper and his orange shoulders stood around the building and waited to see if there were any patrols walking around. After five minutes, he saw six guards walk out on the opposite side. Jesper looked up at his blue shoulders and pointed at the patrol. Litzer and his men stayed low, getting into position to shoot when the time was right. Jesper whispered. "Let's go in." Jesper opened the door and saw two men playing cards.

One of the men threw down his cards, barely taking notice of them. "Look, you idiots you are supposed to stay outside, Thorg's orders." Jesper and his men pointed their spears at the two guards, and their mouths dropped open in surprise. "Well, I'll be damned. You actually made it this far!"

"Where are they?" asked Jesper.

"Why should we tell you?"

"Because if you don't, I'm going to rearrange your face!"

The guard sat, wide-eyed. "Take it easy, their down the hall." Jesper motioned his head toward the guards, and the orange shoulders bound their hands and gagged their mouths. They dragged the guards down the hall and found a closed door. Jesper put his ear up to the door and heard voices.

"This is taking forever. Why does Thorg make us do this?"

"Do what?"

"Be prisoners!"

"Stop your bellyaching. Besides, the last two groups never made it to the fort and we're getting paid, so shut up!" Jesper searched the guards and found a key. He opened the door. There sat three men around a table with their hands bound. "Please tell me you caught Thorg's pets?"

"Well his pets are here to get you out, though we can leave you here all night if you like," said Jesper.

The prisoner's eyes widened. "How did you get past all the guards?" Jesper cut the prisoners loose and his men threw the guards in the room, locking the door.

Jesper looked at the prisoners. "What do you know?"

"We're not supposed to tell you anything, but since you made it this far, why not? Thorg and his men are hiding in the trees near the lake." Jesper's expression changed, thinking of how his blue shoulders got past them.

Jesper pointed his wooden sword at the prisoners. "You're lying and I will not take any chances." Jesper raised his sword up to knock out the prisoner.

"Wait, wait! I don't know where they are!"

"Fine, but I still don't trust you. Bind their hands and gag them!" Jesper opened the door slowly to see if it was safe and saw no movement. Jesper's men did as ordered and carried the prisoners outside. They were walking toward the gate when suddenly a patrol rounded the corner.

Suddenly arrows flew over, painting the guards. Jesper and his men dragged the prisoners to the gate. He whistled for the gate to open as Plonus approached with the wagon. All of Jesper's men ran to the wagon, and when the last man was on board they took off at a full run.

Litzer laughed in relief. "We did it!" All the men began to cheer, but Jesper was uneasy.

"What's wrong, Jesper?" asked Plonus.

"It was too easy. Something about this does not add up."

A low but familiar voice said, "You're paranoid, Jesper, but that is why you succeeded."

"STOP!" Jesper bellowed. Plonus pulled back on the reigns and all the men sat in silence, watching Jesper.

Litzer grabbed him. "What the hell is the matter with you?"

Jesper stared at the men, and then he began to laugh. "Can you not count? We have an extra man with us. He has been with us since the forest."

Plonus looked around wildly. "Who?" One of the blue shoulders stood up and took his helmet off.

The men gasped and saluted as Thorg laughed for some time without saying a word. The men remained motionless. Abruptly, Thorg's laughter ceased as he glared fiercely at them.

"You morons stole clothes from citizens and left them tied up in the middle of the night!" The men sat in fear, sweat rolling down their faces, waiting for their punishment. "You tied up the prisoners and gagged them…what the hell is the matter with you, Jesper? This was a training exercise, not an actual mission!"

"Sir, I take full responsibility for what has happened tonight. The men were carrying out my orders."

Thorg rubbed his bald head. "Exactly right. You are responsible for their actions no matter what the outcome. As for harassing the citizens, you will be…rewarded." All the men's faces went blank and they sat silent, thinking it was a trick. Thorg smiled. "You are the only group to consider the citizens part of the equation and treat this as if it were a real mission." The men still did not move, and Thorg smirked. "You'd better start celebrating or I'll think of something else for you to do." The men relaxed and started cheering once again. Plonus snapped the reins and the horses continued pulling the wagon back to the training grounds, the delighted shouts of the men ringing through the night air.

Seraph Lands

After their strange encounter with Jumbar, they continued heading east, catching their first glimpse of Samha Castle as the sun set behind them. The walls surrounding the castle were slightly shorter than Bezinar's and made of a dark stone. High above their heads were gaps in the wall, set evenly about every five feet for archers. Catapults were mounted along the top and were guarded by soldiers. The houses were made of aged dark wood that seemed older than the land itself, which was flat and dull with little plant life due to the sandy soil. They rode through the villages where they were greeted warmly by people dressed in various types of animal fur. It was clearly market time along the road, which was lined with vendors with various foods giving the air a sweet aroma. Naughton recognized some nuts and berries on shelves that came from the swamp. Meat from lizards, snakes, and giant rats were hanging from strings. Children followed them for a while, curious. "The people here are very friendly," said Airah.

Eirmosa looked at the land which was once her home. She recognized a few faces but none recalled her, for she was young when she had left with her parents. "They should be filled with joy after what happened here. If King Irus had never sent the

Centores to stop the previous king's tyranny, this place would be in ruins. The people here were terrified as their homes were pillaged. Now these lands are peaceful, and filled with friendly folk."

"Did you miss being home, Eirmosa?" asked Naughton.

"Bezinar is my home now, though part of me still lives here."

Anor led the group through the villages to the castle gate. A guard dressed in light armor and armed with a long spear approached Anor. He bowed. "Greetings, Anor. Welcome back. What can we do for you?"

"We have come from Bezinar with a message from King Irus."

Anor handed the letter to the guard and he examined the seal, two crescent moons with a leaf in the center. The guard handed the letter back. "You may enter." The iron gates rose, creaking loudly, and the group entered. Within the walls were small shops and houses similar to those in the surrounding villages. Samha Castle was made of dark stone and vast towers. They approached the castle and found it guarded by a few soldiers dressed in black and white armor.

Once again the group was questioned. The guards took their horses and led them through the stone doors. The inside of the castle was warm and dry, and the air was filled with an unexpectedly sweet aroma. As they walked through the halls, Naughton noticed the vast wooden pillars engraved with animals. The guards escorted them to a room with chairs and a small fire. The girls ran to the fire and almost smothered it trying to get warm. Everyone took off their cloaks and gathered near the fire.

"Well, we made it," said Bane.

"You talk as if you thought we wouldn't," Anor said, removing his armor.

"I'm just glad to be out of that swamp."

"Yes, but we're still soaking wet!" yelled Airah.

"I'm sure they're preparing rooms for us. Have patience, my Lady," said Anor.

"I'll show you patience, Anor!" Just then a man dressed in a brown robe walked in.

"Greetings, my name is Quint. I will show you to your rooms where dry clothes await you. The King will see you for dinner tonight." Quint led each one to their rooms.

After they were settled, the group met in the dining hall where they waited anxiously for their host.

Quint entered the room and announced the King. The group stood up as King Mel entered. He was dressed in black and white robes. A silver crown, with a green jewel engraved on the front with a large tree, adorned his head. He was tall, with long red hair and a full red beard. He sat down and the group followed suit.

"Greetings, Anor. I see you did not come with Centores this time."

"Yes, your Highness. I am a Guardian now and I have been sent on a quest with my companions."

"I see...and what are their names?"

Anor slapped himself in the head. "My manners! This is Bane and Zealot, our scholars for this journey. These two young ladies are Eirmosa and Airah."

The King raised an eyebrow. "The Lady Airah?"

"Yes, your Highness."

King Mel clasped his hands together. "I knew your father long ago. He was the bravest and wisest man I have ever known." Airah smiled but did not speak, for it was still painful to discuss. "And who are your other companions, Anor?"

"This is Tirus, one of King Irus's royal guards. And last but not least, Naughton, son of Berton."

"Berton, you say?" King Mel tapped the table with his fingers. "I know this name. He was a Shadow Scout, was he not?"

"Yes, sir," replied Naughton.

"From what I remember of his features, you look nothing like him, but I'm sure you possess his talents."

"Somewhat, Sire."

The King clapped his hands and food was brought to the table. It was not what they expected. The table was covered with snakes, alligators, lizards, and frogs. Anor and Naughton started to eat with gratitude, but the others were hesitant. Naughton looked at Eirmosa. "It's good! Try the frog legs." She picked up the roasted meat and tasted a small bite. Hot and moist, it almost tasted like chicken, with spices that gave the meat a wonderful flavor.

The King noticed the confusion on the faces of his guests. "I take it you eat different foods at King Irus's table?"

Airah took a drink. "We are not accustomed to such meals, your Highness, but this is delicious. I need to tell my uncle about this."

The King laughed and continued gnawing on his alligator tail. After the feast was over they sat conversing among themselves. King Mel raised his hand to gain their attention. "So, Anor, what brings you to Samha?" Anor leaned back in his chair and rubbed his belly, exhibiting a satisfying grin.

"Well, your Highness, this may sound crazy, but we need a guide to get us through Mara valley."

"Why in the world do you want to go there?" asked the King, taking a drink.

"To get to the Seraph Lands."

The King choked and coughed, spraying the contents of his mug on those seated next to him. "Come again?"

"The Seraph Lands, sir."

The King sat his mug down while drying his mouth and stared at Anor. "No one goes to the Seraph Lands and returns, Anor. What's there that you would be willing to risk your lives?"

Bane answered, "Apparently, there is a warrior of some sort that has great powers. As you know, the Geols are becoming very powerful and our defenses will not hold them."

King Mel scratched his beard. "I am planning to send my army to Bezinar."

Anor sighed. "With all due respect sir, it will not be enough. These Geols are powerful. We don't know who is leading them and they have large, fierce creatures. Our only hope lies in the Seraph Lands."

The King drank from his mug and set it lightly on the table, contemplating his next statement. "I have heard this tale, and from what I gather it's a myth.

What makes you think such a being truly exists?"

"Berton gave a detailed account of his previous journey, and we have ancient scrolls that lead us to believe that this being dwells there."

The King readjusted his crown and ordered a servant to bring a map of Mara valley. Moments later, the servant returned with the map and laid it on the table.

The King spread the map out to study it. "This map is not entirely accurate, and I have no scouts that know the current terrain. Underneath Mara Valley is an active volcano, which causes the terrain to constantly change. The lava reaches the surface in different locations and hardens leaving deep trenches. There is no plant or wildlife for the land is parched. After you go through Mara valley--if you survive--lie the Seraph Lands, and that is a place that has no maps or known paths. How do you plan to navigate through?"

"The last time we sent a team, Naughton's father learned of riddles that led them safely," said Bane.

"Riddles? What riddles?"

"Berton was the only man to come back from the Seraph Lands, but his mind was wiped clean and he could not remember certain details." King Mel sat deep in thought. After a long moment, he snapped his fingers.

"There is one man I know who use to travel Mara valley, but his son disappeared during a trip. He searched for him for years. Now he has become a hermit, refusing to talk to anyone. His name is Bojah."

"Where does he live?" asked Tirus.

"Several leagues from here, but as I said, he refuses to speak to anyone. Ever since his son's disappearance he has become quite mad. However, he is the best metal worker I have ever known. With me conversations are short, but each visit presents hope. Lately, rumor has it that he is devising new armor and refuses to let anyone see it. One of my servants will take you to his dwelling tomorrow. But be warned, he's known to become violent."

"Thank you, King Mel," said Airah.

"Well, I'm off to bed if there are no more questions." Naughton lifted his hand, and the King gestured for him to continue.

"Would you mind having these two ladies escorted to Fort Estmere tomorrow on the river?"

"Not at all. I will have some of my personal guards go with them. Is there anything else?"

"No, Sire. Thank you for your hospitality," said Anor, lowering his head.

The King stood up and bowed. "The pleasure is all mine. I will never forget what King Irus and his Centores have done for this kingdom." Everyone stood up as the King retired to his chambers.

The group made their way to their rooms, but Eirmosa was reluctant and refusing to go home. She entered Naughton's room, slamming the door. Her face was red, and her jaw clenched as she stared at Naughton, who was fiddling with his deer horn necklace. "Who are you to decide my fate? I have the right to go if I wish, and I was doing fine on my own before you came along. If I remember correctly, I took care of you while you were on death's door step!" Naughton sat in a chair, patiently listening and watching her pace back and forth. "What hope is there for me and my family when the Geols attack? We will be shown no mercy, and if there is a chance I can help stop the Geols then I am willing to risk my life! Why can't I help you, Naughton?" Naughton lowered his necklace.

"Eirmosa, you are helping me, and there is no doubt you could help us in the Seraph Lands. But there is something I have to tell you."

She crossed her arms and stood with a stern look on her face. "What?" He stood up and held her hands.

"When I opened my eyes in Bezinar for the first time, I thought you were an angel watching over me. Being in your presence brings me peace. I have never felt this way before. I don't want you in harm's way. The thought of losing you brings darkness to my heart." He put the necklace around her neck, pulling her in close. Looking into her eyes, he finally told her. "I love you."

As the gold rays pierced through the clouds, Airah and Eirmosa were waiting at the dock for the boat to depart. Naughton came to see them off. "What is the favor you wanted to ask of me?" Eirmosa asked.

Naughton pulled off the Crescent ring and handed it to her. "Please send a messenger to my mother to let her know all is well. I'm sure she's worried."

Eirmosa smiled. "It will be an honor. Where is she now?"

"A village called Doldram, alongside the Shaboot River to the north of Valkry. She is staying with her mother Ruby."

"It will be done." She gave him a sideways glance. "But you are sure you don't want me to come and keep you safe?"

He laughed. "You never give up."

"Neither did you."

The boat captain announced that he was ready to make way.

Naughton hugged Eirmosa. "I will return to you, I promise."

Airah and Eirmosa walked the ramp to the boat and it casted off, the long oars piercing the river. He waved, watching the ship disappear into the mist.

When Naughton returned, Quint had everyone gather in the great hall in preparation for their journey to see Bojah. "If you are ready, we can go to the stables." Everyone nodded and Quint led them to their horses. They mounted, and Quint led the group towards Bojah's house.

They kept a swift pace through the villages to avoid questions from locals. The days were gloomy and overcast as a cold breeze blew from the north. They began to notice fewer trees, and the ground began to harden as the grass thinned. As they rode further east, the land turned to tall, jagged rock formations the color of rusty crimson. In some cases, the boulders were balancing on tall narrow stones as if they were placed there. As they rode, a strange odor filled the air that they had never smelled before. Naughton waved his hand in front of his face. "What is that smell?"

Quint replied, "Don't worry, you will get accustomed to it. As long as the wind is right we have nothing to fear."

"How can Bojah take this foul stench?" exclaimed Bane.

After several hours of riding, Quint led them to a rock formation that surrounded a house made of stone with a small chimney coming from the top, a wooden door, and no windows.

Anor jumped from his horse and walked toward the door, but Zealot stopped him. "Wait, let me."

Anor raised an eyebrow. "By all means, Zealot, let's hear your communication skills." Quint signaled for everyone to step back. Zealot walked up to the door and knocked, but no one answered. He knocked again, waiting for a reply.

Zealot turned around. "Maybe nobody's home." Suddenly, the door opened and closed within a flash, making him jump back. Zealot banged on the door again.

There was no reply and Anor started laughing. "You certainly have a way with people, alright!"

"Mr. Bojah, we have traveled far. We have come to seek your council."

Quint crossed his arms. "I'm afraid you're

wasting your time scholar, we will have to find another way to the Seraph Lands."

The door opened, and out poked a man's head, wearing a strange metal hat. His face was adorned with large glasses that made his eyes look huge. "Yur asken fur trouble. Go away!"

The door slammed once again, but Anor had had enough. "Listen, old man, I did not come all this way to be stopped but some nut!"

The door opened once again. "Who ya callin a nut, nut? Yur the ones talkn about goin to tha Seraph Lands." Bojah stared at Zealot and blinked, baffled. "Did he call ya a shoolar?" Bojah asked, poking his head out once more.

"If you mean scholar, then yes."

Bojah's eyebrow lifted, and he looked warily at the others before stepping out of the house. He wore a large leather cover over his chest. He was short and stocky, with a plump face and a long scar on his neck. "I'd be willin to talk to ya, but not these others." Zealot looked at his companions, and with a shrug of his shoulders he entered Bojah's stone house.

To his surprise, the house was nice and cozy. He had a small fire in the fireplace and strange objects on the mantle. Zealot walked over and looked at them with wonder and curiosity. One device was a large jar of glass that had red bubbles bouncing around in it. The next device was a large spring that was coiled up tightly, yet had no tension. Then he looked inside the fireplace and saw a shiny device hanging above the fire. It had multiple flat, thin blades twirling around like a windmill, and was attached to a bolt in the center. Zealot turned around and saw that Bojah was eyeing him closely. "Those are me son's. He used to play with em when he was a youngster. So yur name be Zealot, eh?"

"That is correct."

"And yur a shooler?"

"You mean a scholar."

"That's what I'd said. Look at this here, shooler, and tell me what this might be." Bojah led him toward the back, past a massive metal door. At the end of the hall there was a table covered with a thin sheet. He pulled the sheet and dust filled the room, making Zealot sneeze. He looked at the wooden table at a piece of sandstone the size of a plate. It had three smooth sides and a fourth side was jagged, as if it were broken from a tablet. He rubbed his hand over it and felt small indentions. He blew on it and engravings appeared. Zealot leaned down to closely examine the tablet with excitement.

"This is Hebrew. I can read this!"

Bojah was standing in the corner of the room. "I was hopin so, you bein a shooler an all."

Zealot studied the words. "It says 'the way.' But there are words missing."

Bojah pulled off his hat, revealing his bald head, and hung it in the corner. "I figured as much."

Zealot scrubbed the sandstone, looking for more words, but all other markings were scratches. "Where did you find this?"

"On the outskirts of those blasted Seraph Lands."

Zealot rubbed his hand over the stone again. "This could be one of them, but how did it break off?"

Bojah glared at Zealot's muttering. "What are ya blabbin about?"

"Don't you see? This is one of the riddles. It must be! You must take us where you found it!"

Bojah crossed his arms and put his hard hat back on his head. "I'm doin nothin of the sort."

Zealot threw his hands in the air. "But why?"

Bojah's lip twitched. "I have no desire and thur aint nothin you can say to convince me."

"Then why did you show me this?"

"I figured you'd want it. Now if ya don't mind, I have work to do, so off with ya. Take yur treasure and leave!"

Zealot grabbed the stone. When he did, the rest of the sheet fell to the ground revealing a book. Zealot stared at it. "What's this, Bojah?" he asked.

Bojah grunted. "That ain't nothin but a stury book."

"May I look at it?"

"Burn it for all I care, that book is worthless now!"

The book was maroon and appeared very old. When Zealot opened it, he gasped. "Do you realize what this is?"

"Whut? Its nothing to me now. Take it and leave!"

"Bojah, listen to me. This is an ancient document. There is only one other known copy."

Bojah spat on the ground. "That ain't nothin but a goofy stury book me son used to read."

Zealot gripped the book. "This is not just some story book, it's the Bindings of El! It reveals the truth about where we come from." Bojah grabbed Zealot and started dragging him out the door. "Bojah, wait! Listen to me. There is much to discuss!"

"Rubbish, I say. I ain't listening to lies. Get out!" Bojah threw Zealot from his home and he slammed the door. The group ran to Zealot and pulled him off the ground.

"I would say your meeting failed," said Bane.

"What's all that stuff in your arms?" asked Naughton.

Zealot held the items tight. "Quint, can you take us to a building with some shelter nearby?"

"Of course. Follow me."

Anor gritted his teeth, holding his hands up. "Wait a minute, I'm in charge of this operation! What's going on?"

"Not now, Anor, trust me," said Zealot. The group got on their horses and rode back toward Samha, stopping at an old shack by a heap of rocks that had been piled up about a league from Bojah's house. They went inside and it was full of pick axes and large hammers for mining. Inside were several wooden chairs and a small table covered with tools. Zealot cleared the table and laid the piece of sandstone and the book on it. Bane picked up the book and opened it. His eyes widened and his face turned white as he gasped for air.

Anor's face turned red as he clenched his fists. "What the hell is going on around here?" The group gathered around the table waiting for Zealot to explain.

"Gentlemen! Needless to say, we're on the right

track. These two items you see before you are priceless."

Tirus touched the stone. "Well, get on with it then!"

Zealot slapped Tirus's hand. "The words engraved on it say 'the way'... and now that I have your undivided attention, I will say this: this stone has been broken off, and that's not all. In Bane's hands are the Bindings of El!"

The group was speechless, realizing that Bojah was indeed very special, and he knew the location of the first riddle. Bane flipped through the pages and suddenly stopped, his face perplexed.

"What is it?"

"There are more pages in this copy. Pages I have never seen before."

Zealot snatched the book from him. As he read, his lips twitched, and he gripped the book tightly. "What is all this?"

Bane took the book back in wonder. When he reached the end he flipped it around, and found words written on the back cover. He began reading out loud.

"My father refuses to believe me, but I know he is still out there. I only wish my father would open his eyes and see that I am telling the truth. I will pray every day to meet him again." Bane closed the book, eyeing the others before settling on Zealot. "Zealot, we must find a way to get Bojah to help us."

"The man is clouded by anger. I don't see how we can convince him." It was getting dark, and Quint suggested that they should stay for the night. They all found a corner and curled up, fighting the cold. Naughton felt strange all through the night. He thought about all the stories he was told and asked himself, "Could it all be true?"

Upon waking, everyone spent the next morning trying to find a way for Bojah to help them. Eventually, Tirus stood up and started pacing. "Does anyone have an idea?"

"Nothing comes to mind," said Naughton, stretching. "I guess we need to just give it a try for ourselves."

"That is unwise. I have lived here for many years and few dare to venture in Mara valley. Even fewer have returned," said Quint.

"No matter the danger, we must push on. I can't sit around and wait for some wacko to decide to help us," said Anor.

Quint shook his head. "You don't understand. The valley shifts constantly, and the toxins will kill you if the wind is not in your favor. Bojah has discovered a way to avoid the poisonous fumes. None of you will make it a hundred yards without him."

Naughton put his cloak on and geared up. "I agree with Anor on this one. Do all concur?" The group agreed, and went outside to mount their horses.

Quint threw Naughton his water bag. "I doubt you will have the opportunity to use it, but take it just in case. I will tell King Mel of your decision. May good fortune find you." With that, Quint kicked his horse and headed west back to Samha. Anor took the lead and took them back toward Bojah's house.

They passed by Bojah's house. Zealot insisted on knocking on his door one more time, but there was no answer. They continued on toward Mara valley, and once they finally saw it, Anor felt doubt begin to creep in. Before them was the dark haze of a black and grey landscape, with smoke rising from the earth. The igneous rock covered the land with its various surfaces.

Bane gazed at the landscape. "So, mighty Guardian, how do you plan on us getting through without getting scorched?"

Anor got off his horse. "Keep that up and I will use you as a draw bridge! Get off your horses, we're walking for a while." Naughton jumped off and the ground crunched underneath his feet.

"I don't think we should take the horses. They'll lose their footing."

"We must take them. We don't have time to walk this journey," said Tirus.

Zealot knelt down and touched the rough black surface. The rock crumbled to ash in his hand. "I think we should consult with Bojah once more."

"Enough grumbling," said Anor. "Tirus, bring up the rear and I will try to lead us through this wasteland." Anor took the lead, looking for the easiest path. The earth was cracked and rocky. Often, steam blasts would blow out of a crevice and the horses would startle and squeal. The terrain never stayed the same. As they continued the air grew hotter, making it difficult to breath. They covered their mouths with their cloaks to filter out the hot air and the horses constantly slipped, chipping their hooves.

Naughton stopped and patted his horse. "This is ridiculous, the horses can't do this!"

Anor turned around. "I'm beginning to agree with you. I don't see how your father did this."

"There is no other way!" yelled Tirus. "We must push on and hope for the best." Bane agreed with Naughton.

"We are not using our brains! We will go back and convince Bojah to help us." They turned to go back, and their mouths dropped open as they caught sight of the terrain. Red ooze was flowing across the ground, and the heat was unbearable.

Tirus swallowed to wet his throat. "You see! It's too late, let's just keep going!"

"Yep, yur nuts, alright," said a familiar voice. The group looked to the right and saw Bojah standing on a rock above them. He was wearing his metal hat and glasses, but now had a strange mask over his mouth. He wore a tan jacket and dark leather pants, and his boots were solid black with metal attached around the edges. "Yur fortunate the wind is in yur favor. I caint believe ya brought those dumb beasts out here with ya!"

"Well, if somebody would have--"

"Shut up, Anor," Zealot interrupted. "Don't you dare finish that sentence. Bojah, have you come here to help us?"

"Well I'm not here fur breakfast! I will help ya under one condition: take me with ya so I can see if that bein be real and I'll killem myself!"

Bane stepped toward Bojah, gesturing to the group. "I don't think you understand; we are going to ask for help. Why do you want to kill him?"

"That be my business."

Zealot took the book from Bane. "Bojah, do you know what your son wrote in the back of this book?"

"Yep, and it means nothin to me."

"That does not make sense," said Bane. "He helped your son."

Bojah spat. "He filled me son's head full of that rubbish gettin him killed, and I will gut'em like fish if he be real!"

Anor shook his head. "We can't have you messing up our plans, Bojah."

"Then ya cun stay out hur and be burnt alive for alls I care."

"Wait!" Naughton looked behind him, observing the steam coming from the ground. He looked at Bojah, putting his hands on his hips. "If you show us the way to the Seraph Lands, you can do as you will--as long as we can speak to him first. Just promise you will do nothing until we are done talking to him."

Bojah put a hand on his chin and thought. "Ya have me word."

"Very well, then. Lead on, Bojah."

Bojah jumped down and walked up to Anor. "Them beasts have to be freed."

Anor looked at Bojah, reluctant to release the reins. "Are you mad? We need our horses to travel."

"There be no travelin with them horses."

"Can you explain why?" asked Naughton.

"Furst of all, yur standn on a thin layer of rock. Them horses are too heavy and will break it, exposin laves tunnels. Second, I got no material to protect em from the toxins."

Naughton wrinkled his nose. "What is laves?"

Bojah pointed. "Ya see that red stuff over thur? That be called laves. The heat can melt iron and other metals in a sec. In other wurds, ya skin will burst inta flames just bein near it and ya horse will be glue! Now get rid of them hairy beasts!"

Anor shrugged his shoulders and unpacked his horse, the others following his lead. When they finished, the horses took off and disappeared into the smoke. "Don't wurry, they will find thur way home." Bojah gave each of them a mask made of silver that covered their mouths. "Do not take these off or yur lungs will turn to mush. I've devised a way to filter them toxins usin special leaves wrapped in cloth." He took the lead and began walking southeast, toward some giant black rock formations. The group followed with their packs and saddle bags, taking cautious steps over crevices. Anor, Tirus, and Naughton took off their armor, which had slowly begun to cook them due to the heat. They packed it away, relieved, but the weight of the packs was agonizing.

Naughton caught up with Bojah. "How do you

know all this?"

"I've been studyin this place ever since the volcano erupted."

Naughton looked around but did not see any mountain. "What volcano?"

"It's beneath us."

"What?!"

Bojah laughed. "Yep, yur standn on an underground volcano. Why, the laves is right under yur feet as we speak, flowing under us in hollur tubes. But that aint nothin, wait till we reach that ridge over thur." Bojah led them to the top of a ridge. The rocky layer was hot to the touch and their boots became sticky. When the group looked down they saw laves flowing in small rivers. Chunks of rock were being carried along like small boats, and in some places the laves spewed in the air.

"You expect us to cross that?" asked Anor.

"Of course not, I'm no nut like you," said Bojah, without looking back. "Were goin around that mess and then towards that plateau."

"Wait Bojah, the soles on our boots are melting!" yelled Naughton, examining his left boot.

"Then I suggest ya keep a quick pace." The volcanic rock was razor sharp as Bojah headed south on the ridge. Their hands were cut and burned as they followed Bojah, struggling to hold on. They reached the bottom of the ridge where the ground floor was smooth and looked like snake scales. The heat had subsided, and Naughton found himself mesmerized by the melted rock flowing through the land. He tried to get a better look, but the heat quickly intensified the closer he got. "Mind yurself, ya goof, it gets mighty soft around nem edges."

"So what interests you about this place, Bojah?" asked Bane.

"Well, thur be many elements in this here molted rock suches iron and other ores. Sometimes I can chip it out once it hardens and sell it. The heat allows me to put strong ores next to it, so I cun shape the metal how I want it. Where do you think yur new Centore armor came from, eh?"

Anor cocked his head to the side. "What new Centore armor?"

Bojah readjusted his glasses. "Ya mean yur King has not used it yet? That be odd. I sent him fifty suits to try out as prototypes."

Anor raised an eyebrow, scratching his head. "Why would King Irus withhold such armor?"

"How'd should I know? He paid me well and said we wud do business again."

"When did you give him this armor?"

Bojah took off his hat and rubbed off a black smudge. "Oh, let's see...bout a year ago. I been makin more, figurin he was comin back soon, but I've hurd no word."

Anor became very interested, but Tirus interrupted. "I hate to break up your conversation, but we are, after all, standing in a lake of fire!"

Bojah pointed a chubby finger at Tirus. "Don't be rushin me, ya savage. The plateau is just over yonder. Thur we'll be safe. We'll sleep tonight and then make our way to tha Seraph Lands." Bojah continued on until they reached sight of the plateau. He lead them up the steep embankment to the flat top.

"What caused this?" asked Zealot.

"This here useta be a laves field, but a small shift caused this here hill to form. Now settle down and get sum shut eye. We ain't far from tha Seraph Lands." They all laid down, using their blankets as pillows. They tried to sleep but the heat made it difficult.

Naughton woke up in the middle of the night to a bloom of fire illuminating the dark sky. He jumped up to a loud hissing sound and saw more flames erupting in the distance. Sweat beaded on his face and he wiped it with his sleeve. The corner of his eye caught another red glow to the north. He walked to the edge of the plateau and saw Mara valley glowing red as lava spewed into the air from where they came from. He noticed Zealot and Bane were sitting on the edge, looking toward Mara valley and having a discussion. He wiped his face again and walked over to them. "Can't sleep, Naughton?" asked Bane.

"How can I in this blasted heat?"

"We're struggling ourselves, and I'm sure the desert will be no better," said Zealot.

"We were wondering if this is what hell looks like."

"What are you talking about?"

Zealot opened the Bindings of El. "We have been reading."

"And?"

He cocked his head to the side. "It concerns me how little we know."

"Go on," said Naughton, as he sat crossing his legs.

"If this is the true copy of the Bindings of El, then I must believe in it."

"How do you know that it's the true copy?"

"Apparently there are two parts to the Bindings of El. You see, back at Bezinar, the one we protect is obviously missing the second half. This copy is identical to first portion back home. This whole time we have been missing the other half!"

Naughton's eyes widened. "But how is that possible?'

Zealot flipped through the pages. "I don't know. We have been reading the very last part of the Bindings of El, and it's frightening. It talks about a lake of fire, a dragon, and the end of the world."

Naughton gaped and wiped his brow again. "What else?"

He flipped toward the back to a certain page. "It says here, 'If anyone's name was not found written in the Book of Life, he was thrown into the lake of fire.' I don't know about you, but I'm sure it looks somewhat like Mara valley--what's underneath, anyway."

Naughton stared out at the laves fields, watching them flow along with smoke rising in the distance. "So you think it's real?"

Zealot laughed sarcastically. "Is it worth the risk to be thrown in that and not die?"

"Good point. But how do you avoid hell?" Bane and Zealot looked at each other for a moment.

Zealot closed the book. "We thought we knew, but now we are not certain."

Naughton sat next to them, wiping his hands off while stretching his legs. "Doesn't it say anything in the Bindings of El?"

"That's the problem. We thought the one in Bezinar was complete. However, this new section has baffled us."

"So…you're hoping to figure it all out, right?"

"Yes, but we have not had the chance to translate it yet. Hebrew is a complex language and you must read it right to left. It will take some time."

"I see," said Naughton.

Bane drank some water. "Right now, we must focus on the task at hand." The three sat silently gazing at the parched landscape, watching the red ooze dance in the air.

When the sun began to glow through the grey haze, the group continued on with Bojah leading the way out of Mara valley. The igneous rock was replaced with dry, hard clay and strange, rusty rock formations once again. Some formations looked like animals, human faces, and other objects that the imagination could forge. At high noon they climbed a ridge high above the valley. When they reached the top, Bojah pointed towards the desert. "Behold the Seraph Lands." The desert was vast and empty but for the rolling hills of sand. The heat waves rose upward, blurring the landscape. The wind howled and sand flew into the air, forming small funnels that appeared and disappeared within minutes.

"What are those things spinning?" asked Anor.

Bojah removed his hat and wiped his head. "I heard them things were called devil twisters. I bet it aint pleasant to get caught up in one of em."

Naughton grabbed the sandstone tablet from Zealot and walked alongside Bojah. "Where did you find this?"

"I'll be, I forgot about that thing. Come, I'll show ya." Bojah led them along the ridge, which was lined with only a few shrubs along the way down. They reached the desert floor and saw a few rock formations, one of which was shaped like a bull. As they approached it, the sand became thick, making it more difficult to walk. The rock formation was very detailed, as if it was carved out by hand. It had two long horns going out to its sides, a hole for the mouth, indentions for the eyes, and two small lumps on top forming ears. The group was astonished as they surveyed the stone.

"Do you think somebody made this?" asked Bane.

Bojah examined the formation and slid his hand over the smooth surface. He did not respond for some time. "It's possible. But this here rock is too smooth with no chippin of any kind." He pointed to the ground. "I found that thing right thur." Naughton examined the ground closely, but there was nothing but sand and small pebbles. Zealot and Bane walked around the formation and found nothing either. Zealot walked up to the rock formation and felt around, looking for engravings, but nothing was there.

"You're sure you found it here, Bojah?" asked Tirus.

"Yup, half of it was buried in this here sand." The group examined the formation all day with no luck as the sun bared down on them. That night they made camp, curling around a small fire since there was little wood from the shrubs. The night was cold and silent with no wind blowing. They ate small rations of food and drank very little water.

"Go easy on the water," said Anor. "We don't know how long we'll be stuck out here." Zealot got up and made a small torch, heading back to the bull.

"Give it a rest, Zealot," said Bane. Zealot ignored him and guided the torch along the whole surface, looking for indentions. He climbed the formation and rubbed the horns and ears looking for any clues or grooves, but had no luck and slid back down. When he reached the front where the mouth was, he rubbed his hand in the hole, but only sand fell out. Defeated, he turned to walk away when he noticed the remaining sand crystals reflecting odd shapes. Zealot rubbed the hole again and felt small grooves where it had been filled in. He took a deep breath and blew the remaining sand out. There was a clear outline of a missing stone, surrounded by an engraved message.

Zealot screamed, jumping up and down. "I found it! I found it!" The group was startled, tripping over their gear. Sand flew up in the air as they ran to Zealot. He pointed the torch toward the hole, allowing the group to see the small engravings. Naughton ran back to get the small broken tablet and gave it to Bane. As Zealot held the torch Bane placed the broken tablet along the jagged edges. It fit perfectly.

"What does it say?" asked Tirus. Zealot and Bane examined it closely and then looked at each other with confusion.

"What does it say?" Anor repeated, frustrated.

Bane responded in a low voice. "It says, 'The sword leads the way.'"

Naughton rubbed his hand over the words. "That's all it says?"

"There must be more!" demanded Tirus.

"That's all there is," said Bane. Zealot handed the torch to Bane and walked away to think. The group followed him like stray dogs, desperate.

He noticed them following and rolled his eyes. "What's wrong with you people? Give me time to think. Get over here, Bane!" Bane walked up to Zealot while the others went back to the fire. The group sat in silence, waiting patiently for their companions to return.

Anor pulled out his pipe. "I told my wife I'd quit, but I'll go insane if I don't settle my nerves." Naughton and Tirus began telling riddles to pass the time. Bojah was fast asleep, curled up in his blanket and snoring like a bear without a care in the world.

After three hours, the scholars returned. The group stared at them, waiting for an answer. Anor puffed on his pipe, letting out a ring of smoke. He chuckled and crossed his arms. "Let me guess...you have no idea?"

Zealot shook his head. "No idea."

Tirus threw sand up in the air. "Well, that's just great! All of Bezinar will fall because you can't figure it out!"

Anor blew smoke in Tirus's face. "Shut up! Like you can do any better." Zealot and Bane laid down thinking about the riddle.

Naughton went over and sat next to Zealot. "What sword is it referring to?"

"That's the problem. There are tons of battles using swords in the Bindings of El, but the riddle is so vague."

Naughton began thinking, repeating the words over and over in his mind. Under his breath he spoke. "The sword...leads...the way." He sat up and spoke louder. "A soldier's common weapon is a sword, and it leads the way in battle."

Zealot shook his head. "Spears and bows are used first in every battle, so technically, swords are the last things used for close combat." Zealot yelled, "Anor, wake up!"

"...What it is?"

"In battle you used your swords last, correct?"

"Uh, why?"

"Just answer the question!"

Anor grunted, turning over. "Not us. The Centores use whatever weapon they wished. The common soldiers never unsheathed their swords until the enemy was close, though. Now shut up so I can sleep!" Anor punched his blanket to form a pillow and laid his head down once again. Naughton pulled out his bow, holding it tight, and bent the tips. Time seemed to stand still, yet the stars moved above.

Naughton put his bow away. "So swords don't lead the way in battle. But why does the riddle say that?"

Zealot snapped his fingers. "Perhaps it's referring to another rock formation?"

Bane was listening in. "I saw no other rock formations." They pondered for several hours, their eyelids getting heavy, until eventually the fire burned out and everyone fell asleep.

The next morning brought no answer as everyone shared their thoughts. The heat took its toll on the group, and they found some shade under the rock formation. Finally, the heat subsided as the sun set and revealed the stars. The cold quickly replaced the scalding heat, but the group welcomed it as they stared at the fire. Shadows danced from their silhouettes as they sat and pondered. One by one they laid their heads down, giving in to their weariness.

They were startled when Bojah got up and stretched. "Well, you ain't figured it out, eh?" No one responded. "Well, I'm sure it will come to ya." Bojah looked up. "Them stars sure are bright out here, especially when…oh, what's em group of stars called?"

"What does it look like?" asked Naughton.

"Well, let's see here, he's got a bow in his hand shooting at a bull."

Naughton raised an eyebrow. "He's shooting at a bull?"

"Yup, me son loved em stars. He taught me all about em." Naughton suddenly recalled his lessons with his father about using constellations at night as a point of reference. He crossed his legs and rubbed his chin. "I wonder if--" He cut himself off and looked up at the stars. "The constellation Orion shoots at a--" Naughton's eyes widened with excitement.

Bane woke up. "What are you blabbering about?"

"Bane, does the constellation Orion have a sword in it?"

"Yes, but it--" he paused and his eyes widened. "The sword hangs from his belt."

Zealot jumped up. "That's it! Orion's sword leads the way!" Anor and Tirus woke up to laughter as their friends danced around like wild monkeys.

Anor shook his head. "I told you, Tirus, that the heat would eventually get to them."

"Get up, you two!" yelled Naughton. "We solved the riddle!"

"What is it?"

"Orion's sword."

Bane stopped gathering his gear and looked at Anor, who was sitting still. "What are you doing?"

"You might as well get some sleep and wait for tomorrow night."

"Why?" asked Zealot.

"Are you people that ignorant? We must wait until Orion is on the horizon to get an accurate destination. Besides, I refuse to cross a desert in the middle of the day." With that, the group lay down in wait for the following night.

After fighting the heat all day and hiding in the shadows of boulders, the group watched the sun finally set, revealing the stars once again. Two hours after sunset, Orion began to emerge, revealing his shoulders and bow. The group had their packs on, ready for Orion to reveal their destination with the sword hanging from his belt. Orion's belt came into view, making the group more anxious. "Why is it taking so long?" asked Tirus.

Bane patted him on the shoulder. "Have patience." Finally, the sword's tip touched the horizon.

Anor clapped his hands. "Everybody stay behind me and do not go astray." Anor led the group at a fast pace.

Naughton caught up to Anor. "How far do you think we will have to walk?"

"Hopefully not far. We only have enough water for about four more days. This desert will cook us alive."

The sand and rolling hills made it difficult to keep up the pace. Their thigh and calf muscles began to burn after a few hours and Anor slowed down. Naughton somehow was not getting tired, leaving the group behind.

Anor yelled at him to wait. "What's your hurry?"

"Just anxious, I guess."

"That's a good thing, but keep in mind we have other riddles to solve and we don't know what awaits us. Save your energy. I'm sure your father would do the same thing you're doing." Naughton slowed his pace and looked at Anor concerned. Anor patted his back. "Your father is strong and wise. I'm sure he's fine."

The night was calm as they hiked through the sand, with sounds of heavy breathing and sand moving under their feet. Orion was behind them as the sun's rays pierced the sky. It tired them, knowing the sun was about to be overhead. The group pulled their hoods over their heads to keep the sun from baking them. Anor raised his hand. "We need to stop."

"Stop? What for?" asked Bane.

"I don't want to lose my heading."

"You mean you can't remember the way?"

"I can estimate, but the slightest miscalculation

can lead astray. It's hard to keep a straight heading with these rolling sand hills." Naughton agreed, and convinced the others that it was a wise decision. The group used their swords and bows as stakes, connecting all their blankets to make shelter from the sun. While they hid under their small shelters, Naughton heard a strange howling sound. He looked around, and in the far distance he saw a sand tornado coming.

"Take down the blankets!"

"What for?" asked Anor.

"Can you not hear it?"

"Hear wut?" asked Bojah.

Bane looked at Naughton with wonder. "How did you hear that?"

"I don't understand how you did not hear it! It's so loud!"

Tirus put on his pack. "Run!"

Anor clenched his jaw. "Absolutely not! We will lose our bearing! Dig a hole as deep as you can and cover yourselves with your cloaks. We must take our chances." The group started digging as the twister got closer. They covered themselves and curled up in a ball, staying close together. As it approached, the roar got louder, like a roll of multiple thunders from a storm. The air pressure changed, making their ears pop as the sand started to hit them. The sand blasted their skin through their cloaks like bee stings. Naughton could barely make out any light as the sand covered him, and before long there was total darkness. The ground shook and sand shifted rapidly around them for what felt like an eternity. Then, suddenly, it was over. There was dead silence and Naughton began to move, shifting the sand off his back so he could raise his head. He pulled off his hood and looked around, but his friends were nowhere to be seen. The sky was clear and the ground was smooth, with only a few small ripples indicating what had happened. Naughton's heart sank as he imagined his friends sucked away by the twister, but suddenly, the sand beside him moved and up popped Bojah's head.

"Well...that be a first."

Next popped Anor, his red beard full of sand. "That blasted thing nearly killed us!" They dug for their companions and one by one they found them all.

Zealot spat sand out of his mouth. "This place is cursed for sure!"

"Where did it go?" asked Tirus.

"Who cares as long as it's gone," said Anor. He shook the sand off his cloak. "Let's rebuild the shelter."

After the shelter was constructed, Tirus began

pacing. "This is a waste of time. We're going to get killed sitting around like this."

"Sometimes waiting is a good use of time," said Bane.

"You need to quit walking around," said Anor. "The Seraph Lands are no place to wander."

"Blah blah blah, you people worry too much." Tirus continued walking. He made it about thirty feet away when suddenly the sand slowly shifted from under his feet. He picked his feet up, trying to get out, but he sank faster and faster. "I...have a problem." They ran over and he put his hands up. "No, stop! Don't come any closer."

"Just stay calm," said Naughton.

Tirus's lip curled into a snarl. "Easy for you to say. You don't have sand going up the crack of your ass!" Zealot ran to get rope. Tirus was now waist deep in sand. Anor pulled his long sword out for Tirus to hold on to. He grabbed the blade, trying not to cut himself. "Ouch! Damn you, Anor. Why do you sharpen this thing so much?"

Anor shook his head. "I told you to quit walking around."

"Oh, shut up and get me out of this!" Tirus had sunk to his head, with his arms sticking out like a small gopher. He held onto the blade while Zealot came running back with the rope. He threw the rope to Tirus and the group pulled. Slowly but surely, Tirus slid out of the quicksand. They all lay down under the shelter, catching their breath. Tirus took off his clothes and shook out the sand.

Bane laughed. "I told you waiting is the best option sometimes." Tirus ignored him and continued to shake out the sand.

"I think I've had enough action for one day," said Anor. "Nobody move a muscle."

As they waited for darkness, Anor wanted to finish his conversation with Bojah about the Centore armor he had built. He crawled to him and propped his head up with his hand. "How many more armored suits did you make, Bojah?"

"Well, let's see…I reckon over two hundred now."

"Are you serious?"

"Yup, yur King paid me well so I made more."

"I--I don't understand. Why has the King been silent on this matter? I am certain unit three got that armor, for theirs is different than ours. How is this armor improved?"

"Yur King told me not to say."

Anor was furious but did not pursue the matter. Zealot sat next to Bojah. "Can I ask you a question about your son?" Bojah grunted with little enthusiasm.

"When this book was given to him did he describe who gave it?"

"All he said was that a man dressed in a teal cloak gave it to him. He said his face looked different than ours."

"Different in what way?"

"He said his eyes be a strange gold color, and he saw a glimpse of shiny armor under his cloak." Zealot asked no more questions, fearing that talking about his son would make Bojah angry.

They ate and drank small rations, waiting all day for Orion to reveal their destination once again. When the sword revealed the way, they quickened their pace. Naughton led the way this time, with Anor right behind him. After several hours of walking, Naughton thought he could see an image on the horizon that looked like a mountain range. As the night passed, the group became tired as they fought the sand and rolling hills once again. Naughton did not slow down as the group tired, but then Anor reminded him of their past conversation, making him slow his pace.

By sunrise they had reached the end of the desert, and Naughton found his eyes had not deceived him: a large ridge lay before them, stretching north to south as far as the eye could see. A narrow valley with a ridge on each side was ahead of them, forming a small canyon that had a dead end. The ridges were covered with only a few rocks and shrubs. The group began searching for clues, looking all along the ground and small rocks that sparkled gold. After hours of searching, no clues were found. "I guess I miscalculated our destination," said Anor. Zealot shook his head, refusing to believe that.

"No, you didn't. Have faith. It's here somewhere, we just have to keep looking."

Naughton threw his gear on the ground. "Everything looks the same. I hate this place already."

The day seemed hotter than usual making sweat pour off of them. Before long, everyone was soaked and using their cloaks to keep the sweat out of their eyes. Bane continued to walk around and examine the area. When he got tired, he spotted the only flat rock in the valley and sat on it. He wiped his face again, wringing the sweat out from his cloak. After resting he stood up and glanced around. As he did he saw the wet spots on the rock and his sweat had revealed strange markings. He looked closer and took some water from his pack and poured a little on the flat surface. Instantly, words appeared.

Bane gasped. "I--I found it! I found the next one!" The group ran to him, and Bane pointed at the rock. "Look, there are words here!"

"How did you find it?" asked Naughton.

"My sweat hit the stone and I saw markings."

Tirus wrinkled his nose and crossed his arms. "Nasty."

Zealot looked at it closely. "Pour more water, there are more words." Bane poured small drops of water, being cautious not to use too much. The words appeared as if they were just written. "Those who believe respect Holy ground and will bear good fruit," Zealot translated. The group began to ponder while Anor constructed a shelter. Zealot saw him and laughed. "I guess you think we'll be here for a while?"

"The way you scholars are? Absolutely."

"Ye of little faith, eh?" asked Bane.

"Of course not. I just have common sense," replied Anor, pulling out his blanket for shelter. They built their shelters, trying to stay out of the blistering sun. When it began to set, Naughton and Bojah began building a fire.

"Bojah, I never asked you. What was your son's name?" Bojah grunted, ignoring him, so Naughton left him alone and went to gather wood from nearby bushes. After everyone gathered around the fire, Anor called everyone's attention.

"I hate to bring this up, but if we don't find

water soon, we will be in some serious trouble."

"Maybe I can go looking for water tomorrow if we haven't solved the riddle," said Naughton.

"Absolutely not," said Tirus. "Did you not learn from my predicament yesterday?" The group laughed.

"Don't worry, we'll find it," Zealot said with confidence.

Naughton grimaced. "I'm glad you feel confident about it. This land looks so barren."

The group sat around the small fire, staring at the flames dancing. "Has anyone got an idea about this riddle?" asked Bane. No one said a word, leaving only the sound of the fire crackling. Zealot flipped through the pages, looking for hints.

Naughton said the phrase out loud. "Those who believe respect Holy ground and bare good fruit. What does it mean, 'those who believe'?"

"It is referring to believers of El," said Bane.

"So you're saying only believers can solve this?"

"It seems that way," said Zealot. "The Bindings of El say that true believers bare good fruit."

"What kind of fruit?" asked Anor.

"Not actual fruit, it's talking about the person. Those who believe and do El's will are filled with righteousness, therefore possessing good character--in other words, good fruit."

"That sounds ridiculous," grunted Tirus. "So you're saying that those who believe and have good character are superior to others?"

"Of course not! It's talking about how a believer has the power to show others the love of El."

Anor scratched his head, puffing his pipe. "It can't be just that. There are many elements that can sustain good fruit, such as water, the sun, and good dirt."

Bojah laughed. "Yur sure nuff a nut. Dirt ain't its proper name. It's called soil ."

Anor smirked. "Either way, it allows plants to grow. You of all people should know, working with elements of the earth as you do."

Zealot crossed his arms. "It has nothing to do with actual fruit, I tell you."

"What's this holy ground business?" asked Naughton.

"It means that when El enters an area, it becomes holy ground. Those who believe are allowed to be near or on the ground that is holy." Bane answered, but his tone was unsure.

"So yur sayin that only a righteous person can be standin on this holy ground thing?" asked Bojah.

"I think so," said Zealot.

"But the riddle says those who respect holy ground," said Naughton.

"If you're a believer, you will respect holy ground," said Zealot.

"What if you're not chosen or a true believer when you stand on it?"

"You probably die," said Bane.

Bojah laid down. "In other words, ya better be a bucket fulla of sunshine."

Zealot shook his head and rolled his eyes at Bojah. "Well, at least we have an idea."

Tirus threw another log on the fire and plopped down with a loud thud. "Are you serious? You don't have a clue! How are we supposed to find holy ground?"

Zealot curled up in his cloak. "You have a point. We need to find where the holy ground is in order to reveal the path."

"But how?" yelled Tirus. Anor glared at him, and Tirus crossed his arms in silence.

Naughton tucked his knees under his chin, rocking back and forth. "You said respect holy ground. How is that done, exactly?"

Zealot and Bane looked at each other, murmuring. Zealot cocked his head to the side. "There are various ways, from what I remember.

Sacrificing a pure animal, bringing gifts, giving offerings of gold and other items that are sacred."

"Why don't we just pour more water around that flat rock to see if there are any more clues?" asked Tirus.

Anor yanked the water from him. "Absolutely not! Water is precious to us, and we have none to spare for such actions. Besides, you're just guessing now, and I am not willing to take such risks on a guess."

The next morning the sun was unbearable as it shone down on the group. The water seemed to slowly vanish from their sacks as the day waged on. Naughton gazed at the ridges towering above them on both sides. It began to make him feel trapped, as if they were closing in on him. "Ya better get to solvin before we fry like chickens," said Bojah.

Zealot wiped his face, looking for any indication of holy ground. A stone got in his boot, so he sat down to take it off and shake it out. As he watched the rock hit the ground, he noticed a nearby plant starting to form fruit and flowers in front of his very eyes. He stopped and stared at the plant, mesmerized.

Anor noticed his silence. "What's the matter?"

"Did that plant have fruit on it earlier?"

Anor walked over. "I don't know, why?"

"I think I'm seeing things. This plant did not have flowers or fruit on it before, and now all of a sudden it does."

Anor gave him a drink from his water sack. "I think you're getting too hot my friend, perhaps you should rest."

Zealot took a drink. "Wait, let me try something." He took off his other boot and walked closer to the plant, and it bloomed, creating more fruit.

Anor stood up and rubbed his eyes, astonished. "I'll be--"

Zealot interrupted, "Don't curse, you idiot!" Everyone ran over, wiping the sweat from their eyes.

"Watch this," said Anor, pointing at the plant. Zealot stepped closer to the plant, and instantly the flowers and fruit got bigger. The group stood over him in shock. Naughton pulled a piece of fruit off and tasted it. It was sweet and delicious, like nothing he had ever tasted before. Naughton looked around and the other small bushes had no flowers or fruit.

Zealot got up and looked at the other plants. As he walked, certain plants bloomed with fruit and flowers, all the way up the northeast end of the ridge. Everyone else took their boots off, but nothing happened.

"I would say that solves the riddle," said Bane.

Zealot shook his head and looked at his feet. "How is this possible? Surely there are others who believe."

"Apparently you are chosen," said Naughton. Zealot felt odd and out of place, as if he were an alien among his own kind.

Forged

Jesper's unit came rolling in with the sun peering above the horizon. Plonus stopped the wagon and the men spilled out, cheering while the other leaders and men stood speechless, wondering how they did it. Thorg ordered Plonus to take the wagon back to the goat herders and release them. He gave Plonus some money. "Be sure to pay the goat herders for their trouble, or I'll never hear the end of it from the King." Plonus drove off, and Thorg gave orders for all the men to get in formation. The leaders stood in front as usual, waiting for orders.

Gideon elbowed Jesper, whispering, "How did you do it?"

"I considered the citizens part of the training exercise." Gideon and Marxus laughed, feeling stupid. Thorg and his training Centores stood in front, discussing an issue for several minutes. Thorg faced the men.

"Alright, boneheads. We have orders from King Irus that have been brought to my attention that we must discuss. Leaders, have these men eat, rest, and be in formation in the morning before sunrise." The leaders took their squads and carried out their orders.

An hour before the men were to be roused, a Centore woke up the leaders and brought them to

Thorg. They went into the room that said Red Shoulders Only. In the room was a display of armor behind glass, ranging from the past to the present. The room was full of shields and swords hanging on the wall, with names under them of who used them. On the far end, they saw a red shoulder Centore armor on display and Jesper walked over to it. Under the display it read, In honor of Tulios. Jesper froze, having mixed emotions of excitement and horror. He thought to himself, there must have been another with his name...and besides, I was told he died in Yorben. Suddenly, Thorg entered the room, followed by men carrying three objects covered in sheets.

He gestured at the chairs to the side. "Be seated, gentlemen." They sat down and looked at each other, confused at Thorg calling them gentlemen. Thorg smiled. "Yes, I said gentlemen. We have selected who will be a gold shoulder. Before I say who, I expect all of you to respect one another no matter what, understood?"

"Yes, sir!" they replied in unison.

"Very well. Come forward, Marxus." He stood up and Thorg walked back to one of the objects covered in a sheet. He pulled it off, and before them was silver Centore armor, brightly polished with gold shoulders. Thorg shook his hand. "Congratulations,

Marxus."

Marxus's face radiated joy. "Thank you, sir."

"You will serve with unit eight. They are stationed at the city of Valkry right now." Thorg had Marxus escorted out with his armor. Jesper and Gideon stayed seated as Thorg shut the door and sat in front of them. Thorg gripped the pommel of his sword, looking down at them. "Now for you two." He paused and looked up. "I chose you last because you will be challenged more than any of your companions. Before I show you what your armor color is, I must tell you this: Fort Yorben is under attack by a massive force of Geols and Mohai has requested assistance. Units two and six are there, but Nemian sent me a letter as well, saying that Fort Yorben will eventually fall if they don't get reinforcements. The King has dispatched soldiers there to help." Thorg walked over to the remaining covered armor and pulled the sheet revealing two sets of silver Centore armor with gold shoulders. "Gideon, you are to report to unit six in Fort Yorben." Jesper's eyes began to water as he smiled. "Jesper, you will go with him and report to unit two. You should know that there have never been three gold shoulders selected, so feel honored. Some of the men you trained with will be going with you as well."

Thorg shook their hands, congratulating them. "In two days there will be a graduation ceremony. Your families have been contacted for the event. Keep in mind that your training has been cut short, but I am confident you and the others will manage. Otherwise, I would not send you. Tomorrow you will be given your weapons and have a chance to get acquainted with them. Are there any questions?"

Jesper and Gideon said nothing, but as they walked out the door, Jesper turned around and went back in. "Sir, permission to ask you a question?"

"Took you long enough, what is it?"

"Whose armor is that on display back there?"

"Oh, you mean Tulios? He was a respected Centore of unit three."

"What happened to him?"

"You're one of us now, so I see no harm in telling you." Thorg walked to the display and crossed his arms. "Tulios was a unique man. We graduated together, but we began to clash after I was promoted to my position. He was the best Centore in history, despite his renegade attitude and his disobedience. He was the leader of unit three, and they achieved every mission they set out for. He was crafty--and above all, sneaky. Somehow he could infiltrate forts and cities without ever being detected, and at times, raise hell in the end without losing a single man. Unfortunately, he was killed in a rescue mission." Jesper's heart sank. Thorg looked at Jesper with concern. "What's the matter?"

He cleared his throat. "Nothing, sir. I'm fine. I heard rumors of that name and somehow it being related to Lady Airah."

Thorg swung his arms to his back and clasped them, looking at the display. "In some ways you remind me of him. You think and command your men in the same manner he did. Perhaps one day you will be treated with such honor and be remembered. Is there anything else I can help you with?"

"Why didn't you tell me you were over the training when I first met you?"

Thorg laughed. "That's what makes it fun. Now get out of here and try on your armor."

Jesper smiled. "Yes, sir!" He walked out, followed by a trainer Centore with his armor.

When they reached the room, the Centore hung his armor up. "Congratulations, Jesper."

"Thank you, sir."

The trainer shook his head. "Don't call me sir anymore. My name is Shokan, and it has been an honor training you." He closed the door as Jesper sat on his bed, deep in thought on the armor of Tulios.

Morning came with a knock on his door and Shokan's voice. "Jesper, you have one hour to be dressed in your armor and be outside." Jesper put the armor on, enjoying every minute of it and remembering all the suffering he went through to wear his prize. Holding his new helmet in his hands, he looked in the mirror. His armor fit him perfectly. All the joints were snug, unlike last time when he was clanging about. He looked at the helmet as if it was brand new. It was silver, with polished metal plating all around. He slid it on his head, and it fit with resistance to make it fit firm.

He looked at himself in the mirror, and right then, he knew he was finally a Centore. His cheeks were covered by broad, smooth silver plates that curved from below his chin all the way up the back of his head, where they pointed out. His jaws were protected by other silver plates that were connected to the curving cheek plates. His eyes were covered by mysterious hard glass that allowed him to see clearly from the inside, but the outer glass was solid black, keeping his eyes from being seen. The rest of his head was covered with silver metal plating to protect his skull. He left his room and made his way outside. When he opened the door, he saw his companions dressed in their shiny new armor with various colored shoulders. As he walked up, the men saluted him, and they began congratulating each other.

Litzer patted Jesper on his new gold shoulder. "Well, don't we think we're hot stuff!"

"Alright, knock it off. I see you're wearing some shiny new blue plating yourself." Plonus ran up next, wearing his green plating.

"What unit are they sending you to, Jesper?"

"I'm being sent to unit two." Plonus and Litzer looked at each other, grinning. Jesper raised an eyebrow. "Let me guess, I'm stuck with you two?"

The two laughed. "Looks like you're not going to get rid of us that easy," said Plonus.

Suddenly, Thorg's voice rang through the air. "Get in formation!" All the men darted to their places they had memorized from the very first day, standing proud with their chests poking out. Thorg stood in front while his Centore trainers walked around the group. "I must say, you look like very sharp boneheads now, and I am glad to get rid of you people." A grin began to form on his lips. "I would like to congratulate every one of you today. You have overcome the hardest obstacles in your life. You are graduating early due to recent events, but from this day forward, you are now Centores. You will always be highly honored and feared by the kingdom and its allies. No matter what enemy you face, they will remember who you are after walking over their dead companions." Thorg's face changed to a stern look and his jaw clenched. "Some or all of you may die in battle. Some or all of you will grow old and retire, with your grandchildren sitting on your lap, telling stories of your life. When they ask you what you did during the great Geol War, you don't have to tell them you sat idly by and did nothing! No matter how your days end, your names will be remembered as Guardians in the pages of history. Tomorrow, your family members will be brought here for the ceremony. After five days with your family, you will leave to go to your assigned units. Follow your trainers to the armory and they will equip you with your weapons. After being equipped, you will do drills with your new weapons and armor." Thorg cocked his head to the side with a grin. "Move!"

The men followed the Centore instructors and got their weapons. The gold shoulders were last. They were given their shields first, which were made from a metal ore they had never seen before. It was solid silver with a leaf symbol in the center. Shokan handed Jesper his sword, which he recognized as the sword given to him at Fort Yorben, with a few modifications. The sword's hilt was polished, with a gold emerald placed on the bottom of the handle. The curved blade was so polished that he could see his face in it. He slid the blade along his arm and it shaved the hair off. The teeth on top curving back toward the hilt were sharpened as well. He sheathed it, going back outside where he saw Marxus and Gideon talking.

They both greeted Jesper, and Gideon pulled out his sword. "Have a look at this, Jesper." Gideon's blade was identical to Jesper's.

"It's just like mine."

Marxus crossed his arms. "All leaders' swords are identical."

"What's the difference between ours and the other swords?" asked Jesper.

"The others have no teeth on top of the blade."

Sometime later, Thorg called the men to get in formation and began doing drills, making them move as a single unit. Their new shields were lighter than the wooden ones, allowing them to be more agile and move much quicker. Thorg continued screaming commands. "Threat left! Threat right! Threat forward! Stride forward! Stride backwards!" The men moved as one, like a giant snake, protecting one another in all directions when the command was given. As they ran through the exercises, they anticipated the command they struggled with the most: the bubble. Finally,

Thorg yelled, "Bubble!" The men bunched up, remembering their places and putting their shields up to form a giant ball that allowed nothing to get through. Thorg and his trainers walked around them, looking for gaps, but no hole was discovered. Thorg bellowed, "Recover!" The men got back in formation in seconds, tireless. Thorg was smiling, clearly pleased with the men. "Now you see why we ran you so much! Endurance is the key to victory. If one man gets tired and allows one hole in any shield formation, you're all dead! The burning powder has taught you to stay together and cover each other. And, let's say one of you is hit with an arrow or sword. The burning powder has increased your pain tolerance. Gold shoulders, listen well: if one man is slacking, punish him in your fashion. I don't care if he dies during the punishment, I'd rather him die than get everyone killed!"

Thorg had the men dismissed to polish their armor again for the celebration. Not one man slept the whole night in the barracks as they prepared for the ceremony and told stories on each other. While his comrades prepared, Jesper was nowhere to be found. Gideon had an idea where he was. He went to the building with the armor displays. When he opened the door there was no light. He began to close it, and then

413

heard a whisper. "What are doing here, Gideon?" He looked in again and saw Jesper lighting a candle.

"You shouldn't be in here. Thorg will rip your head off."

"How did you know I was in here?"

Gideon closed the door lightly. "You can't hide anything from me. I know you too well. I saw your face when you saw this display and I knew something was going on."

Jesper returned to staring at the display. "To be honest, I don't know what to think." Gideon stood beside him, waiting for an answer. Jesper touched the glass.

Gideon squinted, looking at the name plate at the bottom. "Did you know this man?"

"I'm not sure."

"Was he a relative or something?" Jesper heard footsteps and blew out the candle, grabbing Gideon and hiding behind the display. The door opened, and in walked a Centore trainer carrying a spear. He put it in the corner of the room and walked out. "We need to leave, Jesper." Jesper lit the candle again and stared at the armor. Gideon became agitated. "How do you know this man?"

"Can you keep a secret my friend?"

"Yes, yes, but hurry up! We need to leave

before we are discovered!"

Jesper glared at the helmet and then blew out the candle. "I think this armor belonged to my father."

"Your father...now it makes sense. You're afraid of dishonoring him?"

"Yes, and if this was my father, how can I keep such a secret?"

"I strongly suggest you leave it be for now. Let us be off!" Gideon and Jesper snuck out without being discovered and reported back to the men.

Marxus saw them walking up from the darkness. "Where have you two been?"

"Talking about upcoming events, why?" asked Gideon.

"A Centore trainer came by and did a head count, but he seemed to not care that you two were missing."

Jesper shrugged his shoulders. "We're gold shoulders now, so we have some flexibility, I guess. Let's go finish getting ready for tomorrow." The three joined the rest of the men and had a small celebration in honor of their last night together.

By mid-morning a crowd had gathered, with wagons still coming in full of people. The forty-two men were getting anxious as they peeked from the windows of the barracks, seeing their families waiting. By noon, the last convoy was the King's open chariot, with his royal guards along side. Thorg entered the barracks dressed in his armor. His silver armor was brightly polished and his red-armored shoulders were the color of blood, with a silver sword imprinted on each side. He stood with a different demeanor than what they were accustomed to. His face had a smirk and his chest poked out with pride.

"Get in lines!" The men got in three lines with the gold shoulders in front, then the blue shoulders, the green shoulders, and finally the orange shoulders. Their weapons were strapped on, and they were ready to march out into the crowd. Thorg got in front and made his last statement to the men. "Gentlemen, today is the last day you will all be together, unless we are all united again in battle. Remember what we taught you and always remember the code. It has been an honor training you. Let me finish by saying this." Suddenly, Thorg started singing the song that he taught them while they were training. Al the men instantly joined in as the doors opened and they marched outside.

"Call out the army, call out the calvary, we will be standing long after they're dead! Death before dishonor, glory to the Creator, Centores never die!

We are the leaders, we will defend, we will never surrender, we would rather die. Death before dishonor, glory to the Creator, Centores never die! Centores never die...!"

The sun beamed in Jesper's eyes, making him squint. His stomach felt tight with anticipation, and joy filled his heart knowing the training was all over. Yet, he felt all alone. Not one relative was present, nor was Lady Airah. He had never felt so nervous, for every eye was on him and his brothers. The crowd watched in awe as the new Centores marched in unison, their armor shining in the sun. Thorg marched them into the middle of the crowd, making them move to give the Centores space for their upcoming display to the crowd.

When Thorg was satisfied, he yelled, "Formation!" The Centores got in position, ready for battle, holding up their new silver shields with leaf imprints on them. Thorg took several paces back and gave commands to the unit. "Threat behind! Threat left! Stride right! Advance! Hold!" The new Centores moved as one, all shifting to protect each other with a quick graceful motion. The light flickered from their moving shields as every command was given. The men's nerves settled as they concentrated on the commands. "Bubble!" Thorg finally yelled. This time, the men moved as fast as lightning, remembering where to go to create the impenetrable defense.   The crowd stood in awe as the Centores formed a shiny silver bubble that had no holes or gaps. Thorg waited for a minute to let the crowd examine the bubble defense and then yelled, "Recover!" The Centores recovered in seconds, standing back in formation, ready for orders. Thorg raised his hand and the Centores relaxed with a loud cheer from the crowd. Thorg went up on a wooden podium overlooking the crowd.

"Greetings, Bezinarians! It is an honor to present to you today your forty-two new Centores. These men have overcome the hardest training ever known to man, and they will become the finest warriors the world has ever known." Thorg gestured his hand to the men and to the crowd. "These men, including you, will be highly honored for the rest of their lives. They have fulfilled the requirements of being Centores. You should be proud of them, not only because they became Centores, but because they are willing to risk their lives to protect what we hold dear--our freedom. May our mighty El, the Creator of all things, watch over them and give them the strength to smash our enemies into dust!" Thorg looked at the men. "As of today, you are officially

Centores. Make us proud. Death before dishonor! Dismissed!"

The crowd cheered as the men disbanded banging their shields with their swords as they made their way to their families. The families gave hugs to their new heroes as conversations began. Jesper looked around, feeling hollow, for no one was there to congratulate him except the King. He walked over to Gideon. "I'll see you in five days."

Gideon punched his shoulder. "Five days, brother." Jesper went to King Irus, taking off his helmet, and the guards allowed him through.

The King stood up. "Well done, Jesper! I must say, that was an excellent performance, and I am sorry that Airah is not here to see your graduation."

Jesper bowed. "I am grateful that you came."

The King smiled. "Which unit were you assigned?"

"Unit two, sir."

"I see. And how long do you have before you are due to report?"

"Five days, sir."

The King clasped his hands. "To the castle! We must celebrate!" Jesper gave a big smile and sat next to the King as the royal guards took positions around his chariot, escorting them back to the castle.

As they approached the front gate, cheering could be heard on the streets. The gates opened and petals fell all around the chariot from above. As they entered the kingdom, the people surrounded them, cheering. Chants filled the city as the chariot went down the street. Joy filled Jesper's heart. "They honor you, Sire."

"No, Jesper, it is you they honor. They knew today you were graduating."

"But I don't know these people."

The King laughed and patted Jesper on the shoulder. "They know you. Stand up and see for yourself." Jesper stood up and the people cheered even louder and started clapping their hands. Jesper felt tingly all over, at a loss of what to do. The King nudged him and motioned for him to wave. Jesper began waving to people in all directions as the chariot went down the main street, back to the castle. Children were chasing the chariot and the guards allowed them to run along side, shaking Jesper and King Irus's hands. As they started to leave the main street, a bouquet of flowers landed on Jesper's lap. He looked up, and there on a balcony stood his little friend Nihyah, waving at him. Jesper blew a kiss to her and waved.

After the warm greeting, the chariot went

through the castle gate. Jesper noticed that the guards were saluting him. The guards escorted them to the main doors as the King entered the castle. Jesper followed, with the royal guards taking positions all along the great hall.

The King turned around before going up the stairs. "Today is about you, Jesper, for I know what challenges await you. Tonight we will celebrate in the dinner hall, and I have something in store for you." The King continued going upstairs to his chamber. Jesper went to his quarters, finding his room cleaned with fresh clothes awaiting him. As he went through the clothes, there was a knock on the door. He opened it, and there stood a servant holding a black robe with a shield patch on it, just like what Thorg wore the first day he saw him.

The servant bowed. "You forgot your robe, Centore."

He took it and smiled. "Thank you."

"The pleasure is all mine." The servant left, and Jesper noticed that his black robe was slightly different from the one he'd seen on Thorg. There was a gold sword patch on the left side of the chest with his name on it. He took off his armor and put on the robe. It fit perfectly, covering his whole body and hanging just above the floor. He left his room to take a stroll around the castle. As he walked, the guards saluted him, allowing him to go wherever he desired. He went to Airah's room to see how his gifts were doing. As he entered, he saw the flowers he left her were dead. The very sight of them made him sulk, but as he started to leave, he saw the Curado plant on her balcony. It was ready to burst open its red and gold petals. The green leaves looked fresh and were broad, soaking the rays from the sun.

He left the room and a guard saluted him. "She will return, sir." Jesper smiled as he walked down the stairs and went to the main hall. He stood there staring at the giant pillars of old kings. He gazed at them for a few moments, wondering who they were, and then he felt a tap on his shoulder. He looked around and saw Felden, standing with a big smile. He was dressed in a light brown coat with a green tunic underneath. His hair was well groomed with a short pointy beard.

"Well, I see you're something special now."

Jesper hugged him. "It's wonderful to see you! Where have you been?"

"I've been traveling back and forth from cities and forts to keep track of the Geols' movements."

"I heard they're massing a large force to take Fort Yorben, is that true?"

Felden cocked his head. "Where did you

acquire this information?"

"From Thorg."

"He is correct, somewhat. The Geols have two large armies, one at Fort Yorben and the other at the city of Valkry. They will take Fort Yorben one way or another, but I know Mohai will not make it easy for them. Valkry, on the other hand, will be a great challenge for the Geols. The army gathered there is of no concern. I think they're trying to distract us from their other objective. It would take a number beyond reckoning to take Valkry."

Jesper gave a smirk. "I will be seeing Mohai soon, and I will be helping him with that task."

Felden's face went blank. "You're going there to fight?"

"I'm certainly not going there to play card games."

Felden was speechless at first, but finally spoke. "Which unit are you assigned to?"

"Unit two, and this time, I will be ready."

Felden raised an eyebrow, concerned. "Nemian has killed many Geols with his unit sneaking across the Suriu River at night, and has only lost two so far. That is incredible, I must say, but our army is losing men every day holding the river. Our archers are making it difficult for the Geols as they build more bridges, but it won't be long before the Geols overrun the Suriu River and attack Fort Yorben. I will be returning there in six days to get reports from my Shadow Scouts."

"Perhaps you can come with me and my men. We're leaving in five days."

Felden shrugged his shoulders. "I don't see why not. It would be great to travel with an old friend. I hear tonight you're having a celebration for your graduation?"

Jesper nodded. "I can't believe the King is doing that for me."

"It is no secret he favors you, Jesper, and I will plan on being there. For now, however, you must excuse me. I have a few errands to run." Felden bowed and left, going out the back door of the main hall.

Jesper continued walking around the castle and decided to take a detour through the city. As he walked out, he and the guards saluted each other. He walked to the stables and pet the horses for a while, thinking about the first time he met Airah. He laughed to himself, thinking about what she said to he and Naughton the first time they met. He walked down the city streets and enjoyed the scenery of folks smiling, coming and going. It reminded him of how

Sturkma use to be before it fell. He continued on, forgetting the troubles of the world. As he approached the center courtyard full of markets, he felt a pull on his cloak. He looked down, and there stood Nihyah, smiling at him in an orange dress. "Mr. Jesper, I see you're wearing a fancy robe now. Turn around and let me have a look at you!" Jesper smiled as he turned around. "I must say you look spectookalar--um, I mean spectugalar--oh good grief, you know what I'm trying to say."

Jesper laughed. "Thank you for the flowers."

She smiled as she bowed. "It was nothing, Mr. Jesper. Oh, by the way, did Lady Airah like her flowers?"

Jesper hid his sadness. "I'm afraid she has not returned from her trip."

Nihyah put her hands up to her face. "Wow, I bet those flowers look like dirt clobs now, ha ha! We need to fix that. Come with me." He followed her back to the store, and as he entered, Nihyah's mother hugged him.

"My goodness, Jesper, you look wonderful. I am honored that a handsome gentlemen like yourself is in my store once again."

Jesper felt himself turn red. "I believe I owe you money." He handed her fifty shekels.

She looked down. "But you already gave me thirty."

"I know, but it's the least I can do for all the service I'm getting from Nihyah."

Jesper patted her on the head, but she pushed his hand away. "What are you doing? I'm no dog. Shake my hand, goofy!"

"I'm terribly sorry."

Nihyah's mother stuck out her hand. "I didn't get a chance to introduce myself last time. My name is Sarai."

Jesper shook her hand. "The honor is mine, and thank you for your generosity."

Nihyah came running up with red roses. "Here you go, Jesper. Make sure she gets them before they die this time!"

He took the roses. "How much are they?"

"This one's on the house, brave Centore," said Sarai.

Jesper bowed and Nihyah hugged him as he started to leave. "Come back to see us."

"Always," he replied, with a big smile.

Jesper made his way back to the courtyard. By late afternoon he reached the castle and went straight to his quarters. He put the roses in a vase and filled it with water. He started to leave for Airah's room, but changed his mind. Instead, he put them on the table and lay down. "I think I will enjoy them, she won't see them anyway."

He fell asleep, enjoying the soft bed and pillow, which were unlike that hard bed he had during training. His mind flashed to all the pain he went through and he remembered his first day on the Centore grounds. He began to dream he was back in Sturkma, chopping wood and inhaling the smell of fresh cut timber.

Several hours had passed when he woke to a knock on the door. "It is not custom for one to be late to their own celebration," Felden said, once Jesper opened the door.

Jesper shook his head. "I must have passed out." They went downstairs and walked to the feast hall. Jesper could hear people talking and laughing, and when they opened the door, the people started to cheer. Jesper looked around, recognizing a few faces. Jesper sat down and the people followed suit.

The King held up his hand. "Jesper, I know you don't know most of these people, but alas, we can still celebrate. I am very proud of you becoming what you are, and we will eat and drink until we burst." The King clapped his hands and food was brought to the table. Everyone, including Jesper, began eating to their heart's content. Jesper missed the taste of good food, and ate slowly, enjoying the taste of every bite as the flavors soaked his tongue.

Eventually, Thorg came to sit next to him. "How does it feel to be one of us now?"

Jesper took a swallow from his mug. "It feels great, sir!"

Thorg patted him on the shoulder. "You don't have to address me like that today, Jesper. This is your day. I will be gone when you leave to go to Fort Yorben, so I will say it now: take care of yourself, and remember your training. The unit will give you trouble at first, only because you're new, but do not let them get the best of you. Remember, you're next in charge after Nemian, so act like it!" Thorg went to the King and resumed talking.

The meal came to an end and the King made a final announcement. "I appreciate all of you coming to Jesper's graduation ceremony, and I will close with this." The King stared at Jesper. "You are like a son to me, and your family raised you well. I would also like to announce that a rescue team is being organized to save Berton. It will be some time before they are ready, but perhaps you, Jesper, will be able to help them when the time comes. Thorg tells me you're good at deception and strategizing." The King winked at Jesper. "When you go to Fort Yorben, have no fear, for it is in your blood to be a great Centore."

The King looked down for a moment and readjusted his crown. "War is about to consume our lands from every angle. I advise everyone to be cautious. As you know, we have spies among us, and I am sure assassins will make attempts." King Irus gripped his sword. "So don't be surprised if I am hard to get in contact with." With that, King Irus stood up and the group made a toast. Everyone left after the feast, and Jesper made his way outside, taking a breath of fresh air. As he stared up at the stars and the full moon, he made a decision to make the night useful. He made his way to the stables and borrowed a horse. He rode through the streets and through the market, going to the south gate. The guards saluted him as they opened the gate. He rode through, turning left along the wall and heading to the eastern foothills enjoying the serenity.

Around midnight, the guards spotted a group approaching and stopped them at the gate. "We're sorry, but the gate is closed during night hours. You will have to wait for morning." The stranger pulled off the hood and revealed herself to be Lady Airah. The guards bowed low, apologizing as they opened the gate. Airah went first, followed by Eirmosa and four Samha guards. They made their way to the castle and put the horses they had borrowed from Fort Estmere in the stables. When they entered the castle, the royal guards bowed and allowed them passage.

The lead royal guard, McBran, approached her. "My Lady, how was the trip to Samha?"

"The journey there was well, but our return was depressing. While we traveled the Suriu River we passed many families going north leaving their homes. They said the Geols were massing at Fort Yorben. Does my uncle know of this?"

"Yes, my Lady, the King is dispatching more soldiers and Centores there."

"I see…and where is my uncle?"

"He is resting, my Lady, from the ceremony."

Airah's face was puzzled. "What ceremony?"

"Why, Jesper's graduation ceremony, of course."

"You mean they are done training?"

"Yes, my Lady. The word is Jesper leaves in four days to Fort Yorben."

Airah looked down. "Where is he now?"

"I don't know, my Lady. Perhaps in his quarters resting."

Eirmosa interrupted. "My Lady, I suggest we find a room for King Mel's guards."

"I'm sorry. McBran, see to it these men are treated as if they were one of our own."

"It will be done, my Lady."

Airah went upstairs to her room, followed by Eirmosa.

They entered and Airah paused, looking at her night stand. "He's been here." Eirmosa looked where Airah was staring and saw the dead flowers. Airah continued looking around, and then saw a plant on the balcony. She touched the leaf. "What kind of plant is this?"

Eirmosa laughed. "I'm surprised you don't know this plant. It's a Curado plant. It is a unique flora that has the power to heal, and it blooms red and gold petals."

Airah observed the plant closely, touching its soft leaves. "It seems special."

"I would say he cares for you, Airah. This plant is not easy to find, and I'm sure he had difficulty with it."

"He is kind."

Eirmosa's nose wrinkled. "Kind? Is that all you have to say?"

"What else is there to say?"

"You have no feelings for Jesper, my Lady?"

"I...don't know. I have many obligations and

other tasks to perform. I have no time for romance."
Eirmosa did not press the matter and prepared Airah's
bath.

As she went to the door to give Airah privacy,
she spoke in a low tone, "It's not my business...but if I
were you, I would at least tell him thank you in
person." With that, Eirmosa closed the door.

After taking her bath and considering Eirmosa's
words, she went to Jesper's quarters. Before knocking,
she examined herself and readjusted her red dress. She
knocked several times with no reply. She cracked the
door open and entered slowly. She saw Jesper's
Centore armor hanging up along with his shield, but
the sword was missing. There were fresh red roses
sitting on the table. "What will I tell him?" she
whispered to herself. She left, closing the door, and
started searching for Jesper.

She asked multiple guards if anyone had seen
him, but no one knew where he was. After hours of
searching, she went back to her room to find solitude.
She stood on the balcony, admiring the Curado plant
and gazing at the horizon. She looked out across the
kingdom with its empty streets and small flickering
torches. Sleepiness was coming upon her as the moon
revealed the landscape. In the far distance on one of
the foothills to her left, she saw a small glow. She

continued gazing and then looked at the plant. "I wonder…" she said to herself, before grabbing her cloak. She went downstairs going to the stables to find her horse. She jumped on with no saddle and made her way to the south gate.

The guards were shocked. "My Lady, what are you doing out here this time of night?"

She pulled the cloak over her head. "All is well, just open the gate."

The guards hesitated. "My Lady, perhaps an escort should go with you?"

Airah became agitated. "Open the gate or you will rue this day!" The guards rushed to open the gate and she trotted through, going toward the eastern foothills.

As she approached the campfire, she slid off her horse and tied it to a nearby tree. As she slowly approached the dimming fire, she saw a man lying on the ground, curled up in a blanket. She moved closer until she was almost on top of him, and then suddenly she was on the ground with a blade to her neck. Jesper was ready to thrust the sword into her, eyes glazed with sleep, before he realized who she was.

He removed the blade and backed away slowly on his knees in shock. "Airah…I could have killed you! That was--was--"

"--Stupid, I know." She leaned up, dusting herself off, and sat on the ground.

He sheathed his sword and crawled up to her. "I'm sorry, you just startled me."

She gave a warm smile. "Don't apologize. I'm the dumb one who snuck up on you."

He sat stunned and unsure of what to say, even though he had practiced his speech a hundred times. "Did you see your flowers and the plant? I was going to replace the roses, but I--"

Airah put her finger over his mouth. "I know, Jesper. I saw the flowers in your room. You don't need to do that. Suspicion will rise if you keep pursuing me like this."

Jesper stood up. "Why did you come out here?"

"I was worried about you and I haven't seen you in weeks. I heard you graduated and you are a gold shoulder. I wanted to tell you congratulations."

Jesper threw more wood on the fire to give himself time to think. "Well...thank you. How is my cousin?"

"He is well. He is on his way to the Seraph Lands. There is a team with him to help, and my uncle would not allow me or Eirmosa to go further than Samha, so here I am."

Jesper was not sure what Airah's true intentions

in coming to see him were, and he was tired of playing cat and mouse. Thinking was causing him more pain than necessary, so he went straight to the point. "Is there hope for me to win your heart, Airah?"

She stared at him, stone-face. "I'm afraid not, but I do want to be your friend if you wish it."

Jesper kneeled down, poking the fire. "I see."

"Do you? I do not wish pain upon you, Jesper. I care about you, and I will always be your friend, but I cannot offer you what you seek."

Jesper felt a cold, piercing ache go through him, as if his heart was being ripped into pieces. He wanted to scream. "Then how am I supposed to suppress my love for you?"

Airah lowered her head. "Perhaps my very presence is conflicting you."

"Don't tell me that. I'm having a hard time as it is!"

"If you cannot put aside your feelings for me, then we must not see each other anymore. I will not allow you to throw away what you worked so hard for."

Jesper tensed with anger. "It is my choice who I love!"

"Love is a strong word, Jesper, and I am flattered, but love must be returned as well. You know

I care about you. Please don't make this more difficult than it already is. You made an oath and it cannot be broken. Remember what you are now. Your loyalty is to your men and to the King. I have many responsibilities, and the war is not helping any. I have made my choice, Jesper. Please honor that."

He stood up, looking her in the eye. "As you wish." He walked away into the darkness, leaving Airah sitting by the fire.

Secrets unfold

Jesper awoke lying in a patch of grass under a tree. The sun was just above the tree line, and as he leaned forward, he saw a convoy of people walking in the southern gate. He walked back where he'd left Airah, and all that remained was the smoldering fire. He readjusted his belt and sword. "I should have known better." He got on his horse making his way to the southern gate. As he approached, he saw that the people looked exhausted and famished. Children were being carried on the shoulders of their elders with bags on their backs. The crowd moved slowly through the gates, and the streets steadily filled up as people took to laying on the sidewalks. Jesper took his time, avoiding them as he made his way to the castle. He jumped off, handing the horse to a guard as he walked in.

McBran spotted him in the grand hall. "The King has been looking for you, Jesper. He is in his throne room having a meeting." Jesper nodded and made his way to the throne room. When he entered, people were standing and facing the King, who had guards all around him. Generals and council members were close by as well, trying to aid the King with all the questions.

"My King, we come here to plead with you. These people coming from Yorben and villages are eating our food in the market without paying. How are we supposed to feed ourselves with all of these thieves walking around? We demand justice!" The King sat calmly on his throne as the villagers grumbled, loudly and angrily. Finally, he had enough.

King Irus stood up. "Silence!" he bellowed. His jaw clenched as he gripped the hilt of his sword. "You come into my hall, you yell and complain about your food, and all with such disrespect. These so-called thieves are your fellow countrymen. They have lost homes, gardens, livestock--some have lost family. You dare to come here and gripe while they starve! Why don't you help your fellow Bezinarians in the time of chaos? How would you feel if your lands were taken and you were driven from your homes?" The villagers stood in fear, looking at each other. The King put his back to the people. "That's what I thought! Leave me be and come back with proper attitudes toward your kinsmen!" The guards escorted the villagers out and the hall was left with generals and councilmen, as well as a few others.

"My King, what if we--" The King raised his hand, silencing Thorg.

The hall was silent, until finally the King let out a long, exasperated breath and looked at Thorg. "You were saying?"

"What if we set up small tents for each family in Centore Valley. There we can ship food to them and supplies for the time being."

"Make it so. Have the people informed." Thorg dispatched a messenger. The King looked at Winsto. "Have you and your fellow physicians see to the people who are ill or injured." Winsto bowed, leaving the chamber. "General Hollis, how much longer can we hold the Suriu River?"

"My King, I am not sure. The Geols--"

The King interrupted. "Answer the question please."

"Five days at the most, Sire."

"Very well, have the army fall back to Fort Yorben in four days, with Centore units two, four, and six in position to counter attack when our soldiers retreat."

Thorg interrupted, gesturing his hand. "My King, unit four is not present at Fort Yorben."

"Then have them notified immediately!" Thorg bowed and made to leave the hall, but the King stopped him. "Before you go, where are the other Centore units?"

"Unit one is here for your protection. Units five and ten have been relocated to the city of Valkry with units eight and nine after the fall of Fort Coralis.

Unit seven is stationed at Fort Estmere awaiting orders. You know where unit three is, Sire."

"Very well, you may go." Thorg bowed again and left. The King sat for several moments, thinking, while the remaining people waited. "General Abrum, can Valkry hold if the Geols strike?"

"It depends on the Geols' numbers, Sire. For now, Felden and his Shadows report a small force residing nearby. However, our army is hidden to the west, prepared to flank the Geols when signaled. As you know, Centore units are in Valkry as well, ready to fight alongside the Valkry guards."

"Very well then, dismissed." Everyone left the hall except the King and Nellium. Jesper began to approach the King, but as people filed out of the hall, he noticed Airah's presence out of the corner of his eye. He ignored her. "Ah, my niece, you had me worried. I see, however, you were well protected by the Samha guards."

"Yes, Uncle. Here is a letter from King Mel." King Irus took the letter, breaking the seal, and began to read. When he finished, he gave the letter to a servant. "King Mel is sending five thousand soldiers to aid us. They will be here in ten days. Nellium, see to it that arrangements are made for Mel's soldiers when they arrive." Nellium bowed and made his exit. As he left, he hit Jesper in the leg with his cane, giving a wink. The King wiped his face. "I'm sorry, Jesper, but it seems you will be leaving sooner than I thought."

Jesper gave a humble smile. "I expected that, Sire, and I am ready. When should I leave?"

"Tomorrow night. I will send messengers to the others." Airah's heart sank, and she wished Jesper would not leave on bad terms with her. The King slapped his forehead and waved Airah over, whispering in her ear.

She bowed. "Very well, Uncle." Jesper raised an eyebrow, but remained silent. The King stood up, leaving the throne room, followed by his royal guards. Airah gestured to Jesper to follow her.

"Where are we going?" asked Jesper.

"Patience, young Centore."

She took him to the stables. When she entered, she walked up to a horse with the coloring of dry maple leaves and a touch of orange gold. His mane was gold and he stood fifteen hands tall. She began rubbing his neck. "His name is Moonfire. He is a Palomino Appaloosa, one of the King's stallions, and has many sons to replace him."

Jesper looked at her, confused. "What are you saying?"

She smiled and grabbed a saddle. "This is your

graduation present."

Jesper's mouth dropped open. "You're kidding! I don't deserve this fine beast!" She threw the saddle on him and he squealed.

Airah rubbed his neck. "Steady, Moon, this is your new master." Moonfire looked at Jesper with wide eyes, unsure about his new companion. Airah grabbed Jesper's hand and they rubbed his forehead together. Moonfire relaxed and allowed Airah to continue getting him ready.

"Airah, I'm telling you I don't deserve this horse. The King has made a mistake. Why is he so kind to me? What is it that makes me unlike others?"

Airah looked sharply at Jesper. "You are like a son to him. He believes in you and what you will become. Naughton has chosen his fate and now you must choose yours. Now take this horse before I order you to!"

He gave a smirk. "Yes, my Lady." He started petting his new friend while he brushed him.

When Airah finished, she held the reins for Jesper. "Now get on him with confidence. He can sense fear." Jesper climbed on without hesitation and Moonfire did not move, but when Airah handed Jesper the reins, the race was on. Jesper ducked before getting his head slammed into the railing as Moonfire raced out of the barn into the streets. Jesper pulled back on the reins, but Moonfire quickened pace. People were jumping out of the way before they got trampled by the renegade horse.

Jesper laughed, delighted. "I see! A test, is it?" Jesper rose up and took proper position, letting his heels down and centering his balance. "Let's see what you've got!" Moonfire raced through the streets, heading toward the north gate. The guards saluted, thinking the Centore was on an urgent errand. They raced through the villages and up the foothills. Moonfire was not slowing pace as he ran up and down the rolling hills, and then he started bucking. Jesper hung on, using his legs gripping the horse. He continued laughing as his new friend jumped side to side, trying to shift Jesper's balance. After time, Moonfire tired and stopped moving as air rushed in and out of his flared nostrils. Jesper wiped the sweat from his brow. "I take it you have submitted?" Moonfire snorted in answer. Jesper waited to let his friend catch his breath and started walking down the foothills.

As he approached the gate, Airah and Eirmosa met him on their horses. "Are you alright?" asked Eirmosa.

Jesper patted Moonfire. "We're fine, just had a

little discussion." As they returned, they watched the people from Yorben preparing to relocate to the Centore plains for shelter.

Eirmosa's eyes began to water. "When will we have a chance to avenge all this evil?"

"We will strike back soon, and when we do, it will be like a wind in a hurricane," said Jesper, with confidence. After turning a corner, Jesper heard his name being called. He turned around and saw Nihyah running to him. "Greetings, Nihyah. How are you today?"

"All is well, except for all these strangers. They seem sad." Jesper smiled as he lowered his hand to her. When she grabbed it, he lifted her up on the horse in front of him.

"Ride with me for a bit. There is someone I want you to meet." Nihyah smiled from ear to ear, feeling very tall as they rode above all the people down the street. They caught up to Airah and Eirmosa waiting in a corner.

"I see you picked up a hitchhiker," said Airah.

"Indeed. This is a dear friend of mine that I would like you to meet," replied Jesper. Airah rode up next to them and Nihyah stretched out her hand to shake it.

"You're Lady Airah, aren't you?" Airah smiled.

"I knew it was you!" yelled Nihyah. "It is an honor to meet you face to face. All I ever hear is what Mr. Jesper tells me and when I see you with the King sometimes."

Jesper laughed. "Airah, I would like you to meet Nihyah. She helped me with your gifts."

"Did you now? Well, they certainly were fine flowers, especially the--"

Nihyah interrupted, "--the Curado plant! I know, isn't it goredus--I mean, gurdus--oh, blast it! I'm all nervous." Airah winked at Jesper, and he put Nihyah behind Airah on her horse.

"How about you ride with me for a while?" said Airah. Nihyah nearly burst with joy as she held on to the princess, riding through the streets. Guards bowed and saluted as they passed by posts, and the people were too busy to notice them. "So where do you live?"

"I live at the flora shop called Petals. It's five blocks down on the left."

As they turned the last corner, Nihyah hollered, "Mother! Mother! Come out here and look at me!"

Sarai stepped out, and her face went blank before she swept herself into a low bow. "Lady Airah! I hope she has not pestered you?"

"Of course not, she is a fine young Lady."

Airah slid Nihyah off the horse and Nihyah bowed. "Thank you for the ride, Lady Airah."

Airah put her hand over her chest. "The honor was mine. Try to stay indoors until all these people leave, okay?"

"As you wish, my Lady."

They rode back to the stables, giving their horses to the caretakers. Jesper patted Moonfire on his neck. "I'll see you tomorrow." They walked back inside going to the feast hall. As they ate, Jesper questioned them about their trip to Samha. "So, I guess Naughton has reached the Seraph Lands by now?"

"And he would not let me go with him!" said Eirmosa, clenching her jaw.

"I'm sure he had good intentions for his decision."

"So he says."

Jesper noticed the deer horn hanging from her neck. "If he gave you that necklace, I'd say he has very good intentions, indeed." Eirmosa blushed and Jesper chuckled. "It seems he finally said the magic words. It took him long enough. He's felt that way for a long time."

"He has?" asked Eirmosa.

"Don't play stupid. You saw how he was

looking at you all the time, and you played games with him."

Eirmosa narrowed her eyes at Jesper. "I had to make sure I was ready. Stop pestering me!"

He smiled. "I am happy for you both. Love is a powerful force, I hear, and I will never understand it," said Jesper, not looking at Airah. He dropped the subject before he received a taste of Eirmosa's fist. "So how long will it be before they return?"

"We are not certain," said Eirmosa. "It depends on what the supernatural being says."

Jesper cocked his head to the side. "How so?"

"The King has ordered the group to keep Naughton from returning if this supernatural being says no."

Jesper froze. "But why?"

"We don't know, my uncle won't speak of his reasons," said Airah, hesitantly.

Jesper stood up. "Ah, of course. More secrets. Why is it that I always surround myself with those?" Jesper drank from his mug. "I have errands to run before I leave to Fort Yorben. Thank you for the food." Jesper stood up, and then paused. "Take care of my cousin when he returns." He walked out and did not look back, pushing Airah out of his mind.

Fear of the Unknown

For the rest of the day, the group followed Zealot like a shepherd as the plants bloomed with beautiful flowers and fruit. The blooming plants led them up and down mountain ridges with scattered rocks and plants, but no trees. Zealot's bare feet caused him agony as the rocks tore his flesh. At sunset, they reached the top of a mountain ridge and decided to rest. Anor and Tirus set up camp while the others gathered what little dried brush they could find for a fire. Bojah was staring into the distance, looking at the mountains to the east that extended from north to south. The tallest peak was covered in snow, and at its base were many trees. "I reckon we'll be goin to them mountains."

"It's possible," said Bane.

"Why do you say that, Bojah?" asked Zealot.

"Have a look around. There's not much else to look at."

They gathered around the small fire, eating small rations of food. The water was becoming scarce. Anor looked into his water sack. "We will run out of water tomorrow."

"Don't worry, we will find water when we reach the mountains," said Naughton.

"How can you be so sure we're going to those

mountains, and what makes you think we'll find water?" asked Tirus.

"Like Bojah said, there are no other landmarks, and for some reason I just feel like that is the direction we will be going. As for the water, there will be a few streams from the melting snow. The Mountain of Colonies has several."

"You know what I think?" asked Tirus.

"I already know what you're going to say, but go ahead and tell us," said Bane.

"We're all going to die!"

Anor shook his head. "You and those negative ways." Tirus curled up in his blanket, ignoring Anor. Deep down inside many of them thought Tirus was right, and that their quest was in vain, looking for phantoms or ghosts. However, Naughton had sense of peace and no fear of failure.

Anor roused the group just as the horizon began to glow, in fear that the heat of the day would drain their water sacks in hours. Zealot continued leading the way down the ridge as he fought the pain in his feet. The loose rocks gave no firm grip as they fought step by step. Several times, they had to catch one another as rocks slipped out from under their feet, tumbling down the steep ridge. But despite the obstacles, the bushes ahead continued to bloom without fail, making the group press on. Bane was shaking his head. "I don't understand how he alone has the power to do this."

"There is more here than what meets the eye, Bane," said Anor. "I am certain this is going to get more peculiar as we get closer to our goal." By noon they were heading east down the ridge toward the mountains, and there was a cool breeze blowing which helped them beat the heat. Finally, they reached the bottom of the ridge and walked through the valley near the mountain. The ground was soft with dark clay, and more plants started to appear along with trees. As Zealot walked, the plants continued to bloom and point the way to their destination. By nightfall, they were halfway through the valley. Once again, they built a fire and Bojah threw a sack on the ground.

Naughton opened it and found it was full of fruit. "Where did you get all this?"

Bojah had a small bag and was eating the various fruits. "Ya ain't too bright are ya? This whole time ya left the water we needed which is in this here fruit that Zealot has been bloomin."

Bane took a sniff wrinkling his nose. "I don't think we should eat them. Whatever force is doing this can turn on us."

"Yur a superstitious buffoon. These here plants not only show the direction we're supposed to be goin, but also provide the nutrition we need to survive. Ya mama's dropped ya one too many times."

Zealot laughed. "You're right Bojah! But I must ask, how is it you have such faith, and yet you say you don't believe?"

Bojah stopped eating and looked at Zealot with stern eyes. "Faith has nothin to do with it. It's common sense to salvage what ya can and when ya can, nothin more." The group ate the fruit and drank the juices from them. They filled their water sacks by squeezing the fruit, getting as much juice as they needed. The group slept in a deep sleep from eating all the fruit, and they did not wake once all night.

The sun was well above the horizon when Anor woke with a fly on his head. He swatted it away and, staring angrily at the sky, realized the sun's position. He jumped up, kicking everyone awake. "Get up! Bezinar is counting on us, get up!" They roused sluggishly, and then as they started walking they felt much energy flowing through them.

"That fruit was amazing!" said Tirus.

"You mean you're being optimistic? That's odd. Something was definitely in that fruit," Bane joked. Zealot's feet felt much better, allowing him to quicken pace, and he did not miss a beat as he followed the plants to the mountains. Nightfall came, but the group did not stop, instead using the crescent moon's light to see where they were going. By midnight they reached the base of the mountains, and Anor decided to stop.

"That's far enough, Zealot. We have no idea what's waiting for us up there."

"No, we need to press on," said Bane.

"I agree with Anor," said Naughton. "I have made many mistakes traveling on mountains at night. A crescent moon is not enough light and believe me, it's not worth it." The group agreed and prepared for camp. They built a big fire and ate until they were stuffed, drinking until their bellies started to slosh full of juice. Anor decided that they should take turns on watch, fearful that some beast may sneak up on them. The night held no surprises, and Naughton had last watch. He took a small walk trying to stay awake. He could barely see as he made a circle around the group. He noticed large dark objects and walked closer, it was trees, similar to Hightop forest. He sat on a small rock next to a mound watching over his companions from a distance.

As he waited for sunrise, the air turned cold and he could see his breath. The air was still, and it was so quiet he thought he could hear his heart beating. He pulled his cloak around him, trying to stay warm, and decided to walk back to the fire. As he jumped off the rock, the fire went out with a hiss. Naughton pulled the bow off his back, terror gripping him. He struggled putting an arrow on the string as his hands shook from the cold and fear. He did not move for some time, feeling something or someone was looking right at him. He strained his eyes, looking harder, and thought he could see a face a stone's throw away.

Suddenly, a slight breeze hit his face and he heard a faint whisper. His very soul went empty and cold, as if he'd been buried alive. He then saw the sun starting to rise and it filled his heart with hope. As daylight approached, the fire burst back onto the logs and the cold air dissipated. Naughton's face beaded with sweat. He slowly put the bow on his back and leaned against a tree, speechless.

Anor woke and began packing. "Naughton, why did you not wake us?" Naughton did not respond, and Anor looked at him and saw that he was pale. He walked over to him, putting his hand on his shoulder. "Don't tell me you saw a giant snake again."

Naughton looked at him. "I--I don't know what happened. I heard...something. Did you not feel the cold air rush in?"

Anor looked at him oddly. "What cold air?"

Naughton shook his head. "It was nothing."

"I think you will take first watch tonight this time and sleep. Come on, we need to rouse the others and push on."

The group packed and began following Zealot up the mountain. The spruce trees were thick and smelled refreshing. Animals gave alarm calls as they scurried away in holes. As the day progressed, colder air surrounded them, and they noticed taller trees and a few shrubs. Tirus threw up his hands. "Now what?" Naughton continued walking up the mountain.

"Wait, where are you going?" asked Zealot.

"We will continue the direction the plants have been leading us." Anor shrugged his shoulders and followed him as the others filed in behind him. They continued walking as snow started to appear on the ground. As they marched up the mountains, the snow got deeper, making it difficult to keep a good pace. The trees seemed to get shorter and the wind increased. Their feet began to numb as the cold gripped them, and they started feeling light-headed from the lack of oxygen. The wind was blowing in their faces and was going through their clothes, making their skin feel like ice. Anor, Naughton, and Tirus put on their armor, hoping it would help, but

Anor was not satisfied.

"Okay, this is far enough! We are not prepared to make an ascent like this. We will freeze to death!"

Bojah laughed. "Yur not afraid of a little snow, are ya?"

Tirus whipped around to glare at him. "You call this a little, you four-eyed maniac?" They began to argue among themselves if they should go back, but Naughton remembered Eirmosa and knew all would be lost if they turned around. He knew his father would not stop, nor would he. He took a steadying breath and continued up the mountain, lifting his legs high to get through the snow. The group fell silent, staring at him as though he'd gone mad.

Zealot caught up with him and stopped him. "Naughton, this is suicide."

Naughton patted him on the shoulder. "Then go back. I will fulfill my father's quest." He continued marching up. The group was reluctant and Naughton knew it. He turned around, looking at them with wrath in his eyes. "I refuse to go back after we have come so far! I, for one, would rather freeze to death than let everyone I know died because I dared not continue into the unknown." He looked upward as it began to snow again, and then looked back at the group. "Do as you wish, but I am continuing forward!" With that, Naughton turned around and continued trudging up the snow bank. Anor admired his bravery, and in his heart remembered what it meant to be a Guardian. He grabbed his pack and followed Naughton. The others strapped on their bags continuing up the mountain as well.

By midnight the temperature plummeted and it began to snow harder, covering them. They could not see five feet in front of their faces. Naughton's body started to slow as he began to go into hypothermia. His companions felt the same, but Anor knew that there was no going back. Naughton stopped and looked at Tirus. "Give me your sword."

He reached behind to grab it, but it was frozen to him. "I can't break it loose. We're all going to die up here!"

Naughton turned him around, eventually pulling the sword free, and began cutting limbs off the trees. The others got the idea and started gathering wood. They used their numb hands to dig a hole for the fire, and as they dug, Bojah pulled out a small collapsible device and began deepening the hole.

"What in the world is that?" asked Bane.

"This here is called a shovel that I designed, and I have an idea." He kept digging, but eventually tired and handed the shovel to Tirus. "Here, start diggin a tunnel for us."

Tirus's eyes opened wide, "we are not gophers!"

"Just quit yur naggin and dig!" Everyone took turns digging, and when the tunnel was deep enough, Bojah took over and started making a cavern. The others hauled the snow out until the cavern was big enough to fit them all. "Now then, ya goofs, go get tha wood!" They brought it in while Anor set to banging two rocks together, starting the fire using pinecones and dead pine needles lodged in the limbs. As the flame got bigger they added more wood, and the flame started to roar. The fire melted the snow at first, before hardening back to solid ice, making an ice cave. They huddled around the fire as the ice glittered. As their bodies heated up they could finally feel their appendages. Their skin started to sting as if ants were biting them.

Anor was rubbing his hands together and smiling. "Bojah, from now on you have my complete support."

"I still think ya people are nuts," said Bojah. "What imbecile would tackle a mountain without proper clothin?"

The group looked at Naughton and he shrugged his shoulders. "I guess I owe you one,

Bojah."

"Yep," he replied, putting more wood on the fire.

"How did you learn to do this, Bojah?" asked Zealot.

"Me uncle was a miner and he told me stories of how they useta do this in tight situations. Turns out he was right." Tirus pulled out his water sack and the juice was frozen solid, so he put it next to the fire to melt. They pulled out what food they had left, only to find it was frozen as well.

Bane laughed deliriously. "Well, this is a first...and maybe our last."

"I'll say," said Tirus. "I have to admit, I didn't think we would survive this long."

"That's no surprise there," said Naughton with a chuckle. Snow steadily fell throughout the night, but the heat from the fire continued rushing out of the hole, keeping it clear. One by one they fell asleep, enjoying the cozy fire and eventually eating and drinking their melted beverages.

Early the next morning, Naughton woke up to a light purring sound. He flipped over, looking out of the hole, and saw a mountain lion staring at him. When Zealot moved, it darted away, startled. Zealot put his hands to the embers of the fire.

"I bet he's wondering what in the world we're doing up here."

"I'm thinking the same thing now. There have been no more clues."

Zealot continued warming his hands. "Relax, I'm sure we'll come across something. How about you go take a look outside while I get them up?" Naughton nodded and gathered his gear. He crawled out of the small hole and when he reached the top, he pushed the snow aside so he could stick his head out. When he did, he started laughing hysterically. The group woke up at the sound of him cackling, and they crawled up the hole to see what the fuss was about. There, three hundred feet away, was a cave at the base of the mountain, with white peaks towering above them. They all looked at each other, and laughed until their stomachs hurt.

Bojah readjusted his hat. "Well, that figures!"

They gathered their gear and Naughton led the group through the snow to the cave. As they entered, they found there was barely enough room for all of them. Bane rubbed his hands over the walls, but felt no grooves of any kind that resembled writing. Anor and Tirus built another fire and the group huddled around it, thinking of their next move. "Please tell me somebody has got an idea?" asked Tirus. No one spoke as they stared into the fire.

"Perhaps this itself is another riddle," said Bane.

"Maybe, but we need something to get us started and there is nothing here," said Naughton. After a couple of hours, Tirus started banging on the walls with a stick.

Bojah crossed his arms. "I knew he would go first."

Tirus paused. "First?"

"First to lose ya mind."

"First off, my mind is sound--unlike you morons--and secondly, how about you get off your asses so we can get out of here!" He continued beating the wall until Anor had enough. He stood up, grabbing the stick, and yanked it out of Tirus's hands.

"There is no hidden wall, you big dummy!" He threw the stick in the fire, and Tirus became even more agitated.

"Look, just for once let me just goof around. I am bored to death." He grabbed his stick that had caught on fire and used it as a torch. He examined the walls closely, and when the flame hit the rock wall, there was a burst of flames. They all jumped back and watched the fire zig zag along the wall. With a final burst the flame vanished, leaving black marks. Tirus put the flame up to the wall again, but Anor grabbed it from him.

"Don't do that again, you idiot!"

"Wait!" yelled Bane. "Give me the torch." Anor handed it to him and he started to examine the burnt markings. Bane started laughing. "Out of all people, you found it, Tirus!" The group stood speechless as they realized they were staring at the next riddle.

"How is this possible?" asked Anor.

"Ya mean you never heard of powder?" asked Bojah. The entire group stood baffled.

"Explain it to us."

Bojah crossed his arms. "It's a type of powder that ignites when a fire touches it. I've been workin with that there stuff and believe me, it aint worth messen with unless you know what yur doin." Zealot and Bane looked at the black writing, and together they translated the next riddle aloud.

"Provide the force that brings life."

Suddenly Bojah yelled, "BANG!" The entire group jumped and Bojah started laughing. "Haha! Ya fellas need to loosen up. Life just happens, ya can't explain it."

Zealot clenched his fists. "One cannot concentrate being loose, Bojah."

Bojah crossed his arms, not saying another word. Zealot turned back around and continued to examine the words.

"What is the force that brings life?" asked Anor. Bane and Zealot looked at each other, clueless once again. Anor suddenly chuckled. "Scholars, indeed." The group sat down, thinking of an answer. "What about water?"

"That is a possibility. Let's try it." Bane stood up and took some snow from outside, melting it beside the fire over a water sack. He filled it up and started splashing the wall, but nothing happened.

Anor poked the fire. "Well, that was a waste of time."

"Quit being pessimistic," said Naughton.

Anor glared at him. "Don't ever compare me to Tirus."

Tirus crossed his arms. "At least I found the riddle."

Anor poked his chest out. "Blah blah blah. You got lucky, that's all."

"Is it the sun?" asked Tirus.

Zealot scratched his head. "The sun does provide us what we need to survive, and without it, life would not exist." The group pondered until Naughton spoke.

"Even if it is the correct answer, we cannot capture the sun."

"Perhaps we can," said Zealot. The group looked at him curiously. Zealot stretched his hand out to Anor. "Give me your sword."

"For what? You are no swordsman."

"Just give it here and let me try something." Zealot walked out of the cave, looking up at the sun. He angled the blade so the sun would reflect the rays into the cave. The beam hit the cave wall, but nothing happened. He walked back in and returned the sword to Anor. "Thank you for sharing," he said with a smirk.

"An excellent effort," said Bane.

Nightfall came and once again the temperature dropped, the wind howling. They gathered more wood for the night and got settled in. "Well, at least we're dry and warm," said Anor, humbly.

Zealot drank some water. "That is true, and at least we can melt the snow and have plenty to drink as well. Hey Bojah, you wouldn't happen to have any more fruit, would you?"

He shook his head. "Nope. You dopes ate it all already and I ain't goin lookin, either."

Tirus stood up and began pacing. "I can't stand this. I have to move around or something."

"Remember what happened the last time you went moving around," said Bane with a sarcastic grin. Tirus put his hands against the wall and pushed against it, stretching his legs. As he stretched, he let out a puff of air. Suddenly, the wall began to move. The cave shook and pebbles fell all around them. Everyone froze in fear, and then glared at Tirus, ready to strangle him.

Anor walked up to Tirus with a stick held high. "I should beat your head like a drum!" Tirus put his hand over his mouth to shut him up, and then blew on the wall again. The cave shook once again, small rocks falling around them. The group leapt to their feet, ready to run, but stopped when they noticed Tirus and Anor were still frozen in place, staring at the wall as it crumbled before their eyes and revealed a tunnel.

Zealot slapped his forehead. "Of course!"

"Of course what?" asked Bane.

Zealot put his hands on his hips. "Don't you see? What is the force that brings life?"

"Wind?" asked Anor.

"No! The breath of El."

"Uh...speak plainly," said Naughton.

"Oh, good grief. Look here." Zealot pulled out the small copy of the Bindings of El, pointing at the page. "Look here, it says El formed man from the dust of the ground and breathed into his nostrils the breath of life, and the man became a living being. You see? The breath of life! All we had to do was breathe on the wall."

"I knew the answer all along," said Tirus. "I was just waiting to see if you got it."

Anor laughed sarcastically. "Like you ever read that thing. I just hope your luck holds out for us. Come on." The group packed their belongings and constructed torches with Anor taking point.

The group slowly entered the narrow tunnel, decidedly in no hurry once they saw the interior. The walls were jagged with sharp edges, and the floor had lumps of rock sticking up like annoying little stumps. They were stumbling as they went down the tunnel, and it seemed like hours until they came upon an opening. When they entered the cavern it was vast, like a void in the earth. Their torches revealed beautiful rock formations filled with columns that stood over seventy feet. Along the floor were stalagmites that rose up, reaching the ceiling that was surrounded by water puddles. They looked up, seeing stalactites dripping water down to the stalagmites. "Is this how those giant columns formed?" asked Naughton. No one answered him.

Bojah examined the stalagmites closely and touched one. He tasted the moisture that gathered on his finger and spat. "Tastes mighty salty."

"I don't think you should touch them," said
Bane. "We don't know what we're getting into down
here."

"I must agree with him, Bojah. This is not
exactly a safe place," said Anor.

"Can we at least drink the water?" asked Tirus.

Anor leaned over and smelled it. "Let me put it
this way: if Bojah won't drink it, then I wouldn't
chance it either. Just stick to your water sacs." Anor
led them through the cavern, trying to avoid the water
puddles. As they approached the other end he saw a
tunnel, but heard a little chirp. He held up his hand for
everybody to stop, and then looked around. Suddenly,
something hit his shoulder. He reached over, thinking
it was just a drop of water, but his hand revealed
otherwise. It was a dark, soft pebble, and suddenly it
dawned on him. He put a finger over his mouth and
spoke very softly. "No one move or talk."

"Why?" whispered Zealot. Anor raised his head
and slowly looked up. On the ceiling were hundreds
of bats. When the group realized what was going on,
they lowered their torches, trying to keep the light
from shining too bright.

Bojah whispered. "What are them things?"

"They're bats, and I heard their bites can cause

sickness," answered Anor. Bane's torch began to shake as his nerves started to get the best of him. Anor slowly started walking toward the tunnel. The others followed, holding their breath and trying to make as little noise as possible. Naughton noticed that the ground was soft and he pointed his torch down to look. The ground was covered with bat droppings. He breathed in a little and the smell made him gag.

He whispered, "Don't breathe through your nose." Despite the warning, curiosity got the best of Tirus as he looked down taking a sniff. The stench took his breath away and he had to sneeze. He covered his mouth and nose and tried to hold it in, but just as they reached the tunnel, he sneezed. The bats went ballistic, flying in all directions.

"Run!" screamed Anor as he pointed the torch toward the tunnel. The group ran hastily, trying to avoid the flying rodents as they flew all around them. They swatted at them like annoying flies in an attempt to scare them away, but it did not faze the bats. Bane was bringing up the rear, and as he swatted at the bats, he lost track of his direction and ran straight into a wall. Naughton heard the loud thud and ran back, spotting Bane out cold with a red lump on his forehead. He picked him up and ran down the tunnel as it angled down further into the abyss, with only the small glow from Anor's torch leading the way.

An hour later, Bane opened his eyes and winced at the pounding in his head. He looked up at Tirus. "He told you not to breathe through your nose, you moron." He touched the walls. "Where are we?"

"In a cave," said Bojah.

"I know that, you ass! I mean how deep in the earth are we?"

"Deep enough," said Anor, sharply. "Let's go."

Bane rubbed his head. "Fine, but somebody help me up. I'm feeling dizzy."

Naughton pulled him up. "I can't imagine why."

The group continued through the tunnel, noting how narrow it became as they went. In some places, they had to turn sideways just to fit. Anor's armor kept getting wedged against the walls, and eventually he had to take parts of it off and carry them. After several hours of walking, Anor noticed that everyone except Naughton was lagging behind, so he sat down. "Why are we stopping?" asked Naughton.

Anor leaned against the wall. "Look at them. They are exhausted. Let's rest a bit." Naughton sat next to him, and eventually the others came up and sat down without hesitation. They drank water from their sacks as they leaned their heads against the walls. Anor blew out his torch.

"What are you thinking? Light back that torch!" yelled Zealot.

"We need to save our resources. The rest of you blow yours out, we don't know how long were going to be in here."

They blew out their torches, but Bojah refused. "I aint doin no such thang. You don't know what's in here."

"Bojah, if we run out of light we all die." Bojah snarled and blew, instantly consuming them in darkness. It was as silent as a tomb, with the exception of their breathing.

Something touched Naughton's leg, and he kicked.

"Ouch! That was my foot, Naughton!"

"Oh, sorry Zealot."

Zealot rubbed his foot. "What are you afraid of?"

"After what I've seen this journey--especially the giant snake--there is no telling what we will encounter."

"I second that statement," said Tirus.

"Try to get some sleep. I will take first watch," said Anor.

Tirus laughed. "And just how do you plan on

taking watch? You can't see your hand in front of your face."

"I swear, you and your negative ways are going to be the end of us. Relax. We can hear a great distance in here."

The group lay down on their blankets, but the stone floor made it impossible to get comfortable. Naughton started to shut his eyes, but there was no point because it was dark anyway. Well, that is something new, he thought to himself.

He tried to relax, thinking about Eirmosa and his family. He wished he'd heard news about his father before he left, and wondered if he was back yet. If only he could have somehow spoken to his mother and sister before he left. He thought about the time he'd spent with his father as a child, and how he had taught Naughton how to track. He eventually fell asleep, the sound of his company's breathing echoing in the darkness.

Naughton woke to the sound of rocks banging together. He opened his eyes and saw sparks flying around him as Anor tried to light his torch. He stopped to readjust the rocks and tried again, but could not get the torch to light. After several more attempts he took a break, setting the rocks down. "The torches are a bit moist, I'm afraid."

Naughton sat up and was surprised to realize he could see Anor's silhouette. He rubbed his eyes and looked again, and the outline remained. "Anor, can you see me at all?"

"No, quit messing with my head."

"I must be hallucinating."

"Why?"

"Because I think I can see you."

Anor took a deep breath. "There is no way you can see. If I can't see you, I know you can't see me. Relax, your eyes are playing tricks on you." Naughton blinked and could tell he was not hallucinating. He then put his hand in front of his face and could see it, if only slightly. He crawled up to Anor, taking the rocks from beside his hands. He slammed the rocks together over the torch. Suddenly, the torch caught fire. Anor picked it up, looking at Naughton with wide eyes. "How did you know where the rocks were? And how in tarnation did you see where the torch was?"

"I told you I could see you somehow."

Anor wrinkled his eyebrows, thinking to himself, and scratched his red beard. "I think it's best if we keep this to ourselves. They'll think we're losing our minds, but I believe what you say." They stood up, waking the others, and together they all continued down the tunnel.

"How long did we sleep?" asked Bane.

Anor shrugged his shoulders. "There is no way of knowing for certain in here. I can only guess several hours."

The tunnel was straight for the most part, though every so often it would curve and angle up, sometimes very steep. The tunnel was wide enough for two people, and was so tall they could reach their hands up and not touch the ceiling. The walls changed from a rough surface to smooth, with little moisture dripping down the sides. The floor began to get slippery as they continued down the dark abyss. It seemed like hours of fighting wet floor until finally they could hear a loud roar. Anor stopped the group. "Do you hear that?" The group held their breath and listened.

"It sounds like a waterfall," said Naughton.

"Impossible. How can a waterfall be down here?" asked Zealot.

Anor shrugged. "We will find out soon enough." The roar got louder and louder, and it muffled the soft sounds of the torches. The tunnel opened up into an enormous cavern, and there before them was a giant waterfall coming from a large hole in the ceiling. The water was splashing into a pool that had foam forming around it. They walked around the cavern, looking for an exit, but none could be seen. They met back where they came in, and Anor looked at Naughton, perplexed. "What now?"

Naughton put his hand to his ear. "I can't hear you!"

Anor yelled, "I said, what now?" Naughton held up his hands as he walked toward the pool. As he stared down, he thought his eyes were playing tricks on him again. He could see light.

He waved his companions over. "Can you see that light?" The group stared into the pool, and they too thought their eyes were deceiving them.

Zealot shook his head. "You have got to be kidding!"

Bojah started laughing. "You ain't afraid of a little water, are ya?"

"Why is everything little to you?" exclaimed Tirus. Anor began taking the rest of his armor off.

"You're not seriously thinking of swimming down there?" asked Bane.

Anor dropped his armor with a loud clang. "Is there a choice?"

"The hell you say! I am not swimming that!" yelled Tirus.

Anor re-tied his sword belt. "Fine. Stay here and rot with our armor."

Naughton took off his armor and stuck his foot in, reeling back with a jolt. "It's freezing!"

"What did you expect, a nice day at the beach?" asked Anor with a wink.

Naughton dove in and his head popped up. "I...prefer the...beach!"

"Go on and get it over with," said Zealot.

Naughton took a deep breath and dove down. One by one, they jumped in after Naughton, carrying their weapons, water sacks, and what little food they had. After going down, Naughton opened his eyes and found he could see clearly. The current forced him down, pushing him away from where they entered. As he went down he felt pressure building in his ears. He swallowed, popping them, and the pain faded. When he reached the sandy bottom, he grabbed a stone to keep from drifting into a dark hole. He looked up and saw the opening where the light must have come from. He tried to swim up, but the current began to sweep him away toward the hole. His heart raced as he realized he was about to drown. Just then, he saw stones leading toward a rock wall where the light was coming from. He pushed from the rock and started kicking as hard as he could, finally reaching the next stone. He had three left that were about ten feet from each other before reaching the wall. The others followed behind him, fighting the strong current from one stone to the next. By the time Naughton reached the wall he felt weak, and his body was screaming for air. He began climbing the wall, and suddenly a current grabbed him, forcing him up to the surface.

When he surfaced, he breathed in the fresh air, coughing. He grabbed the edge and laid his head on it, breathing deeply to gain composure. He lifted his head up, and there before him was another cavern with light coming from a hole far above him, at least two hundred feet high. As he looked around, his eyes locked on four stone pillars with flat surfaces. They stood three feet tall and had writing on them. Behind the four pillars was a smooth wall that also had writing it. Soon after, his companions appeared beside him.

Naughton noticed two missing. "Where are Tirus and Bane?"

"I don't know what's keeping them," said Anor.

Naughton took a deep breath and dove down, grabbing the wall. The current was so strong that water rushed into his ears and pushed his eyelids back. As he pulled himself down, he saw Bane and Tirus lagging behind two stones away.

He waved them on to hurry up, and then suddenly Bane slipped. The current took him, making him hit Tirus, and then they both were flying through the water toward the dark hole. Tirus reached for the bottom, trying to grab onto a stone. Right before going into the hole, he managed to grab a rock. He saw Bane coming over him and grabbed him. Naughton swam, trying to reach them. Tirus tried to drag Bane up to the rock, but the current was relentless. Bane looked into Tirus's eyes, and with a slight grin, let go of his hand. Tirus, however, was not letting go that easily. He refused to let go of Bane and continued to hang onto the rock.

Eventually, Tirus's fingers began to cramp and his lungs began to burn, craving air. Naughton made his way closer and Tirus saw him coming. After several more attempts at gaining ground, Tirus realized there was no hope. He looked up at Naughton and, with a small, regretful smile, released his grip on the rock. Within a blink of an eye they were gone. Naughton's heart filled with grief and sorrow all at once. He turned around, making his way back to the wall. His body screamed for air and he hurried up the wall, kicking and climbing with all his strength.

He reached the top, splashing and gasping for air, trying to catch his breath. "No!"

Anor pulled him up, immediately understanding what happened. "It's not your fault,

Naughton."

"I could have helped them! But--but I was too late!"

Anor gripped Naughton's shoulder with sadness in his eyes. "The current would have taken you along with them, and our quest would have been in vain."

Naughton's voice shook. "Bane wanted Tirus to let go of him, but he refused, and instead he let go of the rock." Zealot's eyes watered, for he had lost not only his mentor, but his friend.

Anor felt a tear go down his cheek for the loss of his companions. "What they did was brave. They knew you would try to save them but did not want to risk your life. Tirus may have been annoying at times, but he was a man of honor." Naughton was shaking all over, full of anger and sorrow.

Bojah felt sorrow as well, but gathered his wits. "Ya should honor thur sacrifice and make em proud."

Anor nodded. "Indeed." He picked up Zealot. "On your feet. We must finish what we began." Zealot wiped his eyes and trembled all over from the cold water. Anor walked up to the four pillars and looked down. "There is a skeleton here!"

The group slowly made their way over with Naughton, kneeling over and observing the skeleton. He saw a necklace around the neck and pulled it slowly. The skull detached, falling to the side with a crack. The group was startled, but then observed the necklace. It was a medallion, with two crescent moons facing away from each other and a leaf in the center.

Zealot took it from him. "This was one of the King's scholars. How did he die, I wonder?"

Anor looked at the stone wall with the ancient writing. "Ready when you are, Zealot."

Naughton grabbed Zealot's forearm. "Come on, my friend." Zealot looked at the wall and translated the old Hebrew writing with a shaky voice.

"Ye be warned, mistakes dim thy light. And I looked upon the throne and saw four living creatures, and they were covered with eyes, in front and back." Zealot looked down at the four pillars and saw a dial on each one. There were symbols of animals around the dial and an arrow pointing down to a riddle below it.

He looked at the first dial's riddle on the far left pillar. "Thy mouth was closed by angels to spare the innocent." The second pillar dial's riddle read, "Enjoyed rest along their masters on the Sabbath." The third pillar read, "I am created after His image." The fourth pillar, "Behold the proud symbol of Qanas."

After Zealot translated, his heart sank, wishing

Bane was there. "I have no idea what the four creatures are around the throne. We must guess with each riddle."

"Where are the Bindings of El?" asked Naughton. Zealot pulled the book out of his pocket. It was soaking wet, with the ink smeared over many pages.

Bojah walked up to the smooth stone wall, feeling for edges. "There be no signs of a door here. What you reckon that warning was about, that dimmin the light stuff?"

"I would rather not find out," said Naughton.

Zealot walked around examining the dials. Each one had symbols of over twenty animals. "I don't see how we're going to get this right, and I don't think we're allowed too many mistakes."

"We will take our time with each pillar. We are in no hurry," said Anor.

Zealot shrugged his shoulders. "We can just swim back out if we can't get the riddles."

"No, we can't!" said Naughton, frustrated. "That current is too strong to go back. We have no choice, so clear your minds and let's get this done. We will start with the one on the far left. What does is say again?"

It says, "Thy mouth was closed by angels to

spare the innocent."

"It's obvious this animal is a predator."

"Well, of course it is!" exclaimed Anor. "But there are many."

Naughton looked at the dial with all the animals. "It must be a big one."

"That is very likely, but what predator's mouth was closed by angels?" asked Anor.

Zealot closed his eyes, remembering stories he had read. He gasped, and his eyes flew open. He snapped his fingers. "Of course! I forgot about that story, and it was one of the most famous stories in the Bindings!"

"Out with it then, eh," said Bojah, putting his hands on his hips.

"There was a story about a man named Daniel who was thrown into a den full of lions, and angels came to help him."

"Well, that sounds good enough to me. Give that there dial a turn then."

Anor raised an eyebrow, crossing his arms. "Are you sure of this, Zealot?"

"I am certain. That was one of my favorite stories growing up."

"I guess there is only one way to find out," said Naughton. Zealot put his hand on the dial and slowly started turning it, putting the lion over the arrow. He stopped it over the arrow and nothing happened. "Are we not doing it right?"

Zealot put his hand on his chin. "I'm not sure. Perhaps it only works when all four are lined up."

"That's a thought," said Anor. "Let's do the others then, shall we?"

Zealot walked over and read the second riddle. "Enjoyed rest along with their masters on the Sabbath."

"What is a Sabbath?" asked Naughton.

"It's a day of rest. El commanded that no man or animal is allowed to work. For it is written, keep the Sabbath holy."

Anor scratched his head. "So what animal did they use to work with?"

"What about them mules? We always used one in our fields growin up," said Bojah.

Anor nodded. "Many gardeners use mules to pull their plows. I must agree with Bojah."

"Very well," said Zealot as he turned the dial, placing the mule over the arrow.

Zealot walked over to the third pillar and read aloud. "I am created after His image." Zealot started turning the dial without hesitation.

"What are ya doing!" yelled Bojah.

"Relax, my odd friend. I know the answer to this one."

"What animal is it then?" asked Anor.

Zealot laughed. "It is the one to rule over all animals. It's us. Man." Zealot turned the dial, putting the man over the arrow. They walked over to the last pillar with Zealot reading the riddle. "Behold the proud symbol of Qanas."

"It's a snake," said Naughton.

Anor wrinkled his nose. "What? No it's not, it's an eagle!"

Naughton put his hands on his hips. "I know for a fact it is a snake! The Geols wear a flame and snake on their armor. I have seen it myself."

Anor threw his hands up. "Fine, but I'm telling you it's an eagle. Zealot, you must choose between the eagle or the snake."

Zealot looked at Bojah. "What do you think?"

Bojah adjusted his hat. "I ain't sayin a word on this one. I haven't got a clue." Zealot thought for a moment and started turning the dial. He stopped it over the snake and closed his eyes, waiting for the results, but there was only silence.

He opened his eyes. "Is it broken?"

Anor gripped the hilt of his sword. "You're killing me, Zealot! You will drive me to drinking again! Are you sure you know how to work that damn thing?"

Zealot whipped around. "No, and your yelling is not helping our situation!"

Naughton and Bojah were looking over the pillars and dials, searching for any clues. After several minutes, Bojah propped his elbow on the first dial. "Well, I reckon we're stuck here for a while." Suddenly, the dial started to go down. It gave a click, and Bojah froze. There was a loud sliding sound coming from the smooth rock wall, and then it stopped with another loud click.

"Seems the lion was the right answer," said Zealot rubbing his short black hair from stress. Naughton walked over to the second dial and pushed down. The ground shook, and above them, the light was covered almost half way. The dial lifted back up with a click and all was quiet.

"And obviously that was the wrong answer!" yelled Naughton.

"Maybe it's a horse," said Zealot.

"That's possible, but let's think about this a tad longer," said Anor, sitting down. He sat, deep in thought, and tapped the floor with his fingers. "What in the world could it be, then? Let's see here now, there's pigs, horses, goats, and, um...oh, what's that thing called?"

"What does it look like?" asked Naughton.

"It has long horns and is very strong."

"Yur talkin about an ox. Me uncle use to have one to pull his wagons," said Bojah.

Anor snapped his fingers. "That's it, an ox. Try that one."

Zealot put his hand on the dial. "Are you sure about this, Anor? We're running out of light."

"If you have something better in mind, by all means."

"I say we take a vote," said Naughton.

Anor stood up. "Fine, then."

"Those in favor of ox, raise your hand." Only Anor raised his hand. "Those in favor of a horse?" The rest raised their hands.

Anor crossed his arms. "Alright, let's see who is right, then." Zealot turned the dial to a horse and pushed down. The ground shook, and with a loud boom, the light was almost gone. Anor started laughing. "A horse, indeed!"

"How can you laugh at a time like this?" asked Zealot with wide eyes. "This could be our death!"

"I have found that in tense situations, it's good to laugh sometimes."

"You Guardians are crazy," said Naughton.

"And just think, my cousin is going to become a Centore." Zealot regained composure, turning the dial to an ox.

"This is it," he said as he pushed down the dial. There was a loud click, and then another loud sound came from the smooth wall. "Whew...okay, two down and two to go!" He walked over and pushed the third dial down without hesitation. Once again, a loud grinding sound came from the smooth stone wall. "Ah ha! I told you it was a man." They walked over to the last pillar, but Zealot became nervous. "You all realize if we miss this, we are doomed in here for all eternity?"

Anor leaned back and put his hands behind his head, seemingly relaxed. "I'm telling you that the symbol of Qanas was an eagle."

Zealot clenched his fists. "But Naughton said that the Geols hail from the land of the south, which is where Qanas was located."

"Then leave it on the snake," said Anor with a smirk. Zealot looked at Naughton with a humble grin of hope and slowly pushed down the dial. The ground shook, followed by a loud boom, and then the light vanished, leaving the group in blackness.

Zealot exhaled shakily. "Somebody light a torch!"

"Them torches are useless," said Bojah. "That water soaked em."

Zealot collapsed to the ground. "We're going to die in here."

Anor chuckled. "Seems I was right. Remember I said was, past tense." He stood up. "Alright, Naughton, get it over with. Just remember I got it right." Out of the silence they heard the dial turning, and then a loud click was heard. The sound of grinding was heard again, and a small door opened from the smooth rock wall underneath the riddle.

"Let's get moving," said Naughton.

Zealot stood up. "Wait a minute, how did you see the dial?"

"Indeed!" yelled Bojah.

"I'll explain later! Let's get through the door before it closes," said Naughton.

"What door? I can't see my hand in front of my face!" yelled Zealot.

Naughton grabbed each of them. "Everyone hold a hand, I'll lead you through the tunnel."

"Ya got some explainin to do here, Naughton," said Bojah.

"I can see," said Naughton, calmly.

"But how?" asked Zealot.

"I don't know. I noticed it when Anor was

trying to start the torch a while back."

"That explains it," said Zealot. "That's why you weren't afraid the whole time, Anor! You knew Naughton could see in the dark this whole time, and you had me and Bojah worried to death. You big meathead! That goes for you too, Naughton!"

Anor chuckled. "It was worth watching you sweat."

As they approached the small door, Naughton stopped and listened. "Can you hear that?" The group paused and listened as well. A slow roar began to build up, and water suddenly rushed around their feet.

"Is that what I think it is?" asked Anor. Naughton looked behind them and saw that the water was rushing out of the pool where they came from. The water exploded out of the pool, rushing toward the group.

"Run!" yelled Naughton.

Anor felt the air rushing by. "Run where? I can't see--"

With sheer force the water swept them off their feet, flushing them down the tunnel. The water carried them, twisting and turning through the dark tunnels. Naughton was laughing with excitement, for he could see and was enjoying the ride. The tunnel was tight, and they often hit their elbows and knees on the sides as the water carried them through the stone pipes.

Zealot put his hands over his mouth. "I'm going to be sick! Make it stop!" Within a flash, they were flying through the air in broad daylight, falling down into a lake with the echoes of screams coming from them. The group plummeted into the water with giant splashes. One by one, their heads popped up like corks.

Naughton shook his head. "Wow! That was fun!"

"Fun?! Fun you say?" asked Zealot. "We almost got killed!" The group looked up as they swam to the shore. They had fallen from a giant waterfall that was over a hundred feet high.

"We should be dead," said Bojah.

"You think?" yelled Zealot, sarcastically.

Anor splashed water in his face. "Give it a rest. You're starting to sound like Tirus." Zealot got quiet as they swam to the shore.

When they reached the soft sand they sprawled out, trying to catch their breath. Naughton got out of the water and when he saw what lay beyond the tall grass, he froze. The others noticed that Naughton was not moving. They gathered around and stood motionless, filled with excitement, fear, and anxiety.

Before them was giant temple made of gold and marble, covered in moss and vines. It was massive and stood over one hundred feet. They looked around and saw that it was surrounded by mountains that were taller than any of them had ever seen, with peaks covered in snow. "We did it. We actually found it."

"We have done nothing," said Anor. "Our mission is to get help."

Bojah's face was angry and began to grit his teeth. "Just wait till I get me hands on him!"

Naughton turned around to face Bojah. "You will do no such thing. You agreed to wait until we are done talking with him."

"I remember me oath, but don't take long when we find him. Me tongue will only remain still for so long." Naughton nodded and walked toward the temple.

"Wait a minute," said Anor. "I'm not doing anything until I get dry." He started gathering wood to build a fire and the others came to help. While drying their clothes, they ate the last of their food and stared at the temple.

Bojah drank water from his sack. "So who's goin to do tha talkin?"

Zealot gestured his hand at Naughton. "I imagine him, since he carries the sun jewel."

"What do you plan on saying? That is, if we find him?" asked Anor.

Naughton cleared his throat as his stomach tightened. "I don't know yet, but I'll think of something."

"What? You mean this whole journey you haven't considered what to say?" Naughton looked at him and shrugged his shoulders. Anor pulled out his pipe, but the last of his tobacco was soaking wet. "Figures! Bah, it's a bad habit anyway." He put away the pipe. "Well, choose your words carefully. You will only get one chance, I'm sure."

After drying their clothes, they approached the temple and went up the golden steps. They climbed several feet until they reached a door with pillars on either side. The door was ten feet wide and fifteen feet tall with writing and symbols all over them, plated in gold.

"What does it say, Zealot?" asked Naughton.

"I am not certain. There are a variety of languages on here, but the one I can read are warnings not to disturb this temple and many quotes I have never heard of."

Anor rubbed his hand over the giant gold door. "Does it say how to get in?"

"No, I don't see anything of the sort. Perhaps

there is another entrance."

"Alright, let's have a look around then. Naughton, you come with me. You two walk around on that side and we'll meet you at the back."

Naughton and Anor went to the left, walking along the side of the temple. The walls were beautiful, made of solid marble and covered with gold symbols. There were no windows. The vegetation was sprawling, covering the wall with vines and flowers. When they got half way, they saw on the wall several symbols, with letters made from red, sparkling diamonds. They continued walking toward the back of the temple, which had no markings of any kind. Zealot and Bojah met them on the other side.

"Did you see anything of interest?" asked Zealot.

Naughton broke a nearby limb, releasing his frustration. "No! Just a bunch of words again."

"Show me." They led him and Bojah to the wall where the red diamonds glittered in the sun. "This is a language similar to the front, but I cannot read any of these." Naughton kicked a rock.

Anor patted him on the shoulder. "We will find a way in."

The group made their way to the front and eyed the giant door again, looking for handles. They pushed and banged on it, hoping it would magically open. Anor raised his hands. "Open sesame!"

Naughton crossed his arms. "Are you serious?"

"It was worth a shot. Besides, you're not doing any better."

Zealot sat on the stone floor, examining all the words on the door. "There must be something I'm missing, a clue at least."

The sun began to set and they built a fire in front of the door so Zealot could continue to study the letters. Zealot pulled out the copy of the Bindings of El he found at Bojah's house. The ink was smeared everywhere, but some parts were readable. Everyone was asleep but Naughton and Zealot. Naughton sat more wood to the side and took his boots off. "Any luck?"

"No! I have no clue how to open this thing. I have been doing a lot of reading each night since Mara valley on this new section of the Bindings of El."

Naughton crossed his arms. "Is it different than the first half?"

Zealot chuckled. "You have no idea."

Naughton clenched his fist, then relaxed. "Well, explain."

"It would take too long. First I must solve this puzzle." He strained his eyes, looking at the door. "I only see one part that seems like a riddle."

"Which part?"

"At the top it says, Out of all the tongues of men, three remain, but only one is greatest of all. I have read these words recently during our travel, but I don't know what it's referring to."

"How do you know it means words?"

"Because it says tongues of men, which means words...but one is more powerful than the rest it seems. Only El knows what it's talking about!"

Naughton leaned back against the pillar with his cloak covering him. "Relax, we've come this far. I'm sure you will think of it."

"If only Bane were here," said Zealot with a low voice. He put the smeared Bindings of El away. "Ah, what's the point? I'm too frustrated to concentrate. Naughton, I want a direct answer. How is it that you can see in the dark now?"

"I told you I don't know." Naughton stretched his neck, moving his head side to side. "I noticed it in the caves."

Zealot moved closer to the fire. "There must be an explanation of how it happened! You're not an owl."

"I can hoot like one."

"Stop joking around. It's not a natural to see in

the pitch black," said Zealot, with eyebrows raised. "Has the sun jewel affected you somehow?"

Naughton looked at the jewel, but it was the same. "No...nothing." He shrugged his shoulders. "I must admit, I learned a great deal when I met Nellium, but how can I believe in something I can't see?"

"It's called faith, my friend."

"Faith?"

"Yes, faith. For example," Zealot picked up a rock and then dropped it, letting hit the ground. "Now, can you explain why the rock went down?"

Naughton looked at Zealot with a sarcastic grin. "Nellium has already given this lecture to me about not being able to understand everything."

Zealot raised his finger. "So, you understand what I'm talking about?"

"No."

Zealot wrinkled his nose, looking at Naughton like he was an idiot. "No? If Nellium can't explain it to you, then how can I?"

Naughton stared up at the stars. "I don't know." He glanced around and then looked at the fire. "So you're saying that all I have to do is have faith, and El will take care of me?"

Zealot spread out his arms. "Exactly. It is the

same reason why your parents took care of you--love, my friend." Zealot froze, arms still held wide, but now with a puzzled expression on his face.

Naughton looked at him, worried. "What's the matter with you?" Zealot lowered his arms slowly and stood up, looking at the words on top of the door. His mouth started to twitch and then he began speaking out loud.

"I remember a quote I read. How could I forget such words!"

"What are you blabbering about, you goof?"

Zealot closed his eyes. "I remember now. The three words it's describing are Faith, Hope, and Love. The greatest of these is Love."

As soon as Zealot said love, a mighty wind came and blew the fire out, the cold air rushing in around them. Bojah and Anor woke up, startled. Cold air filled their lungs, rendering their breath visible, and a cold chill went through them as fog formed all around. The trees were bending over from the violent wind. Clouds rolled by as if a hurricane was approaching, and lightning bolts struck around them, though there was no thunder of any kind. The lightning struck so close they felt the heat, but they remained standing. The group stood still and terrified, wondering if the storm would pass as their hearts pounded in their chests. Slowly, the giant golden doors began to open with a loud roaring sound, as if two mountain volcanoes were erupting beside them. They approached the door, and as soon as they entered, the doors closed behind them with a loud boom. The ground quaked, making them fall, and then all was silent.

Darkness surrounded them, and they could hear each other breathing. "Zealot, what did you do?" asked Anor.

"I found out how to open the door."

"That is obvious!"

"How bout a little warnen next time!" yelled Bojah. Naughton blinked and rubbed his eyes, trying to see, but his night vision failed him, leaving him as blind as his companions.

"I can't see," said Naughton in a shaky voice.

"Everybody just calm down and slow your breathing so we can hear," commanded Anor.

After everyone was breathing normally, Naughton noticed a light glow in front of him. "Hey, I can see a glow. I think my vision has returned!"

"We all can see that," said Zealot. Anor took point, leading the group toward the glow. As they got closer, a tunnel was revealed, its floor illuminating the walls and ceiling. They approached it slowly, and

Zealot noticed writing on the wall. "There are more words here."

"What does it say?" asked Anor.

"Question of my life." he grunted. "I can't make it out. It's another language or dialect that I have never seen before." They continued down the tunnel, led by the glow, until they reached a set of stairs leading to a lower floor.

"Hold!" Naughton hissed, his voice sharp and tense. "My father's story describes this part. He said when they reached the bottom of the staircase, everyone around him died."

Anor took a deep breath. "We have no choice but to take our chances." Anor led them down the glowing stairs. Down and down it went, making the group more nervous by the minute, until finally they reached the bottom. The glow ceased, leaving blackness all around them. They stared into the abyss and waited for their fate. Suddenly, two golden eyes appeared in the distance. A low, calm voice full of authority came from the same direction as the eyes.

"I see one righteous heart."

Naughton screamed, "Wait! I was sent here by my father. Behold, the sun jewel!" Naughton pulled out his father's sun jewel. Instantly, the golden rays around the diamonds glowed brightly, and then faded.

The voice returned. "You come uninvited."

"How? My father told me that you said only the sun may return, and the jewel says Honor the Holy."

"You were summoned, but these others were not."

Naughton's voice changed with anger. "If you kill them, then you must kill me as well. They helped me find you!"

The golden eyes blinked. "I admire your bravery, Naughton, son of Berton. However, only one of you bares a righteous heart."

"Who?"

"The very man who opened the door." Zealot shook in fear. "Do not be afraid," said the voice. "Zealot, son of Galvus, the one you call El is with thee."

"How do you know my name?" asked Zealot, voice wavering.

"I know many things. I know why you have come, and the answer is no."

"At least hear our plea!" yelled Anor.

The golden eyes closed for a moment and then reappeared. "You, Anor, son of Boronus, are the bringer of death. Those who live by the sword die by the sword, just like your Centore brothers. What good is a warrior without proper morals? Glory belongs to my King alone, and no others. The king you serve is made of flesh and bone. The King I serve is King of all. He created all things, even you."

"We come here with hope," said Zealot.

The golden eyes disappeared. "Ah, hope. A powerful word. What is your hope?"

"The hope that you will aid us against the Geols. They are killing everyone--women, children, and the old. How can El stand aside and let such evil reign?"

The golden eyes returned with a stern voice. "Evil will never reign. My King is allowing this to happen."

"But why?" demanded Zealot.

"They have forgotten who their shepherd is."

"I don't understand," said Zealot. "I remember in the Bindings of El how there were a few in the city who were spared because they still believed. Surely there are others who believe?"

"You speak with wisdom, but understand this: those who believe will not perish. They will be taken up to El where they belong." Zealot pondered how to counter, but could think of nothing.

"At least tell us who you are?" asked Naughton.

The voice became even more firm. "You may call me a Calvaryman. However, son of Berton, you are not like your companions. I killed many of your kind in Qanas, and not even you have the authority to know thy given name."

"What do you mean?"

Anor interrupted, gripping the hilt of his sword. "So you did destroy Qanas! Was it because they became wicked?"

"Yes, but why do you grip your sword? Do you consider yourself wicked?"

"No!" yelled Anor. "I am angry because you will not rise up and help us in the hour of need. If this so-called El loves us, then why let us die?"

Zealot threw up his hands. "Forgive him! He does not know what he is saying!"

The golden eyes disappeared again. When the being spoke, it sounded very calm, though further away than before. "A prime example of why my King refuses to hear your pleas. They do not believe. Now leave this place, or death will be upon thee."

Bojah became furious. "Now wait justa minute, I have come here on another note! Where is me son?"

The voice returned, filled with joy. "He is safe. He is none of your concern now." Bojah, filled with rage, drew his sword and charged toward the sound of the voice. Suddenly there was a flash, and Bojah's sword was gone, the hilt still in his hand. After the flash, the glow on the stairs returned. The group stood still, feeling hopeless.

Zealot gritted his teeth. "We have failed. We must go back and tell the King."

Anor shook his head. "No. Remember the King's orders of what must be done with Naughton."

Naughton jerked his head around. "What are you talking about?"

Anor started up the stairs. "We will discuss that later, but for now let's leave this cursed place."

They walked back upstairs, following the glow, and Naughton became more agitated as they walked. "What order did the King give you?"

Anor shook his head. "Zealot, you should have kept your mouth shut."

"You're the one who mentioned it. He has the right to know," said Zealot.

"I want an answer!" yelled Naughton. They ignored him as they approached the entrance. The doors opened with clear and beautiful skies on the horizon. As soon as they stepped out, the doors closed swiftly with a boom. Naughton took his Osage bow and hit it on the pillar, making a loud clang. "I want an answer, or I am not leaving this spot!"

Anor turned around. "We will tell you nothing, because the King has sworn us to an oath!"

"I will not go on with this any longer," Zealot said, resigned. "Naughton has the right to know and I don't care what oath I have made, because all is lost now. The Geols will destroy all that we love, and before I die, all secrets need to be unveiled."

Anor shook his head. "We're not dead yet! We keep our oath for reasons I will explain later. The King gave me specific instructions on what to do in case this happened."

Zealot looked at Naughton with pity in his eyes. "I'm sorry, I should not have said anything."

Naughton was so full of rage, blood vessels could be seen bulging from his forehead. "So the Calvaryman was speaking the truth?"

Anor whipped around with anger, but then suddenly relaxed, hesitant to answer. "Yes."

Naughton felt hollow. Everything he knew was a lie. Zealot went to speak, but Anor intervened. "Not another word from either of you." Naughton put his hands over his face, feeling alone, betrayed.

To War

The next morning, Jesper woke to Litzer loudly banging on his door before barging into the room.

"Jesper, we have been ordered out!"

Jesper slowly opened the door rubbing his head, "I thought we were leaving tonight?"

"Shadow Scouts have spotted Geol reinforcements on the way to Fort Yorben. Thorg has ordered us to leave immediately!"

Jesper stretched his legs. "Alright, give me a second."

"Yes, sir."

"Don't call me that when we're not on duty." He gathered his gear and put on his polished armor. Before walking out the door, he heard a soft voice as faint as a whisper.

"Take care." He turned around, stunned, and faced Airah.

"Did you watch me sleep the whole night?"

"Of course not."

Jesper cocked his head to the side. "Is there something you want?"

"I came to wish you a safe journey. Moonfire will take care of you."

Jesper's heart pounded and he wanted to scream when he thought of their last discussion, but he kept his composure. "I thank you for your concern. Please watch over my cousin when he returns." With that, he threw his bag over his shoulder and walked out the door, never once looking back at her. When he reached the stables, a servant was there holding Moonfire. Litzer and Plonus were there as well, sitting on their horses.

"Where did this fine horse come from?" asked Plonus.

"It was a gift from King Irus."

"You a relative or something?" asked Litzer.

"No, he gave it to me as a graduation gift."

"That is a fine gift indeed," said Plonus, patting Moonfire. Jesper jumped on Moonfire, looking up at Airah's room, wondering if she would be on the balcony. He strained his eyes, but saw only the small green Curado plant.

He lowered his head and whispered to himself, "Farewell, Airah." He pulled the reins, pointing his new friend toward the south gate. With a kick, they took off. People cheered as they rode through the streets and out of the south gate, making their way to Fort Yorben.

They continued riding through the night to the south, occasionally passing villagers from Yorben and Iona. As they rode, they saw a group of men in an open field under the moonlight. They approached the men, weapons ready in case the men were not their allies. Instead of trouble, they found Felden, Rubus, and Gideon and his men, all on horseback.

"Greetings, Jesper. I thought you would ride through the night," said Felden, sitting upright.

Jesper shook his hand. "We have no time to lose, from what I hear. Is it true the Geols are amassing a great army to attack Fort Yorben?"

"Yes. They will cross the Siriu River in five days, and Yorben will be overrun."

"Then what are we waiting for?" yelled Gideon as he kicked his horse, their forms fading in the darkness as they rode.

Jesper shook his head. "Someone is a bit anxious."

"Indeed," said Felden. "But the battle will change his mood when the screaming starts."

After a few days of riding, they reached the town of Iona during the night. They watched as the townspeople ran around frantically, grabbing their belongings and preparing to leave. Felden stopped one of them. "What is going on?"

"We heard the Geols are going to destroy Yorben!" the villager shouted, and then dashed away with his bags.

Plonus was patting his horse. "We should rest, Felden."

Felden gazed at the town. "We will not stay at the inn. These people are in panic! We will sleep in the fields away from all this disarray." Felden led them to an open field away from the town, watching the people run around like angry ants.

"Do you think we can win this war?" asked Rubus.

Litzer drew his sword and started to sharpen it. "With that kind of attitude we won't."

"You have no idea what we're up against, kid."

"I am no kid!" he yelled.

"Just because you're a Centore does not make you a man." Litzer stood up, walking toward Rubus with a menacing stare.

"Stand down, Litzer!" yelled Jesper.

"You mean you expect me to sit here and take that from him?"

"No, I do not." Jesper looked at Rubus. "We must work together. Felden and I will not tolerate such nonsense."

Felden nodded. "I agree. Keep your mouth shut, Rubus."

"Felden, have you heard any more news of

these creatures?"

"No, but I do know they hold many cities such as Carasin under captivity, using the people as slaves. Apparently, the soldier that Naughton found dying was telling the truth. The other cities that we know of are located to the southeast, but we are not certain how many the Geols control. My Shadows say that the Geols are jumping from one city to the next and taking control of them. Sturkma was one of several that were demolished and rebuilt for their purposes. The map your uncle and I discovered reveals a massive stronghold far to the south. The only way we're going to win this war is to flush out the enemy from these villages and cities as well."

"Why don't we retake the cities first?" asked Gideon.

"I am sure that's the plan along the way, but the stronghold is a key factor. As of now our primary goal is Fort Yorben, it must not fall." Felden looked around to make sure they were alone. "It is the key to the King's campaign."

"Didn't Nemian say that Fort Yorben will fall?" asked Jesper.

"It will, unless we plan a great defense. If we can hold them, the Geols will retreat back to Sturkma. Hopefully the King will be ready to launch his campaign by then. But rumors are spreading that Valkry will soon be tested. If that is the case, then we will be back on the defensive."

"What if Yorben falls?"

"Then we are to report to Fort Estmere and wait for further orders."

"I must object to this idea," said Flitzer. "If we go marching off chasing these Geols, we will leave Bezinar exposed. Fort Coralis has fallen, and if the City of Valkry is tested, we will be too far away to assist."

"He has a point," said Gideon. "The question is, where did the Geols that destroyed Fort Coralis come from?"

Felden bit his lip, deep in thought, and finally spoke. "We believe they're using ships in the west. Nevertheless, we can only hope Valkry holds them. Sometimes the best defense is a good offense."

Rubus stood up. "I don't like this plan."

Litzer sheathed his sword. "What's to like? The King issues orders and we follow."

"I understand that, but we know so little of the Geols locations!"

Felden grabbed Rubus's cloak and made him sit down. "Calm yourself. Assuming things gets us no where. We can talk all night of such things, but we must rely on what we know at the present."

The group sat in silence, thinking more on the situation, until Jesper threw his armor to the ground. "We can only hope Naughton returns with help." With that, the group fell asleep, each taking their turn keeping watch.

Felden woke the group at sunrise and they rode swiftly to Fort Yorben. The closer they got, the fewer people they saw walking the opposite direction. By mid-afternoon, Fort Yorben was in sight with dust further south. As they approached, a horn sounded, announcing their arrival. The gates lifted, allowing them passage. Soldiers ran in all directions and the smiths pounded away on the anvils, repairing armor and weapons.

Captain Ruros waved his hands at them, getting their attention. "Greetings, Felden! It is good to see you...and what is this? Jesper is a Centore now, and he is a gold shoulder!"

Jesper jumped off of Moonfire's back, shaking Ruros's hand. "It warms my heart to see you, Captain. Where is Mohai?"

"He is in his headquarters with the other captains and Centore commanders. I will take you to him." Felden and Jesper followed Ruros to Mohai's headquarters. Once again, Jesper heard Mohai yelling, shaking the walls.

"We will not retreat!"

"Mohai, nobody is going to think you are a coward. Retreat is a form of strategy," said a Centore commander.

"I refuse to let this fort fall to those Geols! I have lost many men holding this fort, and their deaths will be in vain by just retreating without a fight." Mohai saw Felden and Jesper walk in, and his mouth dropped open. "It can't be...It is you! Jesper has returned to us!" The others turned around to look at Jesper, proud in his polished armor.

Nemian smiled hugely, laughing. "I knew you would make it. I see you're a gold shoulder. Which unit are you assigned to?" Jesper gave a smirk, and Nemian's eyes widened. "You're kidding! You mean Thorg put you under my command? I am deeply honored. You must have impressed him! Come sit." Jesper sat next to him and readjusted his sword. "Jesper, I would like you to meet Kenaf, commander of unit six, and Zanah, commander of unit four." Jesper shook their hands.

"Did Thorg send us some men?" asked Kenaf.

"Yes, sir. They are waiting outside."

"Felden, what news from the King?" asked Mohai.

"Our orders are to hold Fort Yorben, if possible."

"What's his intentions?" asked Hubin.

"He and his council are creating a counter offensive, and Fort Yorben is the key to the whole operation. However, if we fail we are to go to Fort Estmere."

Nemian scratched the side of his missing ear. "I see. So, how do we proceed? We are greatly outnumbered, and the Geols are building several bridges over the Siriu River which will allow them to overwhelm us."

Felden sat down. "We will use that to our advantage. They are expecting us to retreat, more than likely, so we must make it seem that way." Felden pulled out a map of the fort and region. "We make is seem the army is retreating, but actually, we will hide men here in the fort and make the army hide to the west. That way, when the Geols come in range, we can bombard them with arrows and catapults while the Centores keep them away from the south and north gates. When we stop their advance, our army can come around to flank them with cavalry and infantry."

"May I make a suggestion?" asked Zanah.

"Of course."

"I recommend we put all our blue shoulders on

the walls with your archers to pick them off while we hold the gates. We won't drive them back, but we can keep the Geols still for our archers and our catapults to bombard them."

Ruros waved his hand for a question. "How many Geols are we expecting?"

Felden clasped his hands and put them on the table. "My Shadows tell me at least ten thousand."

"Ten thousand!" yelled Mohai. He looked at the Centore commanders. "Gentlemen, I honor you greatly, but three hundred Centores will not stop ten thousand! It's suicide!"

"You underestimate us. All we have to do is hold the gates," said Nemian.

Mohai rubbed his beard. "If we are overwhelmed, there will be no escape. Are you sure of this plan?" The red shoulders stared at each other and all agreed, nodding their heads silently. Mohai stood up. "Captain Hubin, have our army informed of the plan. Tonight we will order our army to retreat from the Siriu River; the cover of darkness will help us hide our activities in the fort. Captain Ruros, notify the men here in the fort. Centore commanders, prepare yourselves, for tonight for you have the hardest task of all." Mohai and his captains stepped out, leaving the Centore commanders to their thoughts.

"So, Jesper. How did the training go?" asked Nemian.

"The first night was the hardest, I have to say. You could have warned me." All the commanders laughed.

"Ah, yes. The first night is hell, sure enough, but necessary."

Kenaf interrupted, "So, which one of us will hold the south and north gate?"

"We will hold the south gate," said Nemian, without hesitation.

Kenaf gripped the hilt of his sword. "Then we will hold the north."

Zanah stood up. "After I dispatch my blue shoulders to the walls, I will split the rest of my unit to aid you at the gates. I will assist Mohai in the fort for the time being."

The rest stood up and shook hands, nodding solemnly. "Death before dishonor."

Jesper followed Nemian down to the small courtyard. When the men of unit two saw Jesper walking up, they all began to laugh. "Turtle? Hey, it's Turtle!" Some saluted him. "Attention, it's a gold shoulder--oh, we mean a Turtle!"

Nemian winked. "You will have your hands full, but they will respect you."

Plonus and Litzer approached Nemian and saluted. "Plonus and Litzer, here to serve, sir."

"Excellent, we need another archer and scout."

A Centore stepped forward. "So what's the plan, Commander?"

"Our orders are to hold this fort. The King has something special in mind for our guests, but I will discuss that later. We are to defend the south gate, and our brothers will hold the north gate and walls. Archers will pick off the Geols when they come in range while catapults commence bombardment."

Flitzer rose his hand. "Sir, how many Geols are we facing?"

"Ten thousand strong." Flitzer and Plonus's mouths dropped.

The others slapped their backs. "That's nothing. You should have been with us in the battle of Samha!"

Nemian gestured his hand for silence. "Flitzer, you will go to the wall to help Mohai's archers."

Flitzer snapped to attention. "Yes, sir!"

"As you know, brothers, we have new men with us, so watch over them. More importantly, we have a gold shoulder now, and you already know him. You will all respect the chain of command, following Jesper's orders in my absence. I want all men battle ready by dark, with your shields and armor looked over. This battle will last all night, so get some sleep. Dismissed."

Throughout the rest of the day, Mohai and his men made preparations for the battle, stocking arrows and catapult ammo for the bombardment. The walls were armed with long, rotating spikes to keep enemy ladders away from the wall. Wooden and metal plating were put on the catapults to protect them from fire arrows and Geol catapults.

Night came with the sound of silence, peace before a storm. The Centores took positions at the gates within the fort. Jesper's stomach tightened nervously, and his hands shook from anticipation. Nemian noticed that Jesper and Plonus were on edge. "Come here, you two."

"Yes, Commander," they said in unison.

"I have ordered your brothers to watch over you, because the first battle with us is always nerve-wracking, but I promise that once the fighting begins, you will remember your training. I know it's easier said than done, but do not think about if you're going to live or die. Instead, think about why you're fighting and what we're protecting. This is what you are trained for. Remember, we are all in this together. Jesper, have the men get in formation."

Jesper gave the order and the Centores lined up.

Nemian walked out in front of his men wearing his silver armor and bright red shoulders. The skull on his shoulder glowed from the surrounding torches, and he seemed like another man altogether, a warrior full of rage with no fear in his eyes. Jesper noticed that the other Centores looked the same, as if their previous battle experience had made them incapable of fear. They stood ready, heroes of Bezinar.

"My brothers, once again we are asked to do the impossible, but I would rather die than see our country fall to darkness. We will hold this gate as long as it takes, understood?" The Centores began banging their shields, chanting. "Rest assured, blood will soak our swords and armor, but we will walk over their dead corpses. Death before dishonor!" The Centores roared loudly, and Nemian was satisfied. He ordered the gate to be opened and they marched out, continuing to chant.

Mohai greeted them. "Nemian, we are about to signal our army to retreat. We will commence bombardment when the enemy is in range. If your men are overwhelmed, form a bubble defense. We will pour hot oil around you and light it on fire. Your armor should protect you."

"What?" Jesper asked in shock.

Nemian looked at him, perplexed. "You mean

Thorg never told you?"

Jesper looked at his shield and armor. "...tell me what?"

"Jesper, our armor is modified. It is a stronger alloy and is lighter than normal armor. It can handle high temperatures and heavy bombardment."

"What about arrows?"

Nemian laughed. "Arrows are like flies to us. You will never feel it."

Jesper's mouth dropped open. "Why would Thorg not tell us?"

"Perhaps he did not want you and the others to feel invincible. As long as we work together, we can hold these gates."

Mohai patted Jesper on the shoulder, laughing. "It seems you're a turtle after all!" Mohai walked back in, closing the gate and locking the Centores outside.

"What do we do now?" asked Jesper.

Nemian winked. "We wait."

After a few hours, Jesper sat down, leaning against the wall with knots in his stomach. He could hear faint echoes of squealing horses and loud booms in the distance. "Will this night ever begin? I am tired of this waiting! It makes it worse."

Plonus was chewing on a blade of grass. "Just think of something else."

"Like what?"

"I don't know, perhaps about your family or a loved one."

Jesper chuckled with sarcasm. "Love? Ha! It is for the birds and the bees!"

Plonus looked at him oddly. "How can you think such a thing?"

"It's simple. Love can easily backfire on you any time, much like war. It is better to not love at all than feel pain."

Plonus crossed his arms. "You are very odd, Jesper, but your situation is somewhat understandable, being a gold shoulder and all." Jesper said nothing, but felt anger deep in his heart.

As Jesper looked down, he saw a small pebble begin to bounce around. He looked up, seeing dust stirring in the distance. In less than a minute, he saw the beginnings of the Bezinar army begin to close in on them. Jesper anxiously stood, blood rushing back through his body. The others stood up, grabbing their shields. Within minutes, the Bezinar army reached the fort, running around it like a herd of wild deer evading a predator, before heading east. Silence followed, with nothing in sight for almost an hour. Finally, at midnight, the Geols were sighted closing in slowly, as if they were stalking their prey. Nemian gave the order to get in formation.

"My brothers, stay close together. Do not let them split us apart or we will be torn to pieces." Jesper stood beside Nemian, heart pounding and sweat going down his face. As the Geols got closer, they increased their speed and closed in on the fort. "They have taken the bait!" He turned around to look at his men and yelled, "What are you?"

"Centores!" they bellowed.

"What are you?"

"Centores!"

"Then show them!"

The Geols came charging in with infantry when suddenly, Nemian yelled, "Night arrows!" The entire unit lifted their shields in unison as the arrows rained down on them. Jesper's heart was racing as he lifted his shield without hesitation. He could hear the breathing of his brothers and it was nothing like his, for theirs was slow and smooth. Not one arrow got through as they clanged against their shields.

"Recover!" They regrouped at once, forming a crescent barrier around the gate with men three rows deep, ready to fight and die as one. The Geols, clad in gray armor that bore a snake curled around a red flame, came charging in with swords held high, spears pointed directly at them. With a loud clash, they hit the Centores, giving no ground. The pressure on Jesper's shield increased every second. Once the bulge stopped, he and his brothers pushed simultaneously, throwing the Geols back. Instantly, the Centores began cutting the Geols to pieces.

Jesper looked for openings, like he was trained to do, and began attacking those exposed. His blade became a part of his arm, slashing at every leg or torso he could reach, his blade tearing their flesh open. When a Geol stabbed at him, his reflexes engaged and he blocked the attack, returning the blows. He realized that in the realms of chaos, he was in control. His body moved without thinking, allowing his reflexes to act. Jesper realized then how important all the training was, and he was thankful for Thorg and the other trainers.

Suddenly, Mohai's voice rang through the air. "Fire!" Arrows from the fort rained down on the Geols, filling the battlefield with screams of pain. The catapults commenced, launching balls of fire that exploded on impact, hurling Geol soldiers through the air. Despite the fort's defenses, they continued charging, bringing ladders and battering rams.

The Geols encircled Fort Yorben and headed to the north gate, but unit six was waiting for them, along with Gideon and Kenaf. The Geols began their raid and tried to take the fort, but the soldiers and Centores on the walls kept them at bay, shooting them one by one. Mohai gave the order for the men to start rotating the blades. Over and over, the ladders kept coming, but the blades shattered them into pieces. Next came the battering rams, and Nemian saw their plan.

Nemian screamed, "Battering ram!" Instantly, the front row knelt, digging their shields into the ground. They leaned back to create an angle with their shields. The second row put their shields on top of their brothers' shields, the rows behind them following suit, to create an arch. Jesper locked his muscles as he leaned back, ready for the jolt. The battering ram hit, sliding over the Centores and exposing the Geols. The Centores ripped them to pieces with their spears and swords. Nemian gave the command to regroup, and in unison, they formed a crescent wall once again, killing all who were close enough with the reach of their weapons. Jesper's training continued to take over as he moved with his brothers without having to think as the orders came. His heart was pounding as he jabbed his sword over and over, killing the enemy without hesitation. Blood hit his helmet and fear left him as he stabbed away, only to be replaced with concentration and anger.

Fueled by the remembrance of his cousins and the deaths of his friends in Sturkma, he slaughtered every Geol in his path.

The Geols slowed for a moment, shocked at the loss of their battering ram, before beginning another ground assault. The Centores showed no mercy as the came running at them wildly. Both units two and six held their defenses, not giving a foot of ground to the enemy.

Meanwhile, Flitzer and Zanah of unit four held the walls alongside Mohai and his men. The Geols were relentless, trying to scale the walls, but were unsuccessful. The catapults continued bombardment, killing rows of Geols by lighting them on fire. The archers picked them off from above, filling the ground with blood and corpses all around the fort. Suddenly, a horn sounded, and the Geol infantry retreated. The air was silent, giving no indication of what was to come next. Jesper raised his head from behind his shield. "Is it over?"

Nemian stood up from his defensive position, and the rest of the unit followed suit. "Not hardly. They are regrouping. This is when it gets difficult, because now they know we're here."

"Hey, you guys okay down there?" asked Felden, looking down from the wall.

Nemian looked up. "Not one of us has a scratch!"

"I suppose they're regrouping. Here, take this water." He and other men dropped water sacks to them.

Suddenly, Mohai's voice rang through the air. "Incoming!"

Everyone looked up as balls of fire came streaming down. Everyone took cover and the Centores formed a bubble defense. The balls of fire exploded, killing several archers and soldiers. Flitzer formed up with several other Centores on the wall, but they were not enough to protect one another as a fireball came down on them, exploding on impact. The collision threw them in the air, launching them off the wall. Flitzer hit the ground and was knocked unconscious as the other Centores were skewered by spikes. Others perished as they plummeted to the ground, crumpled at the bottom of the fort. The archers ran downstairs, getting off the walls and trying to find cover as the Geols bombarded the fort. Jesper felt the ground shake as fireballs crashed into Fort Yorben, screams echoing within its walls.

After an hour or so, the bombardment ceased, and the men tried to douse the fires in the fort. Jesper banged his shield on the ground to smother the fire as the Centores around him tried to recover. He looked into the distance. At first, he thought his eyes were deceiving him, but then he realized Nemian was right. In the far distance were five siege towers rolling toward. They stood over a hundred feet tall. Nemian yelled up at the wall. "Where is Mohai?"

A guard replied, "One minute, sir!"

Moments later, Mohai appeared and looked down at Nemian. "What do you want? My hands are full as it is!"

"Mohai, do you have something to block the gates with?"

"Of course not! You would not be out there in the first place if that were the case!"

Nemian looked back, frowning. "Will you be able to handle the siege towers?"

Mohai laughed. "Are you kidding? Siege towers are my speciality. We will bring them to the ground in seconds, wait and see!" Mohai took off toward the catapults, giving his men orders. "Be sure to bombard the men pushing the towers!"

"Yes, Commander!"

Mohai ran to Felden. "Felden, have your Shadows ever operated a tilter?"

"A what?"

"A tilter. It's a device I designed to take down

siege towers."

Felden smirked. "You designed something? That's a scary thought."

"Quit being a smartass and have some of your men meet me at the southeast tower. I will show you what I'm talking about."

"Very well, give me a few minutes." Several minutes later, Felden and some of his Shadows met Mohai on the tower. "What do you have in mind, Mohai?"

Mohai gestured to a large object hidden under a sheet. He pulled the sheet down, uncovering the device. "This is called a tilter. It launches a long metal spear that deploys spikes around it with a rope attached to it. It goes through the siege towers, and then you pull this lever. That unlocks a boulder down below, which pulls the siege towers over."

"This is incredible, Mohai!"

"I am excited to see the results! This will be the first time ever to be used."

Felden's eyes widened. "Say what? You have never used this device in battle?"

"Of course not, but there's a first time for everything."

Felden shook his head. "I'll say!"

Mohai's face went stern. "Just be sure to shoot

the damn thing at the towers right before they reach the wall. Each tower has one of these devices, so dispatch your Shadows to each one."

Felden bowed. "It will be done." Mohai ran off, leaving Felden and his men to operate the tilters.

As the siege towers approached, the Geols began their bombardment once again. The men hid, waiting for the towers to close in. When the siege towers were in range, the fort's catapults fired at the men, pushing the siege towers. For every one they killed, another took its place. Once the towers got close, the Geol bombardment ceased. The archers ran back to the walls and started shooting at the men pushing the towers. The Centores held their ground, protecting the gates as the towers approached from the south. However, the Centores noticed that the Geols were not that concerned with the gates but the walls.

Once the siege towers were in range, the Shadows fired the tilters. The spears went through them like butter and then released the boulders, pulling the ropes. The results were staggering. One by one, the siege towers toppled to the ground, killing the surrounding Geols in the process. Unfortunately, despite their efforts, the fifth siege tower reached the wall. Geols poured out of it in droves, and the fight was on at close quarters. The Centores and fort soldiers on the walls switched to their swords and shields, trying to keep the Geols at bay.

Three creatures squeezed out of the siege tower after the Geols had vacated. They were at least nine feet tall and covered in thick black armor, with spikes coming out of their necks. Though they were weighed down with hammers and huge, pronged spears on their backs, their blood red eyes showed no mercy. In the distance, Felden spotted them, and a cold chill ran down his spine as he remembered the night he first saw one at Crubitz.

"Spikers on the wall!" he yelled. He drew his sword and ran at the Spikers as men were slung off the walls like lifeless dolls. The Spikers swung away wildly, killing all in their path. The archers were shooting arrows at the Spikers, but they bounced off like leaves against a stone wall. Two blue shoulder Centores charged at them and stabbed them with their swords, but their blades did not penetrate the armor. One Spiker grabbed his spear and pinned a Centore to the ground. It laughed with a deep hollow chuckle and bit the Centore's head off.

The men panicked, fleeing from the Spikers, but Felden stopped them. "Turn around and fight them! We must work together. Their weakness is their necks!" A few Shadows joined in, helping the soldiers of the fort to fight the Spikers. Together, they jabbed at the creatures, taking their attention away from the second Centore that was pinned against the wall. "Make them fall so we can stretch their necks out!" yelled Felden. Out of nowhere, Rubus appeared with rope, knowing exactly what to do.

Rubus and a few other Shadows were trying to rope the Spiker's feet to make them fall, but while they tried, the Spikers were killing dozens of men with their giant hammers. Geol soldiers tried to help the Spikers, but a squad of blue shoulder Centores kept them at bay while the others fought the Spikers. Finally, after several attempts, Rubus and his men were successful getting the ropes around their feet.

"Pull!" yelled Rubus. When they pulled, the Spikers fell to the ground and Felden grabbed their spears, pinning their heads and stretching out their necks. When the men saw the exposed orange flesh, they stabbed wildly, orange blood flew everywhere. Two of the Spikers let out a horrific scream that was heard to the river. One Spiker, however, broke free and jumped off the wall, landing in the center of the fort. The fort soldiers charged in, stabbing the Spiker, but his armor was impenetrable, snapping the swords and spears. The Spiker grabbed his spear and began stabbing soldiers left and right, as if they were small rabbits. Blue shoulder Centores closed in as a single unit, using their shields as one. The Spiker jabbed and swung his spear, but the Centores held their ground.

Felden looked down, putting his hands to his mouth. "You have to make him fall!" Several Centores ran behind the Spiker, kneeling low behind his feet. All at once, the rest of the unit charged, knocking the Spiker to the ground.

"Push its head up! No, no, I said its head!" The Centores pinned its head and pushed up, exposing the flesh at its neck. They stabbed deep into the Spiker, and once again the fort and battlefield echoed with a shriek that pierced everyone's ears. Mohai signaled for the Bezinar army to flank. Instantly, the army charged in with cavalry and infantry from the west, catching many Geols off guard. After the wave of Bezinar soldiers, a horn sounded in the distance and the Geols began to retreat.

Mohai screamed, "Continue firing! Show no mercy!" The catapults and archers continued bombardment, killing many Geols as they ran for their lives to the river. Once they were out of range, Mohai gave the order to cease fire. At sunrise, the men cheered and celebrated as the Geols faded toward the Siriu River.

The gates opened and units two and six walked

in, blood from the enemy all over them. Zanah, Kenaf, and Nemian greeted each other with handshakes.

"My brothers, well done!" yelled Mohai.

Felden ran up and saw Jesper covered in blood and dirt. "You okay?"

Jesper's eyes seemed dazed, as if he were in a trance. "I'm fine. I have never seen so much blood." Jesper looked at the creature on the ground as he walked up to it. "What is that?"

"That is a Spiker, the same type of creature that captured your uncle."

Nemian looked around and saw many of Mohai's men dead. "It killed all these men?"

"Yes. Their only weakness is just below their heads when the neck is stretched out."

Mohai leaned over, examining the carcass. "Perhaps that's what these spikes are for. Protection."

Felden circled the dead Spiker. "Notice how its armor is part of its body. Our weapons are useless against their armor. We have tried countless times."

Kenaf spat on the body. They are demons."

"Their blood looks real enough," said Nemian.

Rubus came walking down the steps, covered in orange blood. "I can vouch for that statement. Look at me! This is the second time I've been covered in this filth."

Mohai got closer, looking at the Spiker. "In all my battles, I have never encountered such strength."

Felden leaned over next to him. "No one has." Jesper poked it with his sword and the Spiker's leg moved abruptly. All the men jumped back, drawing their weapons. Rubus jumped on top of it and stabbed it in the neck, sending a spray of blood into Mohai's face, but the leg was still moving.

"You moron!" yelled Mohai. "It's just twitching!" Everyone started laughing. Mohai wiped his face, glaring at Rubus. "Just for that, you are in charge of cleaning up!" Rubus continued laughing as he walked off, gathering the men. Mohai addressed everyone. "I want all Captains to oversee the injured. Centore Commanders, if you don't mind, have your men secure the area. Felden, have your Shadows do a recon on the Geols. After completing these tasks, we will have a meeting in my headquarters." Mohai walked away, continuing to wipe the orange blood off his face.

After everyone did their duties, Jesper was on his way to headquarters when Plonus came running up. "Jesper, I thought you should know that Flitzer is injured."

Jesper's heart sank. "What happened to him?"

"He has a concussion. Apparently, he was knocked off the wall during the bombardment."

"I will come see him after the meeting. Thank you, Plonus." Jesper made his way to headquarters and the guards saluted as he walked in. When he entered the meeting, everyone was already seated.

"What took you so long, boy?" asked Mohai.

"I was being informed that one of our men was injured."

Nemian raised an eyebrow. "Who?"

"Flitzer, sir, our new blue shoulder."

"We will see him after the meeting. Come, let us begin." Jesper sat, and Mohai started the meeting.

"Well, gentlemen, it seems we were successful, but I don't think we can hold them again if they get reinforcements. They know what we're capable of now. The question is, what are they going to do?"

Felden stood up. "My Shadows report they are retreating to the south, probably back to Sturkma to regroup. If the King is going to do a counter-offensive, the time is now."

"I agree," said Kenaf. "We need to come up with a plan."

"I wish we could act, but our orders are to wait for the King's messenger to come with the plans."

Nemian slammed his fist on the table. "We

can't afford to wait! The longer we wait, the more organized they will get. We must attack now!" All the Centore commanders agreed, but the captains were not so devious.

"We don't know what Sturkma has for us," said Ruros. "If we go marching up there, we could get massacred."

Mohai rubbed his dark beard and changed the subject. "It's irrelevant. Orders are orders and we must wait, but somebody explain to me what a Spiker is?"

Felden went to speak, but then stopped, remembering when the Spiker spoke to them near city of Crubitz. "I don't know, but we came across a village when we were following a squad of Geols. We watched as one of those Spikers killed and drank the blood of one of our men."

Zanah's face turned white. "Drank? Did I hear you correctly?"

"Yes, I said drank! That damn creature stabbed one of my men and drank his insides!"

The room fell silent until Jesper spoke. "Do they thrive off our blood?"

"I am not certain, but I will tell you this: right before we killed one, it said it follows the last of his kind."

"Who is that?" asked Captain Hubin.

Mohai gripped his sword. "Who cares? They will soon be extinct! But for now, my concern is what we haven't faced yet."

"I agree," said Kenaf. "These Geols we're fighting now could be just regular soldiers under the Spikers' control. I am sure there are other forces at work that we have not encountered yet."

Mohai gritted his teeth and then relaxed, leaning back in his chair. "Captain Ruros, how many men do we have left in the Bezinar army?"

"Reinforcements came in today. As of now, we are twelve thousand strong."

Mohai tilted his head, confused. "Where did the King mass that many men?"

"I don't know, sir. Perhaps it's part of the plan we are waiting for."

"Very well, see to it that everyone rests. It seems the King may have us launch a counter-offensive soon." Mohai stood up. "Is there anything else we need to discuss?" The room was silent. "If anyone needs me, I will be monitoring the repairs to the fort." Mohai walked out, followed by his guards.

Everyone else began filing out, but Jesper remained seated. Nemian noticed. "What is on your mind, Jesper?"

"I'm just reflecting."

Nemian sat next him. "Speak your mind, then."

"I never thought war was so…"

"Horrible."

Jesper nodded. "It was nothing like what I expected. The men I killed did not die quickly. They slowly bled to death, fear in their eyes as they coughed up blood and grabbed their wounds. I had pity for them."

Nemian leaned back, crossing his arms. "War is a dreadful thing, Jesper, and anyone who thinks war is glorious is a fool. I have fought for many years, and I still see the faces of the men I killed."

"Do they ever go away?"

"No, but it gets easier to push them out of my thoughts when they appear. The key is to think what the world would be like if you had not done your duty. Our kingdom is still here today for what you and countless others have done to protect our freedom. Unfortunately, some forget the price that was paid for what we have today. Above all else, keep in mind that it is either you or the enemy."

"I see your point," said Jesper. "May I ask you a question?"

"By all means."

"Was my father a Centore?"

Nemian leaned back, reluctant to answer. "What makes you think that?"

"During training, I went into a room that had armor and weapons on display. I saw the armor of Tulios."

"I see." Nemian crossed his arms. "Very well, Jesper, I see no reason why I should keep it from you any longer. The answer to your question is yes."

Jesper lowered his head. "I knew it."

Nemian grabbed his shoulder. "You should be proud."

Jesper's eyes started to water. "How can I be proud of him when I can't claim him?"

"I can understand your frustration, Jesper, but remember that he lived a secret about you as well. I'm sure many times he wanted to tell his men and friends about you and your sister. However, I knew he was up to something since he was making many trips to Sturkma. It finally occurred to me that he had children after your arrival here. You look so much like him, and as far as I know, there are only three people who know that you are his son."

Jesper wiped tears away from his cheek. "Who?"

"Me, Naughton, and King Irus."

Jesper's face went pale. "How do they know?"

"Your father died saving Airah, and somehow, the King found out about you. I know of this for certain because the King's actions toward you speak louder than words. Why do you think he treats you so well, as if you were a son? As for Naughton, do not be angry with him. I had him swear to secrecy, and believe me, I had a hard time keeping his mouth shut. As of now, Airah holds the sword of Tulios in honor of him. She hoped one day she would be able to give it the rightful owner."

"You mean, she knew this whole time about Tulios and never told me?"

Nemian's eyes narrowed. "Do not be angry with her, Jesper. The Centores made her promise to never discuss the event. Besides, she does not know that Tulios had children, as far as I know."

Nemian released Jesper's shoulder. "Now, I will only speak of this once, so listen well. Word has reached my ear of your affection toward Airah. I know you like her, so do not deny it. Your emotions give you away. If you want to become a Commander like your father, you must obey our laws. You must suppress your feelings for her. Otherwise, your heart will lead you astray.

Nemian sighed. "I know it's difficult, because I

am in that position. One day soon, I will retire and raise a family of my own. But now, when my men need me most, is not the time. I do not agree with the Centore laws about Commanders not being allowed to get married. However, I also understand why. Commanders must focus on their men at all times. Red shoulders have the huge responsibility of leading the finest warriors in the world. War has a way of manipulating minds, and it is our duty to keep our men in check when they get out of hand."

Nemian stood up. "That is your first lesson from me, Jesper, but as of now, I want you to rest today. That's an order." Nemian began walking out, but then stopped, smelling the air. "And for El's sake, take a bath." He continued, leaving Jesper to his thoughts.

Jesper put his helmet on the table, looking at the blood stains. He thought about Naughton and wondered if he had completed his quest, for his was only beginning. His mind then reflected on Airah. I wonder if she knows who I really am, he thought. He began wiping the blood off his helmet, staring into the black eye pieces. He saw his reflection and, with a start, realized he didn't recognize himself. "I will never know what he looked like, save this reflection," he murmured to himself.

After a hot bath, he put on his cloak and went to the wall. He stood facing northeast, looking into the distance as the sun beamed down on his face. He began to worry about his cousin, despite the peril he was in himself. He then pondered on the supernatural being, hoping it was going to help them. If not, Jesper knew he would never see his cousin again, for Jesper held a great secret--one that his mother had shared with him before she died, though he had never understood its relevance.

Until now.

In loving memory of:
Julian Kavanaugh Thomas II

Through him we found the true King.

I would like to thank my wife Blanca, family, and friends who have supported me on this journey. Thanks Whit, for helping me like you always have. Special thanks to Mr. Blakeney and Mrs. Rose who reviewed it, gave me advice, and pointed me in the right direction. Kayla Martin, thank you for doing a great job in editing and for wanting to continue this journey. To Mike Welch of *Unique Image*, thanks for the support and encouragement. Many of the characters represent those who have made an impact in my life, and this is how would like to express my love and appreciation for them. This is only the beginning. Thank you for taking the time to go on this journey with me.

Sincerely,

Adam Love

CPSIA information can be obtained at www.ICGtesting.com
Printed in the USA
LVOW07s0437180515

438859LV00002B/166/P